Sacred Music

Felicity Luckman

To Alba
with a hug

Felicity
January 29 2018

First published in 2012 by ActiveSprite Press.

This edition published in 2017 by Endeavour Press Ltd.

Table of Contents

Chapter One

'No popery! No slavery!' As the cry was taken up by more and more voices, burning brands were thrust into the base of the effigy, which leered unsteadily from its cart. The fire took at once, and the shout of defiance from hundreds of eager young voices echoed the length of the High. The undergraduates had gone to great pains with their leering depiction of the Pope, which they now proceeded to burn. Clad in a voluminous crimson robe, the mottled face had been painted into a snarl, which clearly pleased those of the crowd who could see it.

'No popery! No slavery!'

A momentary hush fell as Great Tom tolled nine o'clock, and the East Gate was shut across the High. The whole procession was now within Oxford, and began to move further up the hill. Booted feet, shod feet, bare feet, all tramped the cobbles of the High, intent on proving their unswerving Protestantism, their faith in a Protestant God.

Francis pulled his gown more closely about his shoulders, and turned to his companion.

'Come,' he said. 'We are too far from the antichrist. We need to proclaim ourselves loyal Protestants – and besides, it is burning well now. It will be warmer.'

Christopher laughed. 'You can be hemmed in by so many people and yet complain of feeling cold?'

'I am never cold when I am singing. But this is perhaps not quite the place.'

'Entirely not! If you start bursting into one of your anthems now you will give some of these fellows here strange ideas.' Christopher linked arms with him, though the press of bodies made it difficult for them to move.

'Impatient, are ye?'

'Wait yer turn. We'll get there soon enough.'

Francis allowed Christopher's superior strength to propel him forwards, keeping his fists firmly to himself. But they both had bundles of faggots strapped to their waists, and were eager to dispose of them. With some difficulty, and a few bruises, they found themselves almost behind the cart, to be greeted by several of those about it. Some of them carried banners painted with crude flames, others, like Francis and Christopher, were intent on keeping the cart burning.

'Thought you were a Tory.'

'Practically a Papist, aren't you?'

Francis' fists bunched themselves at the implied criticism, but Christopher laid a restraining hand on his arm.

'Let it go. I've told you before that red hair of yours will get you into trouble some day.'

Francis grinned. 'Just as well you're not the redhead. Your strength and my quick temper would be a lethal combination.' He put his hand to his hair, of which he was inordinately proud. How many times before had he and Christopher held this conversation?

Somebody hurled a faggot towards the cart, scattering a shower of sparks as it landed. Francis wrinkled his nose.

'What on earth is burning?'

'Rancid meat, I fancy,' said Christopher. 'Or perhaps offal. No worse than we might suffer if Antichrist came to rule us.'

'Something has to burn,' agreed Francis. 'It could well be us if the Papists come to rule us.'

'Hot pie, sir? Sweetmeats? Very good, sir.'

Francis turned in surprise to the stallholder who obviously thought he would have a brisk trade as the procession moved up the High. Most of his fellows had shut up shop and gone home, but this rather bedraggled figure was still plying his trade. The stalls along the High in front of the colleges and University buildings had long been a bone of contention, narrowing the street considerably in some places. Francis had grown used to the fact of the stalls being there, but he was surprised at one being manned so late.

'Keep your sweetmeats,' he said to the pedlar in some irritation. 'I have other things to consider.' Fortunately they had moved on before an argument could develop.

They were almost level with St Mary's now, and the glow from rush-lights inside the church proclaimed that it was not empty.

'Let us pull out these trucklers to Rome!' The youth who had accused Francis of being a papist moved towards the church, but this time Francis was quicker, and barred his way.

'No! These are loyal men, and true. They mislike popery as much as any.' He bunched his fists again and his adversary, seeing him side by side with Christopher, obviously decided on discretion.

As though to prove Francis' words, two clerks came out of the church and joined the procession, shouting 'No popery! No slavery!' as lustily as any. Francis' adversary inclined his head in acknowledgement, and turned to feed the hungry cart with faggots.

'Still rather be making music in your room?' Christopher's query was laced with amusement.

'I cannot imagine a world without music. Had my origins been different I might have been a clerk in the choir. But I am not a tory or a papist. I shall knock down the next man who says I am.'

'You scarce have room. If you can manage, turn and look behind you.'

Francis followed his friend's advice, and looked back down the High towards the river. Though daylight had long since gone, it was easy to see the press of bodies, as most were waving torches and banners in the air, creating the illusion of a host of fireflies moving up the hill. The variety in dress was enormous, from velvet and lace to simple broadcloth, from bare heads to elaborate feathered hats. Enough light was shed by the torches to see that there were some prepared to defy University regulations and wear swords.

'As though breaking one regulation was not enough,' remarked Francis. 'We are all out after curfew.'

'I hardly think the authorities will begrudge us our loyalty,' said Christopher. 'It is, after all, the anniversary of the great queen's accession.'

Francis shivered suddenly. 'Why did the old Queen have to die in November? And it was over a hundred years ago. You would think, in that time, our faith would have become better established.'

'It would, if the papists were to stop meddling. Never trust a papist, Francis.'

'I have never met one. My father tells me they are just like us, and it is all nonsense.'

'Then why are we doing this? It is over thirty years, now, since his present Majesty was restored to his throne, promising us freedom of religion. The papists would deny us all our freedoms, and force us to bow down to their idols. We must not let them rule over us. Look, we are almost at Carfax now.'

The procession paused as it began to spread out onto the cobbles of Carfax, and Francis and Christopher were near enough to the front to see what the delay was. They looked north along the Cornmarket, where another procession, similar to theirs, was approaching.

Francis and Christopher, with two of their fellows, advanced to meet three of the townsmen, carrying between them an enormous banner depicting a blazing St Peter's.

'Let us pass,' said one of them, in surprisingly civil tones. 'We wish to pray for our deliverance at St Martin's.'

'Your prayers will be heard where you stand,' said Francis. 'Perhaps better, for God does not love a hypocrite.'

'Perhaps you think he loves a papist better,' said one of the townsmen. 'He will protect you if he does.'

'Papists! They call us papists!' cried Francis, turning to his fellows. 'Can we let that pass?'

'No!' was roared back at him. 'Let us have at these canting hypocrites!'

The university cart, fortunately still burning, was brought to the fore and given a shove which sent it hurtling into the ranks of the quailing townsfolk. The young men of the university followed it eagerly, now full of the lust for battle. Anti-papalism was now largely forgotten in face of the urgent need to outdo a hated rival. Nobody knew the origin of the animosity between Oxford and her university, but it was none the less real for that.

The town cart was pushed towards Carfax, where the students caught it easily and soon extinguished it. But there were many people in both processions, each now intent on vanquishing the other. The university cart was soon extinguished by the townsfolk, and lay on its side in the gutter. Many were still holding torches aloft, however, shedding enough light for their fellows to begin fighting.

Fortunately, perhaps, those of the University wearing swords were not minded to draw them; the battles were clearly going to be decided by fisticuffs. Within minutes, it seemed, there were a hundred separate battles raging from Carfax to St Giles.

Francis had thrown himself into the fray as soon as he had hurled his defiance. His fists had been itching since the procession began, and now he could put them to good use.

His first fight seemed too easy. A portly though shabby townsman had just time to call him both papist and tory before Francis' fist swung into action, and the man was sprawling on the cobbles.

'About time I knocked down somebody who called me that,' he remarked to the inert form, and looked about for another victim. He realised that he would need to keep his wits about him, as people were rushing in all directions, and the noise was deafening. Shouts and insults were traded, and the cries and groans of the combatants filled the air.

A scrawny young man was scurrying towards him, and Francis was minded to ignore him until the familiar insult roused him, and he casually knocked the youth down. He glanced ahead towards St Giles, and realised that several more fights lay between him and his bed, which he would have earned by the time he reached it. They were still heading away from Magdalen.

'Keep at it, Trenoweth,' called a young man he recognised as an undergraduate in his own college. 'At least no-one from the university will call us papist after tonight.'

'They'd better not,' shouted Francis. 'Look out!'

He was just in time to alert his friend to approaching danger, but hearing his shout the townsman concerned obviously thought better of his tactics, and disappeared into the shadows.

He was beginning to wonder what had become of Christopher. His friend was a thoroughly peaceable man, and despite his obvious strength was not a natural fighter. In fact Francis knew they had an advantage that had nothing to do with superior strength. Though they were breaking University regulations, in any dispute with the town it was nearly always the University which won. Many of the townsfolk knew this too, he suspected, and the knowledge made them easy targets.

He had been moving slowly towards St Giles, aware that the fight was unlikely to go on all night. But he was determined that his own part in the affair should be a worthy one, and as yet he had only knocked down two. He was advancing on a third when Christopher at last caught up with him.

'Enough, Francis! Prudence dictates that we should now return to college.'

'We are not going to get there down the High,' replied Francis. 'We would have to pass so many of these ill-favoured citizens.' He hurled a punch at the man approaching him, but it was ill-aimed, and a sudden thrust to his shoulder caused him to lose his balance. His opponent aimed a boot at his head, but Christopher dived for the man's legs in time and brought him to the ground.

'Thank you, my friend,' said Francis, rising and dusting himself down. 'This night is far from over yet.' He looked about him, and saw dozens of separate fights going on wherever he looked. Torches were gradually extinguished, and the light grew less. In truth, few of the fights were being instigated by the townsfolk, but Francis was hoping to vanquish more of the citizens before he had finished. He saw a sharp-faced man dressed in ill-fitting breeches and a torn jerkin trying to creep past him, and at once aimed a blow to the man's chin.

His opponent fell to the ground with a satisfying grunt, but he was up again almost at once, and Francis quickly realised that he knew how to use his fists. He landed a punch to the side of Francis' head, and Francis whistled with the pain of it. It was a moment before he could stand; it seemed as though he was seeing stars, and knew the headache already beginning was going to get worse.

He managed to straighten himself, and his fist shot out again, but he was dizzy with the pain of the earlier blow and it did not connect. The man fetched a sudden hard blow to his belly, and Francis was doubled up.

He was vaguely aware of Christopher not too far away, but Christopher had become involved with a comrade of Francis' opponent, and was clearly unable to come to his friend's aid.

Francis' legs began to buckle, and he could feel himself subsiding to the ground, but even as he fell he twisted his body to head-butt his opponent. Whether or not the citizen was confident in his own victory and had begun to relax Francis could not tell, but they fell in a tangled heap together and were soon wrestling on the ground.

The man he was fighting was heavier, but Francis was more nimble, and was soon using his greater agility to good effect, catching his opponent under the chin even as he started to rise. The man fell back, knocking his head against the cobbles, and lay still.

Francis extricated himself, realising that he was now feeling thoroughly dizzy, no longer certain if he could sustain another fight. Returning to college as a victor suddenly seemed preferable to spending the night in the gutter.

But he felt unable to return without Christopher, and looked around to see what had become of him. With some alarm he saw his friend leaning against a wall, blood pouring from his nose, looking as though he was about to collapse at any moment.

'Christopher! I am sorry. I did not mean to involve you, not in this. I had been called papist and tory once too often. Lean on me, we will get you back to college.'

Christopher put his arm round Francis' shoulders, and together they began to stagger slowly towards a narrow alley that they both knew would lead them eventually to the safety of Magdalen College. The air around them was sharp with the cries of combatants, and the acrid smell of blood was prevalent. There were a number of inert forms in the gutter, and Francis wondered if all would rise again. It was impossible for him to have walked away from a confrontation with the townsfolk, but his greatest need now was to get Christopher back safely.

This was not altogether straightforward, as they were still some little distance from the college, and although they could both still walk, neither was very steady, and they might well present an easy target to any townsman who still had fight left in him.

Fortunately, perhaps, they were moving away from the main area of combat, and though Christopher subsided twice to the cobbles he managed to rise again, and Francis was not, as he had feared, obliged to carry him. He tried to set his own dizziness aside as he concentrated on the important task of getting his friend to safety.

'You'll have to give me some boxing lessons,' said Christopher, as the familiar pale walls of the college came into sight.

'I'd sooner teach you to sing,' said Francis. 'My blood was up just then; they were mocking us. Are you badly hurt?'

'I don't think anything's broken. I shall be a pretty colour in a day or two. But this nosebleed is already easing.'

By the time they had managed to get Christopher into his room at the college the nosebleed had stopped. Christopher did not have his own servant, so Francis fetched a bowl of water and a cloth to clean his friend up.

'You've a fair few scratches on your face,' he said. 'But I don't see anything worse. 'It doesn't look so bad now we've washed the blood off.'

Christopher sat up. 'What about you, though? You were down on the ground at one point. I thought it would be me bringing you home.'

'Me? Oh, I'm all right. My father does not like me fighting, but my cousin Thomas taught me to use my fists. He probably did not realise just how I would make use of his lessons.' He picked up a towel, and dried his friend's face and hands.

'There. You'll live. You might be needing a new gown, though.'

They looked at the dirty, torn garment making an inadequate effort to sit on Christopher's shoulders, and both of them started to laugh.

'Your own has been looking better than it is now,' said Christopher, and Francis realised that his gown was very nearly torn into three pieces.

'Ah. Mine will cost more than yours, too. I know I have to wear this elaborate thing. Perhaps we'd better rest now, and think about new gowns in the morning.'

Francis helped his friend into bed, then descended the staircase to his own room below, reflecting that Christopher would not be the only one to be showing bruises soon. His attempts at washing himself amounted to very little, and in the end he fell back onto the bed. His body ached in so many places, he knew it would be a miracle if he made it to chapel in the morning. His servant Will was nowhere to be seen, which surprised him, but he could not even summon enough voice to call for him now. He sat up to remove his boots, but the dizziness increased sharply, and he just managed to pull a blanket over himself before he senses deserted him.

*

'Pax vobiscum.'

'Et cum spiritu tuo.'

Eleanor remained on her knees as the priest disappeared, to remove his vestments and return as Uncle Anthony, her father's younger brother. She looked around the small room set aside as a chapel, where Mass had been celebrated. Only she, her father and one or two of the upper servants had been present, but that did not matter, as the bread and wine had become the body and blood of Christ. God himself had been with them, so why should numbers matter? She smiled a little to herself as she remembered the enormous privilege she had, to have been born and raised a Roman Catholic, and to know the certainty of her faith.

The servants had left to go about their duties as soon as the service was over, and she knew her father would be moving soon. But she relished these moments of quiet before she was thrust back into the busyness of running the household. She could simply savour the presence of God with her, and to know that his strength would be sufficient to see her through any tribulation.

Her father touched her arm.

'Eleanor. Robert is to join us for dinner. I would have you looking your best.'

'Hush, Father, not here. It is not right.'

'I only desire what is best for you, my dear. You are so very young.'

'I am almost eighteen, Father. And we are still in the chapel.'

'The service is over. I am sorry that Robert could not join us. Will you go and make yourself ready?'

'I must go to the kitchen first, to see that dinner is proceeding.' Annoyed that her period of calm and quiet had been cut short, Eleanor rose and left the room abruptly.

She walked slowly down the passage, trying to prevent herself breaking into a run, still worse to stamp in frustration. Her father, she knew, was looking for any chance to prove her lack of maturity, despite the fact that she had been running the household for as long as she could remember.

She turned at the corner of the house and descended the stairs to the large, cavernous kitchen.

In contrast to the chill outside the heat was considerable. A boy, his sweat-stained shirt clinging to his shoulders, was turning a large capon on a spit, the fat sizzling into the fire beneath. Delicious smells emanated from the oven; the other side of the room a kitchen maid, eyeing the cook warily, was cutting pastry on a wooden board. Eleanor reflected that she would have made a better job of it if she had kept her eyes on what she was doing, not on the cook.

In the centre of the room, her ample frame swathed in a once-white apron, Cook stood before the large scrubbed table, up to her elbows in flour. Eleanor immediately realised that the coming meal would be nothing if not substantial. As she came nearer she caught the spicy scent of the mixture in the bowl.

'Cookie!' she exclaimed excitedly. 'Jumballs?'

'Miss Eleanor.' The cook looked up and smiled, the severity of her expression suddenly softening. 'I know as how you like them. Don't know whether it's the aniseed or the coriander, but they make rare cookies. Your father's not averse either, I daresay.'

'It's the coriander,' said Eleanor firmly. 'It gives it just the right flavour.'

'Yet there's some as say it spoils the aniseed, and won't use it.' The cook bent to her task again. 'There's Italian pudding too, and the beef is baked so like deer he'll think it's venison. Mass is over, then?'

'Yes. My father tells me Robert Carey will be joining us for dinner.'

'There'll be plenty. Get on with your work, girl,' she said to the kitchen maid, without turning her head. 'You'll be pleased to see him, no doubt?'

'I'm – not sure.' Eleanor smiled at the woman on whom, over the years, she had come to rely so much. Her father did not know, of course, but then there was much about his daughter that Sir Henry Somerville did not know. 'It is pleasant to see somebody younger, but my father seems to vary between treating me as a child and marrying me off. I am not ready to marry, and even if I were, I am not at all certain that it would be Robert.'

'He's a handsome youth.'

'I know. And he can be very entertaining. A Catholic, too. What more could I want?'

Cook raised her eyes from her bowl again, and Eleanor saw the question in them.

'I don't trust him. I can't say why, but I don't. Married to him – I would never feel safe.'

'Aye, well, as ye said, ye're young yet. Yer father's not going to press ye.' Cook returned to kneading her dough, and Eleanor realised the moment of intimacy was over. But knowing the old servant as well as she did, she knew she could return to it.

'I can tell my father that the preparations for dinner are proceeding smoothly, then?'

'Get along with ye! When have I ever let ye down?'

'I know. I'm not coming down here to inspect your work. To prove something to my father, perhaps – but more because I enjoy it.'

'I hoped ye did. Ye need other women sometimes.'

'My father will most likely suggest inviting his sister here soon,' said Eleanor. 'How does he think I have managed for female company all these years?'

The cook grinned. 'Ye'd best be getting back to your father now. He'll be wanting his little girl.'

Eleanor shot her a look that was part amusement, part mock reprimand, and heard Cook telling off the kitchen maid again as she turned to leave the room.

She went up to her room next. She had not intended to change; the gown she had worn for Mass, she felt, was quite good enough for Robert Carey. But when she saw her maid laying out her sky-blue satin she weakened. She did so enjoy wearing it, and she knew she looked good in it.

'Very well, Sarah,' she said. 'But it is for myself, not for Mr Carey.'

'Of course, Miss.' Sarah helped her into it and efficiently tied the laces, arranging the overskirt to show the cream silk of her petticoat. 'Shall I brush your hair, Miss?'

'Yes. Thank you.' Eleanor seated herself on a stool and prepared for a ritual they both enjoyed. Vigorous brushing seemed to bring out the copper lights in her hair. It was fortunate, she mused, that her hair was naturally curly. It made it easier for her to look fashionable. She wanted to look her best, and despite what she had said to Sarah, a small part of her wanted to impress Robert Carey.

'There, Miss. Whoever it's for, you look a picture. Those satin slippers go with your gown a treat.'

'Thank you, Sarah. You should get a good dinner in the kitchen yourself today. Cook is making jumballs, as well as Italian pudding. There looks to be far too much for us to eat.'

She made her way to the formal downstairs parlour, and her hand was already on the door handle when she heard her father's voice from inside the room, and her whole body stopped moving. She could scarcely breathe.

'You need have no worries on that score. I am sure she suspects nothing. She is just a child. And her faith is solid. You have seen to that.'

'Nevertheless – ' Eleanor heard the measured tones of her uncle. 'This is a matter of the greatest importance. Nothing, but nothing, must be allowed to hinder our plans. Do you not wish to see our faith accepted throughout this country?'

'Of course, of course. But surely, as a good Catholic, she would wish it too?'

'She is a woman. That makes her dangerous.'

'You have never married, and therefore perhaps do not understand women. Even though I am a widower...'

'I am a priest, and therefore celibate. But I hardly think my understanding need be called in question.'

Eleanor took her hand off the door handle and tiptoed away, returning to enter noisily so that her father and uncle would not suspect she had overheard anything. The two men were standing by the fire, which was sending strange shadows leaping up the tapestries on the walls. They broke off their conversation as she entered, but Eleanor could not detect any hint of guilt or unease in either of their expressions. It could have been mere politeness, so that they could greet her.

'My dear. That blue becomes you. Will you have some wine with us? We were just waiting for Robert to arrive. Something would appear to have delayed him.'

'He will be here soon enough.' Eleanor noticed the pride in her father's face as he handed her a glass of wine. He must be eager to impress, she thought. The Venetian wine glasses were not used very often. She knew that her father was mightily proud to possess them at all.

She also noticed the reluctance on the part of his knee-length coat to remain fastened. She made a mental note to speak to Cook about limiting the supply of jumballs. Her father had put on more weight than she had realised. The purple velvet did not sit well on his frame.

Anthony, by contrast, was spare, almost slight, and dressed in black, only relieved by a fine silk shirt with a deal of lace at collar and cuffs. Eleanor did not believe that the black was in deference to his priestly role, but did think the shirt unnecessarily ostentatious. However, she said nothing, and seated herself on a comfortable upholstered settee to the left of the fire.

'I was pleased to see you at Mass this morning, Eleanor.' Anthony inclined his head towards her as he spoke. He looked so like a raven pecking for crumbs that Eleanor had difficulty in preventing herself from giggling. She found it difficult sometimes to separate his two roles of her father's younger brother and their resident priest. She addressed the latter.

'I do not miss Mass unless for very good reason. My duties about the household do not normally prevent me.'

'Of course, of course.'

Eleanor looked up at her father, standing before the fire, and as she did so heard the unmistakeable sound of horses' hooves on gravel.

'Ah, here is Robert.' Sir Henry sounded relieved. 'From the sound of things he is not alone.'

'I expect he has brought Tom with him,' said Eleanor. 'Now that he is in service to the Duke of York he likes to travel with a servant.'

'As is only proper.' Anthony poured himself more wine. 'And it is surely safer. A young man cannot be too careful these days.'

It was not many minutes later before the door was opened and a manservant stood aside to allow a tall young man to enter the room. Eleanor watched him as he crossed the room. Her knowledge of London fashions was small, but she realised that his elaborately embroidered coat made her father look positively dowdy. It was made of silk, she believed, and reflected that he must have taken at least a couple of minutes to change before presenting himself. He had surely never ridden in that coat, and those high-heeled shoes would have made for a very difficult journey.

Robert bowed with just the correct deference to her father, and Eleanor wondered why it was that she was so set against marrying him. Cook was right when she had said that he was handsome. His features were regular and pleasant, with a firm straight nose and deep brown eyes. Thick chestnut curls rested lightly on his shoulders. He had adopted the Court fashion of a wig, but he had chosen well. Even the smell of horse that accompanied him was not altogether unattractive.

'Sir Henry. My apologies for my late arrival. My horse shed a shoe, and though we were near enough to Woodstock to take him to the farrier, it was an unavoidable delay.'

'No matter. You are here now. It is not quite the hour for dinner.'

Eleanor was surprised when Robert gave a more elaborate bow to Anthony, then decided it must be on account of his priestly role. But then Robert had turned to her, and raised her hand to his lips.

'Miss Somerville. It is, as always, the greatest pleasure to see you.'

Eleanor allowed him to touch her fingers to his lips, then returned them demurely to her lap.

'You are most kind,' she murmured, as the silence stretched and Robert seemed to expect a response. Uncle Anthony busied himself with finding Robert a glass of wine.

Very soon they were seated about the heavy mahogany table; the beef was, as the cook had told her, baked with herbs and spices in such a way that Sir Henry pronounced it to be excellent venison. Eleanor smiled. Perhaps she could cope with a meal.

'And how was His Grace when you last saw him?' asked Anthony. Robert smiled.

'Well, insofar as I was able to tell,' he answered. 'Sometimes I wonder if he even notices whether I am there or not. But he is a good man, and faithful. I hope that I may find ways to show him how useful I could be. At least he allows me sufficient time to come here, for which I am grateful.'

'I am not acquainted with the ways of the Court,' said Sir Henry. 'Do your duties bring you into contact with the King at all?'

'Very rarely. Much to my relief. His Majesty is not – steady as his brother is.'

'You are free to stay with us for a little?' enquired Sir Henry. 'Only I should be glad of your advice on some matters pertaining to the estate.'

'I should be glad to. Perhaps Miss Somerville might take a turn in the garden with me, if it is not too cold.'

Eleanor raised her face to him, and managed a pale imitation of a smile.

'Yes, of course. But I cannot be too long. I need to sort some linen with Mrs Barnes.'

'Eleanor!' Her father laid down his knife. 'On a Sunday?'

This time it was easier for Eleanor to smile. 'Robert may well have no bed linen if I do not.'

Robert smiled. 'I admire your household efficiency, Miss Somerville. But I fear I cannot stay too long. A couple of days, maybe, and then it will be necessary for me to return to London.'

Sir Henry reached across and helped himself to some of the jumballs, as well as a large portion of Italian pudding. Eleanor frowned, but took care that her father did not see.

'Will you go straight to London from here?' Sir Henry asked Robert. 'It would be a long ride.'

'I could manage it. But no, I am minded to visit my cousin in Oxford. It is only about twelve miles, and it would be pleasant to see him.'

'I did not know you had a cousin in Oxford.'

'Yes. He has been there for two years now, though I have not visited him before. He is younger than me, by about a couple of years.'

'But you get on together?'

'Oh, Francis is all right. His father and my elder brother are very close and, as you know, I have had my differences with Thomas.'

'You have described that as being mainly over matters of faith.'

'Mainly, yes. But since our father died he has become very much the head of the family.'

'Surely that is as it should be?' put in Eleanor. Robert favoured her with his most dazzling smile.

'Of course. But he tried to rule my life – too hard. I used the money left by my father to set myself up in London, when he wanted me to go to university. And when I converted – '

'Indeed.' Anthony bestowed the warmest smile Eleanor had ever seen him give on Robert. 'We are most glad that you remain within the true Faith.'

'This Francis is your cousin.' Sir Henry, wiping his lips fastidiously with a napkin, made it a statement. 'Who is his father?'

'Lord Bodmin. He is my brother's godfather. And, of course, a Protestant.'

'I do have some Protestant friends,' said Sir Henry. 'Acquaintances, at least.'

'His mother is related to the earl of Bath,' continued Robert. 'He has the Grenville red hair to show it.'

'Indeed? You interest me. I suppose the whole family is in a ferment against those of our persuasion?'

'My brother, yes. It is another source of discord between us. I cannot speak for Francis. But I believe his father holds this whole "Popish Plot" to be nonsense. So at least Thomas tells me, on the rare occasions when I have seen him.'

'Why do you not introduce your cousin to us?' asked Eleanor suddenly. 'We should be delighted to meet him, should we not, Father?'

Sir Henry carefully finished the piece of apple he was eating, and laid down his knife.

'Of course,' he said. 'Bring him to meet us, Robert. Some more wine?'

Anthony turned to Eleanor in surprise. 'You have just made a very worthy suggestion, my dear. I have met Lord Bodmin – only last year – and should be delighted to meet the son. A sound gentleman in many ways – saving his faith, of course. I believe he is a close friend of the King?'

'Yes. During Cromwell's time they were both exiles on the Isles of Scilly – as were my parents. I was born there. The islands are small, to say the least.'

'So exiles would naturally be drawn together,' said Sir Henry. 'Your family continues to intrigue me, Robert. I should be delighted to meet your cousin.'

Chapter Two

Eleanor felt a sense of relief when the meal was over. She was about to go to her room and put on a more practical gown, but Robert followed her into the passage and reminded her of her promise – that was how he described it – of walking with him in the garden.

'I have not sorted the linen yet,' she told him.

'Can you not do that later? It will be dark soon.'

Her whole being urged caution, but she had not been out of the house that day, and knew that a little fresh air would be welcome.

'Very well. Half an hour, then. I will go to fetch my cloak.'

Some few minutes later they were walking in the formal rose garden, now cut hard back for winter, and looking rather sorry.

'Your garden seems almost dead,' said Robert.

'But it is not! If you do not cut roses back in the autumn, they will not bloom nearly so well the following year. I hope you have not brought me out here to criticise my stewardship of my father's household.'

'Indeed no. I apologise. I know little of gardens, and thought perhaps that your gardener had been neglectful.'

'There is no gardener here. I tend the rose garden myself.'

He turned to look at her. 'You do?'

'Why do you find that so strange? I enjoy it, I like a reason to go outside, and yes, I like getting my hands dirty sometimes.'

He put his hand to her elbow to steer her round a corner at the end of a walkway. She managed – just – to avoid flinching.

'I am so very glad that your uncle introduced me to your household,' he said. 'As you may have gathered, I am not particularly close to my own family, and I feel as though I have been accepted into yours.'

'But this is only the third time you have been here!'

'A tribute to the warmth of your hospitality. I feel I know you well already.'

'Have you known my uncle long?' she asked.

'Quite some years. He instructed me in the Faith, and helped me to gain my present position. I owe him a great deal.'

Eleanor shivered, and they began to walk back towards the house.

'Why did you want to invite my cousin here?' Robert asked.

'I was curious, I suppose. Why have you never mentioned him before?'

'As you pointed out, this is only my third visit. I did not realise I was expected to give you full details of all my family.'

Eleanor laughed. 'True. I suppose I am keen to show my father that I am not a child any more.'

'That you are not. But then I have not known you long. To me you appear a very beautiful young woman.'

Eleanor did not rise to the compliment. 'I have never met a Protestant.'

'They are mistaken,' said Robert. 'Of course, they do not think so, and hold it against us that we would try to save their souls.'

'I have been told that they are little better than pagans.'

'As a former Protestant, I would not go as far as that. But they are in error. There can be no doubt on that score.'

'I see. I look forward to meeting your cousin, all the same. I think my faith is firm enough to withstand possible contamination. And now I must discuss the linen with Mrs Barnes.'

It was with a sense of relief that Eleanor escaped upstairs, determined to shed the blue satin, now sadly marked about the hem, before resuming her household duties. She was still not entirely certain why she had encouraged Robert to bring his cousin to the house. Perhaps the answer she had given Robert was nearer the truth than she had realised, that she was trying to assert some independence from her father.

She believed, as she had been told, that no Protestant could inherit the Kingdom of Heaven, any more than a pagan or a Turk. Yet the stories she had heard of burning people to save their souls filled her with a sense of unease. Perhaps if she could, simply by persuasion, bring about the conversion of such a one, her place in Heaven would be assured.

Sarah helped her change into a practical broadcloth skirt and bodice, then defiantly Eleanor fastened an apron about it.

'I'll take it off for supper,' she said, smiling at Sarah's shocked expression,' but I'm going to be working, so I might as well wear working clothes.'

'Working, Miss?'

'I told my father it was just to sort out some bed linen for Robert. But we'll see if we can make it more than that. I'm in no hurry.'

She climbed the stairs to the linen store at the top of the house, where Mrs Barnes was briskly folding sheets.

'Ah, Miss Somerville. I thought I might see you here. Mr Carey is to stay?'

'Yes. Can the blue room be made ready?'

'It almost is. I was just sorting the linen. And there is space above the stable for Tom.'

Eleanor looked out of the small gable window. The sun was setting amid fiery darts of apricot and cerise, looking ready to set the sky and clouds on fire.

'It will be a cold night, I'm thinking,' she said. 'Have we plenty of blankets?'

'Now, Miss. Have you ever known us go short of blankets? There's plenty and more.'

Eleanor moved further into the room and touched the soft wool of a canary yellow blanket.

'I will help you out the bed ready for Mr Carey, then,' she said. 'It need not take us long.'

They carried the linen down to the blue room. It was a pleasant room, looking out over the rose garden that Robert had so recently derided. Eleanor felt some small satisfaction at that. They arranged the covers on the bed, saw that the fire was lit and a warming pan placed in the bed to dispel any clamminess of the sheets. Eleanor might have her doubts about marrying Robert, but he was not going to be allowed to call into question her abilities as a housekeeper. It was almost with reluctance that she left Mrs Barnes to finish making the room ready and went down to the parlour to join the men, shedding her apron on the way.

'You have changed your gown, Eleanor,' said her father in a tone of disapproval. 'That one does not become you as well as the blue.'

'It is more practical, Father,' she said at once. 'Mrs Barnes was waiting for instructions concerning a room for Robert. The blue room has been made ready for you, Robert. The fire is lit and the bed prepared. I hope you will be comfortable.'

'I'm sure I shall. You are very kind.'

'Supper should be ready soon,' said Eleanor, moving towards the door. 'I will just go – '

'Eleanor!' Her father's voice was sharp, and she turned in surprise. 'Come and sit down for a little. Supper will be ready whether or not you go to the kitchen.'

Eleanor moved slowly to a settee beside the fire, on which Robert immediately joined her.

'I enjoyed our walk this afternoon,' he said. The settee was just large enough to accommodate two people seated side by side. Eleanor realised she could not move away without appearing rude. 'I live in too much of a male environment,' continued Robert. 'I hope I may see more of you. We could be good for each other, I'm thinking.'

'I also live in a very male environment,' said Eleanor. 'My father's sister comes to visit sometimes, but apart from that the only female company I have is the servants. My mother died when I was born.'

'That must be hard for you.'

'I seldom think about it. After all, I never knew her. The cook has been here since before I was born, and is more like a friend than a servant. My maid Sarah has been with me for many years. She even scolds me sometimes.'

'I am sure that can never be necessary.'

'Perhaps you might be surprised. But what of you and your male society? Surely there are ladies at court?'

'Oh yes. But I have never really got to know any of them well. Most of them, indeed, appear empty-headed and silly.'

Eleanor had a sudden vision of one of these empty-headed and silly ladies cavorting herself in Robert's bed, and she pushed the thought away before she was tempted to giggle, and sought for ways to steer the conversation into safer waters.

'What made you become a Roman Catholic?' she asked suddenly.

He looked sharply at her, clearly surprised. But she kept her face as devoid of expression as she could.

'I think it was the colour at first,' he said. 'That and the smell – I love the smell of incense.'

'Now you are not being serious.' She made as though to rise, but he took her hand and pulled her down.

'I assure you it was. Curiosity as well, perhaps. But then I had the good fortune to meet your uncle, and we began a series of conversations. He convinced me of the truth of the Church, and arranged for me to be received.' He turned towards her, becoming suddenly animated. 'That was the first time I felt true to myself. I hope to work towards that glorious day when all of England may know such a truth.'

'What did your family say?'

He grinned. 'My brother was extremely angry. He said I was only ever interested in myself, and was driven solely by ambition. Though how I can advance my career by adopting a faith that bars me to public office in so many areas, I confess I cannot understand. You are truly fortunate in your family. Your uncle is the wisest man I know.'

'What of your uncle – this Lord Bodmin you speak of?'

The grin faded, and Robert looked awkward.

'It's difficult to say. He didn't accuse me of ambition, or selfishness. He just looked – so sad. It was much worse. Thomas and I have never really understood each other, but since my father's death my uncle has been like an adopted father to me. I was thirteen when my father died, and my uncle and I grew really close, or so I thought. But he does not speak to me nearly so much now. I should have realised that he and Thomas were always more companionable than ever he was with me.'

Robert looked almost bitter. He stood up and began pacing the room, so that Sir Henry broke off his conversation with his brother to ask if anything was the matter.

'What? Oh, not really. I have difficulties with my family, that is all.'

Sir Henry smiled. 'There are times when Eleanor and I have our differences, are there not, my dear? Perhaps, after all, it would be as well if you visited the kitchen to ascertain that all is well there.'

Eleanor took up the suggestion at once. She was glad to escape from the room. The kitchen, though there was noise, heat and bustle, seemed tranquil in comparison.

'Aye, Miss, supper's on its way,' said Cook. 'Coming to check up on us, are ye?'

'You need no checking, Cookie,' said Eleanor. 'It was a welcome escape. Let's just say I needed some female company.'

The cook let out a roar of laughter. 'And what of that did you expect to find here?' Then her tone softened and she touched Eleanor's cheek. ''Tis all right, my pretty. He'll not be marrying you yet.'

This time it was Eleanor's turn to laugh, and she returned to the parlour in a calmer frame of mind. Supper was a light meal after the large dinner they had eaten earlier, and it was not late when Eleanor was able to retire to her room and allow Sarah to unlace her bodice and brush her hair.

'I am afraid, Sarah,' she said. 'I am sure my father sees Robert as a husband for me – and I do not want to marry him.'

'Then say so, Miss,' said Sarah simply, moving the brush rhythmically.

'If I said so now, my father would simply ask what put such an idea into my silly little head.' Eleanor sighed. 'No, we need to be cleverer than that.'

'We, Miss?'

Eleanor suddenly turned to face her, so that the brush nearly landed on her nose. 'Yes, Sarah. Are you happy here?'

Sarah put the brush down. 'You know I am, Miss.'

'You would not rather be with your mother?'

'My mother has seven children and a drunken husband in a tiny cottage in Charlbury, Miss. I would much rather be here.'

Eleanor touched the girl's arm. 'And I am glad to have you, Sarah. Here I have position, security, enough to eat and drink. But no friends. I do not think I can live without friendship. I am lonely, Sarah, and afraid.'

'Afraid, Miss?'

'Yes. Afraid for my father, afraid for myself, for our faith and what it may lead us into.'

'I do hear talk of a plot sometimes, Miss. But I reckon 'tis just that – all talk.'

'Oh, there is a plot, Sarah. A very real one. Men have died because of it. I just hope my father will not be one of them.'

*

After the rest of the household had retired for the night, Robert and Anthony sat by the embers of the fire. Robert took a cautious sip of the wine in his hand, and looked up at Anthony.

'Why are you so anxious that I impress Eleanor?'

'Can you not see? If you were able to marry her, then you would be part of the family. And I am sure her father would approve.'

'Yes, but – how *can* I? I can never love her in the way that she will expect. Would it be fair to her?'

'She is a good Catholic. If she understands that it will further the faith in this country, then I am sure she will oblige.'

'Will she not expect children? I am sure Sir Henry will want to be a grandfather.'

'Surely, if you married her, you would be able to father a child on her?'

Robert took another hasty swallow of wine, and almost choked.

'F-father a child on her? But that would mean – '

Anthony took a leisurely swallow of wine, and smiled. 'We do not need to go into details. Of course it would mean – intimacy.'

Robert turned anguished eyes towards the older man. 'I owe you a great deal. You have changed my life in so many ways. But this – would this be to repay you for all you have done for me? If so, I – I am not sure that I can manage it!'

Anthony leaned across and put his hand on Robert's arm. 'Why must you bring such sordid notions into this?' His hand travelled up Robert's arm, fingered his neck, and came to rest on his cheek. 'It would be a service, not to me, but to the Faith. But there would be another, more personal advantage in it for you.'

Robert covered Anthony's hand with his own. 'And that would be?'

'Why, membership of this family. You would be expected to provide for Eleanor, of course, but with your connections that should not be a problem. And as a member of the family, we should be able to meet, not only here, but in many other places as well.'

Robert removed his hand, fumbled for his wine and drank some more.

'Is this not a little soon? I have only met Eleanor three times.'

Anthony laughed, and refilled his goblet. 'I am not suggesting that you marry her tomorrow, or next week. Take your time. She is not yet eighteen, but I know that her father will want her to be married soon. And who better to fulfil that post than you?'

'She may not have me.'

'She is biddable enough. She will do as her father expects. And he will do as I suggest.'

Robert drained his wine, and set the goblet down carefully. 'What is it that you want?'

'I thought you knew. I would see this country brought back to the obedience of Rome, I would see my niece well married and provided for. I would also – '

'Yes?'

'I would have you by me, my dear boy, for as long as I am able.' He placed his goblet on the table, and stood up.

'Come. It is late, and you were talking about riding to Oxford tomorrow. And, Robert, make sure your cousin accepts my brother's invitation. I believe he could be useful.'

Robert looked at him in surprise, but it was clear that Anthony was not going to enlighten him any further.

*

Francis sat at the back of the college chapel. The choir had filed out, and most of the undergraduates, for whom daily attendance at chapel was a duty grudgingly fulfilled, had gone. The organ played for a little longer, then that too fell silent. He had been vaguely aware of Christopher's tap on his shoulder, but he had not responded, and Christopher too had now left.

There was chatter in the ante-chapel and St John's quadrangle, but Francis was only dimly aware of it. He looked up as the organist came across and sat beside him.

'Lord Trenoweth. It is always a pleasure to speak to somebody prepared to wait until the music has finished.'

Francis smiled. 'Forgive me. It was not so much the organ music that held me, I fear – it was the anthem. I have never heard its like before. What was it?'

'Ah. I acquired a copy of this only recently, and thought it might be interesting to try. The composer is young, only twenty-one, and has recently been appointed organist at Westminster Abbey. His name is Henry Purcell.'

'It was sublime. I hope we hear more of him. Even from that I believe that he is a new voice in English music.'

His companion stood up. 'I fear we did not altogether do it justice. The boys were rather wayward today. I shall have to speak to them. And it would be even better with strings, rather than the organ. Have you seen the latest Playford? Purcell has some music in it you might enjoy – particularly his Ode on the death of Matthew Locke.'

'I have heard a new Playford had been issued,' said Francis. 'But I have not been able yet to obtain a copy.'

'I have only recently acquired one. I will gladly lend it to you, if you would like. I have heard the music coming from your room sometimes, and it is excellent.'

Francis left the chapel and made his way towards the cloisters, his head still full of the music. He was about to turn to the staircase leading to his own rooms when a hand on his shoulder caused him to turn.

'Francis! I thought if I stayed near the chapel I should catch you. Thomas told me you could hardly be kept away from it.'

Francis stared, trying to make his brain believe what his eyes told him he was seeing.

'Robert! What does my elegant cousin in Oxford, pray? I thought you were busy at Court.'

Robert laughed. 'Do I need a better reason than to visit my cousin? We have not seen each other for too long, Francis. And what on earth have you been up to recently? I knew that my brother had taught you to use your fists; it would appear that you have been trying out the success of his lessons.'

Francis put his hand to his cheek, aware that the bruising, which no longer caused him pain, was probably still very noticeable.

'Oh, that. It is only a week since November 17. We had to mark the anniversary. It would have passed peacefully, but that we met a similar procession organised by the townsfolk.' Francis had been about to embrace his cousin, his childhood playmate, but the moment had obviously passed.

'A pope-burning procession.' Robert sighed. 'I had thought you wiser than to get caught up in the current hysteria. Do you really believe that all Roman Catholics are a danger to the country?'

'Not all, no. But some, yes. I would not have this country changed by force.'

'No more would I. But come, Francis, I did not seek you out to get embroiled in an argument with you. I am glad that Thomas told me that you are diligent in your attendance at chapel, else I might have been hard put to find you.'

'When there is music I cannot stay away. I have a group of friends coming tonight to sing and play together. But now I am in need of other refreshment. Come up to my rooms for a little. Hopefully Will can provide some wine or ale.'

'Ale! Surely you don't drink that horse's piss? But you mentioned wine, so I will come.'

Francis led the way round the Cloister and up the staircase to his rooms, which he showed Robert into with some pride, slipping out of his gown and dropping it onto a settee.

Robert looked about him. 'Francis! Is this the best you can manage?'

'It is a great deal better than most.' Francis tried to keep the hurt out of his voice. 'I can have Will with me, and I do not have to share. The servitors are several to a room.'

'But you still have to share with Will?'

'How else could he look after me? He has a small truckle bed. And I have this second room, so really I have plenty of space. Will!'

'My lord?' Will appeared silently from the bedchamber.

'You remember my cousin Robert? Perhaps you could find us some wine. Oh, and go upstairs and ask Christopher if he would like to join us.'

Christopher was very soon clattering down the stairs, no doubt delighted at the thought of Francis' wine. Though he was a gentleman commoner, Francis knew that he had very little money. He shared the services of one of the servitors with three others, and did not see him all that often.

'Francis!' He came in beaming. 'I thought I was never going to drag you away from the chapel this time. Oh.' He looked across and saw Robert, elegantly lounging in Francis' favourite chair.

Francis stood up and smiled. 'Come in, Christopher, sit down. This is my cousin Robert, who has turned up here unexpectedly.'

Robert stood up and bowed fractionally to Christopher, who returned the salute and sat down, eyeing the newcomer warily. Francis, still delighted with the recent turn of events, did not notice. As a child he had always been slightly in awe of his dashing cousin, though Robert was but three years older, and the younger son of a knight, while he himself was heir to an earldom.

Will came in with the wine, and Francis, suddenly self-conscious, handed a tankard to his cousin and his friend. Robert looked up.

'Do you not have glasses? Surely your father can afford them?'

'I don't have any here. Breakages and so on can be a nuisance. My father has some at Pelistry, of course, but even those he does not use very often.' Francis was determined not to be affronted.

'What kept you in the chapel so long?' Christopher sipped his wine and smiled across at Francis.

'Surely you heard the anthem? I realised at once that this was something very special. It seems there is a new young composer in Westminster. I hope we are going to hear a great deal more of him.'

'I'm afraid I do not listen to the music with the same attention that you do. You have some people coming here this evening, I believe?'

'Yes. I'd better make sure there is enough wine for them. Julian and Mark are both fiddlers, but the others are singers, and that can be thirsty work.'

'You sing yourself, do you, Francis?' Robert sounded surprised.

'Of course. Surely you remember me singing in Cornwall, all those years ago.'

'I thought that was just a high-spirited boy.'

'That too, perhaps, but I cannot remember a time when music has not been important to me. That is why I persuaded my father to register me at

Magdalen, when he assumed I would go to Exeter College, where most of his neighbours' sons are. But I had to be somewhere with good music, and managed to get my way in the end. Will you come down this evening, Christopher?'

His friend smiled. 'Perhaps not. I understand your enthusiasm, but I cannot understand the music. I shall hear it through the floor, no doubt, while I try to resume my acquaintance with Tacitus.'

Francis turned to his cousin. 'Where are you sleeping tonight, Robert? I was not aware that you had been in Oxford before.'

'I have not. Does this city boast a tavern where I would be unlikely to encounter fleas?'

Francis and Christopher both laughed. 'I should try the Mitre, halfway up the High. Magdalen is outside the city walls, of course, but you should have no difficulty. What does bring you to Oxford?'

'As to that, I have been fortunate to gain an introduction to the household of Sir Henry Somerville at Coneybury, not far from Charlbury. It seemed churlish to be so close to Oxford and not visit you here. Thomas has never quite forgiven me for not coming to university myself.'

'I suppose you see more of Thomas, now you are in Westminster much of the time.' Francis turned to Christopher. 'Thomas is Robert's elder brother, and shares a house with my father in Westminster when Parliament is sitting.'

Robert sighed. 'No, I do not see a great deal of Thomas. Let us say – our ways seem to have parted, and we no longer have a great deal to say to each other. But, Francis, I have an invitation for you. How should you like to visit Coneybury with me?'

'I? But what for?'

'I was there recently, and when I mentioned I had a cousin in Oxford Sir Henry asked me to invite you next time I visit them.'

'But – why? Until two minutes ago I had never heard of this Sir Henry.'

'And now you have.' He took another sip of his wine, and put the tankard down. 'This wine is reasonable, I grant you, but Sir Henry's – now that is something worth tasting. His younger brother Anthony goes to London quite frequently, and usually beings back excellent wine.'

Francis frowned.

'I still cannot understand why he should want to invite me to his house. It sounds – odd.'

'What is odd in a cultured gentleman inviting another such to his house? There you would find, besides the wine, excellent food, good company, stimulating conversation. You cannot tell me you are sufficiently well supplied with all of these?'

Beside him Francis felt Christopher stiffen. 'The university is a very stimulating place at present,' Francis replied evenly. He reached for his gown. 'It is nearly time for our supper, Christopher. And then my friends will be arriving.'

Christopher stood up and looked directly at Robert. 'This invitation,' he said. 'Could it have anything to do with the fact that Francis is the elder son of an earl?'

Robert looked hurt. 'Is that what you think, Francis?' Suddenly his expression changed and he was almost pleading. 'Truth to tell, I am indebted to Sir Henry, and he has expressed a wish to meet you. I shall be out of favour if I return and tell him I have failed. In fact it was his daughter Eleanor who first suggested your coming. You are surely not so ungallant as to refuse a young lady?'

Francis sighed. 'I shall get no peace from you until I agree. Very well. I will come. But I will need to be back in Oxford by dusk.'

Robert looked relieved. 'You will not regret it, cousin. There is more to life than Cornwall and your precious university.' He stood up and reached for his hat. 'I understand that you two have other things to do now. I will not detain you longer.'

As they sat in the Hall to eat their meal Christopher turned to Francis with a serious expression on his face

'Do you trust your cousin?'

'Trust? Why yes. As boys we always got along famously. It always seemed that he did everything better than me, and I wanted to emulate him. I had not seen him for some time, but we were always the best of friends.'

'H'm. Be on your guard, Francis. For all you are handy with your fists, you have such an open, trusting nature.'

Francis laughed. 'I take that as a compliment. But I shall come to no harm with Robert. I was surprised at first when he made this suggestion, but it seems perfectly reasonable.'

'Take Will with you, then. I have never met your cousin before, but there was something about that conversation that made me feel uneasy. I cannot understand what it was.'

'You worry too much. But I need to get back upstairs. I have been looking forward to tonight's music – and I want to know what the others thought of Purcell's anthem.'

Christopher laughed. 'Are you an undergraduate, or a musician?'

'Both, I hope.' Francis stood up. 'I hope Will has made the room ready.'

Chapter Three

'Let me fill your glass, Lord Trenoweth. This Canary is really very fine, do you not think?' Anthony Somerville poured more wine into the glass Francis held.

'It is very good, certainly.' Francis fingered the Venetian glass uneasily. He knew his father possessed better, but rank sat lightly on the shoulders of Lord Bodmin, and Francis had seldom seen it used. The room, too, was considerably grander than any at Pelistry. There were two upholstered settees either side of the fire, and elaborate tapestries depicting Orpheus and the death of Eurydice.

Anthony smiled. 'I am fortunate to be able to go to London from time to time. I usually fetch some wine back for my brother. I have a dealer on whom I particularly rely. I expect you go there yourself on many occasions. I have had the pleasure of meeting your father there. A fine gentleman.'

Francis inclined his head. 'My father does go sometimes to London, to speak in the House of Lords. But I do not have occasion to.' He sipped the sweet white wine. 'I divide my time mainly between Oxford and Cornwall.'

'I have never been to Cornwall.' Eleanor, sitting opposite Francis on a carved high-backed chair, spoke quietly. 'I am told it is very beautiful.'

Francis turned towards her and smiled. 'The most beautiful county in England, for my part. But I must not be discourteous. Robert and I had a wonderful ride here through the woods.'

'I am getting to know it quite well.' Robert, exquisite in a deep blue silk coat, with an abundance of lace at collar and cuffs, looked up and smiled cheerfully. 'It took us little over an hour today, even though it had snowed a little in the night. At least my horse did not shed a shoe on the way.'

'You were here even earlier than I expected.' Sir Henry moved somewhat ponderously to help himself to more wine, and sat himself down beside Francis.

'You surprise me, Lord Trenoweth, in having so little inclination to visit London. Surely with your connections you could make many interesting introductions?'

'It is true that I have recently decided that should I ever go to London I should like to meet Mr Purcell. I shall be sure to seek him out when I do go there.'

'Mr Purcell?' Sir Henry frowned. 'It is not a name I recognise.'

'He is little known as yet.' Francis smiled. 'But I believe he may well be seen as the finest composer this country has ever produced. The choir sang an anthem of his in the chapel recently. I truly believe he is a new voice in English music. It is sublime.'

'If it is better even than William Byrd, it must be fine indeed.' Eleanor was suddenly animated. 'I had not heard of Mr Purcell.'

Francis smiled at her. 'I am sure that you will. I have only heard this one anthem, but he is young – barely twenty-one, and I am sure that there will be many more. For me, music is like a breath of fresh air. I could not live without it.'

'Oh, I see.' Sir Henry was clearly not interested. 'I thought you meant somebody of influence.'

'But indeed he is.' Francis leaned forward, and did not see Robert's warning glance. 'If ever I were in London for any length of time I should hope to be able to make music with him.'

'An odd ambition, perhaps, for the heir to an earldom?' Anthony's question was phrased with the greatest courtesy.

'I cannot see it like that. Music is the most civilising influence we have. If everybody understood its power maybe even the Papists would see how it could unite us.'

The room went suddenly very still. Francis looked around, but found there was nobody prepared to meet his gaze. Sir Henry coughed and went puce about the nostrils; Robert took another swallow of wine with the greatest concentration, while Eleanor gripped the carved arms of her chair so that her knuckles showed white.

It was Anthony who spoke first. 'An interesting observation. You think music could make brothers of us all?'

'I do. When I am singing, I am one with the music. Nothing else matters.'

'Not even your faith?'

'My faith is expressed through the music. We have a glorious Christian heritage, and it is expressed most perfectly through music. Forgive me. I had not intended to cause offence. It is a subject on which I feel strongly.'

'So it would appear. I commend you. Beliefs should be held with passion, or they are not worth having at all.'

Eleanor stood up. 'The afternoon has turned quite mild. Would you care for a turn in the garden, Lord Trenoweth ?'

'Eleanor!' Her father's tone of voice was sharp.

'Father, I shall come to no harm. There is very little snow left, and we shall not be very far from the house. I will go to fetch my cloak.'

Some few minutes later Francis was walking with her in the rose garden. The bare twigs of the bushes each held the lightest dusting of snow, and Francis thought they were quite beautiful.

'You have a gardener who knows how to look after roses.' He touched one with the tip of his finger.

'Your cousin thought they were dead. As to the gardener, I tend the rose garden myself.'

'Then I commend your skill. My mother always looks after her roses herself. I used to follow her with a basket when I was a child.'

'I had to learn from the gardeners. My mother died when I was born.' Eleanor shivered and drew her cloak closer about her shoulders.

'I am sorry. It must have been hard for you.'

'Harder for my father, I suspect. After all, I never knew her.'

Francis slowed his pace, aware that he was tending to outstrip her. 'Tell me, because I clearly embarrassed your family just now. What did I say that was so very terrible?'

Eleanor stopped walking and turned to face him. 'I was certain that it was not rudeness. Robert has clearly not told you.'

'Told me what?'

'That we are Roman Catholics.'

Francis gulped. 'All of you?'

'All of us. My father's brother Anthony is our priest.'

'And Robert?'

'Robert is your cousin, and you did not know? But then I believe he was only received into the Faith last year. My uncle played a significant part in his conversion.'

'He told me that he had met your uncle in London. But he conveniently left out further information.' Francis turned and began to walk again, trying to still the turmoil in his mind. *Papists*! People who would enslave them, force them to bow down to false idols, to worship in the way they commanded. He wanted to run away from Eleanor, to grab his horse and ride back to Oxford, to wash the taint of the experience from his soul and body. He felt shocked to the core of his being, yet curiously excited as well. So *this* was the enemy? She did not seem exactly dangerous.

After a few moments he turned, aware that Eleanor was keeping pace with him, clearly waiting for him to speak. Francis sensed her unhappiness, and knew then that he felt no revulsion, no animosity towards her. She was unhappy, and yet he was powerless to help. He was suddenly aware of was several pieces of a puzzle falling into place, and laughed uncertainly.

'And only two weeks ago I took part in a pope-burning procession.' He sensed the sudden tremor through her.

'Then indeed you must despise us.' She said it entirely calmly, as though it were a simple fact.

'Despise? Why, no. It is true that we cried "No popery! No slavery!", but only because the two seemed securely linked.' He glanced at the bench near which they had paused, but decided it was too damp to suggest sitting on it. 'Until now I had never met a pa... a Roman Catholic. I had learnt that all papists were traitors and worshippers of the anti-Christ. Yet you do not seem to be in any way a traitor.'

'Indeed, I hope not.' She turned to face him. 'There are some of our faith, we are told, who are so zealous that they would even resort to acts of treason to achieve what they perceive to be laudable ends. But we are not among them.'

'I am sure you are not.'

She smiled. 'And until now I had never met a Protestant. I had been taught that they are heathen who had turned their backs on the one true God and would desecrate our churches.'

Francis put his hand toward her elbow, and together they turned and began walking towards the house. 'Then perhaps it is you who would despise us.' He spoke quietly.

'You hardly seem evil. I think perhaps we both have a great deal to learn. But we had best get back into the house. My father will wonder what we are doing, and I know you have to go back to Oxford soon.'

'Why did your father invite me here? I was minded to refuse at first, but Robert was very persuasive.'

'It was I who suggested it in the first place. Robert mentioned he had a cousin in Oxford.' She looked up at him, and this time the smile was almost a grin. 'I suppose I was curious.'

'After today I hardly think I will be invited again.'

'Why should you think that? We know we are not popular in this country. We know there are those who believe we want to subvert true religion and kill the King. You have just furnished proof of such beliefs.'

They both slowed their pace as they approached the house. 'Only last week I said to a friend that I had never met a Papist. He said I should never trust one.'

'If there were truth in these allegations of plots and treason, then people would be entirely right to persecute us. If such plotters exist – and I do not know of any – we are not among them. All we wish to do is to practise our faith.'

'As many of us would say.' Francis concentrated on where he was placing his feet. The ground on which he was walking no longer seemed secure, and it helped avoid the thoughts chasing each other in his head. He tried to envisage a conversation with Christopher, and could not. And Robert? Where was Robert in all this?

'How long have you known Robert?' The question was almost abrupt.

'Not long. He has been here three or four times. My uncle introduced him, and my father appears to like him.'

'And you?'

'I have not yet got to know him well.' She appeared reluctant to say more, and Francis did not press her.

They were almost back at the house now, and Eleanor smiled at him.

'Come. My father will not eat you. He knew of your faith before he invited you here.'

Sir Henry, Anthony and Robert were sitting in the parlour, each apparently immersed in his own thoughts.

Francis went straight up to Sir Henry. 'My apologies, sir, for my earlier rudeness. I can only plead that I spoke out of ignorance.'

Sir Henry smiled. 'A well-mannered Protestant. I share your ambition, young sir, that in matters of faith we should all be united.'

Anthony stood up. 'Now that you know of our persuasion, I should welcome a discussion with you. It is important to have firm beliefs, but it is also important to be able to listen to the views of others. Do you not think so?'

Francis inclined his head. 'Undoubtedly, sir. I have just had a most interesting conversation with Miss Somerville. It is clear that the University is not the only place where I can expect to learn.'

*

'Why did you not tell me?'

Robert and Francis were riding back to Oxford through the last of the snow, now turning to a brown, slippery slush. There was clearly not going to be a frost that night. Will and Robert's servant Tom were a little way behind them.

'And what good would it have done if I had? You would simply have refused to come at all. Now you can see that your so-called papists are people, just like you. We live, we love, we laugh, and all we ask is to be allowed to worship in peace. Do you have a problem with that?'

'I – no – a – that is – of course not.' Francis ducked to avoid an overhanging branch, and straightened himself slowly. 'But surely you can see how difficult it was for me, finding out from a stranger that you, my cousin, have converted in this way.'

'I am sure that Eleanor was the soul of tact. She is a sweet girl.'

Francis looked sharply at his cousin. 'Yes. I still feel I was led into unpardonable rudeness.'

'You extricated yourself with aplomb of which your father would be proud.' Robert quickened his pace, and Francis pushed his horse to a canter to keep up.

'I certainly find myself with a great deal to think about.' Francis reached his cousin and slowed his pace, hoping that Robert would do likewise.

'Then you will come again?' Francis turned in surprise at the eagerness in Robert's voice.

'I have already said so.' Francis was aware that he sounded almost curt. 'Though – I am not at all sure what it is I am accepting.'

'An invitation to a house where there is culture, conversation, ideas, yes, and music too. You did not hear Eleanor play.'

'That is certainly worth looking forward to.' They were through Woodstock now, and had set their faces towards Oxford. 'Does Thomas know of your conversion?'

'He does; and of course he is far from pleased. But I truly believe that I have now embraced the one true Faith. I wish you could see it, Francis. The day I met Anthony Somerville was the most fortunate of my life. He opened my eyes to so much that is wrong in this country, and could be glorious.'

'Anthony.' Francis was thoughtful for a moment or two. 'I did not feel that I got to know him at all well.'

'Nobody does. You quite properly deferred to Sir Henry as the head of the household. But Anthony rules at Coneybury, make no mistake about it. You may not have got to know Anthony, but he will have been watching and assessing you.'

'That does not sound altogether comfortable.'

Robert laughed, and Francis was suddenly reminded of the times they had played together on a Cornish beach. Robert could always manage to get his way then, but something in the laugh this time had alerted Francis to the fact that it might be dangerous to be pulled under his cousin's sway now.

'We shall be in Oxford soon. Did you not want to spend the night at Coneybury?'

'I knew that you could not, and it seemed civil to return with you. The Mitre you suggested is really quite reasonable. And, Francis – '

'Yes?' Francis was acutely aware of the childish, dangerous pull.

'You need not fear Anthony Somerville. He is a very wise gentleman.'

'So you keep telling me. But a Roman Catholic priest – Robert, that takes some thinking about.'

'He is also a man of great courage. Though he is not a Jesuit, and therefore not committing treason even by being here, his position as a priest is still a difficult one. As Anthony Somerville, younger brother to Sir Henry, he is safe. But as anything else – his position could be distinctly uncomfortable.'

Francis nodded slowly. 'I understand. I believe he is also a very clever man.'

'He certainly is. He may appear cold to you, but do not let that deceive you. He is passionate about things he truly believes in.'

'He said as much, though it is true I saw little of it. But then I have only just met him.'

Robert patted his horse's neck. 'We are almost at Magdalen Bridge already,' he said. 'But I am sure we shall meet again soon, cousin.'

'Oh, yes I am sure of that. Will!'

'My lord?'

'Take the horses to the stable. I think I am just in time for chapel, if I hurry.'

'Very good, my lord.'

It was not until after chapel and supper that Francis was able to talk to Christopher. His friend's expression changed from mild interest to consternation to alarm as Francis recounted what had happened during his visit to Coneybury.

'You are surely not going there again, knowing what you know?' Christopher had now reached bewilderment.

'I have been thinking a great deal.' Francis leaned forward excitedly. 'Robert has been clever, it is true. Had he told me that they were papists I would never have gone. Yet now – there is something about that household, Christopher, that makes me want to know more. 'Don't you see what a signal service I could perform if I could discover anything resembling a plot?'

'I thought you said they were all above reproach.'

'I only said that of Eleanor. What chance has she had, being raised in a household like that?'

'And this would have nothing to do with her blue eyes?'

Francis took a pull at his ale. 'I mentioned several things about Eleanor, but not, I think, the colour of her eyes. In fact I believe them to be brown.'

Christopher gave a shout of laughter. 'Oh Francis, if you could see yourself! You look positively pompous. It does not suit you.'

Francis smiled. 'I shall go back there. I believe it could be important that I do.'

'And Robert? Is he still your idol?'

'I tried to get him to explain himself as we returned, but he became all high and mighty with me, claiming that he had converted to the one true faith. No, he is not my idol. When I was a child he seemed to be the ideal, but we are treading very different paths now.'

'A least that is a relief.'

'You know he is in service to the Duke of York?'

'That makes sense. Was that before or after his conversion?'

'I really don't know. I was so startled by the whole turn of events that I forgot to ask.'

'He is wily, your cousin.'

'Yes. I see that now. I had not seen him for nearly three years, remember. Much has changed in that time.'

'So what are you going to do now?'

'We do not have a music evening tonight. I think Tacitus might benefit from a little further study if I am to make any sense of disputation in the morning.'

'Disputation! I had forgotten. My appointment with Tacitus, I think, is equally urgent.'

Will brought them some more mulled ale, and they agreed to study together, but Francis knew that his thoughts were not really on his work, and he suspected that Christopher's were not either. He smiled as his friend looked up.

'Be careful, Francis. I realise you think you know what you are doing, but we live in dangerous times.'

'Which is why I need to go back. I think I may have gained Eleanor's confidence; if I do not go back soon I will lose it.'

'You never were one to do things by halves. It seems there is no dissuading you.'

Francis grinned. 'Decidedly not. I know I was reluctant to go there at first, but now – I have become intrigued, Christopher, and I want to know more.'

*

Daylight had long since faded, and the bare branches of the trees looked bleak outside the parlour window where Sir Henry and Anthony Somerville sat. A few candles had been lit, but more light came from the fire burning in the hearth, sending ghostly shadows chasing up the walls, and putting the trees outside into stark relief.

Anthony cradled his glass of wine thoughtfully, and looked up at his brother.

'I think we can congratulate ourselves. We are doing well.'

'I m not happy. It looks as though Eleanor is about to care more for a heathen Protestant than a good Catholic we have brought into the family.'

'Tush, man, they have only met once! Young Lord Trenoweth has connections that could be of great importance to us. Trust me, I know about these things. You look after your estate, which I own you do well – and try to find out more about this Mr Purcell before he comes again.'

Sir Henry stood up. 'I still think it is dangerous for Eleanor. She is so young.'

'And therefore totally under your protection. Brother, you have nothing to fear. But if our great design is to have any chance of success then we should cultivate Lord Trenoweth. He is intelligent but naïf – an ideal combination.'

Sir Henry stood up, frowning. 'Despite your calling, you seem to revel in danger.'

'Henry, think! If we do nothing our lazy monarch will pass this exclusion bill, and agree to his brother being denied his rightful place as the heir, for no better reason than that he shares our faith. Surely you see that we must have York on the throne?'

'Certainly he would be better for those of our persuasion than his brother. Yet the last Exclusion Bill was thrown out.'

'This one may not be. We would never have thought of a plot if these Whigs had not invented it for us. But with their talk of Exclusion, they force it on us. We face extinction else.'

'Surely you exaggerate.'

'I do not think so. If the Whigs get their precious Exclusion, they will sweep all before them. We will have the dour Prince of Orange as our King, and we will face much more severe penalties than the Test Acts, which merely forbid us public office.'

Sir Henry poured himself some more wine. 'And Robert? Are you going to use him, as you would use Lord Trenoweth?'

'Sit down, Henry. I do not like you towering over me. This talk of using people is absurd. It was Eleanor who first suggested Lord Trenoweth coming here. Do not forget that. And you seemed happy enough with the idea.'

'He seems a pleasant enough young man. Perhaps you could bring about his conversion, as you did Robert's.'

'Perhaps. Though I do not think it likely. This young man is of an altogether different stamp. But even for us to show him that we are not as prejudiced as he believes, as he probably is himself, could be extremely useful to us.'

'H'm.' Henry drained his wine, stood up and moved towards the door. 'It grows late. It is time to retire.'

'Let me ask you one final question, brother. Do you wish to see this country brought back to the true Faith, to the obedience of the Holy Father?'

'Of course. I would be failing in my duty as a Catholic if I did not.'

'Then leave the means by which it is to be achieved to me. I am a priest; do you really think I would do anything that would endanger either of our immortal souls?'

'No. I just do not like the road on which we are travelling.'

'The darkest hour is always just before the dawn.' Anthony was smiling as he stood and flicked dust from his lace cuffs. 'But what a dawn it will be!'

Chapter Four

Sir Henry and Eleanor stood outside the house, looking at a line of beech trees bordering the drive.

'Those two,' said Eleanor. 'They are going to have to come down.'

'But why?' Her father was clearly irritated. 'It will spoil the line. The approach to the house is particularly fine at the moment. My father planted those trees. It will look ragged.'

'We can replant. But beeches are shallow-rooting trees, Father. Why those two are dying when all their fellows seem healthy enough I don't understand. If we do not fell those two they will fall down in the next gale.'

'H'm.' Sir Henry was clearly unimpressed. 'You spend too much time out here, I'm thinking. It is not seemly for a young lady.'

'Father, I desire what is best for the estate. John and I have inspected all the trees, and it is plain that those two are not safe.'

'Oh, John.' Too late Eleanor remembered her father's opinion of his steward was not high. 'What other trouble is he stirring?'

'He cares a great deal for the estate. Particularly the trees.'

'I know you think so. I'm not convinced. I shall give my answer when I am satisfied.'

Eleanor sighed, and began to walk towards the house. Then she stopped, and turned back to her father.

'When is Lord Trenoweth to come again?'

'On Thursday. Robert will not be able to come. It seems His Grace needs him in London.'

'So he does do some work.' Eleanor spoke quietly, but her father looked up sharply.

'Robert is very conscientious. I value his opinions – and his friendship.'

'And Fr – Lord Trenoweth? I would have thought you would no longer welcome him.'

'He spoke in ignorance, and his apology was genuine. Besides, I would not have him think that we act only out of prejudice. You have few enough companions of your own age. You can never share his faith, but he is of good family, and I have no objection to your seeing him again.'

'I shall look forward to it.'

'But you need a female companion. Your Aunt Mary arrives tomorrow.'

'Father, I can manage. I am sure she would rather be in her own home.'

'On the contrary. She has never been one to shirk her duty. For a long time now she has seen herself as a substitute mother for you.'

Eleanor's mouth set in a tight line, and her father smiled.

'You do not like your aunt?'

'She treats me as a child, and would have me sitting inside with embroidery, when I would rather be tending the garden or out riding.'

'You always were headstrong. Your aunt thinks I spoil you.'

'Spoil me! What a strange idea. But she will not take the running of the household from me, will she? I enjoy it, and I believe you are satisfied with the way I arrange things. And the servants are used to me.'

'Of course you may continue with your work. But your aunt thinks I am too easy-going.'

'You are.' Anthony appeared suddenly beside them. 'It will do you good, Eleanor, to listen to your aunt. We all desire what is best for you, but your aunt is right. Your father is too lax. A little strictness in your life would be most beneficial to you.'

'You speak as though I am still a child.' Eleanor was dismally aware that she sounded petulant.

'You are. Until you are of age you are subject to your father. If within that time your father gives his consent to your marriage you will be subject to your husband.'

Eleanor opened her mouth, closed it, then opened it again.

'I need to go and talk to Cook about dinner.' She began to walk towards the house, only to hear her uncle say to her father 'Not before time. She needs taking in hand.'

She quickened her step, managing not to run, but regained the house with her head held high. But when safely indoors she headed, not for the kitchen, but for the sanctuary of her room.

Sarah was there, tidying the drapes on the bed and laying the fire. At the sight of her round, comfortable face Eleanor flung herself into a chair and burst into tears.

Sarah left off what she was doing and came across to her.

'What is it, Miss?'

Eleanor coughed, steadied herself and smiled up at her maid.

'My aunt is to arrive tomorrow. My uncle thinks I "need taking in hand".'

'He said that to you?'

'No, to my father. But I think perhaps he wanted me to hear. They all think I'm just a child.'

'But you can show them you're not, Miss. Don't you let the old dragon get the better of you.'

Eleanor laughed then, and took Sarah's hand in hers.

'I won't, Sarah. My father has no idea who I count as truly my friends.'

*

'So you are determined to go to Coneybury tomorrow?'

Christopher's brow was furrowed as he looked up at Francis over his pot of ale. It was a cold evening, and the two of them were sitting by the fire of Francis' room, ostensibly to look over their disputations, but the volumes of Plato and Virgil lay unopened.

'Yes. There was a particular reason behind the original invitation, and I want to find out what it is. The atmosphere in that house – there is something going on.'

'You think there is a plot?'

'It seems absurd. But I don't know, and I shall feel thoroughly uncomfortable until I do. It is unlikely, of course, that it would be confined to one household, which makes it all the more dangerous.'

'Shall you take Will with you?'

'Yes. I shall be glad of the company, and it is safer that way.'

'Then look after him, Will. You know what a hothead your master can be.'

Will appeared in front of them, apparently unruffled. 'I will that, sir. No harm shall come to him that I can prevent.' He left the room quietly.

Francis took a long pull at his ale and wiped his mouth with the back of his hand. 'The place will be buzzing with the news that the Lords have thrown out the bill. It touches them very nearly.'

'They will be pleased, surely? If it had been passed then York would no longer be his brother's heir.'

'At least that danger has not materialised.'

'But will it still not be dangerous for you? You have already told me you made an embarrassing remark. Next time it could be worse.'

'I don't think it will be more dangerous. They want something of me, and I think are unlikely to do anything that would make it difficult for me to go there – yet. I have to know what it is they want of me, Christopher, I have to.' He yawned, looked at his Virgil, and looked away again.

'Will!' he called. 'Surely you have some more ale in there! Would you have the two of us die of thirst in here?'

Will came in with a fresh jug of ale.

'Your ale, my lord.' He set it down on the hearth. 'Will there be anything further tonight?'

'Stop being so infernally pompous, Will. I'll see you in the morning.'

Christopher reached for the jug of ale as Will left the room.

'Is Will your friend, or your servant? I never quite understand.'

'Both,' said Francis at once. 'Though not a friend in the sense that you are. But he serves me well, and faithfully. I would trust him with my life. Come, let us to Virgil. I hope to see my tutor early, before leaving for Coneybury.'

*

The next day dawned clear and bright, with a hard frost on the ground. Francis was up early, and after breakfasting discovered that his tutor was entirely amenable to an early visit from him. It was not a comfortable hour; Francis left acutely aware that he ought to be working harder, even though he had little intention of taking a degree.

He returned to his room, to find that Will had laid out his thick wool riding cloak and breeches, together with the high leather boots that Francis often thought were something of a luxury. Curiously, he never thought to view his riding gloves in the same light.

'I'll come round to the stables with you, Will,' said Francis cheerfully. 'It's easier than bringing two horses back here.'

'As you wish, my lord.' They were soon ready with their saddle bags packed, while Christopher looked on anxiously and warned Will to look after his master.

Francis rested a hand on his friend's shoulder. 'We'll be all right. It's just the morning for a ride.'

'And did your tutor agree with that?'

Francis laughed. 'Riding wasn't mentioned. He has told me I must work harder. Fortunately he omitted to say what at.'

Before long Francis and Will were riding out of Oxford, turning their horses towards Woodstock. The sun was starting to melt the frost in places, but anywhere still in shadow was still iron hard with it.

'I miss a Cornish winter when we're here.' Francis pulled his cloak about him. 'The trees are just as bare, but it's gentler somehow. Less menacing.'

'The sea is always near, my lord. Makes it milder.'

'It's certainly cold enough here. I'm surprised the sun has melted any of that frost.'

In Woodstock they turned themselves towards Charlbury, riding through the woods in all their winter majesty.

'Nearly there.' Francis turned in his saddle. 'What did you think of Coneybury on our first visit, Will? I forgot to ask you.'

'It's a grand enough house. Bigger than Pelistry, yet Sir Henry's only a baronet, while your father's an earl, in with the king and such.'

'My father never wanted to rebuild Pelistry. It held too many memories for him. And which of the two do you prefer?'

'Oh, my lord, that's not a fair question to a Cornishman.'

Before long they were through Charlbury and trotting down the hill past the Cornbury estate, and eventually into Sir Henry's park. Despite the cold they were both now pleasantly warm from the ride.

Once they had seen their horses into the care of Sir Henry's stables, and Will had helped Francis into the broadcloth suit he had brought with him, they parted.

'Enjoy yourself in the kitchen, Will. Don't eat all the food.' And with that admonishment Francis set off for the parlour.

A fire was burning cheerfully in the grate. Sir Henry stood in front of it, thereby preventing its warmth from reaching the others in the room. Seated side by side on one of the settees, but looking far from comfortable, were Eleanor and a lady Francis did not recognise.

Sir Henry came forward. 'Lord Trenoweth. It is good to see you again. May I introduce my sister Mary, who has come to give us the benefit of her company. My brother will be joining us shortly.'

The lady in question turned icy green eyes in Francis' direction, and he was momentarily unnerved. A narrow face was surrounded by thick, dark hair; as he raised her hand to his lips Francis felt as though she were seeing into his very soul.

'You are a cousin of Robert Carey, I believe.' Francis was surprised at how deep her voice was, almost masculine. 'An excellent young man. You could do a great deal worse than follow in his footsteps.'

'Robert and I have been the greatest of friends since childhood.' Francis sat on a stool close by, and wondered if Sir Henry ever really relaxed. Eleanor shot him a look that comprised both sympathy and understanding.

That blue velvet becomes her very well, he found himself thinking. It is exactly the colour of her eyes. He had not been entirely truthful with Christopher. They were blue.

'Have you heard any more of Mr Purcell's music since we saw you?' Eleanor's smile was entirely without artifice.

'No. Though I am sure that I shall. But we had a wonderful evening of music in my rooms some days ago. I was able to sing, and I have friends very capable on both violin and lute.'

'I did not know that you sang.' Eleanor looked up in surprise.

'I enjoy music in any way I can. Singing, playing, listening. Had things been otherwise I might have gained a place in the chapel choir.'

Sir Henry stood up. 'It wants still an hour to dinner.' He fingered his lace collar. 'And the frost is almost gone. It is almost mild. Why do you young people not take a turn in the garden for a little?'

His sister shot him a look of consternation, which he answered with the smallest shake of his head.

'Thank you, sir.' Francis stood up and offered Eleanor his arm.

'I will go to fetch my cloak.' With the merest hint of a smile Eleanor left the room.

A few moments later Francis and Eleanor were walking along a broad path that led to a small folly he had not noticed before. He was glad that he was still wearing his leather boots, and was relieved to see that, as well as wrapping herself in her thick woollen cloak, Eleanor had exchanged her soft slippers for a pair of robust boots.

Eleanor led him straight to the folly, then turned to him with a smile.

'I have always loved this,' she said. 'When I was small I would pretend that it was my house, and that I could do anything I liked in it.' She touched the stone affectionately. 'Whatever else changes, it is always here. Always the same.'

'And much in your life is not.' Francis looked up at the folly, not at Eleanor, as he spoke.

'How did you know?' He looked at her then, saw the anxiety in her eyes, the tremble at the corner of her mouth.

'I saw the way you looked when your aunt spoke to me. I saw the eagerness with which you accepted your father's offer.'

She smiled then, her face suddenly looking slightly mischievous. 'I don't know if my father thinks he is being kind to me or not. My aunt has come here to provide me with some female company, I am told. I believe it is to chaperone me and see that I behave myself.'

'You do not like your aunt.' It was a statement, not a question.

'She has her own ideas and values. She was married and widowed a long time ago, but has no children. As far as she is concerned, I am simply a disposable asset.'

'And you do not wish to be disposed of.' Again the statement.

'Not without my own consent.' She suddenly took his hand between her two gloved ones. 'How do you like your cousin?' The question was abrupt.

Francis allowed his hand to remain where it was. 'Robert is a little older than I. As a child, I always admired him and wished to emulate him.'

'And now?'

'Now – there is something about Robert that I do not understand. I have always known that he was ambitious. I wonder just how much – and how many people – he will sacrifice on the altar of his ambition.'

'I think he is being groomed as a husband for me.'

'And you do not want to?'

'In many ways he seems ideal. Good family, a Catholic, young, presentable.'

'And yet?'

'And yet I do not feel safe with him. Marriage to Robert would not be comfortable. I doubt whether I could love him.'

'I had not known of his conversion. No doubt that makes him more attractive to your family.'

'Undoubtedly.' Eleanor released his hand, and Francis was conscious of a small pang of regret. 'Though it was I who suggested it, I am still a little puzzled as to why you were invited here.'

'I am glad that you did. Only one person in Oxford knows I am here, and he certainly counselled caution. I think he believes that I am courting danger.'

'And you?'

'I am having to revise so many of my ideas as to what a Catholic is.'

'And I of Protestants.' Eleanor gave a small laugh. 'I had been taught that they were little better than pagans. Yet you seem to me to be a man of faith.'

'As I hope I am. But you think your father may have some particular reason for inviting me here?'

'I am sure of it. Rank is important to him, and you are of noble family. That could be enough.'

Francis smiled. 'My father was ennobled by the present king. My grandfather was a baronet, as is your father.'

'But my father may not have known that. He probably sees you as old established Cornish aristocracy.' She giggled slightly.

'Do you think that is why he invited me here?'

'No. No, not really. But be on your guard, Francis. There is an atmosphere that makes me uneasy. I hardly know what it is. I relax more with my maid than I do with my own family.' She laughed, but to Francis it sounded brittle, false.

'Come.' Eleanor turned around and began walking towards the house. 'We must return, or we shall be late for dinner, and then Aunt Mary will grumble. And that is a great deal worse than my father.'

Sir Henry was in expansive mood at dinner, though his sister sat very still and only picked at her food.

'As your father sits in the House of Lords, no doubt you have heard that the Exclusion Bill has been defeated.' Sir Henry turned smiling towards Francis.

'Indeed. My father would have voted against it. He believes strongly that, whatever his beliefs, the Duke of York should retain his position as his brother's heir.'

'Your father is well acquainted with the King, I believe?'

'They understand each other.' Francis smiled. 'It was a friendship made in adversity, and they are much of an age. But by all accounts they are very dissimilar.'

'By all accounts?' It was Anthony who picked up on the phrase.

'I have never met His Majesty. My father enjoys his company, though I think he knows he will never share his confidences.'

'But your father is often in London?' Anthony seemed to have taken on the role of questioner.

'He and my cousin Thomas, Robert's older brother, share a house when Parliament is sitting. They hold very different political views, but are the best of friends.'

'Different? How so?' This time it was the deep voice of Mary that broke into the conversation.

'Thomas is a Whig, and will vote for Exclusion. He believes that the risks of the Duke of York on the throne are simply too great.' Francis noticed the pained expression on Mary's face, though her two brothers remained outwardly impassive. 'My father believes that we meddle with the succession at our peril.'

'A wise gentleman, your father.' Anthony leaned across the table. 'I met him at court last year, as I think I mentioned. But is not Sir Thomas Carey something of a hothead?'

Francis helped himself to a jumball and munched at it thoughtfully. 'Thomas, I believe, would describe his brother Robert in very similar terms. He regards Robert as the rebel.'

'I would hardly describe Robert as a rebel.' Sir Henry looked puzzled. 'He is a most upright young gentleman.'

'Robert and I were childhood friends.' Francis was acutely aware of Eleanor's injunction to be on his guard. 'As he is the elder, I found myself deferring to him a good deal. I always admired him.'

'You use the past tense,' said Anthony quietly.

'Our paths have crossed less in recent years. He is much occupied at Court, and I am busy with my studies in Oxford.'

'And what do you intend to do when you have finished your studies?' Mary turned her penetrating gaze towards him.

'Return to Cornwall, I expect, to manage my father's estate when he is not there.'

Anthony looked up sharply. 'You will not miss the academic life?'

'I should miss the music. But I love our home at Pelistry. Perhaps I may tempt good musicians there. I have a little ability myself.'

'You do yourself an injustice, Lord Trenoweth.' Sir Henry took a swallow of wine. 'I heard you singing earlier, when you thought you were alone. You have a fine counter tenor voice.'

Francis smiled, and turned to the mutton in front of him. The leaping flames from the fire seemed suddenly hot. 'You are kind, sir. I could live without many things, but not without music.' He turned to Eleanor. 'I must return to Oxford shortly. But I have a little time before that. You have a spinet, I believe. Would you consider playing for me?'

Eleanor's eyes sparkled mischief. 'If you will sing for me.'

The afternoon's music, held in the first floor parlour, was enjoyed not only by Francis and Eleanor, but by Sir Henry, Anthony and Mary. This was a smaller room, less ornate than the one he had been shown into earlier, but Francis found it comfortable. It was clearly mainly a family room, and not designed to impress guests. But Eleanor's spinet was kept there, so they adjourned to this room to make music.

A fire burned in the hearth, sending beams of light flickering over the tapestries, so that Francis almost lost his note more than once, watching the light change. At the end of half an hour's singing he was surprised to receive polite applause from his audience.

'My brother was right, Lord Trenoweth.' Anthony's smile was almost wolfish. 'You do indeed have a fine voice. Is there much music in your family?'

'Not really. My mother sings a little, but my father is happier riding, or hunting with his hawk. He has adapted to Whitehall well enough, but his heart is still in Cornwall.'

'As yours is.' Eleanor rested her hand on the lid of her instrument.

'Why, yes. We all have somewhere to belong, do we not? Until I came to Oxford I had not been out of Cornwall. Crossing the Tamar was a major adventure.'

'The Tamar?' Sir Henry looked puzzled.

'It is a river that separates Cornwall from Devon. And I am a Cornishman.' He could not keep the pride out of his voice. 'We Cornish are an independent people.'

Mary looked up and fixed him with a commanding stare, which he suspected she thought was a smile.

'You speak as though you were Cornish rather than English.'

'Sometimes it feels as though we are.' Francis tried to speak lightly, but he felt uncomfortable.

'And Robert.' Again Anthony appeared to have taken on the role of inquisitor. 'Is he not also a Cornishman?'

'Indeed. Though perhaps he is less enamoured of it than I am. I think perhaps that Cornwall is too small for his ambitions.'

'Does that mean you think the less of him?' There was no mistaking the critical edge to Mary's voice.

'Not at all.' Francis seated himself by the fire and smoothed the broadcloth of his breeches. 'Our friendship goes right back to our childhood. We are just taking different paths now that we are no longer children. Robert is a younger son, of course, and his father has died. He needs to make his way in the world.'

'And you do not?' Francis was now certain that he had made a very poor impression on Eleanor's aunt, chaperone, dragon.

'In one sense, no. I love Pelistry, and think I could look after it well. I am sure I shall go to London soon, but Cornwall is my home.' He looked across at Eleanor and relaxed in the warmth of her smile. It had been worth coming. But he knew the time had come for him to leave. He must return to Oxford.

To his surprise, after he had taken his leave of his hosts and walked round to the stables, expecting to find Will there, he found them deserted apart from Eleanor.

He moved towards her. 'I did not expect to find you here. Will not your father be surprised?'

'He will not know. But I wanted to speak with you away from my father, my uncle and my aunt.'

'In that order?' He tried to keep his voice light.

'Do not make fun of me.' She moved forward, and he saw the anxiety in the lines about her mouth, her eyes lacking their sparkle. 'They will try to use you, Francis. How, I do not know; my uncle in particular will have his reasons.'

'I did not have to come here. And your father is hardly going to keep me here by force.'

'No. It is my uncle you should fear, not my father. He is a priest, and I must respect him for that. But he is ruthless, and will not hesitate to sacrifice a man – or a woman – if he believes it could lead to the greater good. I do not want it to be you.'

'Or you.' Francis took a step closer to her. 'Are you not in greater danger than I? I am here for a short period as a guest. You are not able to mount a horse and ride away.'

She gave an unconvincing laugh. 'I am not in danger – except, perhaps, of suffocation through my Aunt Mary's attentions. But I have my own remedies for that.' Suddenly her eyes sparkled a little. 'My father thinks I lack female company. He even said my aunt sees herself as a substitute mother for me. But our cook, whom my father would probably barely recognise, has filled that role far more effectively for years. We are genuinely fond of each other.'

Francis rested his hand on his horse's flank, and the beast shifted restlessly. 'She is an excellent cook. But she could not save you from danger.'

'I do not believe that I am in danger. Whereas you – ' She swung round suddenly, facing him. 'I cannot tell you not to come here again. Nor do I want to. But – please, be careful. I know that you are a man of courage. Use it wisely.'

Francis was surprised at how difficult he found it to resist the temptation to sweep her into his arms. He took a moment instead to adjust his horse's saddle girths.

'I will be careful. I promise.'

She smiled. One further warning. Look to Robert. Where my uncle leads, he will follow. I feel sure of it.'

'Robert? But – he is my cousin. We played together as children.'

'I know. The warning remains. And now, if you are to start your journey to Oxford soon, you should take your leave of my father.'

'I will do so. But I must find my servant.'

Her laughter was like music to him. 'He is almost certainly in the kitchen. Cook loves an appreciative customer.'

Francis kissed her hand, and left the stable alone.

Chapter Five

As soon they were through Charlbury Francis set his horse to a gallop, so that Will was hard put to keep up with him. He eased off as they entered the thick woodland, inhaling its pungent smell, and let out a long, deep sigh.

'And how do you find Coneybury now, Will?'

'Well enough, my lord. The servants were very pleasant to me, especially the cook. She seems particularly fond of Miss Eleanor.'

'Yes. I imagine that would be the case.'

'My lord?'

'Shall we say there is a certain – atmosphere – between the other members of the household. Are all the servants Catholic?'

'No, my lord. The cook is, though fortunately not the sort who will have nothing to do with Protestants.'

Francis laughed. 'We might both have gone hungry else. Miss Somerville appears very fond of her.'

'The feelings are returned, I know that. If it were not for Miss Eleanor she would have left a long time ago.'

'There is something about that household,' said Francis, 'that makes me feel uncomfortable. I wish I knew what it was.' He looked up at the sky. 'We shall need to get a move on, though. I don't want to get caught out after dark if we can help it.'

The light was beginning to fade by the time they rode up to Magdalen Bridge, and Francis paused.

'Take the horses to the stable, can you, Will? I must get inside. I have missed chapel, which is unfortunate, but I must see Christopher.' He slid from the saddle and handed the reins to his servant.

He walked the few yards to the college entrance, which was deserted. As dusk was fast approaching he saw nothing unusual in this. His mind was full of the events of the day, and his possible future course of action. He was about to go inside when he felt a hand on his shoulder and turned instinctively. A burly apprentice, dressed in rough homespun and woollen hose, now had his arm firmly about Francis' waist.

'Not so soon, my pretty Papist.' Even as he spoke three more sidled out of the shadows and encircled him, pinioning his arms to his sides. Even as he opened his mouth to shout a large hand prevented his making any sound, and he was hustled away towards the bridge.

All this had happened in a matter of seconds, it seemed, and Francis had not as yet even felt anger, only surprise. He tried to wrench his arms free, to be rewarded with a knee in his back.

'You're not running away from us.' The burly apprentice thrust his unshaven, unwashed face close to Francis'. 'We've got a present for you, but we don't want to give it to you quite so near your chums over there.' He jerked his head in the direction of the college. 'But we know we can get down to the river from here. Fewer people to see.'

They were the far side of the bridge from the college now, and Francis' surprise was moving towards full-blown rage, though with four strong apprentices moving him bodily, one still with a hand over his mouth, he was completely unable to do anything about it.

A short way beyond the bridge there was access down to the river, though Francis strongly suspected that the apprentices had no right to be there. But he was pushed and dragged down to the riverside itself, slipping to his knees in the mud more than once, only to be dragged up roughly again. By now the light had almost completely faded, but his attackers were sure-footed. Wryly Francis thought of his cheerful ride home with Will, of Christopher's warnings of danger.

Apart from the burly apprentice his assailants were totally silent, and Francis found this oddly disconcerting. He had no idea why he should have been attacked in this way, but there must have been a powerful reason. The apprentices would be in serious trouble if caught.

He was pulled and dragged a little way upstream from the bridge. Under cover of a stand of trees he was roughly thrown to the ground and a vicious punch landed to the side of his head.

He landed on his chest, the breath knocked out of him. Cautiously he pulled himself to his knees, and found the four of them standing in a circle round him. Blazing anger took control then; he got swiftly to his feet, ignoring the pain, and his adversary reeled against a tree. But Francis was outnumbered, and one of the others seized him swiftly by the shoulders and gave him a powerful push, so that the back of his head hit the rough bark of a tree with a resounding crack. Francis was only dimly aware of the fact that he must have cried out, before he slipped to the mud and lay there, feeling completely dazed.

Even only semi-conscious he was aware of an impotent rage that he was unable to defend himself properly. But this was not a fight; no rules were being observed in what appeared to be a simple desire to inflict pain. Perhaps he had knocked down a friend of theirs during the pope-burning procession. He was hauled to his feet to be knocked down again, he was kicked and punched until he could no longer stand. It was only when, as he lay gasping in the mud and one of them aimed a sudden kick at the side of his head, that he realised the full horror of what they were about. How could he possibly allow himself to be done to death by a small group of apprentices?

He was no longer able to hit back. His only source of safety was the river. Hopefully they did not realise that he could swim. But he was too sick and dizzy to do more than crawl, and it was an easy matter for one of his foes to stop him, almost casually.

'You can go when I've finished with you, and not before. Though by that time you may not think it worth your while.'

'Who – what – why do you wish to kill me?' stammered Francis. He was flat on his back in the mud, one of his foes holding his arms above his head, the other with a knee in his chest. Every muscle screamed at him, but for the moment there seemed to have been a temporary lull in the conflict.

'I'm being well enough paid to see that you never visit your papist friends again.' The pressure of the knee increased, only a little, but to Francis it felt as though he were being crushed. 'Nor shall you,' was added viciously, and suddenly the blows started again, being showered with horrifying ease on to his face, his head, his chest. Blood poured from his nose and streaked his brow, while his eyes were so swollen that he could hardly see. He could feel his senses slipping from him, and knew there was nothing he could do to stop it.

It might have been a few moments or several hours, he could not tell. It was still dark when he woke, or rather when his unconsciousness lessened, and though there was a continual roaring in his ears the buffeting of fist and foot had ceased, and it seemed as though he was being gently caressed. He was frozen to the bone, however, and such clothing as remained to him clung tightly as though in need of protection. Eventually he realised where he was, and even then could see the irony of it. They must have beaten him unconscious and then cast him into the river, assuming he would speedily drown.

Drown? His faculties were suddenly sharpened as he realised that this was precisely what he was doing. His legs were leaden, his arms bruised and almost completely numb, and in his endeavours to breathe he appeared to have swallowed gallons of foul-tasting river water. From a different world came his father's voice telling him how to swim, how to let the water carry him rather than drag him down. In childhood it had been so easy; he had learnt to swim almost as soon as he could walk. But he felt heavy, his chest was tight, both from the beating he had received and for want of air. In another minute, he knew, he would be unconscious again, and from such an unconsciousness, frozen, exhausted and scarcely breathing, he would never awaken.

Perhaps because unconsciousness was already stealing over him, he found himself relaxing, only slightly, but enough to bring him to the surface and air. He knew that he must try to turn himself onto his back, now, for he was growing weaker every second. He brought all his enfeebled concentration to bear on an exercise he had done so many times before without even thinking about it, but to no avail. He could no longer keep his head out of the water and could feel himself sinking again.

But he had been borne downstream round a slight bend in the river where a small muddy promontory jutted out. By himself he could not have achieved it, but the current bore him towards it, and he found that all he needed to do to was to put out a hand to a trailing tree-root. Even that, he found, took all his energies and concentration, but he achieved it, trying to ignore the pain as he hauled himself clear of the water. Unable now to help himself any further, he lay down in the mud.

It was broad daylight when next he opened his eyes. Even before he did so he realised that the night must have ended, for the light hurt his eyelids and made the throbbing in his head worse. In his swollen face he could only open his eyes a fraction, and could hardly take in where he was.

He tried to move, but the dull aches in his limbs and body turned at once into a mass of harsh, shooting pains, and he lay still again, trying not even to shiver, as it made him more than ever conscious of every bruise on his body. By an effort of will he overcame the shivering, though he could do nothing to stop his teeth chattering. He wore neither boots nor stockings, and of the rest of his garments a muddy pair of breeches and a much-torn shirt still clung to him, filthy and wet.

At least for January the weather was comparatively mild, otherwise he might have frozen to death. But the river bank was muddy and slippery, and there was a thin drizzle falling.

How had he allowed himself to be so easily overcome? There were four of them, a voice inside his head reminded him, and he had been unprepared. But on the night of the pope-burning procession he had felled several of the townsmen, and had felt himself invincible.

He tried to take stock of his situation. How his face looked he could not tell, but he suspected it must be badly bruised. Certainly the flesh under his eyes was so swollen that he could only see a little.

He did not think any bones were broken; as he gingerly moved his tongue round his mouth it felt as though even his teeth had somehow survived. He was not ready to end his singing career yet, and he knew how important teeth were to a singer.

From the tightness in his chest he suspected he might have cracked a rib, maybe two, but they would heal. His arms were badly lacerated, probably as a result of contact with trees and stones on the ground. He was bruised in many places, particularly his face and his chest. His legs, apart from being scratched and dirty, did not appear to have fared too badly, but when he gingerly tried to stand he thought otherwise.

His right ankle was nearly twice its normal size, and clearly badly sprained. He was not going to be able to walk. But his greatest enemy was undoubtedly the cold, especially after having spent the night on the riverbank in torn and wet clothing. He must have some body heat left, but he was still soaking wet and shiveringly cold. He tried again to stand, and could hardly keep back a cry of pain.

He knew he would be seriously ill if he did not gain shelter soon. His adversaries probably assumed he had drowned; he did not want to have escaped that only to suffer a more lingering, painful death.

He looked about him. Even with his limited vision he could see that Magdalen Bridge was not far away; just beside it a young alder tree pushed upwards, some at least of its roots clearly visible.

Summoning his courage, he rolled over and tipped himself into the river. The shock of the immersion sharpened his wits, and much to his surprise he found himself standing on the riverbed. It must be shallower here than he had realised, but with the buoyancy of the water standing was not impossible, even with his injured ankle. The water, he realised dully, was not as cold as the air outside, but he was now so chilled he could hardly notice.

Frustratingly slowly, he inched himself towards the bridge, trying to ignore the pain in ankle, chest, face, almost anywhere. As he reached for the tree root he missed his footing and submerged himself for a moment. But he managed to balance on his left foot, grab the root and haul himself out of the water.

He looked at the muddy incline that led up to road level, and realised he would have to negotiate it if he was to reach safety. He crawled forwards on hands and knees, grabbing at roots, stones, stunted bushes, anything to stop him slipping on the muddy surface. He knew he was adding to his tally of injuries, but for the moment that hardly seemed to matter.

How he managed it he would never afterwards understand. Shivering uncontrollably now, he lay in the conduit by the side of the bridge, fighting the urge to close his eyes and let go. He could not even raise his head, and all he could see were feet passing him by. He tried to call out, to shout for help, but all he could manage was a croak.

It was enough. He felt himself lifted up, heard his name exclaimed in surprise, but by now he was incapable of replying. But the voice sounded encouraging, and he decided he could trust himself to his rescuer.

*

Francis awoke in his own room, the winter sun angling low through the window to turn his coverlet gold. He felt an immense lassitude, his mouth was dry and most of his body was too tender to touch. But he was alive.

Will was making up the fire in the grate. Francis raised himself on his elbows to speak to him, but a sudden sharp pain across his chest caused him to cry out, and he lay back again hurriedly.

Putting down the coal shovel, Will came across to the bed.

'You must lie still, my lord. The physician declares you have cracked two ribs. It will be painful until they heal. And your right ankle is badly sprained. You will not be able to walk on it for a little.'

'Anything else?'

'A great deal of bruising. How many attacked you?'

'Four.' Francis closed his eyes as the sickening events of the night before came back to haunt him.

'What day is it?' he asked suddenly.

'Saturday, my lord. You have slept the clock round. Mr Wentworth wanted to wake you to encourage you to drink, but I felt sure you needed to rest. You were so cold when I found you.'

'You found me?'

'Yes, my lord. I could not understand what had become of you. It did not take me very long to see to the horses. I could not find you that evening, so at first light I began searching again. Mr Wentworth came with me.'

'And it was as well that I did.' Christopher's large frame filled the doorway, his eyes filled with concern as he looked towards the bed. 'Will could never have got you back on his own.'

'How – ' Francis made another attempt at sitting up, but the pain was too great and he lay back again. 'But I can't just lie here and be waited on.'

'I don't think you have much alternative.' Christopher perched on a corner of the bed and touched his friend's hand. Francis winced.

'You are a mass of bruises, you spent the night in the open soaking wet, you cannot walk on your right foot and you have to let those ribs heal. Your attackers meant serious mischief, Francis. You are really very lucky.'

'Just wait until I get my hands on them,' Francis growled. 'Two I could have coped with, but four – it was just too many.'

'Francis, this is just what you must not do. As soon as you are able to move we have to get you out of Oxford.'

'Out of Oxford? What on earth for?'

'Because they will strike again if they see you walking about Oxford. They are part of a fanatical sect who genuinely believe it is no crime to kill a Papist, especially if they suspect he is involved in plotting. So much I managed to find out yesterday.'

'I am not a Papist. Didn't my work at the pope-burning procession mean anything?'

'They probably don't know about that. You have visited a Papist household. That is enough in their eyes. They meant to kill you, Francis. Quite possibly they think they did.'

'So you counsel I should run away. Isn't that just letting them win?'

Christopher stood up and began to pace the room. 'Francis, you can be thoroughly exasperating. I am not counselling running away. But nor do I want any mock heroics that would end up seeing you dead. Will, can you get any sense into him?'

Will stood up from beside the fire. 'I think you should have a drink, my lord. I have some mulled ale for you here.'

Christopher laughed. 'Ever practical, Will. But you are right, he must drink.'

Francis raised his head sufficiently for Will to get at least some of the ale inside him. As soon as it touched his lips Francis realised how thirsty he was. He gulped at it, and succeeding in splashing it on his face and the pillow. Christopher came round behind him, and supported his head to help him drink a little more.

Francis grimaced, and pushed the tankard away. 'Can't even have a decent drink. Shouldn't we be in chapel by now?'

Both Christopher and Will burst out laughing. 'You can't even leave your bed, and you talk about chapel!' Christopher's voice softened. 'Your tutor knows you are "indisposed". Nobody expects you anywhere at the moment.'

'Then I suppose I shall have to let you two look after me. As you said, I don't appear to have much alternative. But I haven't agreed to this nonsense of leaving Oxford. Isn't it rather hot in here?'

'The physician was most insistent you were kept warm, my lord.' Will looked at the fire. 'He prophesied serious consequences if you should become chilled in any way. It took a long time to get warmth back to you. I think you should rest again. I will go to prepare you some oatmeal pap.'

'But that is stuff for invalids!'

'Yes, my lord. You need to build your strength up.'

Christopher grinned at Will, and they left the room together. Francis was asleep almost before the door closed.

Chapter Six

Eleanor sat in her room, while Sarah brushed her hair. Normally Eleanor found this restful and soothing, but she was too agitated to sit still for long, and kept jumping up, causing the brush to tug at her hair. The third time this happened she swung around to snap at Sarah, but the girl's eyes were so full of concern that she smiled instead.

'I'm sorry, Sarah. I'm anxious. Robert is coming to dinner, and there have been so many comments, especially from my aunt, that I feel sure I am being pushed towards marriage with him. And I know I do not want to.'

'Is his cousin not coming with him today, Miss? For all that he is a Protestant, I believe that you like him.'

Eleanor's smile was more genuine this time, and she seated herself again, indicating that the brushing could continue.

'Yes. Yes, I do like him. And he was to have come, but a message has just been received that he will not be here after all. Just that. So now I am worrying as to what could have detained him.'

'Maybe he couldn't get leave from his college, Miss.'

'No, I don't think it's that. The message came from Robert. Just a note to say that circumstances kept Francis in Oxford, and he regretted he would not be able to join us. There was no word from Francis himself.'

'Mr Carey will be here soon, Miss. You can ask him yourself.'

'Oh I shall, Sarah. I shall.' She stood up. 'There, that will have to be enough. Do you think I will pass my aunt's inspection? She can be very critical.'

'I don't see how you can fail, Miss. And I'm sure Mr Carey will be impressed.'

Eleanor pouted at her and left the room.

By the time she reached the parlour Robert had already arrived, looking exquisite in a wine red brocade coat, giving no indication of having ridden a number of miles to get there.

'Eleanor.' Her father smiled at her, waving her rather vaguely further into the room. He was moving about restlessly, frowning and looking preoccupied. Anthony and Robert were seated side by side on the settee to the right of the fireplace, deep in conversation. Mary sat, or rather perched, at the other side of the fireplace, clearly expecting Eleanor to join her. She was dressed in deep blue velvet, the bodice shaped in such a way as to make her scanty bosom seem almost non-existent. Her hair was elaborately curled, but its steely grey did nothing to soften the severity of her narrow face.

Resignedly Eleanor sat down beside her, feeling at that moment she would almost prefer Robert's company to that of her aunt.

'We have been expecting you for some little time.' Her aunt's voice was cold. 'Don't tell me you have been to the kitchen in that gown?'

'No, aunt. Sarah was helping me into it and brushing my hair. I had not intended to make myself late.'

'You are not really late.' Her father stopped his pacing and smiled at her. 'Your aunt was looking forward to your company, were you not, Mary?'

'I – no – yes. The men were talking among themselves, and taking little account of me.'

Robert broke off his conversation and looked across to her.

'I must apologise then, dear lady. In no way was the intention to exclude you. Mr Somerville and I had some matters to discuss, but that is finished now.' He crossed in front of the fire and perched on the arm of the settee, looking at Mary so archly that her features softened and she almost smiled.

'I am sure you would rather talk to Eleanor than to me.' She stood up. 'I will go and speak with my brother.'

Robert sat down in the seat that she had vacated. 'Miss Somerville. It is, as always, the greatest pleasure to see you. I trust you are well?'

'I am well, yes, but I am anxious. Why is your cousin not with us today?'

'I fear he is far from well. It would appear he was set upon by a group of apprentices and quite badly beaten. He is in bed in his college, and Will is looking after him.'

The colour drained from Eleanor's face, and she gripped the arm of the settee. 'Is he in pain?'

'He makes light of it, I understand, but yes, I think he probably is.'

'But – but why? Why should anybody wish to harm him?'

He can be handy with his fists, our Francis. He knocked down one or two of the townspeople in the riot a few weeks ago.'

'And you think that is why? That somebody was trying to gain revenge?' Eleanor looked up at him, and was oddly surprised to see the compassion in his eyes.

'No. It would be easier if it were. But the truth is that we are the reason.'

'We are? But – how can we be? I don't understand.'

'The people who attacked him are part of a sect which believes they must punish any who associate with "papists".'

'And yet only a few weeks ago he took part in a pope-burning procession. I was shocked when he told me, yet somehow I understood that he did not mean harm to anybody. Do these people never think?'

'They meant to kill him, I am sure of it. In fact they probably think they have. They threw him in the river and left him. He managed to haul himself out, but spent the night on the river-bank.'

'Have you seen him?'

'No. I tried to call on him in his room, but was prevented by a particular friend of his. At least he gave me some information.'

'He has mentioned a friend – Christopher Wentworth, I think his name was.' Eleanor noticed Anthony looking intently at them, and hoped he did not think that Robert was speaking affectionately to her.

'I am truly sorry,' Robert was saying, 'that I should be the cause of his misfortunes. If I had not brought him here – '

'You are in no way to blame.' Eleanor spoke hastily, and felt herself colouring. 'I think it is time for us to dine. I have not been to the kitchen this morning. Cook will be wondering what has become of me.'

'From what I know of your cook, I believe she will be more than able to cope. But yes, it seems your father is moving now.'

Eleanor stood up, and accepted the arm he offered her.

*

'Why did you have to tell her precisely why your cousin was attacked?' Anthony's voice sounded entirely reasonable, but Robert knew that he was seriously displeased.

'She would have found out eventually. And then she might have thought the less of me for lying to her.'

'I see. I still think you have done your cause no good. Do you not want to be part of this family, Robert?' Anthony ran his hand gently up the inside of Robert's thigh as he spoke, causing the young man to shudder.

'You know that I do. I cannot imagine being away from you. But is there really no other way? It is clear that Eleanor vastly prefers my cousin.'

'Perhaps I should have prevented him coming here.' Anthony was reflective, then bent to nibble gently at Robert's ear, moving his lips suddenly to plant an impassioned kiss on Robert's mouth. Robert responded joyously, then lay back, surveying his own nakedness with mounting disquiet.

'Your cousin's Protestantism will be sufficient barrier to his ever marrying into this family.' Anthony's voice continued reasonable, but Robert recognised its seductive power. 'Unless, of course, Eleanor believes she could effect his conversion. And that, for a man who exulted in a pope-burning procession, is perhaps unlikely.'

'But,' Robert's voice wavered as he felt Anthony's hand on his belly, 'supposing she found out what there is between us? I hardly think I could bear it.'

'Why should she find out?' Anthony's fingers moved lower, and Robert was lost.

'Besides,' said Anthony afterwards, as though he were merely continuing a conversation, 'as your wife, Eleanor would be bound to obey you. Marrying her need not stop us seeing each other. It will make it easier.'

Robert felt as though he were drowning. He owed this man so much, and yet was not sure if he could fulfil what was being asked of him.

'But – marriage – to ensure that Eleanor did not find out – I would have to – '

'We have had this conversation before. It would mean intimacy. I am a priest, Robert, and a celibate, but I do know what happens between a man and a woman to bring new life to birth. I am sure you would be able to oblige her.'

'But – '

'It need not be very often. Think of it as all part of our greater purpose. You would be responsible for bringing a new Catholic into the world. What greater glory can there be than that?'

Robert turned to him, his face a mask of pain. 'I did not realise you would require so great a sacrifice from me.'

'Sacrifice? My dear Robert, most men would consider it a great good fortune if they were offered a bride as attractive as Eleanor.'

'I am not most men. After you and I – became acquainted – I believed that I would never marry. I do not have the taste for it.'

'We all of us have to do things for which we do not have the taste.' Anthony leaned himself on one elbow and looked down at Robert. 'When you were received into the Faith I understood that you would do whatever is necessary to further that faith. I trust I was not mistaken.'

'I would. I mean I will. I just do not see how this will further the faith we both hold.'

Anthony smiled. 'Then I see I shall have to educate you.' He traced a circle round Robert's nipple with his middle finger and Robert moaned, knowing as he surrendered that he was completely in thrall to this man.

*

Any thought of smuggling Francis swiftly out of Oxford had to be abandoned when, three days after the attack, he succumbed to fever, waking in the middle of the night with a raging thirst and an alarmingly high temperature. He thrashed about in his bed, at times so burning hot that he flung the covers from him, at others shivering with cold. Will hardly left his side, apart from the times when Christopher Wentworth almost curtly ordered him to his bed, even insisting that he took the truckle bed out of the room, and sat with his friend himself.

For several days Francis lay thus, warding off imaginary blows in his delirium, and calling out in his sleep or in his wakefulness – there did not seem to be any clear divider. Sometimes his bodily discomfort was so great that he cried out, while at others a curious, almost unearthly peace seemed to pervade his whole being. Afterwards he learned that it was at these moments that he had been in greatest danger of death, for his body was beginning to give up what seemed to be an unequal struggle. But he was young, naturally resilient and reluctant to let go his hold on life. After a week the fever began to subside, and a few days later he was able to sit up in bed and talk intelligibly, for which both Christopher Wentworth and Will Peters were immensely glad.

'I'm glad to see you're letting Will have some rest.' Christopher had brought some mutton broth and a piece of venison pie for him. It felt to Francis like a banquet after the oatmeal pap that had been his main nourishment for the last few days. 'Now we can talk about getting you out of Oxford.'

'Why should I leave Oxford? My ribs are healing, I can put my right foot to the floor, the bruises are going. Have I got to let a few hotheads drive me away from my studies?'

Christopher laughed. 'So it is your studies that keep you in Oxford now, is it? I had thought they rather got in the way of other things you would sooner be doing.'

'You know what I mean. Besides, if I leave Oxford without good reason I could very well be expelled the University.'

'It looks to me as though you have very good reason. But I agree we can hardly go to the authorities and ask permission for you to leave.

Nevertheless, you must go, Francis. If your attackers see you alive and well in Oxford, they will make no mistake a second time. I don't think we should wait until you are strong enough to ride. Go on the public coach.'

Francis sighed. 'You are not going to rest until I agree,' he said. 'Could a message be sent to Coneybury, do you think? I hope this is only a temporary withdrawal; I still believe I have a great deal to learn there.'

Christopher lightly punched his friend's shoulder, and Francis winced. 'They probably know already. Robert came here a few days ago, most eager for news of you. I refused to let him see you, but I gave him what news I could.'

'Robert?' Francis sat up. 'But why did you not tell me?'

'Until today you have hardly been in a position to tell. He was most interested in news of you, and promised he would tell the fair Eleanor. But yes, I will still send a message to Coneybury – after you have left Oxford. You seem to have been born with the concept of danger altogether lacking. Your very survival seems remarkable.'

'It has always been thus, sir.' Will Peters came quietly into the room with a tankard of mulled ale for Francis. 'But I will go with him to London, and do my best to keep him safe.'

'And I will try to minimise the effect of his leaving here in Oxford,' said Christopher. 'Come, Francis, drink your ale, and then you should rest.'

'Nursemaid,' grumbled Francis, but he obeyed.

*

Francis sat in a corner of his room, a blazing fire in the hearth. Around him sat or stood the members of his little music group; he had refused to leave Oxford without one more evening with them, and Christopher had not only agreed, but arranged it for him.

'They weren't exaggerating,' said Julian, as he came in. 'I knew you would not be absent from Chapel without a reason.'

Francis touched his face and smiled. 'I've survived,' he said. 'And not lost any teeth, which is a mercy. Unfortunately, this will be our last gathering for a little. Prudence dictates that I leave Oxford for a while. You are my friends, but please tell nobody of this.'

Murmurs of sympathy and understanding followed this statement. Then with considerable pride, Francis produced the new Playford, and suggested that they try Purcell's ode on the death of Matthew Locke. Francis himself was the only one among them to have seen it so far, and sang as well as playing his lute. Though he knew their attempt at it by no means did it justice, they were all moved by Purcell's soulful lament, and sat in silence for a little when they had finished.

'To think that Purcell was but seventeen when he wrote that,' said Francis. 'He is still only twenty-one. A bright future indeed. Shall we try "I resolve against cringing"? I think we might find it more light-hearted.'

By the end of this song they were all laughing, and Francis resolved in that moment that whatever else he did in London, he must try to meet Henry Purcell.

The next day Oxford awoke to a cold morning, crisp with frost, but with the promise of sunshine enough to dispel it later. Francis was out of bed in good time, ready now to take on another adventure. The coach left from outside the Mitre at six, and he knew it would not wait for him.

He was annoyed in some way that he had allowed Christopher to persuade him of the prudence of flight, and only by regarding it as an enjoyable adventure could he go through with it at all. He realised suddenly how much he hated other people dictating what he should do. And now he had agreed to go to London as a down-at-heel merchant. Francis knew how seriously Christopher took this whole venture, though he was unable to do so himself. He still felt tender in many parts of his body, his right foot ached if he put too much pressure on it, and his chest was uncomfortable where the ribs were healing. He tried to avoid mirrors, as the sight of his bruised face depressed him. Though he had stated to Christopher that the bruises were fading, he knew they had a fair way still to go. At least he had been able to confirm that he had not broken any teeth. He drew considerable satisfaction from that.

He sat down and made short work of the ham and bread Will had put out for him, and washed it down with a mug of ale. Just as he was finishing Will came into the room with a threadbare cloak and a pair of woollen hose. Francis looked at it and raised his eyebrows.

'Am I expected to wear that? I thought I had a better sense of style.'

Will grinned. 'Mr Wentworth insisted. He is most anxious that you should not be recognised. But I have a warmer cloak for you here, which you can use on the journey.'

'Those apprentices are hardly likely to be watching the public coach in case somebody they believe they murdered nearly three weeks ago gets onto it. Still, never mind. I mustn't go upsetting Christopher.'

'I should think not, after all the trouble you've caused me.' Christopher came into the room, holding a satchel which he proffered to Francis.

'Some food and wine for you – and a volume of Tacitus, in case you get bored.' Francis punched his friend lightly on the shoulder, but he was touched.

'The coach will be leaving soon.' Christopher led the way out of the room. 'I will do my best to provide answers to your tutor when he asks them, but I may be unable to prevent your expulsion. At least that is better than the expulsion you so nearly suffered.'

As the three of them walked together to the coach Francis was aware of a sudden, intense joy in living. He was fortunate, he knew, to be able to do so; he realised just how near death he had been, despite all his attempts to pretend otherwise. It was still dark, but even to be outside restored his optimism, his belief in the excitement of life.

He and Will entered the coach as soon as it arrived, with only time for the briefest of goodbyes to Christopher. They tried to make themselves comfortable in a corner. The stench was considerable, and the dust hurt their eyes, but Francis was determined not to admit to Will just how weak he felt.

He sat back in the coach and tried to sleep, but he was none too comfortable, and the smell appeared to grow stronger with every passing mile. He was immensely glad to have Will with him; the temptation to sit back and let him take control was very strong. Francis smiled to himself, then found himself almost in Will's lap as the coach went over a pot-hole.

'Give me riding any day,' said Francis. 'This is quite infernally uncomfortable.'

A large red-faced man looked disdainfully at him, but said nothing and settled himself back in a corner, folding his arms.

'Try to sleep, if you can, my – sir.' Will smiled. 'You must preserve your strength.'

'It seems I must also get used to being told what to do. I don't feel in the least like sleep.' But he sat back and closed his eyes. Despite the gloom in the interior of the coach caused by the leather curtains, he was aware that dawn must have broken. It did little to relieve the stench, though unaccountably it caused his spirits to rise. But then he must have dozed for a little, as he was suddenly aware of Will trying to persuade him to take a little cheese and wine.

'You have slept for an hour or more, sir. We are well on the way now.' Francis drank some of the wine from the flask, then handed it to Will to have some for himself. From the gloomy recesses of the coach it was difficult to see exactly where they were, but they were conscious of the effort the horses needed to bring the coach to the rim of the Chilterns. Francis moved the blind aside and peered out.

'Christmas Common, I think they call it,' he said. 'The trees are thick here, Will. Even outside there is not a great deal of light.'

But soon they breasted the rim of the hills and were conscious of the increase in speed as they proceeded down towards High Wycombe. The coach paused there, to change the horses and to allow travellers the chance of refreshment.

Even in his new persona Francis found it was not difficult to obtain mulled wine and a piece of mutton pie. Will saw to his needs calmly, then at Francis' insistence sat down to share some refreshment with him.

'At least the coach can now get to London in a single day.' Francis finished his wine. 'Though it will be evening by the time we arrive there.'

The fresh horses moved briskly away from High Wycombe, and Francis winced as the coach went over a pot-hole. Will looked up sharply.

'You are far from recovered, sir.' he said smoothly. 'Perhaps we have made this journey too soon.'

'Don't fuss, Will.' Francis saw the look of concern on his servant's face and felt guilty. 'You are right, though. It is mainly my chest and my ankle. My chest feels very tight, and my ankle is throbbing again.'

'It is clearly better, or you would not have been able to walk. And at least we are underway now.'

Francis gave a wan smile, and pulled back the blind to look out on a landscape of winter trees, empty fields and the occasional plume of smoke from a cottage chimney. He shivered.

'I have a spare cloak for you here, sir. You must keep warm – we do not want the fever returning.'

One or two other passengers edged away from Francis at that, as though he could pass his poor health on to them. Even if he could, thought Francis, three inches would not make a great deal of difference. He lifted the blind again, and saw that the short winter afternoon was already fading. He had little idea of where they were. Will handed him a flask of wine, but a sudden jolt meant he spilt some of it on his cloak. He grinned at Will and handed it back.

'Perhaps you'll have more luck, Will. I might try to sleep again.' He settled himself in his corner, but the rigid seat was not the easiest place to relax, and the smell was becoming difficult to endure. He was very tired now, but sleep was proving singularly elusive. Will's comment about the fever caused him some disquiet. He had realised that it was still a possibility.

He must have slept again for a while, despite his discomfort. He awoke with a start to realise that they were now passing through the village of St Marylebone. Several other passengers saw this, and started to fidget as the end of the journey drew near.

By the time they alighted at Charing Cross it was already past seven o'clock, and Francis found himself unable to stop shivering. Will firmly took the satchel from him, which he gripped in addition to that he was already carrying, and they paused in the unfamiliar surroundings. It was a relief to get away from the overpowering smells of stale sweat and unwashed bodies, but despite the cold Francis could still smell the open drains and the rotting garbage. He wrinkled his nose. The smoke from many fires hung like a pall over the city, and he wished himself back in Oxford. He conveniently forgot that Oxford was not the most sweet-smelling of places.

'Come, my lord. It is not far to your father's house, and every moment we spend outside, now, will make you weaker.' Francis noticed that the 'my lord' had returned, but he followed Will in the direction of Whitehall. Neither of them had ever been to the house Lord Bodmin used when in London, but they knew where it was, and Will's ability to find his way with very little information was uncanny. Francis stumbled, and Will immediately slowed so that he was beside his master.

'We should have sent word to my father.' To his surprise Francis was beginning to find that even speaking coherently was becoming difficult. 'He might not – even be there.'

'Somebody will. And Mr Wentworth was afraid that a letter might go astray, and alert those we do not wish to know about your whereabouts.'

'I see.' Francis stumbled again, and Will put his arm out to steady him. 'I think this is not the time for talk, my lord. We must concentrate on getting you safe to your father's house.'

Francis giggled. 'Probably people think we are drunk.' He weaved unsteadily, and giggled again. But Will's support was firm, and together they made slow progress.

In fact the house they sought was not far, in a square set back from the main thoroughfare of King Street, with gardens sloping down to the river.

By now Francis was having to hang on to Will to prevent himself falling, but they climbed the few steps to the front door and Will rapped on it sharply.

It seemed a long time before it was opened; Francis sank to the ground and sat on the top step, curled up in a ball as he tried to keep warm.

'Begone!' said the servant who opened the door. 'This is not the place for the likes of you.'

'But indeed it is.' Will stood up and smiled. 'Don't you know me, Harry? At least you should know Lord Trenoweth, though I grant you he is not looking his best.'

'Lord – Lord Trenoweth?' Harry peered down at the bundle that was Francis. 'Come in, come in, young Will – my apologies for not recognising you. We have to be so careful.'

Will bent down and picked Francis up; it was clear that he was no longer capable of walking. Harry led them into a room where there was a fire burning, and what seemed like a great many candles. Francis thought he recognised the gentleman with the bright chestnut curls, but he could not be sure. He found himself set down on a settee near the fire and immediately slumped.

Lord Bodmin nodded to Harry, who withdrew, and turned a questioning gaze on Will.

'I have often suggested to Francis that he might benefit by coming to London at some point. But I did not expect it to happen quite like this.'

'My lord – ' Will began, but Lord Bodmin held up his hand.

'Whatever has happened, it is clear that my son would be better off in bed than anywhere else. I suggest that this should be arranged, and then perhaps you could explain to me what has been happening.' He rang a bell on a small table, and Harry quickly reappeared.

'Have a bedroom prepared for Lord Trenoweth, Harry. And some hot water for washing.' He smiled, as though this were nothing out of the ordinary, and sat down beside Francis.

'I have little idea, yet, as to what adventures you have been engaging in. But I am sure it will prove interesting.'

Chapter Seven

Sunlight streaming through the window woke Francis, and he lay for a moment in a state of confusion, before the events of the day before started to take shape in his mind.

He looked around the room; it was large and airy, with a fire burning brightly in the grate. Against one wall was a capacious clothes-press; he hoped it meant he would not have to dress in the clothes he had worn the day before.

He slid out of bed, and stood looking out of the window, trying to make sense of what he could see. Before him were buildings of all shapes and sizes, connected by passages, paths and roads but all, in some degree, centring on a large, highly ornate building with deep windows opening on to balconies. Gardens and courtyards were beside it, and an elegant gallery at right angles.

Memory stirred in Francis's mind; he remembered something his father had said, and realised that he must be looking at Inigo Jones's famous banqueting hall. This was Whitehall Palace on which he gazed, and he looked down in fascination. Though he had told Robert he had no need of the excitement of court, now that he was actually looking at it, he realised that getting to know it better might be agreeable.

But even with the fire he was cold in his nightshirt, and he returned to the bed, savouring its warmth. The iron bands about his chest appeared to have loosened, and as he lay back he realised that he had stood on his right foot without it causing him pain.

It was embarrassing to admit, even to himself, that the events of the previous evening were distinctly hazy in his mind. He could remember getting off the coach with Will, and the mixture of excitement and dizziness that accompanied it. Of his arrival at his father's house, which was presumably where he was now, he had no recollection at all.

The door opened and Will came in, with mulled ale and a piece of mutton pie.

'I hope you are up to eating this, my lord. You did not have a great deal yesterday.'

'I most certainly am.' Francis sat up. 'I am thoroughly hungry, and look forward to speaking with my father. I was not able to manage it last night.'

'I have told him what has been happening in recent weeks.' Will set the tray down, and Francis took the mug of ale gratefully. 'I have not seen your cousin yet. I expect he will want an account.'

'Indeed he will.' The door opened again, and a man so clearly an older version of Robert came in that Francis blinked. He had forgotten how alike the two brothers were – physically, at least.

Sir Thomas Carey seated himself on the edge of the bed.

'What do you mean, young Francis, by descending on us like this without so much as a by your leave?' He punched his cousin lightly on the shoulder, and Francis winced.

'I am sorry, Francis. Your father has told me a little of what has been happening. You were set upon by thugs, I understand.'

'They took exception to my visiting a Roman Catholic household.'

'Doubtless you had your reasons for doing so.'

'Robert invited me.'

Thomas frowned. 'Forgive me, dear cousin, but I cannot help thinking that does not sound like the best of reasons.'

'I did not know that they were Papist then. I did not know that Robert is.'

The frown deepened. 'I have not known that for very long. I am thankful that our father did not live to see it. But why should he be so eager to introduce you to this household?'

'I am trying to find out. Sir Henry's younger brother, Anthony, is a priest. It was he who brought about Robert's "conversion".'

'I see. And you think there is purpose behind their evident desire to welcome you into their midst?'

'Yes. I am sure of it. Eleanor, Sir Henry's daughter, is clearly deeply unhappy. I believe she is worried that her uncle is involved in plotting. Possibly Robert too.'

Thomas stood up. 'Then, Francis, family or no family, you should take the matter to the Privy Council.'

'And say what? I have no evidence, Thomas. I have been trying to find some, one way or the other. He would have to have contacts, many of them, to have any chance of success. But Anthony Somerville is a strange man.'

'He sounds it. I am beginning to wonder if I even know my brother Robert very well.'

'It was my friend Christopher who insisted that it was not safe for me to remain in Oxford, when I was not strong enough to resist. I would have returned to Coneybury, to attempt to find out more information.'

'Then I think your friend Christopher is a very wise man. I will leave you for a moment. Will can bring you hot water to wash. I shall be downstairs with your father when you are ready.'

'Thomas, is my sister Elizabeth in London at the moment?'

Thomas paused. 'She and Nigel are in Cornwall. Nigel, I think, is a little piqued that I am a member of Parliament and he is not. How those two have survived four years of marriage continues to amaze me.'

Francis laughed. 'I believe Lizzie thoroughly enjoys being married to somebody with such a resemblance to the Duke of Monmouth.'

'Yes.' Thomas frowned. 'Nigel, of course, is convinced that all our problems would be over if the King would legitimise Monmouth. If only it were that simple.'

Some fifteen minutes later, clad in a suit of deep blue velvet, which he realised Will must have brought from Oxford, Francis sat in an elegant parlour with his cousin.

'Your father will join us directly,' said Thomas easily. 'He had some business to attend to.'

Even as he spoke Lord Bodmin stood in the doorway, his wide boyish grin belying the fact that he had already passed his fiftieth year. His laced cambric shirt was immaculate; his suit, though of broadcloth, was of a deep wine red, showing a satin brocade waistcoat underneath. Even in winter a few freckles danced mischievously on his nose. He had resisted the court fashion of a wig for a very long time, and that he now wore was so like his own chestnut curls as to be almost uncanny.

He was not quite as tall as his son, and though he had never said so Francis suspected that the fact had always galled him. Francis had never quite shed his childish awe of his father, and wondered if Lord Bodmin realised it.

'Good morning, Francis.' Lord Bodmin sat down near his son by the fire. 'I am, as you know, always delighted to see you; but would it be too much to ask what has prompted this curiously timed and precipitate visit?'

'Has not Will told you?'

Lord Bodmin laughed, and the sound was like music. 'A fair amount. Though I am sure there are some parts he left out, or did not know about.'

Francis explained all that had been happening since the pope-burning procession; both Lord Bodmin and Sir Thomas listened attentively.

'I think you know,' said Lord Bodmin, when at last he had finished, 'what my views are on this madness that has gripped the country these past two years. Why should this plot have more substance than thousands of others which are no more than inventions?'

'It may not have. I have not enough evidence to go to the authorities. But I must know, Father; there is something about that household that concerns me, aside from the popishness.'

'Plenty of honest people are papists.'

'I know. I believe that Eleanor is one.'

'Ah. The fair Eleanor. She, perhaps, is the lure that draws you back there?'

'No – that is – alone of that household, I feel easy in her presence.'

'So what do you intend to do now?'

Francis looked at his father, surprised. 'I had not really thought. Without Christopher's persuasion I should never have left Oxford. But now that I am here – '

'Yes?' said cousin and father together.

'You know how much I enjoy both listening to the college choir and making music with my friends when I am able. My music means a great deal more to me than my studies. Recently the choir sang an anthem by Henry Purcell, and I thought it truly wonderful. I should very much like to meet him.'

His father smiled. 'Your passion for music has always puzzled me slightly. It was not entirely what I expected to happen when you first went to Oxford. I have seen Mr Purcell perform his music, though I have not met him. He is young, of course, about your age, but undeniably talented. I had not realised that he had become your hero.'

'I like his music,' said Francis simply. 'And I should welcome the opportunity to talk about it to him.'

'While you are arranging this, uncle,' said Thomas, 'would you take it amiss if I introduced Francis to some of my acquaintances?'

'Seeing that he has become a Whig, he may as well walk among his fellows,' replied Lord Bodmin. 'And now I have business elsewhere.' He laid his hand on his son's shoulder as he walked past him to the door.

'Be careful,' he warned. 'You are about to enter a nest of hornets. Take care their sting be not fatal.' Francis looked up in alarm, but his father had not awaited a reply.

*

Some few days later Francis sat in this same room, unaccountably nervous as he faced the young man opposite him. Henry Purcell wore coat and breeches a shade lighter than black, with a quantity of lace at the collar and cuffs of his shirt. A wig of profuse black curls sat lightly on his head, while his hand drummed lightly on the table beside him; on the third finger was a ring with a single ruby on it which glowed in the firelight.

Francis sensed at once the restless energy of the man; in his wide, sensitive mouth, his clear eyes that seemed to register all that was going on around him, the movements of his hands. Then his companion smiled, and the somewhat severe face was instantly changed to one of great charm.

'I understand that you wished to meet me. What is it that you want of me?'

'I hardly know.' Francis was momentarily taken aback. 'Until recently I have been studying at Magdalen College, Oxford. Not long ago the choir sang one of your anthems in chapel. It was the finest music I have ever heard.'

'So you thought you would like to come and tell me so,' murmured Purcell. 'Which anthem was it?'

'"Behold now, praise the Lord". It was ravishing. Though our organist said it would sound even better with strings rather than the chapel organ.'

'He is quite correct. Do you ever sing at all yourself?

Francis smiled. 'I love to, when I am able. I sometimes have friends to my room and we make what music we can. We have two violinists and a lutenist among our number, and they can sing as well. I prefer my music to my studies.'

Purcell cradled the goblet of wine in his hand. 'What part do you sing?'

'Counter-tenor, usually. Though I can sing baritone if required.'

'You interest me. I have a suggestion to make. It is perhaps unfair to expect you to sing without warning, without music, without instruments. But come to my house in St Anne's Lane – can you manage tomorrow? These defects could be made good then. I should like to hear you sing.'

The following day Francis found himself seated in a pleasant small parlour in Purcell's house in St Anne's Lane. A fire of sea-coals burned in the grate, lending colour to what might otherwise be a rather austere room.

Purcell was again in his dark coat, but looking much more business-like with a sheaf of papers and a lute at his feet. He looked up at Francis and smiled.

'What music have you sung recently?' he asked.

'I have not sung much for a little. Before Christmas, it would have been, before – I fell ill.'

Purcell looked keenly at him. 'I thought you had not been well. Your eyes have a suggestion of the fever about them still. And – your face still bears the suggestion of bruises.'

Francis smiled. 'We had a musical evening last week, before I left Oxford. I have just been lent a copy of the latest Playford, and we sang your ode on the death of Matthew Locke, and "I resolve against cringing".'

Purcell laughed. 'I enjoyed writing that,' he said. 'What did you think of the ode?'

'It was sublime. Though we were hardly able to do it justice. You clearly thought a great deal of him.'

'Locke died less than four years ago. He was a great friend of my father. A sad loss to music.' Purcell picked up his lute and handed Francis a sheet of paper. 'I want to hear you sing. Since you have seen this before it is even better.' He plucked a note of his lute. 'Come.'

Francis looked at the paper, and began hesitantly to sing 'What hope for us remains now he is gone?' Purcell listened in silence, then handed him another paper with plainchant music. With growing confidence Francis sang the anthem 'Gloria tibi trinitas'. Purcell was smiling broadly by the time he finished.

'A little shaky,' he commented. 'But much less than I would have expected. You have an excellent tone, and a real feeling for the music. Where did your learn your singing?'

'My father employed a singing teacher for me when he realised I wanted it. But it was not until I reached Oxford and met other like-minded people that I realised it could become more than a pleasant pastime. It has become a passion.'

'I can see that. I have a suggestion to put to you. I have only recently been appointed organist at Westminster Abbey. We have no vacancies there, but a particular friend of mine is one of the organists at the Chapel Royal. The Gentlemen of the choir are three below strength at the moment, two of whom are counter-tenors. Would you consider becoming a Gentleman of the Chapel Royal?'

'I – that is – of course – why yes,' said Francis, feeling as though his world had turned upside-down yet again. 'It would be a great honour,' he finished.

'You would be required to attend every day,' continued Purcell. 'Though the Gentleman work in shifts, a month at a time. Come to the Chapel tomorrow morning, and I shall introduce you to Mr Blow. Matins is at ten, evensong at four.' He smiled again, and Francis was at once conscious of his great charm.

'One further word of warning.' Purcell's smile remained. 'As the heir to an earldom, your social standing will be considerably higher than most of your fellow choristers. It makes no difference. It is the music that counts.'

'But of course.' Francis was strangely relieved. 'I would not expect it to be otherwise.'

'Until tomorrow, then,' said Purcell, rising and moving to the door. 'There is no need to be alarmed. You have sufficient music. I would not have suggested it else.'

*

The long gallery at Coneybury, only rarely used, was loud with chatter almost drowning the musicians valiantly playing on the dais. Eleanor would have preferred to listen to the music, but her aunt was making sure that was unlikely.

'You are very fortunate, Eleanor, that so many of our neighbours have come to honour your birthday. You must not let Robert monopolise you for the whole evening.'

'No, aunt.' Eleanor was happy to agree with her aunt on that point, though there was little else about the evening she was happy with. Her father had insisted that her eighteenth birthday be celebrated appropriately, and before she knew what was happening neighbours she had not seen for years had been invited, most of them over fifty and not in the least interested in her. She felt as though she were a doll to be paraded for others' benefit.

Robert was deep in conversation with her uncle. She had hoped that Francis might have been well enough to attend, and was downcast when Christopher's message arrived, to tell her that he had left Oxford and gone to London.

'He did not come himself,' she commented to Robert, towards the beginning of the party.

'How could he? He is in fear of his life. His attackers believe him dead. To have been seen about in Oxford would have been to undeceive them.'

'Francis? Afraid? I cannot believe it.'

Robert looked around the room, and Eleanor was suddenly aware of the quiet desperation in his manner, particularly when he looked towards her uncle.

'If it will make you happier, I will try to make contact with his friend Christopher Wentworth. He will doubtless have more information. More than that, when I return to London I will seek out Francis and discover how he fares. Will that content you?'

'Thank you.' Eleanor smiled, and Robert rose.

'I must speak with your uncle now, but after the meal I would be glad if you would walk with me a little, before it becomes too cold.' He moved away, and Eleanor watched him intently as he spoke first with her uncle, then her father, as she accepted the congratulations of people she hardly knew on her birthday.

So now she sat listening to her aunt lecture her, dreading the moment when Robert would come and remind her of her promise to walk with him.

'You have learnt much about the running of your father's household over the years,' her aunt was saying. 'And that is good; it is what a husband will look for. But, Eleanor, I would be failing in my duty if I did not give you this advice. You are spending too much time among servants; you always seem to be going to the kitchen, and you have a perfectly capable cook. Whenever you are late for a meal you say you have been in your chamber with your maid.'

'It is true.'

'Be polite to these people by all means, Eleanor. But never forget that they are servants, and our inferiors. Sometimes it looks as though you are treating them as friends. This is not appropriate. You are a highly eligible young lady.' She looked significantly across at Robert. 'But your behaviour must conform to certain standards.' She patted Eleanor's arm. 'You know I only wish what is best for you.'

Eleanor strongly doubted that. She thought of half a dozen replies she might make, and discarded them all as provocative, contenting herself with 'Yes, aunt'. She stood up with a feeling almost of relief as she saw Robert approaching.

It had begun to rain, which meant they would not be able to walk in the garden. They went instead to the parlour where Eleanor's spinet was kept, and Eleanor's heart sank when she saw that there was nobody there.

Robert closed the door. 'I think you are finding this party difficult,' he said, and smiled. 'These are your father's friends, not yours.'

'I do not really have friends.' She sat on a carved settle, and Robert at once seated himself beside her, covering her hands with his own.

'Oh, but surely – '

'My aunt has just been telling me that I must not make a friend of my maid.' She giggled a little. 'But I fear she is too late.'

Robert turned towards her, and the pressure of his hands increased. Eleanor looked around the room, at the window where the rain was now drumming in earnest, anywhere but at Robert's face.

He stood up, then to Eleanor's horror went down on one knee in front of her.

'I think you know, since I have been welcomed in this household, just how much I value your company. I am a younger son, but I am going to make my way and, as you know, I am of good family. You are still a minor, of course, but I have spoken to your father and he has given his consent. Eleanor, I am asking you if you will marry me.'

There, it was said. Eleanor had realised that this was likely to happen at some point, and though she had rehearsed many answers, she could not call one to mind now it was needed.

'You do me a great honour.' She looked in his face at last, and saw puzzlement, hope and even fear. She took courage.

'I hope you will allow me a little time; this is somewhat unexpected.'

'Of course.' He stood up, and now she read relief. He had not mentioned loving her, she noticed. 'I could not expect an answer straight away. But you will allow me to hope?'

'You may always hope,' she said, and smiled.

*

Francis emerged blinking from the splendour of the Chapel Royal, his head still full of the music they had been singing. The only way to keep it there, he felt, was to return straight away to his father's house and pick up his lute. It was not far, and a walk through the winter sunshine would be pleasant.

The house seemed empty when he entered it, and he was already on the stairs going towards his own room when he heard the front door slam, and involuntarily turned round. Thomas stood with his back to the door, his hat in his hand, his normally genial face ablaze with anger.

'The King!' he shouted, as Francis began to make his way down the stairs again. 'Do you know what our beloved King has done, Francis? We work day and night trying to devise means to protect his life, and what does he do but get rid of his most selfless advisers!'

'Has he dissolved Parliament, then?' Francis followed his cousin into the dining room, where the young baronet flung himself into a chair and called for one of the servants to bring wine.

'He has indeed,' he said, as the man disappeared. 'A week ago, just before you came here, he prorogued it, and we dared to think he was giving us the opportunity we needed – a fresh session in which to introduce a fresh Exclusion Bill. Not he indeed! He waits until all the members have dispersed, and then he dissolves it. A new Parliament is to meet, of all places, at Oxford.'

'At Oxford? But why so?''

'I imagine our dearest King thinks himself safer there.' Thomas flung down his goblet, having tasted only a mouthful of wine. 'Come, Francis, work can be found for every loyal man. You shall dine with me, and I will present you to the earl of Shaftesbury.'

The Sun Tavern lay in the heart of the City, behind the Exchange. The carriage took them up the Strand and Fleet Street, past the King's Head and derelict St Paul's, and so into the width and dignity of Cheapside. Here the houses were taller and grander than elsewhere in the City, where mean dwellings and rude cottages could be seen. Some of the most influential men in the City chose to live here in Cheapside, Thomas informed his cousin.

Past the Exchange they turned down Threadneedle Street and stopped outside a long, low building over which hung a sign depicting a golden sun high in the sky. As Thomas and Francis entered it seemed as though a great many people were gathered there, all wearing in hat or stocking the blue ribbon with which Francis had been provided by his cousin. Apart from this, variety in dress was enormous; some wore plain black velvet or broadcloth, adorned with simple Dutch lace or a plain collar, while others were ornately clad in brocaded waistcoats and buckled shoes, with silver lace that suggested Whitehall rather than Thanet House. No ladies were present, and as Francis followed his cousin further into the room he realised that the Whig cause was very strong indeed.

'You'll be standing again, I take it, Carey?' growled a burly, red-faced gentleman, looking over the top of Francis's head as though he were not there.

'Indeed yes,' replied Thomas, smiling. 'There will be small hope at Oxford if we are not re-elected. Allow me to present my cousin, Francis, Lord Trenoweth – Colonel Mannering.' Francis bowed solemnly, and Colonel Mannering eyed him critically.

'Trenoweth, eh?' he growled – he seemed quite incapable of doing anything else with his voice. 'Bodmin's son, I take it – odd place to find one of your breed, isn't it?'

'I agree with my father in many things,' replied Francis a shade stiffly, 'but I am capable of pursuing an independent line of thought.'

'Aye, to be sure. No offence meant. Shown him to Shaftesbury yet?' continued the Colonel, turning again to Thomas.

'Patience, Colonel. All in good time.' The Colonel moved away, and Thomas murmured to his cousin as soon as he was out of earshot, 'He is a choleric old gentleman, but he can be a tower of strength in times of need.'

Every time Thomas greeted an acquaintance the topic of conversation was the same: the show of resistance they were going to put up at Oxford to force the King to accede to their demands. As Francis realised the depth of hatred against Roman Catholics his heart sank. How could he hope to achieve anything at Coneybury, when there was so much animosity? He suddenly realised how badly he wanted to ride there and take Eleanor away from all the whisperings and innuendoes. It seemed as though her faith alone was enough to condemn her.

Presently they dined, though Francis took little heed of what he ate; his attention was too distracted by the company in which he sat. Thomas at intervals pointed out people of whom he might have heard.

'Over there, with the huge head and over-long chin, that is Titus Oates. Even here nobody can afford to say how much they dislike him, for it was he who first brought the Plot to public attention. He is not a man to court popularity, and not all those he has sworn to their deaths were guilty.'

'Not – ?' Francis looked startled.

'Innocent men have died on account of this Plot,' replied his cousin. 'And some guilty ones too. Why should you look so surprised? Oates is a fanatic, but the lives on which he has trampled are few compared to those that would be lost were York to succeed his brother. Of that I feel certain. Oates's voice has great power still, and for that he is feared.'

'Who is that seated next to him?' enquired Francis.

'Israel Tonge. A strange, morose man, but he has given useful evidence recently. Algernon Sidney sits opposite him; he is a true man, and entirely honest. The gentleman next to him, with the blue velvet and brocaded waistcoat, is Lord Russell.'

'But where is Lord Shaftesbury?' asked Francis, looking round for the imposing figure he expected to see.

'He is looking at you now and wondering who you may be, assessing perhaps whether or not you could be useful to him.' Francis looked up, and found a pair of cold blue eyes directed unblinkingly on him. But instead of the magnificence he had expected to see he perceived a bent old man, who stooped as though his periwig were too heavy for him. He wore a plain suit of sober brown, the coat long and full-skirted showing, however, a waistcoat of deep crimson satin and a finely laced shirt. His hooked nose and small mouth lent fierceness to a face in which Francis had already read determination. This was a man who could be ruthless to achieve his chosen goal; a man whose friendship could be vital, but whose enmity could be a very real worry. Even as an undergraduate Francis had heard of the earl of Shaftesbury: the first of the Whigs, the patron alike of Titus Oates and John Locke. Shaftesbury had become a legend in his own lifetime, and even those who did not admire him frequently went in awe of him. Francis felt uncomfortable under his gaze, and lowered his head.

'He likes to know exactly what is happening among his followers,' murmured Thomas at his elbow. 'You are unknown to him, and he will be curious until you have been introduced.'

The noise, which had been considerable at the outset, was growing rapidly now as men who were well wined became yet more so. Francis wondered if anything could be achieved at such a gathering, and said as much to his cousin.

'You would be surprised,' was the reply, 'to find how much is done in this way. Contacts are made, a confidential word exchanged over a glass of wine. Already, while you have been eating comfits and wondering what you will be singing at Evensong, I have discovered that Shaftesbury and some sixteen other peers are drawing up a petition to the King against the holding of Parliament at Oxford. If you would serve our cause you must keep your eyes and ears open. Come, the meal is all but over – I will present you.'

Francis was glad that he had drunk only a modest amount of wine as he and his cousin moved towards where the acknowledged leader of the movement sat, deep now in conversation with Lord Russell. The earl looked up as Thomas presented his cousin and Francis, feeling flushed and conspicuous, bowed low. Shaftesbury regarded him critically.

'Another convert to our cause, eh?' he said, in a deep but not unfriendly voice. 'But is not your father a staunch Tory?'

'He is,' replied Francis. 'And we are on good terms. But our view of things is not always the same.'

'I will go surety for my cousin's enthusiasm,' put in Thomas. 'He was most eager to come here today.' Francis raised his eyebrows at this, but said nothing.

'Indeed?' Shaftesbury subjected Francis to a further examination. 'Well, well; there will be work in plenty for you, young sir, if you are loyal and a patriot. The Popish Plot is still a very real danger, and the battle must go on. You are lodging with your cousin? I like to know where I can find those who would serve our cause.'

'That is well,' said Thomas, as they moved away. 'If you have the approval of my lord of Shaftesbury then you are safe. His arm is longer than the King's at the present time.'

Several people were leaving the tavern now, many of them paying their respects to Lord Shaftesbury as they did so. Thomas suggested that Francis might like to walk in St James Park for a little, and Francis concurred without really hearing what his cousin was saying. He was the son of a Tory peer, attracted to a papist girl, whose father might well be plotting against the King, and now he found himself virtually sworn to uphold the great Whig cause, and cry death to all papists. In addition to this he had begun singing in what he already believed was the finest choir in the land, firmly Church of England. He mentioned his confusion to Thomas as they entered St James's, and his cousin laughed.

'Things are perhaps a little difficult for you at present,' he said. 'But think. Your father is no less a patriot because he goes about things in a different way. He knows that York's – ecclesiastical prerogatives – must be curtailed if he is to succeed his brother. But he believes that York, as the legal heir, should be allowed to succeed his brother, in preference to the Whig policy of excluding York altogether and naming a different heir.'

'Who would be – ?'

'That is still not certain. Some favour the Prince of Orange, others the Duke of Monmouth.'

'My brother-in-law Nigel can be in little doubt on that issue.'

Thomas laughed. Monmouth is certainly more popular. If the King were to legitimise him – 'He broke off and raised his blue-ribboned cane to a gentleman Francis recognised as having been in the Sun Tavern. He was accompanied, as were several other gentlemen now taking the air, by a fashionably dressed lady with hair piled high and an artificially pale face.

Francis looked about him at the long, neatly gravelled paths, the velvet-smooth lawns, the fountains in various unlikely shapes, the dark green of the evergreen trees which shielded most of the palace from view. Formal gardens were the fashion, of course, since the French King had built Versailles, but Francis had to admit to himself that he preferred the untidy rambling of the Cornish coast. The grass here was untrodden, the paths met each other only at right angles. But as Francis saw the brightly coloured gowns of the ladies, the ankle-length cloaks, the painted faces, he realised how much in the world of men he had been living. His cousin saw his glance and smiled.

'You think we live a somewhat monastic life?' he queried. 'Maybe you are right, though for my part it contents me well enough. I have had my fill of womankind.'

Francis remembered Thomas's proud, domineering wife, now ruling their home in Cornwall, and doubtless instilling fear into their two small children. If I cannot marry for love I shall remain single, and my brother Edward shall be my heir, thought Francis. I could not abide a loveless marriage.

They passed a sundial set in the middle of a small lawn, and Francis became aware of the time.

'I must go,' he said. 'Evensong is at four, and I should not like to be late.'

'Cut through there,' said Thomas, indicating a small path. 'That will bring you directly opposite the chapel. You are still a musician before you are a Whig, are you not?'

'Why, yes,' said Francis. 'How could it be otherwise?'

Mr Blow, noting his blue ribbons, was inclined to think otherwise. 'You have been frequenting the haunts of the Whigs, I see,' he said. 'Take care that they do not lead you from your music.'

Chapter Eight

Francis was up early the next morning, but even so he found Thomas in the dining room before him.

'I have business to attend to,' he said with a smile. 'And you, as a Gentleman of the Chapel Royal, must needs be with Mr Purcell.'

'It is Mr Blow, not Mr Purcell, who has actually given me a place in the choir. But do not mock me, cousin.' Francis helped himself to ale from a jug set at the side. 'Mr Purcell's name will be remembered long after men have forgotten who Lord Shaftesbury was. Of that I feel certain.'

'Perhaps. But you still sport your blue ribbon in your stocking, I see. Perhaps it is as well your father is not here; it would pain him to see me teaching you to be an honest Whig, but I cannot do aught else. I believe it to be of the greatest importance to this country to prevent the Duke of York from succeeding to the throne.'

'Is my father abroad so early?' asked Francis in surprise.

'The King, it seems, has summoned him to Whitehall.' Thomas was unable to keep a vein of sarcasm from his voice. 'He will make a duke of him yet.'

Francis was on his feet in a flash. 'You do not think, surely, that my father acts as he does from selfish motives?'

'Hardly,' replied Thomas with a short laugh. 'Your father is one of the most loyal men I know. I have seen him after five months in a foul-smelling, windowless dungeon; I have seen him forced to undertake a journey few expected him to survive. That is some of what his friendship with, his loyalty to the King has cost him.'

'I have heard the tale,' said Francis hesitantly. 'My father has more courage than I know how to command.'

'You will have ample time to play your part. Already you have joined a pope-burning procession, fought off assassins, and been seen in the company of the most influential Whigs.'

'To say nothing of becoming a Gentleman of the Chapel Royal,' said Francis. 'But – I feel I am here under false pretences, somehow. Have I not simply run away from Oxford?'

'Do you believe that treason is being plotted at Coneybury?'

'I simply cannot tell. Christopher was concerned for my safety, and arranged for me to come here. But perhaps I was merely being weak.'

'You can do a great deal here, Francis. And your music is important.'

'Yes. That is the greatest good fortune. I never expected to be able to sing in a choir at all, let alone the finest choir in the land.'

'And of course this parliament to meet in Oxford will change things.'

'Yes. Yes, of course it will. Thank you, Thomas. I had not thought of that. I must go now, or I shall be late.' He picked up his hat and was gone.

They sang an anthem of Matthew Locke's in Chapel that morning – Mr Blow was sufficiently impressed with Francis's singing to give him a short solo, which he accomplished to his own satisfaction as well as that of Mr Blow. He walked home quickly afterwards, to find his father in the big airy parlour.

'It is good to see you, Francis,' said Lord Bodmin cheerfully. 'Since you came to London you seem to be so busy being either a Whig or a Gentleman of the Chapel Royal that you have little time for an ageing parent.'

'Hardly ageing, Father,' said Francis quickly. 'You look as young as ever I remember you. But forgive me if it appears that I have been avoiding you – I had intended no slight.'

'I am sure you had not, Francis,' replied his father with a laugh. 'And I am glad to see you so well occupied. Thomas expects you to meet him in the King's Head shortly, by the way, so I will not detain you long. I have business of my own to attend to, in any case; you will not be deserting me.'

Francis sat down. 'Do you intend to return to Cornwall soon?' he asked.

'I had thought of it, now that the King has dissolved Parliament. But it is only a few weeks until the new one meets in Oxford. To travel to Cornwall now, only to come to Oxford shortly afterwards, seems extremely tedious. I think I shall write to your mother and explain how matters stand. I believe this Oxford Parliament will be important, Francis; I intend to be present in the House of Lords.'

'And Thomas?'

'Thomas, I believe, will travel to Cornwall so that he may get himself elected for Launceston. He will probably return immediately to London. And what of your own plans?'

'My plans?'

'Yes. You have been in London for ten days now. What are you intending to do?'

90

'I – I hardly know. I feel – I must work to defeat the Popish Plot. And I know I must sing in the Chapel Royal. Yet part of me wants to go back to Oxford, to Coneybury again.'

'Your blue ribbon proclaims you to be a Whig,' said his father. 'And your other two desires I can readily sympathise with. But all three would seem to be singularly difficult to combine.'

'Near impossible,' replied Francis. 'Do you – disapprove of Whiggery, Father?'

'I? No. Why should I? I believe they are mistaken, that there is a better way of going about things, but that is all. You, I take it, have been beguiled by their arguments?'

'York – does not seem to be well suited to be his brother's heir,' said Francis.

'Certainly he is not. But he *is* the heir, and Parliament cannot undo that. The Church, matters ecclesiastical, and matters of conscience, must be taken out of his care. More I do not believe we are able to do. But I'll not stop you working with the Whigs, Francis, if you believe in their aims. Nor will I think any the less of you for so doing. Come, Thomas will be expecting you soon. If you are to be a Whig, you may as well do it thoroughly.'

The King's Head was crowded, but mention of Thomas's name had Francis shown quickly into a private apartment, where Thomas stood by the fire in conversation with two gentlemen. Both were tall, though one, the older by some years, was stout and red-faced, the other pale and slight, with sharp angular features.

'Permit me,' said Thomas at once. 'Lord Cavendish, Mr Standish – my cousin, Lord Trenoweth.' Francis bowed, and was rewarded by a smile from the younger of the two.

Sweet pale Canary wine was brought to them almost at once, and shortly they dined on succulent goose, venison with sparrow-grass, fruits, comfits and nuts. All the while the conversation tended towards the campaign now in progress to elect a Whig Parliament at Oxford, and the relative merits of the Prince of Orange and the Duke of Monmouth as contenders for the position of the King's heir.

'Our position will be greatly strengthened if we turn to Holland,' said Thomas emphatically. 'William of Orange is stronger than Monmouth, and a better Protestant, if it comes to that.'

'I don't know about that,' mused Mr Standish, who Francis guessed was not a great deal older than him. 'Monmouth is extremely popular, and his father dotes on him. And would now appear to have the protection of milord Shaftesbury. Surely, if he were legitimised...'

'Shaftesbury has not committed himself,' said Lord Cavendish at once. 'I agree with you, Sir Thomas – William is after all married to our own Princess Mary, who if her father were to predecease the King would be heir in any case.'

'But he is said to be in close touch with his uncles,' objected Mr Standish. 'What if he were waiting a suitable moment to turn Papist?'

'He would lose Holland as well as England,' said Thomas drily. 'But I hope you two gentlemen are prepared to support me in my candidature?' There was a murmur of assent, and the conversation turned to other topics.

It was still a while before the meal was ended, as the probable outcome of the election was discussed. Eventually Thomas rose.

'Thank you, gentlemen,' he said at last. 'We shall meet in Launceston, no doubt.'

*

Francis slept late the next morning, going over in his mind, not the political tangle that was threatening to envelope him, but the entertainment at the King's Theatre to which Thomas had taken him. He had never been to the theatre before, and was amazed at the sheer bawdiness of it. Much of the time he could not hear what the actors were saying, for the shouts and cat-calls from the pit. The audience were obviously enjoying themselves, and were quick to pick out a favourite actor or actress. The play, he remembered, was a piece by Dryden, and most entertaining, but what he had enjoyed even more was the atmosphere of the place. Actors and audience alike were good-humoured, noisy and cheerful, the orange-sellers were doing a fine trade, and for a while at least Francis forgot the problems that were besetting him.

Now he lay there, enjoying the ease of mind and body, until he realised that unless he bestirred himself he would be late for chapel. He was out of bed at once, shouting for Will to bring him hot water and a clean shirt. He arrived at the chapel breathless and flustered, just in time to don his surplice and earn a mild reproof from Mr Blow. As they processed in and took their places Francis understood Mr Blow's agitation. The King was in chapel today; Francis glanced down the aisle and recognised from portraits he had seen the King's luxuriant curled periwig, his neat black moustache, his aquiline nose and deep-set brown eyes. These seemed to be looking straight at him, and Francis turned his attention to his music in some confusion. By the end of the service he could not even remember which psalms they had sung.

'Well done, Francis,' said Mr Blow as they were disrobing. 'You managed that long sustained F sharp extremely well; not easy with the King's eyes fastened on you like that. I will overlook your near lateness; you are too valuable a counter-tenor.'

Francis walked home in the glow of Mr Blow's praise, scarcely noticing the fact that it had begun to snow. Almost as soon as he was in the house Will Peters handed him a letter. Francis took it and frowned.

'This is Christopher's hand,' he said. 'I trust there is nothing amiss.' He broke the seal, and found himself smiling at Christopher's account of life in Oxford. Even when he mentioned Francis' own expulsion from his college the smile did not waver. Francis had known it would probably happen.

Then he read further down, and the smile faded. He reached for a seat, without taking his eyes from the letter.

'The only topic of conversation here is the Parliament that has been called to meet in Oxford. It seems that most of the students will be sent away, which is a great pity, as it would be hugely enjoyable.

'I saw your cousin Robert the other day. He wanted to know how you were, of course, and said that Eleanor had asked after you. He also said that he had proposed to her, but that she had not given him an absolute answer. But then he spoke a great deal about the Oxford Parliament, and how it would change all our fortunes. Francis, do you think it possible that they will use the occasion to mount some sort of a plot? I must confess that my suspicions were aroused. Coneybury is only a few miles away, and is clearly well known as a hotbed of papists. Robert did not say anything specific, but he was plainly anxious about something, and he was not as circumspect as he usually is. Something has rattled him, and I cannot tell what it is.

'In any case, he said he was coming to London soon, and would be sure to look you up. So don't come rushing back to Oxford yet; or you might miss something useful, quite apart from putting yourself in danger.

'I will write again if I have any further news. In the meantime Tacitus calls. Oxford is a great deal duller without you.

Your friend, Christopher.'

Francis read the letter through three times, as though it were some kind of code and only in this way could he decipher what his friend was trying to say. At the end of the third reading he realised that the news that had stirred him most was Robert's proposal to Eleanor.

'He must not.' Only when Thomas, coming into the room at that moment, said 'Who must not what, Francis?' did he realise that he had spoken aloud.

'Robert. He has proposed marriage to Eleanor. I have just received a letter from Christopher.'

'And has she accepted him?'

'No. Not at the moment, at least.'

Thomas sat down. 'From all that you have said, this would not appear to be an altogether surprising turn of events.'

'No. Yet it feels wrong, Thomas. I am quite sure that she does not want him, and I am not at all sure that he wants her.'

'And you do?'

'I cannot see how that would be possible. But I do care for her. If anybody is plotting in that house, it is certainly not her.'

'But you believe that somebody might be?'

'Before I came to London I was concerned. I am even more so now.'

'So what do you intend to do?'

'If Robert is to come to London soon I had better be here when he does. After that I hardly know.'

'I shall have a certain amount to say to Robert myself.' Thomas's voice sounded cool. 'Though he may not want to hear it.' He stood up. 'Come, Francis, we cannot have you worrying. I believe you are missing your studies.'

'A little.' Francis laughed. 'Though the Chapel Royal choir more than makes up for it. I was not really making music before, Thomas, just playing at it.'

'Will you join me in the King's Head, then? Or is your mind on altogether too refined a plane?'

Francis stood up. 'Gladly. It is good to find I am being accepted for who I am, and not just as my father's son.'

They both arranged their hats, adjusted blue ribbons, and went out.

The meal was leisurely, and involved meeting a number of Thomas's acquaintances, and by the time it was over Francis realised he must make his way straight to the Chapel Royal for Evensong.

He was more than ever glad that he was in time when he saw that as well as Mr Blow, Purcell was there. They were in deep discussion as Francis arrived, but broke off as they saw him. Mr Blow smiled.

'I was just thanking Mr Purcell for introducing me to one of the finest counter-tenors it has been my privilege to meet. You are a great asset to the choir.'

'Thank you.' Francis could not think of anything else to say.

'As soon as I heard you sing I knew my friend here would be glad to meet you.' Purcell clapped his hand on Francis' shoulder. 'We are all united in the desire to improve music in this country, are we not?'

'And you, sir, will be in the Chapel Royal yourself ere many summers are past. We shall need you here. I shall need you here. Come, we must robe.'

After the service Francis realised that there was daylight enough left to walk home through the Privy Gardens, and he set off cheerfully. Though the memory of the attack in Oxford was still vivid, the physical marks had faded. The bruising on his face had gone, his chest no longer felt tight and he could walk normally. He felt secure, and even the memory of Christopher's letter did not seriously perturb him.

He was about to enter the gardens when a hand on his arm made him turn sharply and a well-remembered voice said 'Francis?'

'Robert! I seem to be forever meeting you in unexpected places. To what do I owe the honour this time?'

Robert smiled, and Francis realised that he had lost none of his charm.

'I promised Eleanor that as soon as I was in London I would seek you out. She was anxious as to your welfare.'

'As you see, I am quite recovered. And should I be congratulating you?'

A shadow passed over Robert's face. 'It may perhaps be a little premature. Eleanor has not given me her answer yet.'

'But you have asked her?'

'Oh yes. And her father has given his blessing. It is Eleanor herself of whom I am uncertain.' He looked like a man weighed down with the cares of the world, not one hoping to enter into the state of matrimony.

They were walking along one of the gravelled paths in the gardens; looking at Robert's shoes Francis was glad that the paths were so well maintained, but presumably Robert knew that already. They were only a few minutes' walk away from the house Francis was already thinking of as home.

'Will you come in with me? I know you have your lodgings in Whitehall, but since you are so near you would surely expect to see Thomas.'

'I doubt that he will want to see me. But yes, I will come with you, Francis. I could have come straight to the house, but it seemed easier to meet with you elsewhere.'

'Why so?' Immediately Francis read surprise in his cousin's face.

'You of all people would surely understand.' Robert smiled a little sadly. 'I am sure you are the blue-eyed boy of both your Tory father and my Whiggish brother, whereas I – ' He tailed off, and Francis was suddenly conscious of a certain amount of sympathy for him. This was no longer his childhood hero, but merely his cousin who would appear to have lost his way.

They were on the steps of the house now, and Robert paused.

'Perhaps I should go. I think I am not wanted.'

'And what would give you that idea?' Neither of them had heard Thomas coming up behind them. 'I thought perhaps we should see you here before too long. Robert, Francis, let us get ourselves out of this rather dreary weather.' He pushed ahead of the two younger men and strode into the hall.

'It's even colder here.' Thomas continued straight into the parlour and sank down onto a settee by the fire. Francis sat down beside him and Robert hovered awkwardly in the doorway.

'So, how was Evensong?' Thomas looked cheerful. 'Oh, for goodness sake, Robert, come and sit down. I am sure you have your reasons for being here, and we shall hear them in due course.'

Robert moved into the room and perched himself on the edge of a carved wooden chair.

'Shaftesbury was asking where you were.' Thomas grinned at Francis. 'He seemed satisfied when I told him the Chapel Royal; he likes to know exactly where everybody is.'

'The choir is wonderful.' Francis smiled. 'You should come and hear us, Thomas. The music is sublime. Mr Purcell comes sometimes, when his duties at the Abbey permit. He is becoming quite a friend.'

'You mentioned him at Coneybury.' Robert looked up from studying his fingernails. 'A musician or something, isn't he?'

'The finest composer in the country.' Francis was emphatic. 'And not yet twenty-two.'

'Indeed I must come.' Thomas seemed determined to ignore his younger brother. Robert turned to him.

'You have been instructing Francis in the ways of the Whigs, I see.'

'He needed little instruction.' Thomas at last looked across at Robert. 'Francis is completely loyal.'

'And I am not?'

'That was not what I said. Would you describe yourself as loyal?'

'I would.'

'Then I believe you. But you look forward to the day when his Grace of York is King.'

'His Grace is a Catholic. So am I. But he is the heir, so he will succeed his brother in due course.'

Thomas leaned forward. 'You would not, for instance, look for ways to bring that sooner?'

There was half a second's pause before Robert answered.

'Of course not. I thought you said you believed me. I am no traitor, Thomas. I had not thought your opinion of me was so low.'

'I meant what I said, as I am sure did you. But loyalty can take many forms. Take care that your loyalty to the Duke does not take precedence over your loyalty to the King.'

Robert rose from his chair, his face suddenly flushed.

'Are you accusing me – ' His voice trailed away as the door opened and Lord Bodmin came in.

'Is anybody accusing anybody of anything?' He dropped onto the settee the other side of the fire and smiled genially at Robert.

'Robert. It is, as always, a great pleasure to see you. But would I be mistaken in believing that you are somewhat angry?'

'Thomas believes that I am a traitor.'

Lord Bodmin said nothing, but turned to Thomas and raised one eyebrow.

'I said nothing of the sort. Robert claims to know what I am thinking – how, I do not know.'

Lord Bodmin stretched out his legs and held out his hands to the fire.

'It seems a pity for such a recent family reunion to become acrimonious. I have only walked a short way, it is true, but I am cold. Francis, Thomas, have you yet called for wine?'

Thomas grinned at his uncle. 'It seems an excellent idea. I will do so at once.'

'So, Robert.' Lord Bodmin turned to his younger nephew as Thomas left the room. 'For some time your relations with your brother have been less than perfect. But what makes you think he believes you guilty of treason?'

'He has never thought well of me. He believes that all "Papists" are traitors.'

'That I know to be untrue. A man's belief is a private matter between himself and his conscience. Thomas believes that as much as I do. Treason is a different matter altogether.'

Francis looked up. 'You told me that it was Anthony Somerville who converted you. Do you see him as a man who would lead you into wrongdoing?'

Robert flinched, and held up his hands in horror.

'Of course not. How can you even suggest such a thing?' He stood up and moved to the door, almost colliding with Harry coming in with a flagon of wine and four tankards. Thomas was close behind him.

'I cannot stop. I should not have come.' Robert made to leave the room, but Thomas barred his way.

'Sit down, Robert. You are not a child any more, so stop behaving like one.'

Robert glared at his brother, but he obeyed and took a tankard of wine from him.

Thomas sat down, and stretched out his legs towards the fire.

'Now.' He turned to his brother and smiled. 'I know we have had our differences, Robert, but I had not thought they would cause this extreme unease in your behaviour. As a man contemplating matrimony, I would have thought you would be in a more cheerful frame of mind. Or is it that the thought of marriage does not truly appeal?'

'Marriage?' Lord Bodmin took a swallow of wine, and looked up.

'Robert has proposed marriage to Eleanor Somerville,' said Francis. 'Though she has not yet given an answer.'

'I see. But presumably you wish to marry the young lady because you love her. Or is that not the case?'

'Yes, no, of course.' Robert put down his tankard, and started to pace the room. 'It is complicated. I owe Anthony Somerville a great deal. He informed me that his brother would look favourably on the match. It seems – appropriate.'

'And what are the young lady's thoughts on the matter?'

Robert looked uncomfortable. 'I hardly know. I esteem her, of course, and as a Catholic of good family, I hoped she would see it as beneficial to herself. But I confess I am not certain. She is a lady of independent mind.'

'That I can vouch for.' Francis smiled. 'Her mother died at her birth, Father, and she has run her father's household for as long as she can remember. She even does some of the gardening. Mother would delight in talking roses with her.'

Lord Bodmin smiled. 'She sounds a rare jewel. I hope I may indeed be able to congratulate you soon, Robert. When do you return to Oxfordshire?'

'I think His Grace needs me here at the moment. But yes, I shall be going to Oxfordshire again before very long. Do you have any message for Eleanor, Francis?'

'Not at present.' Francis smiled. 'You may tell her that I am well, and that I look forward to speaking with her again. Perhaps it will not be too long before I am able to do so.'

Robert stood up and reached for his hat. 'I fear that I must leave; His Grace has need of me.' He smiled at them all and walked out of the room. This time nobody made a move to stop him. Thomas turned to Francis as the sound of Robert's footsteps faded.

'When did you meet with Robert?'

'In the park, only a few minutes before you came upon us. I was as surprised as you are.'

'You mentioned before that you doubted his feelings towards the young lady. Do you still?'

'Yes. I am certain that he does not love her. There is something – I cannot understand what it is, but there is something that is not right.'

'Could this have anything to do with your own feelings?' Thomas was gentle.

'I don't know. I am sure she does not want to marry Robert. Though I do not expect ever to be able to marry her myself, I do want to see her happy.'

Lord Bodmin stood up. 'I understand that you care for this young lady, Francis,' he said. 'Is there anything else that concerns you?'

'Yes. Thomas has seen the letter I received this morning. It is from my friend Christopher. He is concerned about what is happening at Oxford at the moment. And if Christopher is concerned, there is probably something to worry about.'

'So what do you intend to do?'

'I think that I must return to Oxford,' said Francis, surprising even himself. He had not known that he thought so, yet now that it was spoken the move seemed obvious. 'I cannot ignore this letter; but what can I do when once I am there?'

His father smiled. 'Would it be to defend the honour of Miss Somerville, or to seek out evidence of treason?'

'I should certainly be glad to see Eleanor again. Christopher mentioned the possibility of plotting. Father, supposing there is a plot, and that by doing nothing I allowed it to happen?'

'And your Whig friends? The Chapel Royal?'

'I am sure Francis' Whig friends, as you term them, would applaud his going to seek out treason.' Thomas was emphatic. 'But the Chapel Royal?'

'That one is harder.' Francis looked crestfallen. 'Yet now it has been spoken I know I must go.'

'I believe you are right.' Thomas looked serious. 'You will be in danger, of course, but I believe that you are equal to it. And if you discover evidence of treason, then you must of course bring what you know to the Privy Council. I do not know whether your father would agree with me.'

'For once, Thomas, I believe I do,' said Lord Bodmin, getting up and standing with his back to the fire. 'I myself am not inclined to believe in this particular plot any more than hundreds of similar ones, but Francis will not rest until it has been proved one way or the other. He is as well equipped as any to find out the truth, and he has at least recovered from the attack that brought him here. Where will you lodge, Francis?'

'Why, at – at Magdalen, I suppose.'

'You have forgotten that you have been expelled?' asked his father gently. 'That way is barred, unless – I wonder – yes, before you leave I shall obtain an audience for you with the King.'

'With the King?' cried Francis and Thomas together.

'Do you have to repeat what I say in that stupid fashion? Francis will be in danger enough if he returns to Oxford, but the King can at least restore him to the University, if anybody can. Royal protection is no bad thing sometimes; if the President knows you have that, he may overlook one or two slight breaches of the rules. You are not afraid, Francis?'

His son stared into the flames with a fierce concentration, as though expecting them to tell him something.

'Yes,' he replied. 'I am. But I have no choice.'

Chapter Nine

Francis, nervous, excited and bewildered, followed his father through a seemingly endless maze of corridors and passages, across courtyards, up and down stairs, pausing now and then as his father greeted an acquaintance. They passed sentries on duty, ladies and gentlemen fashionably dressed, poorer citizens come to beg favours, and hawkers crying their wares. It seemed difficult to remember that this teeming, unruly place was none other than the royal palace. Francis wished he could emulate his father's carefree attitude, his easy laugh, but the object of his journey made him quake; he was going to meet the King. It was easier for his father, perhaps, who had met him first when a boy in adversity, and sealed a firm friendship before power and three kingdoms were restored. All reports agreed that age had contributed to the King's cynicism; in all probability he would brush aside the suggestion of a fresh plot against his life with an amused smile. Francis suddenly found himself wondering if by returning to Oxford he would be putting himself needlessly in danger, whether he would not have been better advised to stay in London, sing in the Chapel Royal and proclaim himself a Whig.

At length their long walk came to an end in a vaulted ante-chamber, where a great many people appeared to be doing nothing in particular. Some of them turned as the newcomers entered, but most did not appear particularly interested. A liveried footman came up to them almost at once and ushered them through into an inner chamber.

'His Majesty will join you presently,' he murmured and withdrew.

'Father – ' whispered Francis, but Lord Bodmin held up his hand.

'Save your breath for the King,' he replied. 'He will not be long.'

Even as he finished speaking a further door opened and Francis recognised the person of the King, whom he had seen in Chapel a few days earlier. Lord Bodmin knelt and raised the King's hand to his lips and Francis, anxious to be correct in all things, did the same, but the King waved aside these formalities.

'I had thought you knew well enough, Lord Bodmin,' he began, 'that I have little taste for such ceremonies where I deem them unnecessary. I am the King, and I will be treated with respect, but I will not have men to fawn upon me.' He sat down beside the fire and looked up at the two men standing before him with a smile of great charm. Lord Bodmin inclined his head.

'So this is your son,' continued the King. 'But I have seen you before. You have been singing in the Chapel Royal. You have a singularly sweet counter-tenor voice.'

Francis blushed, and bowed his head, but the King laughed.

'Royal compliments are not handed out as a matter of course,' he said. 'You should be pleased. But I believe you have a request to make?'

'If it please Your Majesty,' said Francis, 'I wish to return to Oxford.'

The King raised his eyebrows in surprise. 'I do not recall assenting to a Bill which made royal permission necessary for such a journey.'

'No – that is – of course not.' Again that annoying blush. 'Only – it is somewhat awkward – I believe I have been expelled from my college.'

'If your father's account of your departure from Oxford is correct, then I think that not unlikely,' replied the King. 'What would you have me do?' For a second Francis was taken aback, then he noticed the amused expression in the King's eyes, suggesting imminent laughter.

'I think my son has begun things in a rather poor order, Sire,' put in Lord Bodmin. 'He has received information concerning your personal safety while in Oxford. By going there himself he believes he can discover sufficient of the plans of those who wish Your Majesty harm to be able to thwart them. But Oxford being what it is, the protection of the University would doubtless be beneficial to him.'

'And royal protection, you think, would achieve that,' mused the King. 'I am familiar enough with designs against both my throne and my life to place no great weight upon a fresh one. I am persuaded by some that there are people sufficiently misguided to prefer my stubborn brother James as King: they will, I suspect, have time to repent of their folly. But plots there will be by the hundred in Oxford. You think your active presence there might confound one such plot, do you, Lord Trenoweth?'

'I – I do believe so, Sire,' stammered Francis. The King stood up and paced about the room, frowning.

'You would wish also, no doubt, to be present in Oxford while Parliament is sitting?' he enquired after a pause.

'I would, so please Your Majesty. And – if a particular friend of mine, Christopher Wentworth, could also have permission to remain – '

'I see. Well, well. I will ask the President of your college to arrange it. I will not insist, mark you; I expect too many favours from Oxford to make that wise. But you may return, and I wish you success in your enterprise. A lady, I take it, is the fair prize?' Francis was so startled he could find nothing to say, and the King laughed, not altogether unkindly.

'Your venture becomes altogether more comprehensible,' he remarked. 'Complete lack of self-interest among my subjects usually makes me uncomfortable.'

Francis looked intently at his feet, uncertain what to say, but his father smiled broadly. 'It was not so five and twenty years ago, Sire,' he remarked.

'You must not remind me of my mis-spent youth, Lord Bodmin; it will give your son here strange ideas. I may come safely to Oxford, then, knowing my security is in your hands?' he concluded, turning to Francis.

'I will do my best.' Francis tried to speak calmly, but he felt foolish.

'Then I would all Whigs were as loyal as you are. Most of them care not one whit for my safety or my life, but would cheer me on my travels again provided their comfort was assured. Do you not think so?'

'I think, Sire, that you do an injustice to a great many honest men.' His father looked at him in surprise. 'All men want peace in the kingdom – the Whigs have a different way of achieving it, that is all.'

For a moment the King looked taken aback, and drummed as though with the greatest concentration on the hilt of his sword. Then he looked up and smiled at Francis with infinite charm.

'First impressions can often be mistaken,' he said. 'It seems you are no more timid than your father. You will be in danger in Oxford – I can read that in your face, but I believe your courage is equal to it. I will do one thing more for you that you have not asked. I will see that Mr Blow is not offended by your sudden departure. I know that your music is important to you, and it could be that in happier times you will return to the Chapel Royal.'

Francis said nothing, but bowed in acknowledgment.

'And now I fear I must leave you,' continued the King. 'Already the Privy Councillors grow impatient, and soon they will be here to fetch me out. Good day to you, Lord Bodmin; bon voyage, Lord Trenoweth.' With an easy smile he was gone, and father and son made their way back into the ante-room, where they were the objects of many curious stares.

When they returned Thomas demanded to know what they had done.

'Let us walk in the garden, Francis,' he urged. 'We shall see you at dinner, uncle,' he called as Lord Bodmin began ascending the stairs.

'Sometimes I wonder why he comes to London,' murmured Francis. 'He is far happier in Cornwall.'

Thomas turned to his cousin as soon as they were alone. 'So you are going to return to Oxford?'

'I have to find out what is happening, Thomas. It may be helpful if I can get to Coneybury while Robert is still in London. Something is wrong, and I cannot rest until I know more.'

'I can let Lord Shaftesbury know what it is that you are doing. Hopefully he will be pleased, even if you are going under royal protection. But do not be too impulsive. I remember – '

'Yes?' said Francis quickly.

'I was only a boy at the time, but even then I knew that it was his eager impulsiveness that nearly cost your father his life. Be careful, Francis.'

Francis wrinkled his brow as they walked back towards the house.

'My father himself gave me the same warning,' he said. 'Yet you say he is incautious.'

'Of his own actions, not those of others,' replied Thomas. 'You have never known him without position and responsibilities. My earliest memories of him are laughing at a thorough soaking in the coldest sea-water I know, and tearing his breeches on the rocks of St Mary's.'

'Yes, you always did know my favourite hiding places,' put in a voice behind them. 'So you think me impetuous, Thomas?'

'Sometimes,' murmured his nephew, embarrassed. 'And do you not think that Francis has inherited it?'

'Maybe. But I am no longer young, and am grown more mellow – perhaps more patient. It is youth which wants to turn the world upside down; I have known such desire, but now I prefer that it should remain as it is. I have a dislike, however, of abstaining from dinner, and it will be growing cold if we do not go in at once to eat. Francis, Thomas, come and dine; it may be a long time before the three of us enjoy a meal together in peace again.'

*

'The snowdrops are making quite a display this year. Do you not think so?' Mary Somerville turned to Eleanor, who was walking slowly beside her. Eleanor glanced at them, but said nothing.

'I thought you were interested in the garden. Really, Eleanor, you might try to look interested. I offered to come into the garden with you as it is a fine afternoon and you seem a bit down. But all you are doing is hanging your head and moping.'

Eleanor managed a pallid smile. 'I am sorry, aunt. I have a bit of a headache.'

'Mooning after that young Lord Trenoweth, I suppose. Oh yes, young lady, I have seen the way you look at him. Your father should never have invited him here. He is a *Protestant*, Eleanor.'

'I know that. I knew it before ever I met him. Is it so very improper of me to be anxious because he was severely beaten for visiting us?'

'As long as it is no more than that. You have received a perfectly acceptable proposal of marriage from a handsome Catholic young man who has your father's blessing. What are you waiting for?'

Eleanor turned to face her aunt. 'For him to tell me that he loves me, perhaps. I am not at all certain that he really wants to marry me.'

'He has proposed to you, has he not? Is that not evidence enough?'

Eleanor looked at her hands with great intensity. 'No, aunt. I do not believe that it is.'

Mary gave a snort of impatience. 'I think you will find, Eleanor, that love does not have a great deal to do with making a satisfactory marriage.' She began to walk fast towards the house. As they passed the rose garden she stopped suddenly, and gripped Eleanor's arm.

'There are buds on the bushes already.' Mary pointed in the direction of the roses. 'You have looked after it well. Your father says that your housekeeping skills are excellent. You have all the qualities needed to make an excellent wife – but not to a Protestant, Eleanor. We have always been a Catholic family. Why can you not accept Robert?'

Eleanor turned away. 'I am not ready to give an answer yet. It would be wrong of me to make a solemn promise that I am unable to fulfil. And now, if my housekeeping skills are to stay at that level of excellent, I must visit the kitchen and make sure that all is in order for supper tonight.'

Eleanor walked purposefully towards the house. She suspected her aunt knew that a visit to the kitchen was merely a ruse, but as soon as she stepped into the kitchen she felt herself relax. Outside they had been walking in clear air, under the last of the January sunshine, while in the kitchen it was stuffy and steamy, but nevertheless she breathed deeply and smiled. The cook looked up at her.

'Difficult time, chick?'

Eleanor smiled. 'My aunt cannot understand why I have not thrown myself at Robert the moment he proposed. She thinks I am playing for time. I do not want to marry him, Cookie, and I never shall.'

'And you cannot tell him so?'

'Almost I believe I could tell Robert. Even my father might understand. But then there is my aunt, and my uncle. They both seem to think that my marrying Robert is the only possible course of action.'

'And the other?'

'It is true that I care for Fr – Lord Trenoweth. We understand what is important to each other. But I know that marrying him is out of the question.'

The cook looked at her intently. 'Stranger things have happened.' She turned back to her pastry. 'Do you go upstairs and change that muddy gown now, and let Sarah scold you. I've the supper to see to.' And she began rolling pastry as though her life depended on it.

Eleanor went slowly up to her room. It was true that her gown was muddy. Sarah was not there, so she slid out of the gown and left it on the floor, then lay down on her bed in her shift, glad that Sarah had at least ensured that the fire was burning.

A few minutes later Sarah came into the room. She made straight to the fireplace to make up the fire, then turned to the bed.

'Are you not well, Miss? I can see you needed to change your gown, but it is not like you to leave it on the floor.' She gathered it up and spread it out on the clothes press, preparing to sponge the muddy hem. Eleanor watched her for a little, then swung herself off the bed.

'Can that not wait, Sarah? I feel uncomfortable that I allowed it to get dirty, and watching you clean it for me makes me feel worse.'

'It is always easier to do it straight away, Miss. The marks come out so much more easily then. There, it is almost done. See?' She held the dress up and Eleanor saw that though it was now damp around the hem, the traces of mud had gone.

'Have you given him your answer yet, Miss?'

Eleanor smiled ruefully. 'No. I think I know what it will be, but I am putting it off. Is that not cowardly of me?'

'No, Miss. It is difficult for you.'

'I cannot marry Robert, Sarah. I think I shall have to brave everybody's displeasure and say so. They all think it a perfect match. Only I know it would make me unhappy for the rest of my life.'

'Not only you, Miss.'

'No?'

'I would rather you were not married to him. And – do you think that Mr Carey really wants it?'

Eleanor sat up, and pulled the coverlet about her shoulders. 'No. I do not really think that he does.'

'Perhaps I should not be saying it, Miss, but I do not think it either. I have seen the way he looks at – somebody else.'

'He has not made approaches to you, has he? I know that gentlemen in his position often think that servant girls are there for their amusement, but I did not think Robert would do this to me.'

'No, Miss. He has hardly noticed my existence.'

'Then – who? He never sees Bess from the kitchen, and there are no other young ladies in the house.'

'It is not a young lady he is looking at, Miss.'

'Now you have got me thoroughly confused, Sarah. Surely you are not saying that Robert has designs on my aunt?'

Sarah bent to pick up a thread that had fallen to the floor from some sewing she had been doing earlier. 'I am sorry, Miss. I should not have spoken.'

'Now you have said this much, though, you will have to tell me who it is of whom you speak.'

'Watch next time you see him in conversation with your uncle.'

'My *uncle*? You cannot mean – but you do, don't you? Sarah, are you serious?'

'I cannot be sure, Miss, but it is the way they look at each other. It is a sort of hunger. I understand that this sort of thing can happen.'

'But my uncle is a priest.'

'He is a man, Miss. And men have appetites – not always those we can recognise.'

Eleanor lay back, and buried her face in the pillow. 'When she raised it again her face was wet.

'I shall have my meal in my room tonight, Sarah. See that somebody informs my father that my headache is worse.'

*

Francis had never expected to feel such sadness as he robed for evening prayer at the Chapel Royal, knowing that the next day he would be riding back to Oxford. It was his own choice, he kept telling himself, and yet he felt a sense of desolation.

He sang a perfect solo in an anthem by Matthew Locke, and knew that he had done it well. It was a penitential piece, and suited his mood.

Afterwards Mr Blow spoke cheerfully to him.

'You have established a reputation here extremely quickly.' He smiled. 'I shall be sorry to lose you, though I fully understand your reasons.'

'I am sorry to leave, sir.' Francis felt wretched. 'The music here has been all that I could have wished. Yet I know that I must return to Oxford.'

'The other group of Gentlemen is in any case due to take over next week. So if you can conduct your business in Oxford within a month we should be happy to see you here again.'

'Truly?' Francis looked up eagerly. 'I had not looked for such kindness.'

'Hardly kindness.' Francis had not seen Mr Purcell come into the room. 'You are the best counter-tenor any of us has heard for a long time. Nobody is going to want to lose you. You should keep up your singing while you are in Oxford. I am sure you could re-establish contact with your friends. It may not be as good as the Chapel Royal, but at least you will be singing.'

'I had not thought that far, but yes, I will do that.'

'Come with me to St Anne's Street.' Purcell smiled at him. 'I have an hour or two of leisure, and it would be good to drink some wine with you before you go.'

So Francis sat again in Purcell's elegant house and drank wine with him, relaxing in the friendship of the man he believed to be England's premier composer.

'So.' Purcell poured wine for them both, then looked up at Francis with a smile on his face. 'What are you really going to do when you return to Oxford?'

'I hardly know.' Francis sipped cautiously at his wine, and set the goblet down. 'I need to find out more of my cousin Robert's activities – and it would be good to see Eleanor again. My place at the University is restored, so I shall have to do at least some studying. And if I am to make music again I shall be busy enough. I suppose I feel rather inadequate.'

'That you are not. Though I am sorry for the reasons that brought you to London, I cannot be sorry that it happened. I know Mr Blow intends that I should succeed him at the Chapel Royal. I shall need you there with me then, Francis. What a sound we shall make!'

Francis looked up at his host and smiled. He knew he was surrounded by dangers, yet he felt hugely blessed.

The next morning he was up early, delighted that he was now strong enough to ride. He made his farewells easily enough to his father and to Thomas, and then they were off, pale winter sunshine above them, but crisp frost under the horses' hooves.

'We should make Oxford easily before dark, Will.' Francis was cheerful. 'Better than a gloomy coach, don't you think?'

'Indeed, my lord. I am delighted that you are so much stronger.'

They made good time, breaking their fast and changing horses in Beaconsfield, and riding on easily towards Oxford. Francis knew an unexpected thrill of excitement as the city came into view. He had not realised until that moment how much it meant to him.

'Oxford again, Will. I shall miss it when we are no longer here.'

'You are still a Cornishman, my lord.' Will reproved him gently.

'I know, Will, I know. And I never expected to experience London in the way we just have done. Life has so much to offer. Cornwall is a big part of that.'

*

'I am glad to see you with some colour in your face.' Sir Henry came into the small parlour just as Eleanor seated herself at her spinet. 'It is two days since we have seen you at dinner.'

'I could not get rid of my headache.' Eleanor smiled thinly. 'And – I had a lot to think about.'

Sir Henry sat down on the settee by the fire, and patted the cushion beside him. Eleanor closed her instrument slowly and joined her father.

'So. Have you given Robert his answer yet?'

'I have not seen him for over a week.'

'But you have decided?'

'Yes.' Eleanor turned to face her father. 'I cannot marry him. I know you will be disappointed, and I should have told Robert first. Truly, I do not really believe that he wants to marry me. I have been so very unhappy, father.'

Sir Henry put his hand on his daughter's arm. 'He asked you, did he not? That seems to suggest he wishes it. But if that is how you feel, then we must respect it. I know I could insist, but I decided a long time ago that I would not use that right. We are expecting Robert in the next two or three days. Perhaps you will feel better when you have told him.'

'Perhaps.' Eleanor stood up. 'Would you like me to play for you?'

'Sit down for a moment, Eleanor. There is something I wanted to discuss with you – and it is nothing to do with the possibility of your marriage.'

Eleanor sat down again and looked at him questioningly.

'You know that in a few weeks there is a Parliament to meet in Oxford?'

'Yes. But it does not really affect us, does it?'

'Not directly. But there are perhaps ways in which we could affect the Parliament.'

Eleanor's eyes widened. 'Ways? But how?'

'Ways to make quite sure the Duke retains his lawful place as his brother's heir. With the Parliament so close, we can hardly ignore it.'

'But – but – ' Eleanor stared at her father, concern in her mind growing swiftly to alarm. 'Father – please tell me you are not considering treason? Better the Duke should not succeed than that!'

'Better – child, do you know what you are saying? The Duke of York is his brother's heir, and he *must* succeed. Where would those of our faith be if he did not?'

Eleanor stood up again, and looked down at her father, who was stroking his beard with great concentration.

'You have not answered my question.' Eleanor's voice was cold. 'Are you contemplating treason, Father?'

'Of course not. Sit down, child, and stop fidgetting. Whatever put such an idea into your head? You know how important it is for those of our faith that York should one day be King. There are many means we could employ to help that come about.'

'There are?'

'We are only asking that the law be upheld. It is the Whigs who want to play with it. The fact of a Parliament in Oxford may make it easier for us to – well, to show the strength of our opinion. Surely you see that?'

'I don't know what I see any more. I only know that this house, which was once such a happy place, is now full of whispers and intrigue. I am treated as the child I no longer am, expected to marry a man I do not love, and then to look pleased when those nearest to me begin activities that look positively dangerous.' She moved towards the door. 'I no longer want to live here. I shall have my dinner in my room again today. My headache is returning.'

*

Sir Henry sat by himself for some time after Eleanor had left. Not only did he go over their conversation in his head, he went over many episodes in her life. He knew there were times when he had come close to hating her, she looked so like the mother who had died in giving her birth. He had gone through the motions to see that she was cared for: he had employed a wet-nurse, later a governess. He had indulged her, petted her sometimes, but he knew that he had never truly loved her. His brother had seen to it that she was brought up a good Catholic, so he had no worries on that score. He had hoped by trying to take her into his confidence that he could bring them closer together, but he seemed to have driven a wedge between them. Perhaps he should have insisted she marry Robert while she was still a minor, but the indulgent side of him had emerged stronger at that point.

He did not know how much later it was that the door opened and his brother came in.

'Have you spoken to her?' Anthony was plainly impatient as he came to sit beside his brother.

'Yes. She will not marry him.'

Anthony breathed out slowly, but Sir Henry noticed the slight flaring of the nostrils, the heightened colour at the tips of his ears.

'You could insist. She is not of age.'

'What good would that do? It could never be a true marriage. You are a celibate, brother, and perhaps do not understand these things.'

Anthony clasped his hands until the knuckles showed white. 'It is a pity. Even without her whole-hearted co-operation, I believe much could have been achieved. Robert is an ideal son-in-law for you.'

'I know you have always been close to him. I do not feel I know him well.'

Anthony stood up, his eyes suddenly blazing. 'What do you mean, close to him? Are you suggesting – ' He swallowed, took a deep breath, and smiled wanly. 'My apologies, brother. I was disappointed, that is all. It need not affect our great design.'

'You are sure?'

'Of course. The King is offering us an ideal opportunity. We shall have a Catholic king on the throne before too long.'

'I think Eleanor – suspects something.'

'She can do nothing. Our retreat elsewhere will be ready soon. I acknowledge that this house might well become too dangerous. And I believe we have our decoy now.'

'Decoy?'

'I had a letter from Robert today. Lord Trenoweth is returning to Oxford. I believe we shall see him before too long.' Anthony sat down, with a smile of great satisfaction. Sir Henry looked at him, perplexed.

'And when we do see him?'

'My dear brother. All you need do is to play the genial host. Allow him time with Eleanor. Perhaps she can find out what it is that he wants of us.'

'Why should he want anything?'

'He wants Eleanor, that is obvious. But I think there is something else, and I need to know what it is. Do not look so anxious, Henry. Do what you are good at. Be the country gentleman, a kind host, a good father to Eleanor.'

'That is one area where I have failed.'

'Why should you say that? She is a credit to you. It is probably best to humour her if she does not wish to marry Robert. It will be easier if we have her co-operation.'

'Anthony. This plan of yours. You are quite certain?'

The surprise on Anthony's face was plain. 'Of course. At one stroke we can usher in a new and glorious age for this country. Is that not worth fighting for?'

'Why yes. But the danger – '

'All great enterprises carry some danger. If this costs my life lit is not a sacrifice too great.'

'Surely, as a priest – '

'As a priest I see it is my God-given duty to return this country to the true faith by whatever means are at my disposal. Surely you are not wanting to draw out now?'

'No, no. I just wanted to be sure that you had considered the cost.'

'Indeed I have. And if you find the cost too great then I suggest you take Eleanor and Mary to France at the earliest opportunity. There you will be safe until I can summon you home with the news that this country at last has a Catholic king.'

'Will that not make your work harder?'

'It will not make it any easier, certainly. But I must know who those I can count on are.'

Sir Henry stood up, and his normally florid complexion was suddenly pale.

'You can count on me, brother. You can count on me.'

Eleanor crept away from the door as she heard her father's footstep, succeeding in moving quietly despite her distress.

Chapter Ten

Francis sat by the fire in his room with Christopher. Both were cradling tankards of mulled ale which Will had supplied, warming their hands round them.

'So when do you intend to return to Coneybury?'

Francis looked up. 'Tomorrow, I hope. It needs to be as soon as possible. Why do you not come with me?'

'I? But – what for? What could I do there?'

Francis laughed. 'Don't look so anxious, Christopher. I shall come to no harm. But if you would prefer to remain in Oxford, of course I understand.'

'Maybe – '

'There is no need to worry. I have the King's protection, have I not? If they offer a bed for the night I think I will accept. I am sure royal protection will extend that far. And Will can come with me. He does not like the household very much, but the cook – now that is a different matter. At least I know he gets good food when he goes there.'

Francis looked at his friend. Their friendship had always been close, and Francis hoped it would remain so when they left Oxford. 'It grows late. Peter and Julian are supposed to be coming here soon. Mr Purcell encouraged me to keep up my music.'

'You want little encouraging. I can always hear it when you are playing.'

'Why do you not stay? You might enjoy it.'

'I? But what for?'

'Christopher, I'm offering you the chance to listen to some fine music. There will probably be more mulled ale, or there is some wine I brought back from London.'

'In that case, thank you, Francis. I don't understand your music, but it sounds pleasant enough.'

The next morning Francis and Will were ready early for their journey to Coneybury. Francis was impatient, and could hardly wait to eat breakfast before they were off.

Deliberately, he had not sent word to Coneybury of his coming, though he suspected that Anthony at least already knew that he was back in Oxford. But he might to a certain extent have the advantage of surprise.

It was a murky day, with a thin persistent drizzle and the sun hidden behind heavy clouds. Francis was glad of his thick riding cloak and boots, and was pleased to see that Will had wrapped himself up warmly as well.

'I'll swear this damp weather is colder than when we have a sharp frost.' Francis smiled at the horses' breath forming thick clouds in front of them. They set off towards Headington, nudging the horses into a canter as soon as they were up the hill, and pushed on towards Woodstock.

'What do you plan to do, my lord, when we reach Coneybury?'

'It will be interesting.' Francis quickened his pace to keep up with Will, who had pulled ahead. 'This is the first time we have come uninvited. I think that your welcome at least is assured.'

'Yours too, in certain quarters.' Will gave a sidelong glance to his master and grinned.

'Maybe. But I suspect it may be harder now to achieve conversation alone with Miss Somerville.'

In little more than an hour they were through Charlbury and trotting gently down the hill towards the entrance to Sir Henry's park. The drizzle had not turned into the downpour that Francis had feared, but the clouds were still heavy and his cloak felt thoroughly damp. Whether or not he would be welcome at Coneybury he had very little idea, but he hoped that it would extend at least to drying his riding cloak before he returned.

They trotted up the drive and came to a halt in front of the main door. A stable lad, no doubt hearing horses, came running to assist.

'Thank you, Dick.' Francis dismounted easily and handed the reins to the lad. 'Is Sir Henry at home today?'

'Yes, sir, my lord, he is in the parlour. I will rub the horses down for you.' The horses disappeared, and Will went round to the kitchen entrance. Alone, Francis suddenly felt uncertain of himself, wondering if he was wasting his time, or even placing himself in unnecessary danger. Even as he hesitated, the front door opened and Sir Henry emerged. Swathed in a voluminous brown cloak, he stood on the top step as though assessing the weather. Then he saw Francis, and hurried down the steps, his hands outstretched, his face a mask of welcome.

'My dear young man! We had heard that you had returned to Oxford. I am delighted that this miserable weather did not deter you from coming to visit your friends. You will stay for dinner?'

'Thank you. That would be kind. But you were about to go out?'

'Nothing that cannot wait. Eleanor insisted that two trees were felled a few weeks ago, and I am expecting replacements soon. But I doubt that they will be here in this weather.' He held out his arm, indicating that Francis should precede him up the steps.

Francis found himself conducted to the little parlour, where Eleanor and her aunt sat beside the fire, both busy with embroidery. Francis could not tell what Mary was thinking, but there was no mistaking the animation in Eleanor's face as he entered the room.

'Lord Trenoweth.' She curtsied, and Francis saw the beginnings of a smile as she looked at him. 'I am delighted to see you.' She looked past him to her father. 'Robert is not with you?'

'Not at present. I believe he is still in London. But I am sure that he will be here before very long.'

A shadow appeared to fall across her face as she seated herself, indicating that he should do the same. 'I am sure that he will.'

Francis began slipping out of his heavy cloak, which was now distinctly uncomfortable.

'Give that to me.' Eleanor seemed almost eager. 'I will take it to Sarah. She can dry and brush it before you return to Oxford.'

Sir Henry had taken off his own cloak, revealing a coat of plum coloured velvet that looked distinctly tight. Francis tried not to smile, and seated himself beside Mary, who was looking at him rather coldly.

'I trust I find you in good health?' He felt awkward, and held out his hands towards the fire, more for something to do with them than because he was cold.

'I enjoy excellent health, thank you. We are all glad to see that you are recovered from your unfortunate mishap.'

An odd way of describing something that had nearly cost him his life, Francis thought. But he inclined his head towards her. 'I am fully recovered, thank you, ma'am.'

The door opened again and Eleanor reappeared. 'I saw Peter just now, Father, and suggested he might bring some wine for us.'

'An excellent idea. Perhaps in a little you might go to inform Cook that Lord Trenoweth will be joining us for dinner.'

Francis grinned. 'I think it probable that Will has done that already. He seems to receive an excellent welcome in your kitchen.'

Peter came in with the wine at this point, followed almost immediately by Anthony, dressed in his habitual black. He joined Francis purposefully on the settee, preventing Eleanor from doing so.

'Lord Trenoweth. I am indeed glad to see you. It is good that you are recovered. I am hoping to enlist your help.'

'Indeed?' Francis turned towards the priest in surprise.

'Nothing too arduous, I assure you. But you are well placed to find out for me where certain people will be staying for the Parliament in Oxford. I have some acquaintances I have not seen for a long time, and should be glad to see again.'

'I should be happy to help.' Francis felt that his voice sounded false, and wondered if anybody else in the room had noticed.

'I will furnish you with a list of those I should like to contact. And, of course, any other information would be useful. This is an unusual event, and I am interested to see how it is to be organised. I believe Robert will be in the area shortly. If it is in any way – inconvenient – for you to return here, then I am sure he would carry the information here for you.'

'That would make sense, I suppose.' Francis' voice lacked enthusiasm.

'Arrangements are well in hand already, I expect?' Anthony was studiously bland.

'Indeed. The King will be staying at Christchurch.'

'And the Duchess of Portsmouth?' There was the hint of a smile behind Anthony's voice at this point, as he referred to the King's favourite mistress.

'She will be lodged at Merton College, I believe.'

'Ah. How convenient for His Majesty. But the Queen is also coming?'

'Oh yes. The King may even pay her a visit. But his prime task will be to see that Exclusion does not succeed.'

Anthony's eyes glittered. 'You are certain of this? I understand that the Whigs are very confident.'

'They are indeed. My cousin Thomas, Robert's elder brother, is one of them.'

'And you?'

'I have met some of the Whigs when I was in London. But I am my father's son, and my return here has his blessing – as well as that of the King.'

Eleanor obviously heard his last remark, and looked up animatedly.

'You have met the King?'

Francis smiled. The conversation was clearly about to become more general.

'My father arranged it. Without such influence I would probably have been unable to return.'

'Why so?' Sir Henry looked up, plainly puzzled.

'I had been expelled my college. His Majesty – implied – that my reinstatement would cause him satisfaction.'

'Why should you have been expelled?' Eleanor looked positively indignant.

'The circumstances of my leaving were a little unusual.' Francis smiled. 'My friend Christopher Wentworth was convinced that if anybody knew that I was leaving then there might be another attempt on my life. So not even my tutor was told. I was far from strong at the time, and went along with what was suggested. Leaving Oxford without permission is frowned upon.'

Anthony looked up. 'I am in considerable doubt on one point. If you had plenty to keep you occupied in London, why did you return at all?'

'My studies in Oxford are so near completion, it seemed a pity to waste it. And I was glad of the opportunity to visit you here again.'

'Indeed.' Anthony was suddenly inscrutable. 'I am sure that we are most flattered.'

'And did you managed to make any music in London?' Eleanor's voice was eager.

Francis turned to her in relief. 'Indeed. It was magnificent. I sang in the Chapel Royal choir, and I have met Mr Purcell.'

'I envy you there. Is he in charge at the Chapel Royal?'

'No. He is organist at Westminster Abbey. Mr Blow is at the Chapel Royal. But he is older, and may hand over to Mr Purcell at some point, or at least arrange for Mr Purcell to join him. They are friends, and there is work in plenty.'

'And since your return to Oxford?'

'I have been able to make a little music with friends. Both Mr Blow and Mr Purcell believe I should return to the Chapel Royal.'

'And shall you?'

'Maybe. I hardly know yet. So much has happened recently. My thoughts are not at all clear.'

'Which is more important to you, your music or your studies?' Mary's deep voice suddenly cut across the conversation.

'My music, I would say.' Francis was startled. 'My studies will be over soon. Music I hope will always be with me.'

'If your music is so important, why did you not stay with the Chapel Royal?' Mary's questioning, if swift, was inexorable.

'The Gentlemen in any case sing for a month, and then others take over. Next week the other Gentlemen are there for a month, so I may yet return and miss very little.'

'So you will be devoting yourself to your studies at the moment?'

'I certainly need to. I have fallen sadly behind.'

Francis was greatly relieved that shortly after this they went in to dine. Mary had a knack of making him feel thoroughly uncomfortable.

After the meal was over they saw that the drizzle had eased, and a thin winter sun was trying to make its appearance.

'Why do you young people not take a turn in the garden?' Sir Henry was clearly addressing Francis and Eleanor, but he appeared to be looking more towards his brother. 'I know Lord Trenoweth has had an invigorating ride today, but Eleanor has not been out of the house yet.'

'I will go to fetch my cloak,' she said at once. A few moments later Francis was escorting her carefully down the drive.

'I was delighted to see you have returned to Oxford.' Eleanor smiled at him. 'But is it altogether wise? You will be in danger; I can read that in your face, and I understand it from what others have said.'

'What have others said?'

'My father thought that those who attacked you might do so again.'

'I think it unlikely. They believe I am dead already. People have talked about danger, yet I feel strangely blessed.'

'Then I will tell you that I have told my father that I intend to refuse Robert's proposal. I have not had a chance to tell Robert himself yet.'

Francis was surprised to discover just how much pleasure the news gave him.

'Do you think that Robert will be upset?'

'Truly, no, I don't. Do you?'

'When I met him in London last week, he did not speak like a man in love. It sounded almost like a business transaction.'

'According to my maid Sarah, who notices these things, he is in love – but not with me.'

'Has he been making advances towards her, then?'

'No. That is what I thought she meant at first. But she suggested I watch him next time he is with my uncle.'

'Anthony? Surely she is mistaken! Do you believe it is true?'

'I have not seen them together since Sarah suggested it might be so. But the more I think about it, the more I think she might be right.'

'Do you think that your father knows?'

'I am sure he does not. If he did, I do not believe that he would have either of them in the house, brother or no brother.'

'But if it is true, why should Robert have asked you to marry him?'

'I have been searching for an answer. I believe that my uncle suggested it. Perhaps they saw it as a means of bringing Robert into the family, keeping him near. I was probably seen as the demure obedient girl who would do what was required. Even before this was suggested I did not wish to marry Robert. And now – ' she turned towards him, and Francis saw that her face was tear-stained.

His heart gave a sudden lurch, and it was all he could do not to sweep her into his arms and profess undying devotion. He stood still, clenching his hands behind him. In that moment Francis knew just how much he loved her. She might be forever beyond his reach, but that made no difference at all. From being somebody he cared about, she had suddenly become the most important person in the world to him.

They walked in silence for a little. Francis was going over in his mind the information Eleanor had just given him. Anthony and Robert? He would have dismissed the idea out of hand as being totally absurd. And yet – the more he thought about it the more he realised that it was possible. It would explain many glances and remarks of Robert's that Francis had dismissed too easily because he could not understand them. And who better than a servant girl to observe and notice things that family members could or would not?

He turned to Eleanor. 'You really think that it is true?'

She looked up at him, and he could see how very real her distress was.

'I – I hardly know. Since Sarah mentioned it I have thought of little else. But I have not seen Robert since. I do not know what to think.'

'But – forgive me – how could your uncle square it with his conscience?'

She smiled then. 'Oh, my uncle could square it with his conscience if it was in his interests to do so. His conscience is his servant, and he has tamed it.' She looked up at the sky. 'I think we should return to the house. It is going to rain again. Are you staying here tonight?'

'I have not been invited. But it would not be possible now to reach Oxford before dark. And the king's protection will probably extend to one or two breaches of the rules.'

'Stay. I know my father will agree. You are in enough danger. Do not add to it by riding at night.'

They walked slowly back towards the house. 'Why did you return? And why did you come here?'

He smiled. 'I have been asked that question more than once already today.'

'You gave my aunt and uncle answers that you hoped would satisfy them. They do not satisfy me.'

He stopped, and turned to face her. 'I received a letter from my friend Christopher Wentworth. Then I met Robert in London. I became more and more convinced that something that should not happen was being planned for when the Parliament meets in Oxford.'

'Something that has its origins here?' Her voice was scarce above a whisper. He nodded.

'There is no evidence, and yet – I have to know.'

'Then you should know – yesterday, after I had told my father that I would not marry Robert, he spoke to me of how we must see that the law is upheld at Oxford. He denied treason, but then I overheard him talking with my uncle. They spoke of their great design, and my uncle said that if my father found the cost too great then he should take me and my aunt to France until this country has a Catholic king.'

'He said that?' Francis frowned. 'Then you are in danger as much as I. Yes, I know there is danger in looking for information that others might want to keep hidden. It does not seem to touch me greatly at the moment. What do you suggest I do?'

'By finding the information my uncle wants you may help your own cause as well as his. He has not asked you to do anything treasonable.'

'No. And you?'

'Apart from refusing Robert, I think I must be the demure Catholic girl, pleased that the heir to the throne is of our faith. I do not see what else I can do. My father would not hurt me, nor my uncle.'

'No. He would certainly not intend it. Why did your father suggest that we go out together, do you know?'

'No. But I saw him look to my uncle for approval. Somehow you are part of their plan, though I do not know how. Be on your guard, Francis. There is so much danger around.'

'That word again. I shall be forced to believe in it soon.'

The first drops of rain began to fall as they reached the house. Eleanor smiled. 'I have been showing you where the new beech trees are to go. Don't forget.'

'They will look well there.' Francis held the door for her, and returned her smile.

*

Sarah was brushing Eleanor's hair with long, measured strokes. Eleanor sat on the stool in her chamber, enjoying the rhythm of the movement, and trying to resist the urge to turn round and look up at her maid.

'Everything is changed, Sarah. It is all exactly as it was, yet everything is different.'

'Not to all of us, Miss. I know you liked him.'

'Liked him, yes. But this! Suddenly I find that I love him with everything that is in me. As we walked, as he looked at me, it was as though I suddenly knew – I don't know what I knew, except that he fills my very being. And does your infinite wisdom tell you what he thinks of me?'

'He likes you, Miss. I think he likes you a great deal.'

Eleanor sat silently for a little. 'But it's no use, is it? I would never be allowed to marry a Protestant.'

'It has been known, Miss.'

'Not in this family. There, that's enough, Sarah. I can't sit still any longer. I feel as though I want to dance.' She skipped about the room for a few moments, then sat down, looking thoroughly disconsolate.

'What am I to do, Sarah? I don't know whether he loves me or not. If he does that makes it worse, in a way. We shall never be together. For the first time in my life, it seems, I have met someone who seems to want to understand me, to value me as a person. And for his own safety I must send him away.'

Sarah came round and knelt in front of her, putting her hands in Eleanor's lap.

'Miss. He is upstairs in the Blue Room at the moment. Your uncle has asked him for information that means he will have to come here again. You know that your faith teaches you to pray. Pray for him, Miss. If God intended you to be together, you will find a way.'

Eleanor looked at her, and though her eyes were wet, they were bright with hope.

'Do you think so? Oh, I hope you are right, Sarah. I just hope you are right.'

*

Francis lay awake in the Blue Room, his mind too full for sleep. Will had come and attended to him, but though Francis trusted his servant implicitly, on this occasion he felt unable to confide in him. He had fallen in love with a Catholic girl. What was he thinking of? She represented all that he despised in the country, or at least her family did. His father, being both broadminded and wise, would probably give his blessing, but Francis knew there was no way that he could expect Sir Henry to accept him as a son-in-law. And as Eleanor was a minor that meant there was nothing they could do. To change his faith he knew at once was impossible.

He could not tell, of course, whether she felt the same way about him. And yet – and yet – she had confided in him in a way that made him feel elated, then immediately forlorn as he saw how impossible his position was.

Leave now. Do not come back. You cannot taint yourself. You cannot associate with Papists, or be seen to be their friend.

Yes, but – if I can uncover a plot, if by associating with them I can help preserve the peace of the nation, will that not be good?

If that is all. But is it not that you are prepared to abandon your principles because you have seen a pretty girl?

No! Whatever dark secrets may be uncovered in this house, I believe that she is innocent. Perhaps I may persuade her to my way of thinking.

And abandon the faith in which she was reared, the faith of her father, whom she honours, her uncle, who baptised her?

Whatever is happening in this house is making her unhappy. That much is obvious. I believe that she would want to expose treason.

You are placing yourself in great danger, of course. You will be partly on two sides, so perhaps trusted by neither.

That does not matter. I came back here because I suspected treason. It would be wrong of me to be deflected because – because –

You have fallen in love? Oh yes, it is obvious. But can you sacrifice her to the greater good?

I may not need to. She could well be the vital link I need to uncover treason. I cannot draw back now. Yes, I love Eleanor, and care what happens to her. But even that could help the cause I have espoused.

Don't be too sure of yourself. If your cause means as much to you as you say, you may have to sacrifice even Eleanor. Even yourself.

Exhausted, Francis closed his eyes and slept fitfully. He awoke in the night, no nearer solving his dilemma. He found himself thinking instead of this relationship between Robert and Anthony that Eleanor had hinted at. The more he thought about it the more he thought it was not only possible but probable. It answered questions that he had never realised he was asking. What he found surprising was his own lack of revulsion. It merely seemed to be another piece in the puzzle falling into place. Should he tell Thomas? Should he confront Robert? Suddenly he felt immensely alone. What on earth was he trying to do? Single-handedly foil a plot that had already claimed the lives of others? And he was still not certain that the plot existed, though he knew it was becoming more likely that it did.

In the darkness Francis smiled softly to himself. Even as regret for the days when his music and his studies were the only things that mattered to him, he knew that he was content that his life had changed. Eleanor might be for ever beyond his reach, but simply to have known her brought its own reward.

He must try to sleep. The next day he would have to ride back to Oxford, and try to gather the information Anthony wanted. To further his cause it seemed he was going to have to help one he was coming to regard as an enemy. He hoped that at the same time he could shield Eleanor from danger. Because he knew that the course to which he was committing himself brought danger to her family.

Should he, for love of a girl he knew to be innocent, turn away from the actions he had planned? He would not be committing a crime, merely refusing to voice his suspicions. But what would Eleanor think if he behaved in that way?

He fell asleep with the question unresolved.

He woke to find that the damp of the previous day had given way to a hard frost, and knew instantly that he must get back to Oxford as soon as possible. Fortunately his hosts understood his desire to return, even if they attributed other motives to him.

'We look forward to seeing you here again when your studies permit.' Sir Henry was entirely genial. 'And I understand that my brother has asked you for certain information.'

'Yes. I shall be happy to oblige him. I think I can find answers to his questions easily enough.'

'That is good. You are staying in Oxford while the Parliament meets?'

'Yes. It has been arranged for me. Many of the undergraduates will be leaving the city.'

'You clearly have a great deal of influence.' The words were said entirely without artifice, and Francis was glad that Anthony was not there. In all the puzzle that centred on Coneybury, he felt certain that Anthony was at its heart.

He spoke to Eleanor before he left, but not alone, and the words between them were courteously polite. The sight of her, however, cool and demure in her morning muslin, made him want to throw convention to the winds and hold her to him. To counter this his words were politely formal.

'Miss Somerville. I trust you are well?'

'Thank you, Lord Trenoweth. I am in excellent health. I look forward to our meeting again.'

Francis raised her hand to his lips, then released it hastily, afraid of betraying himself. Eleanor curtsied and turned away.

Mary he did not see at all, and Anthony only appeared as Francis and Will were getting ready to mount their horses.

'A good morning for a ride, Lord Trenoweth.'

'Indeed. Much to be preferred than the murk of yesterday.' Francis looked at the man, sleek in his habitual black, and tried to imagine him cavorting with Robert. He almost giggled, and managed – just – to turn it into a cough.

'I trust I shall see you again before very long.'

'I have your list of names safe.' Francis patted his saddle bag. 'It will be a pleasure to be able to help you.'

Anthony looked at him sharply, then he raised his hand in parting, and they were away.

Francis waited until they were around the curve in the drive, then let out a long, slow breath.

'What do you make of this household now, Will?'

'Well, my lord, even the servants can notice an atmosphere. They don't know whether it's Miss Somerville being unhappy, or her uncle behaving as though he were in charge. But some of them are restless.'

'You've made quite a friend of the cook, haven't you?' Will grinned.

'One of the best. Reckon you'd think so too, my lord. She adores Miss Somerville.'

'And that should endear me to the cook, should it?'

'Begging your pardon, my lord. But the way you look at her – I shouldn't have spoken.'

'It's all right, Will.' They were out of the estate now, and turning their horses to the hill. 'I don't think I realised myself until yesterday just how much she matters to me. 'But there it is. I love her, Will, and I cannot tell her.'

'Not now, my lord, but maybe later. Things may well change.'

They rode on in silence for a little, then Will suddenly turned to Francis, rather red in the face.

'My lord. Forgive me if you would rather I stayed silent. It's just – I know there's danger in what you're doing, and I wanted, need, to say – I would count it a privilege to help you.' He looked away hurriedly.

Francis smiled. 'Thank you, Will. I'm very touched. You are right, there is danger; the problem is that I'm not quite sure where it is. But it's good to know that I can count on my friends.'

Chapter Eleven

Robert and Anthony sat either side of a pleasant fire in Anthony's chamber. Anthony was wrapped in a voluminous purple robe of velvet, reaching to his ankles, and which Robert thought became him very well. Robert himself, though he had shed his tight-fitting riding boots, still wore his breeches, and was uncomfortably aware that his coat was travel-stained.

'So.' Anthony poured wine into two goblets, and handed one to Robert. 'Have you seen your cousin recently?'

Robert accepted the goblet and cradled it. 'Not since I saw him in Westminster. It was most uncomfortable.'

'Nevertheless, you will need to meet with him soon.'

Robert took a slow pull at his wine and set it down carefully.

'I no longer know what to say to him. He looked up to me once, and I felt flattered. Now I feel as though I am deceiving him.'

'We all have to make sacrifices for the greater good. Do you not want to see the Catholic faith restored to this land?'

'I – well, yes, that is – of course.'

'You hardly sound certain. I need total commitment, Robert. Nothing less will suffice.'

Robert looked across at him, and saw the glitter in his eyes. He owed this man everything, and had thought he was loved by him, yet when Anthony looked at him like that Robert knew he was afraid. Anthony was adept at spinning webs, and he, Robert, felt as though he were no more than the fly caught at the centre.

Even as the thought occurred to him he felt guilty. Anthony was a priest, and if what he was proposing was a little – unconventional – Robert knew that it was because he cared for the nation's soul. He looked up and smiled.

'I am sorry. Of course I will do what you require.'

'That is good. I have asked your cousin for certain information concerning where people will be residing for the Oxford parliament. The information itself is not important, and I have told him he may send it through you. But I do need to make sure that he returns here. You can perhaps help me in this.'

'In what way?'

'He may come to feel that it is too dangerous for him to travel out here again. I want you to persuade him otherwise. The information I have asked him to obtain could be sent here in many different ways. Take the information he gives you, say you will be happy to give it to me. But then I want you to persuade him that my brother might look kindly on his paying attention to his daughter.'

'But – but Francis knows that she has only recently turned me down. Will he not think that strange?'

'Robert, you must learn to be more observant. Have you not seen how they look at each other? Both are convinced that it is impossible – but if you were to hint to him that it is not ...'

'But would Sir Henry agree? It is hardly likely that even for Eleanor Francis would change his faith!'

'Of course he will not agree! That is not the point. There needs to be a specific invitation to your cousin that will bring him here – after we have left.'

'You mean a trap?'

'That's a rather crude way of putting it. Your cousin is ideally placed to deflect attention from what we are doing. We shall of course need to alert one other if we can get the agreement of your cousin.'

'One other?'

'My dear Robert, you are not thinking straight. The magistrate, of course.'

'You mean – '

'Certain evidence will be placed in the house. When the magistrate finds it he will of course arrest your cousin. Oh, don't worry, he will be acquitted. But it will give us the time we need. Come, it grows late. There is nothing more that we can do tonight.' He looked significantly towards the bed and began to unbutton his robe. Underneath it he was naked.

*

Francis sat at the back of the chapel, conscious of a very real sense of dissatisfaction. The choir had just sung what he knew to be a sublime anthem of Matthew Locke's, but they had fallen far short of what it could be. The boys had been unable to hold the top line, and the basses had growled their way along the bottom. They did not even finish together.

He smiled to himself. At least his dissatisfaction stemmed from the fact that he now knew he could make music on a higher plane. Whatever happened, the friendship of Henry Purcell was infinitely important to him.

Christopher had hurried away, and Francis knew that he must leave soon. His mind felt in a whirlwind, and he was not at all certain which way to turn. He rose slowly, his mind on the wine that Will could supply him with in his room. At least he did not have to go out in the rain.

He had just reached the first bend in the stair when he heard footsteps coming down towards him. He stopped, then Will appeared in front of him, looking anxious.

'My lord. I am glad to see you. I am able to tell you – your cousin is in your room.'

'Robert? What is he doing there?'

'He came looking for you, my lord. I told him that you were at chapel, and he simply sat down and said he would wait for you. I could hardly turn him out.'

'No, of course you couldn't, Will. Don't worry. I'll go and see what it is he wants.'

'He seemed – quite agitated, my lord. As though something was on his mind.'

Francis smiled. 'Robert has quite a bit on his mind at the moment, Will. I shouldn't worry.' He climbed the remaining stairs to his room, puzzled. Will seemed quite agitated himself, which was not like him. He was usually so very calm and competent.

Robert was lounging by the fire in Francis' room when he entered, a tankard of wine in his hand, and looking thoroughly comfortable. He waved the wine towards Francis in a proprietorial fashion .

'I never realised you had wine like this here. It's really quite reasonable.'

'Did Will give you that?' Francis saw the wine sitting on a small table and went to pour himself a tankard.

'Well, no. Will – rather grudgingly, I thought – said I might wait for you, and then went away. Said he had work to attend to. But I saw it sitting there, and I decided you would want me to help myself. Will said you were at chapel, so I knew you wouldn't be long.'

'How so? I don't always come straight back here after chapel. Had it not been raining I might very well not have done.'

'But now you are here.' Robert took a draught of wine, and turned eagerly to Francis. 'You have been back to Coneybury since your return to Oxford, I believe?'

'Two days since. It seemed civil to call on them since I was so near again.'

'Naturally. And how did you find them?'

'Well and in good spirits. Why do you ask? Surely you have seen them yourself?' Francis helped himself to a tankard of wine.

'I have seen them. But – truth to tell, I was concerned for Miss Somerville's health, and the opinion of another would be valuable.'

'She seemed in perfect health to me.'

'Good, good.' Robert cradled his tankard in both hands, then took a long, slow draught. 'Tell me, Francis, you admire Miss Eleanor Somerville, do you not?'

'I esteem her, certainly. What is all this about, Robert?'

'Esteem! That is a cold word. Do not your very vitals threaten to turn to liquid when you see her? Do you not count days wasted when you are apart?'

'She is very attractive. I thought you "admired" her yourself, Robert. Has she not declined to marry you?'

Robert looked at the floor. 'That was perhaps a mistake. I thought – but no matter. You seem most happy, when you are at Coneybury, to spend time in her company. Why do you not consider paying court to her?'

'How can I? Even if I wanted to, there is the small matter of my faith. Even for Eleanor I would not change it.'

'Who says that you would have to? I know that hers is a Catholic family, and that was one reason that I thought might help my cause. Don't worry on that score. It would not have done. But I also believe she would accept you, if you were to ask.'

Francis held tightly onto his tankard, afraid of spilling the wine.

'But – but what of her father?'

'So you do care for her? I thought as much. Why do you not approach Sir Henry, and ask him? You might be surprised.'

'I doubt it.' Francis realised that he had betrayed himself. 'The matter of faith comes between us all the time.'

Robert leaned forward. 'Sir Henry trusts Eleanor. He would not part with her to anybody. But – rank matters to him, quite a lot – and you are the eldest son of an earl. That could make a considerable difference. He would be much more likely to give her to you than to a Catholic pot-boy.'

'Eleanor is still young. Surely he would prefer to wait until a suitable Catholic suitor came along. I am still surprised that you gave up so easily.'

Again Robert refused to look directly at him. 'On reflection I believe Eleanor to have been right. I would not have made her happy. She deserves better. All I am saying is, Francis, that you should come to Coneybury, and ask Sir Henry if you would have his blessing if you were to pay court to Eleanor. I think you might be surprised.'

Francis looked doubtful. 'I cannot understand why you are urging me in this way, Robert. Is there some advantage in it for you if I should win Eleanor? In truth, I cannot see what it could be.'

Robert looked hurt. 'Do you really think so little of me, Francis? I only desire what is best for you. I know you have been gathering information for Anthony, and he is most grateful. I have been bidden to say that if you will come to Coneybury on Thursday of next week with any information you have found, then you will be assured of a welcome.'

'I understood I was to hand any information for Anthony to you.' Francis reached to a table behind him. 'If you are seeing Anthony before me you can give him this. It is the information I have gained for him so far. There may be more by Thursday.'

Robert took the slim package that Francis held out. 'Then you will come? I am sure that Eleanor will be pleased.'

Francis smiled. 'I hope so. And now, if you really desire what is best for me, you will leave me to some studying. I need to see my tutor in the morning.'

Robert stood up. 'Of course, cousin.' he smiled. 'Though I think I hear your large friend on the stairs.' He reached for his hat and opened the door, almost bumping into Christopher as he did so.

Christopher came into the room without ceremony and sat down on the chair Robert had vacated. 'I heard your cousin was here. I thought I would wait until he had gone before I interrupted you.'

Francis smiled. 'Most tactful. Had it not been raining he might have had to wait even longer.'

Christopher grinned. 'And what was he doing here?' He nodded in the direction of the door.

'He seems to be suggesting that I should ask Sir Henry Somerville for his daughter's hand in marriage.'

'What! Did you tell him it was impossible? She has only just turned him down. And I trust you are not thinking of turning Catholic.'

'Christopher! What do you take me for? It's true I – care – for Eleanor, but I cannot see how we can overcome those things that divide us.'

'Are you going to return there?'

131

'I think I must. I have given Robert some of the information Anthony asked for, but there will be more. I think I have nearly enough of my own to go to the Privy Council.'

'Truly?'

'Eleanor has overheard her father and uncle talking about their "great design". She is very worried.'

'Then why do you not go to the Privy Council straight away?'

'I need to be certain. If I went now I believe Anthony at least would be arrested. But supposing the evidence was insufficient and he was acquitted? Where would that place me – and Eleanor?'

'Yes, I see. I still think you should go to the Council.'

'I will; very soon. But there is something else. I should have told you as soon as I returned, but – I could not. I did not know how.'

'Oh?'

'Eleanor knew at once that she did not want to marry Robert. But something her maid said made things look entirely different.'

'And that is?'

'That Robert is beholden to somebody else. Her uncle.'

'You mean – surely not! You do, don't you?' Francis nodded.

'I have thought of little else since Eleanor said it might be true. So much else fits into place if it is.'

'But – two men – and one a priest!'

'A very manipulative priest. That much I do know. It is possible that Robert is in thrall to him, but I suspect that Anthony is merely using my cousin.'

'Take care that he does not use you, my friend.' Francis snorted.

'I am hardly likely to go down that route!'

'There are other ways of using men. When do you plan to return there?'

'Robert also issued an invitation for Thursday of next week. He told me I should be assured of a welcome.'

'You have thought, have you not, that it could be a trap?'

'Of course. But I hardly see in what way they could ensnare me. I know – Eleanor excepted – they want to use me, but I have not yet discovered in what way. Is gathering information in Oxford enough?'

'I doubt it. I know I cannot dissuade you from going, Francis, nor should I. But be on your guard.'

'Of course. I cannot draw back now. And if I cannot be with Eleanor, at least I hope to protect her. I am thirsty. Shall we see what Will can provide us with?'

*

Eleanor looked in dismay at the clothes piled on her bed. She shook her head at Sarah.

'Not that one. I've never liked it.'

Sarah folded up the thick brocade gown that Eleanor indicated. 'But take the peach coloured silk, Miss. We do not know how long we shall be away, and spring will be showing in a few weeks.'

'Surely we shall not be away that long! It is not even February yet. I don't want to go at all.' Impulsively, Eleanor dropped the lace collar she was holding and put her arms round her maid. 'Sarah, I don't even know where we are going. Probably my father thinks I might tell somebody if I knew. I still don't know why we are going at all.'

'I think you do, Miss. I know it's hard. At least they have let me come with you.'

'Not Cookie, though. Most of the other servants are just going to have to stay here. I should have said more to Francis when he was here. Now I have lost the chance. Am I going to have to sit back and watch my father commit treason?'

'Do you think he is about to, Miss?'

'I don't know. Oh Sarah, I don't know. But my uncle has something planned. And after what you said about him and Robert – I don't know where to turn.'

Sarah folded the peach silk dress. 'I should not have spoken, Miss. Perhaps I was wrong.'

Eleanor shook her head. 'No. I have been thinking about it a lot since you told me. I believe that you are right. Robert was here yesterday, and I was watching them. Sarah, I'm frightened.'

'I know, Miss. But the best we can do is to get on with packing these clothes. Your father said we are leaving tomorrow.'

'I wish I could take my spinet. Better still, I would like a harpsichord. I am sure that I could play one.'

'Perhaps we will be back here soon, Miss. Now, what about the pink satin?'

'Yes – no – oh, Sarah, I don't know. You decide. I'm going to go down to the kitchen.' She left her maid to finish the packing, not really caring what she wore at the moment.

In the kitchen all was bustle. Cook was obviously determined that the food provided would be of the best, even if as from the next day there would be only servants in the house. She looked up, saw Eleanor, and smiled.

'All ready, my pet?'

'I've left Sarah to sort my clothes. I can't decide. Cookie, it feels as though we're running away. My father says that because of certain – suspicions – we will be safer wherever we are going. But this has always been my home. Why should it not be safe? I wish you were coming with us.'

'I shall be safe enough here. James is staying too, so between us we'll look after the place.'

'Cookie, I'd trust you with my life.' She kissed the cook's cheek, and the older woman's face became even redder.

'Get along with you. I've the dinner to see to. You go and be the demure daughter. That will keep your father – and your uncle – sweet.'

Eleanor grinned at her and went back upstairs.

In the parlour her father was prowling about restlessly, picking up objects and putting them down again. He looked up uneasily as Eleanor entered.

'Your trunk is packed, I take it?' He seemed reluctant to look her in the eye.

'I have left Sarah to finish. I am not happy about this, father.'

'It is necessary.' His voice was cold. 'I am completely loyal, but certain undertakings of your uncle's could be considered in a bad light by those not disposed to like us. Those of our faith are not popular in this country, Eleanor. To remain here while there are so many Whigs in Oxford would not be wise.'

'Only if you plan something that is against the law, or treasonable. Are you, father?'

'Now you are being fanciful. I have indulged you too much over the years. You had best go to see if your maid has finished packing. We shall be leaving quite early tomorrow.'

Eleanor bit back an angry retort, remembering Cookie's words of wisdom.

'Yes, Father. I shall be ready. You need not worry on that score.'

He patted her on the head, as though I were a child, thought Eleanor.

'I know you will do your part, my dear. I am sorry. It is not easy for you. But then it is not easy for any of us.' He sighed, and Eleanor felt almost sorry for him.

*

Francis was wakened very early that Thursday morning by a distinctly unsavoury smell. He got out of bed to find Will on his truckle bed, leaning over and retching into a bucket. Clearly this was not the first time. Will was shivering violently, and looked extremely pale.

'I am sorry, my lord.' Will managed a pallid smile, then leaned over to retch into the bucket again. 'I shall be right very soon – I don't know – '

'You stay right where you are,' said Francis firmly. 'Can you eat anything?'

'No, not yet. Perhaps – a little ale – '

'I will fetch you some.' Francis went to the large cupboard that did duty as a pantry for them, and came back with some ale. Will tried to sip at it, but despite Francis' help some of it spilled onto the bedcovers.

'My lord, this is not suitable.' Will's voice came as barely a croak. 'You should not be waiting on me.'

'And who else is going to? Come, see if you can drink a little more.' Will managed a couple of sips, then lay back on the pillow.

'My lord – Coneybury – '

'I know. We're supposed to be going there today. You clearly can't.'

'No. Perhaps you should not either.'

'Perhaps I should not. You clearly need looking after.'

'I shall be right very soon.' Will coughed. 'On your own – could be dangerous – '

'As to that, I'm sure I shall be all right. It's you I'm thinking of.'

'It's only a bad stomach. I shall be right again soon.'

'If you're sure.' Francis drew his brows together. 'I really think it's important that I go to Coneybury. Tell you what, I'll get Christopher to look in on you and make sure you are all right. I'm sure he wouldn't mind.'

'My lord – be careful – danger – '

Francis looked in concern as a spasm of coughing overtook Will, then he smiled and left the room.

Christopher, of course, had similar concerns to Will.

'It's madness to go alone. Wait till Will's better. Surely it can't be that urgent?'

'I think it could. The invitation was specifically for today, and time is running out. There is not long to go until the Parliament meets.'

Christopher sighed. 'I'm not going to dissuade you, am I? All right, I'll look after Will. And just you come back safely.'

Francis grinned, and went in search of some breakfast for himself.

Perhaps half an hour later he was leaving the college to go to the posting station. Fortunately the horse offered to him was ready and willing, and he was very soon mounted and heading out of Oxford.

Never had he known such a ride. For sheer exhilaration he knew it could not have been bettered. It seemed he scarcely had time to draw breath before he was over the river and heading out towards Woodstock, the dark woods beckoning him enticingly. The wind tore at his hair and turned it into a mass of confusion; somewhere along the road, he supposed, his hat must now be lying. He felt neither heat nor cold, only an intense desire to be at his journey's end.

He galloped through Woodstock without a pause, then turned the horse towards Charlbury, resolutely undismayed by the gloom under the canopy of trees, though his progress was slowed a little. But then he was out in the open again; trees and fields flew past him; he rose and dipped with the undulations of the land, excitement mounting all the while. His horse showed no signs of flagging, though he might well have been startled at the sudden exercise. It seemed a great deal more than an hour before he found himself heading into Charlbury, and cantering down the slope past Lord Clarendon's estate of Cornbury. He slowed to a trot as he entered Sir Henry's park, dismounting in the wide sweep before the main entrance.

The first thing that made him feel slightly uncomfortable was that nobody came to take his horse. But he knew his way to the stables well enough, and walked the horse round there without being particularly worried. Here he did receive rather a shock; not only was Sir Henry's carriage gone, but so were the two chestnuts who normally pulled it, as well as Sir Henry's own stallion and Eleanor's favourite grey. There were other beasts in the stable, dull, unpromising animals that did not look to be Sir Henry's choice at all. However, a stable lad came in response to his shout, and Francis curtly demanded care for his horse. The lad looked frightened, but not unwilling.

Now definitely uneasy, Francis made his way round to the house. Why should Sir Henry invite him so particularly to Coneybury, and then absent his horses and his carriage? He remembered Wentworth's suggestion that the invitation could be a trap. Could he have been right? Almost Francis turned round to make his way back to the stable.

Almost, but not quite. For surely there must be some ordinary explanation? Perhaps Mary Somerville had taken the carriage somewhere, perhaps Robert or Anthony had need of the other horses. He could not just leave, ride away as though he had never been there. With some trepidation, he walked up to the main door of the house.

It was opened at once by a poorly clad servant he did not recognise, who indicated in total silence that Francis was to follow him. Feeling thoroughly bewildered, Francis followed his guide up to the first floor parlour. The door was thrown open to reveal a portly, florid man stretching his legs towards the fire, glancing in a rather bored way at some papers in his hand. He looked up as the door was opened and smiled, but not in welcome.

Suddenly Francis realised who this was, and knew again that he was recognising too late Christopher's wisdom. For this was Sir William Corner, Oxford's leading magistrate and papist-hunter.

'Good morning, Lord Trenoweth,' he said unpleasantly. 'We have been expecting you.'

Francis started, and looked about himself.

'Where is Sir Henry Somerville?' He hoped he had managed to turn the fear he felt into anger in his voice. 'He invited me here today.'

'No doubt,' said the magistrate. 'I am sure that he did. I must congratulate you upon your acting. I could almost have believed that you expected Sir Henry Somerville to be here.'

'Of course I did! I have told you that he invited me.'

'Indeed. It seems strange, does it not, to invite a friend to your house, and then not be there to receive him?'

'No doubt there is a reasonable explanation. Francis dropped unasked into a chair. 'He must have been called away.'

'It would certainly seem so. Perhaps you can tell me his whereabouts? You appear to be much in his confidence.'

'I am not in his confidence. I think there are very few who are. For some little time now I have been uneasy about certain activities in this house. I was trying to find out more.'

'What activities are you talking about?'

Francis instinctively disliked the magistrate, but he could at least make an attempt to show that they were both on the same side.

'The family are Papists. I believe they were intending to use the Parliament at Oxford to further their own ends.'

'Treason, you mean? If you thought that, then why did you not go to the Privy Council?'

'I did not have enough evidence. I hoped that my visit here today might furnish me with the information I needed. I would then have taken it straight to the authorities.'

'And your reluctance to bring this evidence earlier had nothing to do with Sir Henry Somerville's daughter?'

Francis felt his anger beginning to rise again. 'Why should it?'

'According to information I have received, you were coming here to ask Sir Henry's permission to pay court to his daughter. Perhaps you were intending to turn papist yourself.'

Francis clenched and unclenched his fists. 'You are misinformed. There can never be an understanding between myself and Miss Somerville. The matter of our faith is too great a difference.'

'Indeed. But your coming to this house at this particular time is highly suspicious. My men have already begun searching, and I must ask you to wait in the room downstairs while the search is completed. John will take you there.'

Chapter Twelve

Eleanor looked around the small, dingy room with something approaching dismay.

'Sarah, it's tiny! And you and I are going to have to share it.' She looked again at the brown walls, cheaply panelled, the narrow bed that still managed to take up most of the room, the cracked jug on the washstand. 'There is hardly anywhere to put our clothes. I am glad now that we didn't bring any more.'

Sarah smiled. 'It's not so bad, Miss. We've got somewhere to sleep. It's harder for you than me. This is still better than my mother's cottage in Charlbury.'

'You put me to shame. But I still do not understand why my father has brought me here. He should not have done.'

'I think he had to. I believe your father is afraid.'

'My father? Afraid? Surely not!'

'Haven't you noticed, Miss, that he hardly speaks now without reference to your uncle? Your uncle had his own reasons for bringing us here, and I'm not sure that your father likes them.'

'He seemed set on it when he told me we had to come. I'm not much better than a prisoner, Sarah, and neither are you.'

'At least we know where we are now. When did they tell you we were coming to Marlow?'

Eleanor laughed 'I should think we were nearly two miles from Marlow. We were almost here before anybody bothered to inform me. I feel as though I am no more than a parcel my father and my uncle have to carry around. They tell me so little.'

Perhaps you will be able to walk in the garden. You might even be able to tend it.'

'Garden? What garden?' Eleanor went to the window, which looked over a small and not very clean stable yard. 'I suppose there must be one somewhere. I have hardly had the heart to go out yet.'

'Get your cloak then, Miss. We'll go and walk in the garden now. It is not raining, and surely no-one can object to your taking a little fresh air with your maid?'

Eleanor giggled suddenly. 'You are right. And – you never know, it might be helpful to acquaint ourselves with our surroundings as much as possible.'

They gathered their cloaks and went downstairs. As they passed what did duty for a parlour, they saw Mary sitting close to the fire, apparently busy with some embroidery. She looked up and smiled.

'Are you coming to join me, Eleanor?'

Later, perhaps, Aunt. I feel in need of some fresh air, and Sarah has offered to accompany me on a turn round the garden.'

Mary nodded. 'That is quite proper. Make sure that you do not catch cold.' She returned to her sewing as though it was of the greatest importance.

Eleanor and Sarah let themselves out by the little door at the back of the house. A pale winter sun failed to provide any real warmth, and the wind was rising.

Eleanor looked about her. 'It's not much of a garden. You can see it all from here. I thought our host was a substantial merchant, but his house does not seem to reflect that. Still, at least it borders the river.'

They walked down a path to the river's edge. A wooden seat stood there, and after feeling it cautiously Eleanor decided that it was not especially damp, and sat down on it. Sarah stood beside her awkwardly.

'Shall I fetch you anything, Miss?'

'No. There is nothing I need at the moment. Come and sit beside me.' Sarah obeyed, still looking distinctly uncomfortable. Eleanor looked across at her, and managed a rueful smile.

'Oh, Sarah, what do you think he is doing at the moment? I should so dearly love to know.'

'Perhaps studying, Miss? He is at the University.'

'Yes, but I cannot think he is studying at the moment. Sarah, I love him, and I do not know if he is even aware of it! What am I going to do?'

'I think he knows. I think he knows very well. And I think he loves you.'

'Truly? But how?'

'I have seen the way he looks at you, Miss. Maybe there will be a way for you to be together.'

'I do not see how it could happen. And I think he is in danger, Sarah. Perhaps he is in danger at this moment, and I am doing nothing.'

'Because there is nothing you can do.'

Eleanor stood up, and suddenly there was a light in her eye that had not been there a moment earlier.

'Yes, there is. I shall be the dutiful daughter, the obedient niece. Perhaps there is an advantage to this being such a small house. It might make it easier for me to learn what is going on. For something is, I feel certain. Perhaps if I am seen as eager to fit in with their plans they will not be so circumspect in my presence.'

'But you must be careful.' Sarah looked anxious. 'You spoke just now of danger. Do not go putting yourself in the way of it.'

Eleanor smiled. 'If there is anything, however slight, that I can do for what is right, then I must do it.' Do you not see that, Sarah?'

'Oh yes, Miss. I see it very well.'

*

Francis was conducted to the ground floor drawing room, where he had first met Sir Henry. The tapestries at least kept out some of the draughts, but the servants gathered at one end looked confused and cold.

His two guards led him in, locked the door and stood impassively in front of it. Seeing the cook among the servants, Francis moved towards them and gave her a brief smile. She bobbed an uncertain imitation of a curtsey.

'My lord. I'm that sorry.'

'You are not to blame. But Sir Henry invited me here. I cannot understand what has happened.'

'It were near a week ago now. Sir Henry, or I should say his brother, insisted that all the family left. Miss Eleanor, she were in a right old state. Didn't want to go at all, an' she didn't even know where they was going. Reckon her uncle didn't want her to know.'

'So you don't know where they are?'

'No, my lord. Nobody knew. Something's gonna happen soon, an' I don't think Miss Eleanor liked the look of it. Ferriman, Andrew, Harry, they're not here either. And they're the ones Mr Anthony trusted most.' She glanced towards the guards, who were shuffling their feet and looking bored. The other servants, most of whom appeared thoroughly frightened, had moved away a little.

'I cannot understand why Sir Henry should have invited me, if he knew he was not going to be here.' Francis frowned.

'There's a lot about this family it's hard to understand.' The cook looked up at him. 'My lord. Perhaps I should not be speaking, but I think we have little time. You care for Miss Eleanor, I believe?'

Francis started. 'Is it so very obvious?'

'Not to everybody, perhaps. But I have known Miss Eleanor since she was born, and I believe she trusts me. She cares for you, you know. A great deal.'

He smiled at that. 'I had hoped – yes, I care for her. But so much lies between us. It is no good at all.'

One of the guards looked across to them, but did nothing and resumed a conversation with his companion.

'You are an honest man, I think.' The cook spoke quietly. 'And for all that he is a Catholic, and a priest, I sometimes wonder if that is the case with Miss Eleanor's uncle. She loves you, my lord, and I think you love her.'

'Yes.' The word was barely a breath. 'But what is going to happen now? I think we are all in danger.'

At that moment the two guards stood aside as the door was opened and Sir William, accompanied by several other men and looking thoroughly pleased with himself, strode in. He walked straight towards the group of servants gathered at the end of the room, and the cook reluctantly detached herself from Francis and joined them.

'It is clear that treason has been plotted in this house,' Sir William began. 'Do any of you know where your master and his family are?'

One of the maids began to cry. The cook looked scornfully towards her, then turned to Sir William.

'No, sir. We all knew that they were going away, but none of us were told where. Even Miss Eleanor did not know. She was very distressed.'

'Indeed. Well, there is no evidence to suggest otherwise at the moment, and it seems probable that none of you are directly involved. You may all go about your tasks. As my men in their searches have created some little disturbance, I think you will find there is plenty to do. But you are not to leave the house. I shall leave men at the doors to ensure that you do not.'

The servants began to move towards the door, the cook throwing a rueful look in Francis' direction. He made to follow them, but Sir William held up his hand.

'You, Lord Trenoweth, are a different matter. Your riding at such a time to a nest of Papists is highly suspicious.'

'Sir Henry had invited me here.'

'It is odd, is it not, to invite a man to your house and then deliberately absent yourself?'

'Of course. My fear is that Sir Henry may have realised my true motive for coming here.'

'Which is?'

'Like you, I suspected a papist plot. I was trying to find enough information to lay before the authorities.'

'Most commendable, I am sure.' The magistrate rubbed reflectively at his nose. 'But why had you not already done this?'

'I though I had already explained this. The information I had gained was insufficient. Rumours, thoughts, impressions. I had hoped that after today I should have enough to go to the Privy Council.'

'Perhaps if you had searched more thoroughly you would have found what you were looking for.' Sir William held up a small, leather-bound book that Francis had not noticed in his hand.

'We found this in a room that had clearly been set aside as a chapel. I am aware that this is a missal used, not by all Catholics, but those who call themselves the Society of Jesus. The Jesuits.'

'But Anthony is not a Jesuit!' Francis was startled. 'Yes, I know he is a Catholic priest. But there is no law against that.'

'Are you aware just how many Papists have been executed these last two years? Even were this gentleman not a Jesuit his position would be precarious. As such, of course, it is a great deal worse – as it is for those who harbour him.'

A thought occurred to Francis, so appalling that he thrust it from him. It could not be true. They would not – would they?

He had not time to order his thoughts before Sir William was speaking again.

'You have been here several times, and claim to have insufficient evidence of treason. I have been here but once, and have found clear evidence straight away. Strange, is it not?'

Francis paled. 'I still do not believe that Anthony Somerville is a Jesuit. Had I thought so I should have gone to the authorities long ago.'

'Even though you would have been placing a certain young lady in great danger? Oh yes, we know all about your movements. Our spies have served us well. You did not know you were being followed, did you?'

'I – ' Francis was suddenly uncertain how to reply, and the thought galled him. The magistrate smiled, entirely without mirth.

'It is of course disappointing that we should find the Somerville family no longer here. Perhaps you could tell us where we might find them?'

'I have no idea where they may be. I would scarcely have come riding here to meet them had I known they would be elsewhere.'

'Quite. But you have done so, confirming suspicions I have already entertained of your behaviour. It is now my duty to arrest you on suspicion of treason.'

Francis looked at the magistrate, at the cold sneer on his face, and suddenly found himself completely overtaken by blind, unreasoning anger. He swept the sword that he had worn since returning to Oxford, despite University regulations, from its scabbard and swept it through the air.

'Take me if you can, then. I'll not make it easy for you!'

For a moment the magistrate looked taken aback, then he summoned his men standing awkwardly near the door. Francis at once found himself surrounded by a semi-circle of armed men. He sliced the air with his sword and the men fell back a little, but there were eight of them ranged around him, and he could not face them all at the same time. The man on the far right, braver perhaps than his colleagues, seized a moment he was not within Francis' range of vision and brought the butt of his musket down on Francis' wrist.

The sword fell with a clatter to the floor. Francis' assailant stepped forward to pick it up, handing it hilt first to the magistrate, whose sneer became even more marked. Francis had not time to consider the pain in his wrist before it was seized and efficiently bound to his left with cord.

'I was wrong in my original estimation of you,' said the magistrate. 'I had thought you reasonably intelligent, but most traitors are not as foolish as you.'

'I claim the protection of Oxford's University,' declared Francis. 'I will not be lodged in prison in the town.'

'That no doubt can be arranged. For the moment you will be my guest, and we will send to enquire if they will house you in the Tower of London.'

Francis was silent. Ruefully he thought of Christopher's warning of a trap, of Will suggesting he should not ride alone, of Robert – what on earth was Robert's part in all this?

'Our searches here are more or less complete.' Sir William was looking thoroughly pleased with himself. 'Cooper, West, remain here with Lord Trenoweth, while I make sure there are enough to guard the servants and keep this place secure.'

He left the room and Francis, after glancing at his two guards, decided to ignore them. His wrists were tightly bound behind him, and the right in particular was throbbing, but he stood by the empty hearth as though it were the most natural thing in the world. After that sudden surge of anger he felt a little foolish, but he was unafraid, and strangely calm. His future looked distinctly uncertain, but it was enough, at the moment, to believe that he had a future.

Sir William was not long, and as soon as he returned Francis was roughly led out to the front of the house, where horses waited. His wrists were unbound to allow him to mount, but then they were made fast to the reins and Sir William's men closed about him, with the magistrate himself a little way behind.

They were returning almost to Oxford, Francis realised, and compared this slow, uncomfortable procession with his impetuous gallop to Coneybury only a few hours earlier. He doubted that his wrist was broken, or even seriously sprained, but it was badly bruised, and he knew would be painful for some little time to come.

The magistrate's house was eventually reached, an unremarkable manor house just outside Wolvercote. Francis' bonds were cut, and he was taken to a small room at the back, where there was a narrow truckle bed, a table, a stool and a bucket. The door was locked, then unlocked a few moments later for a hunk of bread, some stale-looking cheese and a mug of small ale to be thrust at him.

Francis took them and set them on the table, hearing the key turn in the lock again as he did so. He looked around the room; there was one small window high in the wall, and from the marks on the walls he guessed the room had originally been used as some sort of storeroom.

He lay down on the bed, which was far from comfortable. At least his thick riding cloak had accompanied him; he suspected he would very soon be glad of its warmth.

I ought to be near despair, he thought. I have been arrested; I am probably going to be charged with treason and put on trial for my life. Yet all I can think about at the moment is what Eleanor's friend the cook told me. She loves me. It seems almost too good to be true, and yet instinctively he knew that it was.

He placed his hands behind his head, cautiously so that he did not add to the pain in his wrist. Surely there was not enough evidence to convict him? Most likely it was just an over-zealous magistrate anxious to be seen to be doing his job.

But Francis knew now that treason had been plotted at Coneybury, and that the prime mover was Anthony. And, of course, particularly in view of Eleanor's revelations, Robert must also be involved.

Francis sat up sharply, two thoughts occurring to him almost simultaneously. Anthony was no Jesuit. He knew that. The missal must have been placed there deliberately. And the invitation to Coneybury had been delivered verbally – by Robert.

'So that is what the trap is!' In the shock of the realisation Francis spoke aloud. He remembered the thought that had occurred to him while he had been trying to avoid arrest. Now it returned with full force. Anthony had placed incriminating evidence in the house and then ensured that he, Francis, would be there when it was found.

Then even Robert must want me arrested, he mused. But why? To have me accused of treason does not prove their innocence.

No, but it shifts the focus of attention to you. Besides, nobody is going to look very hard for the Somervilles now. They will all believe that you know where they are, and will tell them.

But I have no idea where they are.

You will not be believed. Your trial will take attention further away from Anthony and Robert.

So I am to be tried for treason?

Of course. How could you think otherwise?

Surely there can be very little evidence?

That depends. On quite a number of issues.

Such as?

Suborned witnesses, servants' gossip, even your regard for Eleanor. That could go against you.

Eleanor. And only a moment ago I was exulting in the knowledge that she loves me. Surely there must be a way out of all this?

Despite his discomfort and his hunger, Francis slept eventually, the bread and cheese still untouched.

*

'I hope you are satisfied.' Robert looked down at his shabby breeches, threadbare coat and torn shirt. He had set aside his wig, and though he had refused to give up boots altogether, Anthony had seen to it that those he now wore were far from elegant.

'My dear Robert. Surely this is but a minor sacrifice for the cause we all hold dear? You are the one who will need to come and go from this house more than any of us. I do not want you recognised. Nobody will look as this down-at-heel tradesman and see you. It is perfect.'

Robert reached for his wine, and studied Anthony's black velvet, the profusion of lace at collar and cuffs.

'Francis has been arrested.' Robert was surprised at just how hard he found it to say the words.

'I know. You are tardy in your information this time.'

'But – he will be charged with treason. Because of what I have done.'

'He will not be convicted. Robert, dear Robert, do you think so little of me that I would condemn an innocent man to that sort of torture?'

'No, of course not. It is just – could we not simply wait for His Grace to succeed? He is the heir, after all.'

Anthony stood up suddenly and towered over him, causing Robert to shrink back into his chair.

'I hope I never hear you say such a thing again. Supposing we do nothing, and Exclusion is passed next month at Oxford? Then where would we be? Besides, the Duke is only three years younger than his brother. Suppose he died first? No, we must act, to return this country to its true obedience.' He sank back into his chair, and passed a scented handkerchief over his face. 'Forgive me, my boy. I did not mean to alarm you. But I thought I had your total commitment. You still have a vital part to play.'

'I do?'

'We are all under suspicion now. Oh yes, it is inevitable. But you can perhaps keep the authorities from us, to give us the time that we need.'

'But how?'

'Your cousin is being held at the magistrate's house at Wolvercote. Shortly I expect that he will be taken to the Tower of London. You are to confess to your part in a plot – but a markedly different one from the plans I have been contemplating.'

Robert stood up so fast the wine in his goblet splashed onto the floor. 'Surely then I would be arrested too? What purpose would that serve?'

'Sit down, Robert. You are far too excitable. If you do exactly as I say, you will be treated as a valuable witness, not a potential traitor.'

Robert sat down, partly at least because he doubted the ability of his legs to hold him upright. Now indeed he saw how far he was being drawn in, and still he could see no way of escape. He could not go backwards; somehow he had to find a way forward.

'Should I tell Eleanor? About Francis?'

'Eventually it will be necessary. But not yet, I think. I had thought she was in love with him, and would be very angry. I am less certain now. She has been remarkably docile since coming here. She has apparently told her father that she will do whatever is required of her.'

'Does she know what that might mean?'

'I hardly think she can. But by the time she does it will be too late.'

'You're very certain, aren't you?' Robert looked across at his lover/confessor/patron with a mixture of admiration and fear. But the fear which only a few moments earlier nearly turned to panic was already giving the admiration its head.

'Oh yes. Somebody has to be. How long is it since you last made confession?'

'A week, I think. Maybe a little more.'

'Then I will hear your confession now. Our plan needs to be undertaken with a clear conscience.'

'But – will not your brother or your sister come upon us? Even Eleanor?'

Anthony stood up and gently turned the key in the lock. 'We have an understanding that when this room is locked everybody knows that we wish to be alone.'

Robert flinched. 'Then – your brother knows?'

'Of course. Why should he not? Henry is older than me, and therefore holds the title. But in every other respect he has always deferred to me, particularly since I took orders. Whatever I do, in his eyes, must be right. We shall not be disturbed, nor will any opprobrium be cast upon us. Come, there is a prayer desk here that will serve us as confessional. I will withdraw to this side of the room while you make yourself ready.' He stood up, and his smile chilled Robert to the marrow.

Chapter Thirteen

For three days Francis was kept close prisoner, grudgingly allowed a small amount of food, and told nothing of the steps being taken against him. He tried to keep his spirits up by thoughts of Eleanor, of singing in the Chapel Royal and making music with the best in the land.

They have imprisoned my body, he thought, but my spirit is free to soar where it will. And surely the evidence against me will be seen to be negligible. He even sang from time to time, and smiled as he thought of what the surly magistrate must think.

As yet he had been charged with no offence, and he knew enough of the law to know that he could not be held long in this way. Only two years before the King had consented to an Act of Parliament making such wilful imprisonment illegal, and Francis wondered if he would be able to secure his liberty by suing for a writ of Habeas Corpus. But such hopes were soon to be dashed, for on the fourth day after his arrest he was taken to Sir William's study as soon as he had finished the inadequate breakfast the magistrate's pretty maidservant had been able to bring him.

Sir William was seated behind his desk, looking extremely pleased with himself.

'I have here,' he began, tapping the papers in front of him impressively, 'a warrant for your arrest on charges of high treason. You may at least have the satisfaction of knowing that your case is regarded as important, for it seems the Privy Council wishes to examine you. You will therefore ride to London today. I have detailed men to conduct you to the Tower of London. That is all.'

He rang a bell on his desk and four stalwart men entered at once, formed a guard round Francis and marched him out, not back to his prison, but into the courtyard in front of the house. Horses were waiting there, ready saddled, and Francis knew that any last-minute escape was out of the question. Besides, there was a charge of treason against him now, and he could scarcely live out the rest of his life in hiding.

He shivered as they left the house, for the sun had declined to appear that morning, and there was a biting wind. He glanced at the warm riding clothes of his guards, and thought wistfully of his own cloak, lying where he had left it as the only bed-covering he had known these last four nights.

He had scarcely supposed that he would be hurried off so quickly. Fortunately the maidservant had noticed it, and came running out of the house with it even as Francis was curtly ordered to mount. He smiled at her as she put it about his shoulders, and swung into the saddle with an appearance of lightheartedness.

Clearly his guards were determined to do their job thoroughly, for one of them at once seized his wrists, while another bound them firmly to the reins. Even his feet were bound, the cord being taken under the horse's belly. The saddle, Francis noticed, was already made fast by a leather thong to that of one of the guards. Then the guards mounted and they began to move off, one of them holding Francis's reins and the pretty maidservant looking on with pity in her eyes.

The guards were not disposed to talk to Francis during the journey, though they conversed freely enough among themselves. Occasionally a fierce tug was given to the reins if it was felt that he was lagging, sending shafts of pain through his wrists, or the horse would move suddenly, causing a sudden lurch as the leather thong pulled him back, but otherwise he was merely luggage they were obliged to take to London.

At least the movement warmed him, and during the morning the wind lessened and the sun appeared between broken clouds. Almost Francis felt he could sing; the discomfort throughout his body was considerable, particularly in his wrists, but his heart was as light as that of a skylark he heard hovering on the breeze.

Prudence dictated that he kept silent, and in any case he found he needed all his energy for the ride. He wondered how easy it would be to get word to his father, to Thomas, even to Purcell. And had poor Will recovered? Francis was genuinely fond of his servant, and felt a stab of guilt that he had thought so little of him these past days. Will at least must know that something untoward had happened, and might even be able to alert others.

But all the time his thoughts kept coming back to that conversation with the cook at Coneybury. *She loves you, my lord, and I think that you love her.* Without that knowledge, he realised, his present situation would be even darker.

Soon he began to realise that the breakfast with which he had been provided was far from adequate, but he was clearly in no position to ask for refreshment. Some of the men had had the foresight to bring ale with them, and Francis was grateful when a bottle was held to his lips, but he only had time to gulp a mouthful before it was removed, and the gesture was not repeated.

They had breasted the rim of the Chilterns now, and were looking down into the valley to whose side High Wycombe clung. Francis tried to pause for a moment, and the horse to which he was tethered stopped also, but his guard pulled hard at his reins, and Francis could scarcely keep back a cry of pain as the cords bit deeper into his wrists.

'There'll be time to stop later,' snapped the man. 'Till then, you just keep going. Think we're enjoying it, having to take you all this way?'

Francis could think of no reply that might be appropriate, so he said nothing and tried to concentrate on matching his pace to the others', so that the pain in his wrists was not made any worse. He was thankful indeed when the guards decided to stop in the town of High Wycombe. He made light work of the cheese and ale set in front of him, and watched as the saddles were put onto fresh horses, the leather thong very much in evidence. After barely half an hour he was ordered to mount again, his guards taking no notice of his look of pain as the cord lacerated his wrists. Spots of blood appeared on his cuffs, but as they were already dirty and torn, having been worn continuously since his arrest, he decided it made very little difference. The meal had only taken the edge off his hunger, and had done nothing to ease his weariness. The lightheartedness of the morning had disappeared, and he found himself yearning for rest. Dully he noticed the villages through which they passed: Beaconsfield, Gerrards Cross, Ealing. In Gerrards Cross there was a fair in progress, and Francis felt a sudden surge of envy at the pleasure of the fair-goers, their lives uncomplicated by any talk of treason or fear of plotters.

Tyburn now; and Francis looked away hastily, fearful of acknowledging that he found the rotting carcasses on the gibbets so nauseating. The guards seemed entirely unconcerned, and passed them by without a comment. The crowds grew ever thicker as they approached the capital, but few even bothered to turn their heads as they saw a prisoner being brought in to justice. Had they known that he was bound for the Tower on charges arising out of the Popish Plot their interest might have been greater, and they would have turned to jeer at him.

So at last they came to London. The streets were narrower here, and more than once they barely avoided slops being thrown on them from above. But Francis now felt weak and dizzy; his wrists were causing him constant pain, and his legs were numb as, being tied under the horse's belly, he was unable to move them. It felt as though he had been travelling for days rather than hours; almost he felt he would admit his guilt if he could be assured, even temporarily, of greater comfort. His whole body ached, his throat was sore and dry, and he had difficulty remembering why he was in this position.

The light was beginning to fade by the time they came to the site of St Paul's, London's proud cathedral, now a heap of rubble. One or two scavengers were wandering somewhat aimlessly about it, but even as Francis watched they were curtly sent about their business. These would be the servants of Sir Christopher Wren, he supposed; he had heard that London was to have a grand new cathedral.

And now they were at the Tower itself, waiting for the gate to be unlocked from the inside. Above them loomed the formidable grey bastion, daunting, merciless, yet somehow protective. Francis understood suddenly that there was no need to fear the Tower; it was a fortress as well as a prison

So at last his journey was over; the gate was shut behind him, and he was within the Tower of London. The thong about his saddle was removed, and the guards who had conducted him disappeared. He was surrounded instead by gaolers of the Tower, who at once cut his bonds and helped him dismount.

'My apologies, Lord Trenoweth, that you should have been so used,' said one of them. 'The magistrate's men are able and devout, but somewhat officious in the execution of their duty. I trust you have not been used too sorely?'

'I – no – that is, their ways are a little rough,' said Francis, bewildered by this sudden deference, and chafing his wrists where the cord had cut them.

The man laughed. 'You are to be lodged in the Cold Harbour Tower,' he said. Francis was escorted across the courtyard and into the tower, where he found that his surprises were not yet over. He had expected to be lodged, if not in a dungeon cell, then a bare room with a pallet bed, but he found that he was to have a comfortable room with a small bedchamber opening off it. True, the walls were bare stone and the windows were securely barred, but they were large enough to let in plenty of light, a pleasant fire burned in the grate, and Francis saw at once that he could be as comfortable here as in his rooms at Magdalen.

One of the gaolers noticed his face, and smiled sympathetically.

'We are not all as heartless as some would think,' he said. 'It is a little early yet for supper, but I have given word that some should be sent to you directly.' Even as he spoke there was a tap at the door and a maidservant entered with a tray. In his general confusion Francis had forgotten how hungry he was, but the sight of spiced meats, herbs, wine and fruit, coupled with his sudden access of comfort, made him eager to begin. The gaolers laughed and left him to his meal, locking the door behind them.

It was the best meal he had tasted for a long time, and Francis felt enormously improved when he had finished. He walked to the window and stood for a while looking down on the courtyard below. There was little enough he could see, for it was dark now, but he could see the torches of the gaolers going about their duties, and by their light see some ravens swooping for crumbs. Francis realised it was true that, as Sir William had said, he was to be treated with deference. Almost it was possible to forget the finger of peril that pointed at so many here, himself included.

The wine, coming after his uncomfortable ride, had made him exceedingly drowsy. The bed in the little chamber was as comfortable as any he had slept in; there was even a ewer set for him to wash. He took off his boots and lay down, wondering whether he was dreaming that he had woken that morning in the magistrate's manor house, and was now a prisoner in England's most strongly guarded fortress. He was too tired to sort it out; he only knew that he was comfortable, and very soon he was fast asleep.

It was still dark when he woke, and for several seconds he lay still, trying to remember where he was. Then the turbulent events of the day before came back to him, and he remembered that he was in prison. Curiously, the thought did not terrify him; it seemed completely matter-of-fact. For the moment it seemed as though he could no longer influence the course of his own life, that he could watch what was happening to him as though it were a play.

Gradually he realised that, though the chamber in which he lay was in darkness, candles burned in the outer room where he had supped. He slipped off the bed and pushed the door wider, to see his servant Will Peters calmly laying the fire.

'Will!' he cried, when at last he found his voice. 'How – how is it that you are here? I last saw you completely unable to leave your bed.'

'That were soon over, my lord. Later that day I was able to eat, and move around. But when you didn't return from Coneybury I started to get worried, and so did Mr Wentworth. We feared you must be in trouble, so next morning I set out there myself. I thought it best to ask for news at a cottage in Charlbury, rather than go to the house itself. They'd heard of a search at Coneybury, they said, and of a young gentleman taken prisoner. I was sure it must be you; the goodwife said you had been taken to the justice's house.' Will blew on the fire as it started to catch.

'Go on. What did you do then?'

'Came back to Oxford first, to see if I could find where the justice's house was. Fortunately Mr Wentworth knew. Don't know how, but I went there and hid in the bushes until I spied a maidservant who might accept a florin to tell me where you were. She told me there was talk of taking you to the Tower. Mr Wentworth agreed that I should come here directly; I came on Monday, and though you weren't here then they said you were being brought in next day, and I asked if I might be allowed to wait on you.'

Francis stared. 'But – do you mean that you have given up your liberty in order to be with me?'

Will blushed. 'Better here with you,' he muttered, 'than outside wondering what they was doing to you.'

'Will, you're a marvel!' cried Francis. 'I don't suppose – ' he hesitated.

'I stopped at your father's house afore I came here,' said Will at once. 'Your father and your cousin both know where you are.'

Francis sat down. 'I cannot understand this sudden desire for courtesy to one accused of treason,' he said. 'It was not so with the magistrate.'

'You are the eldest son of an earl, remember. And I shall not be with you all the time. But I shall be allowed to bring you your meals, and sleep in the servants' quarters. 'Tis early yet, but there are some cold meats and ale set up for your breakfast.'

Francis thought he had eaten amply the night before, but he found that his sleep had given him a fresh appetite, and he sat down to eat.

'I brought some of your clothes from Oxford,' said Will hesitantly when Francis had finished. 'I knew you had nothing but what you set off in.' He pointed to a clothes-press in the bedchamber beyond, and to his delight Francis found that several changes of clothes had been carefully set there – his crimson velvet breeches, satin long flared coat, silk shirts and lace-trimmed nightshirts. A trivial thing, perhaps, but it seemed to accentuate the fact that he was being treated with great courtesy.

'And only yesterday I thought I was bereft of friends,' he murmured. 'To be tried for high treason now seems to be a little thing, if those who wish me well stand by me.'

Will smiled. 'Let me help you change your clothes, my lord,' he said. 'I can see you spent the night in them, several nights most likely, and when the warder comes I shall have to leave you.' He selected a laced cambric shirt and plum-coloured suit with a wide-skirted coat which Francis donned carelessly, Will straightening it for him. Soon afterwards they heard the key turning in the door and a warder entered, halberd in hand.

'You must leave your master now,' he said. 'You will be able to exercise later in the courtyard, I am sure, Lord Trenoweth.'

Will obeyed meekly and Francis sat back, trying to make sense of the puzzle that surrounded him. But he had never understood puzzles; music, now, that was different. Softly at first, then with growing confidence, he began to sing the counter-tenor line of Purcell's 'Behold now, praise the Lord'.

So deep was he in trying to sing the anthem from memory that he did not hear the door open. He looked up suddenly to find his father sitting quietly opposite him and listening.

He stopped at once and grinned sheepishly.

'It is extremely good, Francis.' Lord Bodmin smiled. 'How you can sing at all under these circumstances I find surprising.'

'If I sing, at least I am concentrating on the music, and not on other things that I find more uncomfortable.'

Lord Bodmin stood up to embrace his son, then sank back into the chair, as though movement had become an effort.

Francis looked at his father, and found himself deeply shocked at the change in him: the face usually so cheerful was pinched and drawn and deeply lined, the sprightly gait had become a reluctant dragging step. Even his clothes, which he usually wore with such panache, hung listlessly from his shoulders. It seemed to Francis that his father had grown old overnight.

'All is not yet lost, Father,' said Francis. 'I can – I must prove that I am innocent of this crime which is charged against me. You know, surely, that I am not guilty?'

'Of course I do, Francis,' replied Lord Bodmin, and the old defiance was there in his voice. 'But it is not as simple as that – you will have to fight against a great deal of prejudice, and the odds will be weighted against you. Tell me – how did it happen?'

'I was invited to Coneybury by Sir Henry – verbally, through Robert. I thought this might be my opportunity to find out what I needed to know, before going to the Privy Council, but when I arrived there was no sign of any of the Somervilles, or Robert. The magistrate and his men were conducting a search of the place. He arrested me that day, and I was taken to his house, where I was kept until he could obtain a warrant and have me brought here.'

Lord Bodmin stroked his beard. 'Do you know the details of the charges against you?'

Francis shook his head. 'No. Only that I am charged with treason. Sir William knew of my visits to Coneybury, it seems, and my meetings with Robert, and somehow he is able to twist that into evidence against me. He made much of my "refusal" to tell him where Sir Henry is, but of course I do not know.'

'And Eleanor?' asked his father gently.

"Her father has taken her away – where, I do not know. I was able to talk to the cook while the house was being searched, who it seems is very fond of her. But even Eleanor did not know where they were going. She was in considerable distress.'

'You are, I imagine, relieved that she refused to marry Robert?'

Francis smiled. 'I doubt we can ever be together, but I love her, Father. And according to the cook she loves me.'

Lord Bodmin sat silent for a moment. 'Your union would have my blessing,' he said. 'Though I imagine her father's might be a little harder to obtain. But the important thing now, of course, is to have you acquitted and released from this place. Thomas will probably come to see you later, by the by; he is busy ferreting out what information he can from his amiable Whigs.'

'Is he elected for the Parliament?'

'Yes, for Launceston. He travelled there when you were in Oxford, won the election, and returned to London directly. Almost I went with him, for it is a while since I saw your mother, and I wished to forget Parliaments and plottings at Pelistry. But it seemed a lot of travelling, if I am to go to Oxford next month, and now I am glad that I remained. A messenger has been despatched to Cornwall to inform your mother what has happened; she will very likely come to London when she knows.'

Francis began to walk about the room. 'It seems hard to believe in danger here,' he said quietly. 'I am well tended, kindly treated, and only the locking of that door reminds me that I am indeed a prisoner.'

'Your courage is at least equal to the occasion,' remarked his father. 'I had not expected it to be otherwise, but I am reassured to see you after the message I received from young Will.'

'I am sorry that my carelessness has put you in such distress,' said Francis.

Lord Bodmin looked grave. 'I think you may find it is the wickedness of others rather than any carelessness of yours.'

'But surely there is not enough evidence to find me guilty? I shall sit with you at Pelistry before many weeks are past, Father; I feel sure of it.'

Lord Bodmin stood up and smiled briefly as he rapped on the door. 'Amen to that,' he said as a warder unlocked the door. 'I shall come again to you, Francis, and I shall use what influence I can on your behalf.'

Francis sat down by the window after his father had gone. Somehow the fact of his father's being let out of the room while he was compelled to remain within it emphasised the fact that he was a prisoner as nothing else had done. He found that he was trembling. Solitude was all very well unless it was imposed on you.

*

Eleanor paced restlessly up and down her little bedchamber, causing Sarah to look up from the shift she was mending.

'Sit down for a little, Miss,' she said. 'You don't want your uncle thinking you are agitated. And in this house he can probably hear.'

'Sarah, I can't help it! I must try to be calm when I go down to dinner, and if I sit still now I don't think I will be. My only hope of achieving anything is to appear entirely happy with whatever is being planned, and perhaps I shall find out more about what it is. But please allow me to be restless now.'

Sarah bent over her sewing. 'You knew that he had been arrested.'

'Yes, but now he is in the Tower! That must mean he is being charged with serious crimes, probably treason. I am afraid for him, Sarah.'

'He cannot be condemned without a tr – oh!' Sarah squealed as she pricked herself with the needle, the blood beading bright on the pad of her finger. With the other hand she moved the shift away so that she did not stain it.

'Leave that for now, Sarah. I am sorry if my anxieties have caused you to hurt yourself.'

'It hardly hurts, Miss.' Sarah sucked at her finger. 'I wish I could do more for you.'

'You already do a great deal, Sarah, but I must go down to dinner soon. How am I to pretend that Lord Trenoweth's being in the Tower is of no great consequence to me?'

'Is Mr Carey here, Miss?'

'I don't think so. That is another thing I find hard to understand. He is looking so ill-kempt all of a sudden. He had always taken such a pride in his appearance. It seems as though he is hardly washing, even.'

Sarah smiled. 'I think I can tell you that, Miss. In fact, I think you know yourself. He does not want to be recognised, or perhaps Mr Anthony does not want him recognised.'

'Yes.' Eleanor sighed. 'I wish I could follow him back to London, see where he manages to become the smart courtier again, even perhaps find out what is happening to Francis.'

'I should brush your hair before you go down to dinner, Miss. You know your aunt will criticise you if you are not looking neat.'

'Your finger will not make that difficult?'

It was my left hand, Miss, and it has stopped bleeding already.' She held the finger up and smiled.

By the time Eleanor's hair was arranged to Sarah's satisfaction they could already hear the clatter of plates from downstairs.

'That's another thing about this house,' said Eleanor. 'You can hear so much from other parts of the house. There is almost no privacy.' But she flashed a smile at Sarah and went demurely downstairs.

There were six of them for dinner: the four of them from Coneybury, their host, Mr Weston, and his wife.

'Eleanor.' Her father looked up and smiled as she entered the oak-panelled dining room. It seemed to Eleanor that it was almost with relief. 'Your aunt was wondering what had become of you.'

'I was still sorting things with Sarah,' said Eleanor easily, seating herself beside Mrs Weston.

They had been with the Westons for nearly two weeks now, and Eleanor wondered if she would ever be able to make a friend of their hostess. She was an ample lady, whose hair hung down in greasy ringlets either side of a shiny face. It seemed she was oblivious to her considerable size, as she always dressed in the most unsuitable clothes. Today it was a vast gown of purple velvet, cut low to reveal a bosom that shook whenever she moved, which was frequently, as she seemed to suffer from an inability to sit still. But Eleanor believed that she was essentially kind, and might prove a useful ally. Already she had tried to tempt Eleanor with titbits and comfits when she did not seem to be eating very much. Eleanor knew that she must overcome her natural repugnance and try to accept the woman's well-meaning offer of friendship. Never before had she felt so totally friendless.

Mr Weston she tried to avoid as much as possible. He was clearly beholden in some way to her uncle, but she did not think he was dangerous. Fortunately he scarcely noticed her.

'There you are, my dear.' Mrs Weston put a plump hand on her arm, and Eleanor attempted a smile. 'I'm sure it must still seem very strange to you here. And I know we are not as grand as you are at home, but we will try to make you welcome.' She had said this every day since their arrival, but Eleanor acknowledged her politely.

'Thank you, madam. You are most kind. I think my maid and I have sorted our clothes satisfactorily now. Sarah was doing some mending for me.'

'You must come and eat a good dinner now. We have beef, and capon, there are dumplings, and all sorts of comfits. You shall not go hungry here.'

Eleanor did not doubt it, and she made a real effort to do more than pick at her food. Her aunt leaned across to her.

'I was wondering, Eleanor, if you would like to accompany me into the town tomorrow. My yellow gown would look so much better with new ribbons, and I am sure we can find something for you too.'

Eleanor smiled. 'Thank you, aunt. That would be most agreeable.'

Mrs Weston nudged her. 'That will bring some colour into your cheeks. I really thought you were quite poorly when you first came here.'

'Eleanor is strong enough.' Sir Henry's voice came booming down the table. Eleanor started. She had not realised that her father was listening. 'She does a deal of the gardening at Coneybury. Does it very well, as a matter of fact.'

'I wonder you can tear yourself away from your beautiful house.' Mrs Weston smiled at him. 'Perhaps one day you might show it to me.'

'I shall be glad to dear lady. Mr Weston as well, of course,' he added, turning to his host, who sat in baleful silence at the head of the table. 'When happier times return, and our country is united in faith once again.'

This brought the first smile Eleanor had ever seen on Mr Weston's face, and it sat oddly there, as though it was a stranger. Eleanor suspected he was as much a fanatic as her uncle. She turned suddenly to her hostess.

'Would you show me your garden before the light fades, Mrs Weston? I have walked in it a little, but I am sure there are some parts I must have missed.'

Mrs Weston beamed. 'Of course. I do not walk very far nowadays – I find it tires me so. But a short way in the garden; now that would be delightful.'

Eleanor turned to her food with fierce concentration. She knew a turn in the garden with Mrs Weston would not be nearly as enjoyable as one with Sarah, but anything that would help her in her present predicament had to be considered.

Chapter Fourteen

Francis was alarmed at the change in his cousin when Thomas appeared before him in the Tower. Had his own ill fortune so badly affected all those he held dear? All Thomas's confidence seemed to have deserted him: he glanced uneasily over his shoulder, and stiffened at the sound of the key being turned in the lock after he had been admitted.

'Francis,' he said, and even his voice seemed muted, devoid of hope. 'What can I say? I knew your return to Oxford carried danger with it, but I never expected to come to you here!'

Francis smiled. 'I am sure the evidence against me cannot amount to very much,' he said. 'A few visits to Coneybury, a few meetings with Robert – what can that prove?'

'Ah. Robert. When did you last see him?'

'It would be nearly three weeks ago now. When he gave me Sir Henry's invitation to Coneybury. It seemed so genuine, Thomas. I never realised – '

'No, no, of course you did not,' said his cousin impatiently. 'And you have no idea where he might be now?'

'None whatever. I know that the magistrate did not believe me, but – '

'But you hope that I do,' said Thomas, and then was silent for a little, studying his hands with great intensity. When he looked up again his face was drained of colour.

'I want you to know, Francis,' he said, and his voice shook a little, 'that if my influence can save either you or Robert, then my brother must look to himself. From what I have already learned I suspect Robert of being guilty of treason. I would not have him evade the consequences by thrusting his burden upon you. Do you understand my meaning?'

'Not altogether,' muttered Francis. 'But I think I would rather remain in ignorance just now.' He paused. 'Thomas, do you know when – I am likely to be tried?'

His cousin shook his head. 'I will find out what I can, though, and come to you again. I will tell you two things, Francis: I believe your case could well affect what happens in Oxford next month, and I am sure that if a verdict can be deferred until after Parliament has met you will be acquitted.' His voice had grown stronger as he spoke, Francis noticed, and the old, resourceful Thomas appeared to be materialising in front of his eyes. He rapped on the door, and so quickly was it opened that both of them realised that the warder must have been waiting outside.

'I cannot stay longer, Francis,' said Thomas, 'but much of my work concerns you. Your case is far from desperate.' With that he swept up his hat and was gone.

Later in the day Francis was allowed to take exercise in the courtyard. His guards were cheerful and polite, and though they could answer most of his questions concerning the Tower itself, they knew little enough about the likely conduct of his trial. Francis knew almost nothing about it; only that he was going to have to fight for his life. How, he had no idea. He had fallen in love with a Papist girl and for this, it seemed, he was to be accused of treason.

But his musings, he found, were to be kept short. He was scarcely back in his prison when the door opened and in swept his sister Elizabeth and her husband, he in wine-red velvet, she in apricot silk.

'Francis!' Elizabeth was across the room in two strides and embraced him. 'You booby, getting yourself locked up here like this. But don't worry, Nigel has influence. We'll soon have you out.'

Nigel seated himself cautiously on a stool and looked up at Francis. His smile was distinctly strained.

'I will do what I can, of course. But – I am indeed sorry to come to you here.'

Francis looked across at the man who had married his sister, the man he knew to be a thorough rake. Perhaps he and Elizabeth deserved each other, however. He knew that she was hardly a faithful wife. She was barely two years his senior, and sometimes Francis felt that he was a long way the elder. Sexual exploits aside, Elizabeth appeared to hold growing up at arm's length.

'Have you – seen Father recently?' Francis asked, more for the sake of something to say than because he wanted to know the answer.

Elizabeth examined her nails in great detail, then stood up and moved to the window.

'Oh yes. Do you know, Nigel and I have been married for over four years now, yet Father still manages to lecture me. Nigel is my husband, after all, yet he never does that.'

Nigel looked up and grinned. 'I wouldn't dare,' he said simply. 'If it's of any comfort, Francis, Jemmy says he is sure no relative of mine could have been plotting with Papists.'

Francis smiled. 'And will he come and give evidence on my behalf? It's all right, Nigel, don't look so shocked. The Duke of Monmouth must keep well away from involvement with such as me.'

Nigel coughed. 'He would not see it like that, of course, but, yes, he must be careful.'

Elizabeth turned from the window. 'It doesn't seem fair,' she said. 'Father lectures me continually about my behaviour, yet when you managed to get yourself locked up in the Tower he gives you all the support you could want.'

'It still may not be enough,' said Francis quietly.

They did not stay long after that; as they left Francis suspected they had only come because Elizabeth found it exciting.

The next day he had scarce breakfasted when he heard the key in the lock again. Into his prison, blue coat set jauntily on his shoulders and black periwig curled luxuriantly strode, not his father or Thomas, but Henry Purcell.

'Mr Purcell!' cried Francis. 'I did not expect – this is an honour.'

Purcell took both of Francis's hands in his own. 'Henry, please,' he said. 'I heard but yesterday of your misfortune, and am come to tell you that I am entirely persuaded of your innocence. If there is anything I can do then I demand to be told.'

Francis smiled. 'Thank you,' he said. 'But why should you be so convinced of my innocence? Influential men, it seems, believe me guilty of treason.'

'I may not have known you for very long,' replied Purcell, 'but I formed an immediate impression of your integrity. Besides – no man who sings as you do could possibly be guilty of treason. It is beyond the bounds of belief.'

This time Francis laughed aloud. 'It is good to hear you speak,' he said. 'Here I am, a prisoner in England's most strongly guarded fortress, about to be tried for my life. Yet I cannot but believe that the trial will be a formality, that I will be acquitted and released.'

'Let us hope so,' replied Purcell. 'It is likely that I shall be taking over at the Chapel Royal this year, and I shall need you there. I have no counter-tenors of your quality. I want this to be the best choir in England, Francis; and you can help me realise my dream.'

'I have not sung for a little,' replied Francis. 'I am afraid that I should be out of practice.'

'Then we must remedy that forthwith,' replied Purcell. 'I must leave for the Abbey now, but I shall come to you tomorrow, and bring my lute with me. We shall ensure that you have not forgotten how to sing.'

True to his word, he was back the following day with his lute and a large sheaf of music, much of it his own. Francis sang for an hour, and took enormous pleasure in Purcell's tuition. For that hour it was possible to forget his predicament, but merely to rejoice in the fact that they were able to make music together.

Not long after Purcell had left him his cousin Thomas was with him again, this time looking purposeful and eager.

'You are to be examined by the Privy Council tomorrow,' he said. 'There is no need to be alarmed; it was bound to happen, though I confess the speed with which they are acting has surprised me. I cannot decide whether you are fortunate or no – you might have had to wait many weeks. There is only one thing that I fear at the moment.'

'And that is – ?'

'That a conviction would be more easily secured before Oxford than after, and that it would benefit Exclusion for this to happen. A Popish Plot unveiled on the eve of Parliament! Think of the stir it would cause; it could well affect voting among the Trimmers. Most of them will follow Halifax and vote against Exclusion, but some might be persuaded to change their minds if the Popish Plot were shown to be a present danger. I am a Whig, Francis, and I believe Exclusion would benefit the nation, but I see now where many of my fellows are become so fanatical – I have been in danger of doing so myself. But it has gone far enough; if Exclusion can only succeed at the cost of your life, then James must be his brother's heir, and we must take the consequences.'

Francis looked at him in bewilderment. 'You mean – the Whigs wish me to be found guilty?'

'Many of them, yes, without considering what is the actual truth. This is a political matter, Francis, but their weakness will be your strength – you cannot be convicted without evidence, and I am hopeful that they may not have enough.'

'I still do not know what their evidence is,' said Francis. 'How can visiting a household, even if it is Papist, constitute treason?'

'We will know more tomorrow,' said Thomas. 'Meantime, try to keep your spirits up. I am told that Mr Purcell has been to see you.'

'He has been very kind,' said Francis. 'He hopes to take over at the Chapel Royal this year, and wants me in the choir.'

'Then we must make sure that you are acquitted,' said Thomas, and rapped on the door for the gaoler.

After he was gone Francis sat back, trying to puzzle out the mystery in front of him. He was a pawn, it seemed, in a dangerous political game where heads were the only stakes. And who were the other players? Robert and Anthony or milord Shaftesbury? Francis had once thought that he had the earl's protection, and now feared that all his deadly venom might be directed against him.

Will Peters noticed his abstracted look when he came in with his dinner, and tried to keep his spirits up by retailing servants' gossip and telling what he knew of other inmates of the Tower, both past and present.

'Some of the older ones can remember when milord Shaftesbury was here,' said Will. 'It was a while ago now, but he created a fine stir, seemingly. Must have his own cook, a great red-faced man who lorded it over all the others because he was cook to a lord.' Will rambled innocently on, and Francis listened with amusement, delighted that for once he could forget his own wretched plight and think of less serious matters.

The next morning he dressed carefully, choosing coat and breeches of brown velvet. The coat was wide and full, and he let it hang open to show his laced silk shirt and deep golden sash. Will had attended to his red periwig, which curled in profusion over his shoulders, and his paste-buckled shoes gleamed with the attention given them. It seemed a pity he was not allowed a sword to complete the picture.

Will brought him his breakfast early – a piece of cold mutton pie with some bread, and a mug of mulled ale which steamed gently. Francis almost laughed as he began to eat.

'How do you mange to keep this so hot, Will?' he asked. 'It must be quite a way from the kitchens.'

'It depends how quick you want to be, my lord,' replied Will. 'I know you like your mulled ale hot, so I make to hurry with it. I daresay some wouldn't bother.'

Francis finished and sat back. 'What would I do without you, Will? Shall you look after me like this when we are both at Pelistry?'

'I'm glad to hear you talk like that, my lord,' said Will. 'But finish the pie – I was told they would be coming for you at eight.'

Certainly it was not long before Francis found himself at the water-gate – Traitor's Gate, he remembered wryly – there to be handed into a barge and conducted up the river to Whitehall. He was not made to suffer the indignity of being bound on this occasion, but he was closely guarded every inch of the way. Nevertheless he enjoyed the river journey, as they pushed slowly past the warehouses of the City, the ruin that was once St Paul's, then – once the grimness of Alsatia was past – the Temple, Somerset House, and the large elegant houses of the Strand, with their gardens stretching down to the river. Soon they would be passing his father's house, thought Francis, and he craned his neck to see if he could recognise it. But Whitehall was soon reached now, and armed guards were waiting to conduct him to the council chamber.

He dimly remembered the maze of courtyards, galleries, staircases and corridors as though from another life. There was the magnificent Banqueting Hall, with the elegant Privy Gallery at right angles to it, but Francis was conducted beyond this to a more functional part of the palace, where at last he was required to wait in an ante-room. There was no fire here, and he felt cold now that he was no longer able to move about, and full of fears as he realised what was about to begin. His guards did not look particularly cold, he mused, but they were not about to be put on trial for their lives. He had but the vaguest notion of the charges against him, and his knowledge of the law was slight. That this was to be an examination by the Council and not a trial in a court of law did nothing to abate his uneasiness.

He was required to wait in the cold for some little time, until at last a footman called his name, and demanded the he be led into the council chamber. This was a large room with a barrel-vaulted ceiling and many windows overlooking the river, but though a fire burned at one end of the chamber, behind the King's chair, Francis, standing at the other, found it almost colder than the ante-room.

His guards had led him in and withdrawn, and Francis found himself standing at the end of the long table, staring down it straight into the dark piercing eyes of the King, whom he had once met as his father's friend and his own benefactor. The King was dressed in the black velvet which became him so well, with fine lace at throat and cuffs. This time, however, there was no smile to relieve the set determination of his countenance. The councillors, perhaps thirty of them, sat grouped about the table, waiting the word of the King to begin the examination of the prisoner before them, but for a long moment King Charles sat silent, as though marshalling his thoughts with the greatest care.

'Well, Lord Trenoweth,' he began eventually, 'things have changed somewhat since we last met. You have either been singularly foolish or particularly wicked.'

'If it please Your Majesty,' replied Francis, 'the folly indeed is mine, but the wickedness I trust I can disprove.'

'Let us hope so,' remarked the King. 'Lord Sunderland, you have a copy of the charge there? Perhaps you would read it to us.'

A tall, elegant man with a well-curled periwig stood up and cleared his throat portentously.

'Francis, Baron Trenoweth,' he began, 'you are accused that between December last and this present time you did wilfully plot and intend to bring about the final death and destruction of our sovereign lord the King, to overthrow the government of England, to alter the sincere and true religion of this kingdom as is by law established, and to levy war on our aforesaid lord the King in his realm of England.'

'But none of that is true!' exclaimed Francis. 'I sought to put an end to a plot, not to take part in it.'

'That is not what our witnesses will say,' said Lord Sunderland. 'Your Majesty, this young man was taken in a house where it is known a Jesuit priest had been in hiding, and where it is believed a plot was being formed for the taking of Your Majesty's life.'

'That in itself does not prove his guilt,' said the King.

'No, Your Majesty; but there is a witness prepared to swear to it.'

'Mr Oates has not been interesting himself in this case, has he?'

Francis remembered the ugly Titus Oates, whom Thomas had pointed out to him that day in the Sun Tavern. The prophet of the Popish Plot, some called him, but Francis felt sure he could not be a witness in this case.

'No, Your Majesty,' Lord Sunderland was saying. 'The witness I refer to is the prisoner's own cousin, Robert Carey.'

'Robert!' The cry came from Francis as he tried to digest such a totally unexpected turn of events. Was this some plan that Robert and Anthony had concocted between them? That the evidence would be perjured he knew even before he heard it, but proving this might not be so easy.

He did at least have the satisfaction of noting that when, a moment later, he found himself looking straight at Robert across the room, it was Robert who looked away first. He was, as always, immaculate, this time in crimson satin, with a luxuriantly curled black periwig, in imitation, it seemed to Francis, of the King's.

Lord Sunderland stood up. 'Your name is Robert Carey, first cousin to the accused?'

'Yes.'

'And as cousins you and the prisoner see a good deal of each other?'

'As children we were playmates. Later our paths drifted apart, but I found myself in Oxford last year, and was minded to seek my cousin out.'

'When was this?'

'It would have been November. I had on a previous occasion met the Somervilles of Coneybury and, anxious to do my cousin some good, suggested that he might accompany me there.'

Francis gripped the table edge in front of him. He knew there was no chance of his being seated, and he was cold, but he also knew it was vital that he learn as much of the evidence against him as possible. Instinctively he sensed that for the moment it would be best for him to stay silent and merely listen.

'So you effected this meeting?'

'I did. I knew, of course, that the Somervilles were Papists; this perhaps gained me my introduction to them, as I am in service to the Duke of York. But I believed it a private matter between them and their consciences.'

'And the position of Anthony, Sir Henry Somerville's younger brother?'

'He is a Papist priest. I discovered recently that he is in fact a Jesuit.'

'And your cousin returned to the house?'

'Many times. Sometimes I was with him, but sometimes His Grace of York had need of my services.'

'Were you aware of your cousin's faith?'

'I was not. He had been raised a loyal Protestant, and I believed him still to be that. But it became clear at Coneybury that he had become a Papist.'

'That would not be enough to have him arraigned here.' Lord Rochester, a portly, red-faced peer, spoke up. Robert turned to him and smiled.

'No. But when I heard him in conversation with Sir Henry Somerville talking about the King's being "taken off" and a large sum of money being mentioned, I believed that treason was being plotted. The possibility of Miss Eleanor's hand was also mentioned.'

'That does put a different complexion on things.' The King turned his gaze directly to Robert, and spoke for the first time. 'You are certain of this, Mr Carey?'

Robert looked slightly taken aback. 'Yes, Your Majesty. At the time, if treason were being plotted, I still hoped I might dissuade my cousin. It seems I failed. But it was clear that the offer of Eleanor's hand would be a very real inducement.'

'And you do not know where Sir Henry Somerville has taken his family now?'

'Not at all. Things would be very different if I did.' He looked straight at Francis. 'Perhaps my cousin knows.'

'I wish with all my heart that I knew,' cried Francis. 'For where he is – '

'His daughter will be also,' finished the King with a smile. 'But you must clear yourself of the charges, Lord Trenoweth, before you rest in her arms again.'

'I would like to hear the prisoner's answers to his cousin's charges,' said Lord Radnor, an elderly, inoffensive-looking peer.

'Then I would tell my cousin,' said Francis, 'that he knows full well there is no truth in what he says. Sir Henry was not the prime mover in this plot of which he speaks, but his brother, Anthony Somerville.'

'So you knew of a plot?' Lord Sunderland was quick to ask.

'I believe that it was possible, yes. I was trying to find enough information to lay before you all when I was arrested.'

'It seems the prisoner has no defence but blank denial,' put in Robert calmly. 'But many times he spoke to me of this terrible plot. I tried to dissuade him from his course of action, but I failed signally.'

Even to Robert he was no long 'my cousin' but 'the prisoner', Francis noticed. He grew weary of the questioning that followed; all the councillors seemed eager to thrust at him. How long had he been a Papist? At what time did he and Sir Henry begin plotting together? What was his reward to have been? There was no mention of the possibility that he might not be guilty at all, and the suggestion that he had continued his visits to Coneybury on Eleanor's account and as a loyal Protestant was greeted with shouts of laughter. It was clear that to many of the councillors his answers were merely evasions; only the King appeared still to doubt his guilt.

Robert had been gone long since, and already it was past noon, though there was no mention of pausing for dinner. The councillors refreshed themselves with wine and sweetmeats, but Francis, compelled to remain standing, grew tired and confused until, answering yet again a question as to when he had first visited Coneybury, he gave a slightly different answer. Much was made of this apparent inconsistency, and several of the councillors believed it added to the count against him. It was with something approaching relief that he heard the King pronounce that he must be committed close prisoner to the Tower; that he would be summoned from thence to answer the charges against him in the Court of King's Bench. He had given a bad account of himself before the Council, he knew; but Robert's treachery had compelled him to rethink his position entirely, and for that he would need time for quiet and contemplation. To be condemned to all the horrors of being put to death for treason on perjured evidence seemed cruel indeed, yet it had happened to others before him. A scapegoat would suit the Whigs, and he had put himself into a very vulnerable position.

He was almost glad to find himself in his room in the Tower again, though he refused the supper Will Peters had brought him, almost brusquely asking Will to leave him. He needed to be alone. How was he to deal with this new threat? He had begun to believe that Robert was involved in plotting with Anthony, but this particular turn of events had never occurred to him. He felt sure that Robert did know where the Somervilles were, though the knowledge in itself was no use to him at all. Had it not been for his brief conversation with the cook, he might now be doubting even Eleanor.

He slept eventually, and awoke to pale winter sunshine. The memory of yesterday's examination by the Council lay cold on his heart, however, and seemed to forbid the awakening of hope. Was it possible to school himself to resignation? He knew now just how much danger he was in; that there was a real possibility that he would be found guilty, and condemned to death for treason. And Eleanor might never know how true his love for her had been.

Will Peters brought him breakfast, but Francis was still too much in shock to say a great deal to his servant. When the gaoler came to tell Will to leave, Francis asked for pen and paper, but was told that under the terms of his committal it could not be allowed. He was alone again, and took to pacing the room restlessly, looking down into the courtyard and watching the ravens, even trying haltingly to pray.

He was not alone for more than half an hour when he heard the key in the lock again, and turned to see his cousin Thomas with him in the room. Thomas glanced uneasily at Francis, and sat down heavily.

'My confinement is not then to be as harsh as I had feared,' said Francis hesitantly. 'I have already been refused pen and paper, and thought that perhaps I should not be allowed to see those who wished me no harm.'

'I am here under false pretences,' said Thomas quietly. 'As a known Whig of some standing, and as brother to your chief accuser – yes, I know all about Robert's perfidy – it is thought I might persuade you to confess. Francis, I know you are not guilty of the charges brought against you, but I fear you will have difficulty in proving it. Robert has told his tale too well.'

'Then – what am I to do?'

'We must try to find some flaw in Robert's evidence, some inconsistency. What exactly did he say?'

'That he introduced me to Coneybury, and that some time later he heard me discussing with Sir Henry the King's being "taken off" and talking about money. He even said I was to be offered Eleanor's hand if I would help in the plot.'

'And they believed that?'

'Some of them, I think because they wanted to. Robert declared that I was obviously a Papist, and that though he was aware that Anthony is a priest, he did not know that he was a Jesuit. Thomas, he is not a Jesuit. I believe that missal was placed there deliberately to incriminate me.'

'Yes. I think you are probably right. If I could find Robert it would help enormously, but he is going to be slippery. He is certainly not in his lodgings in Westminster.'

Francis smiled. 'That would be too easy. I believe he is with Anthony. But where that is – ' He shrugged his shoulders, and the smile faded.

Thomas studied his nails with great intensity for a moment, then looked up. 'Have you any idea why he should have acted in this way?'

'At first I thought it was just to save his own skin.' Francis remembered the disbelief he had felt as Robert had walked into the council chamber. 'But I think it is more than that. I see Anthony's hand behind this. Their plot will still go ahead, I feel certain, and somehow the danger I am in will benefit it.'

'Was Anthony mentioned yesterday?'

'Not a great deal, beyond the fact of his being a priest and, so they declare, a Jesuit. It is Sir Henry I am supposed to be plotting with.'

'And Robert claimed not to know where Sir Henry and his family are?'

'I'm sure he is with them already. It's too late now to have him followed.'

'My dear brother has no doubt thought of that himself.' Thomas smiled briefly. 'Almost certainly you're right. He has gone into hiding with them. I think it unlikely that we shall see him before your trial opens. He has given his evidence to the Privy Council. He will not be needed in London before that.'

'There seems to be very little I can do now.' Francis stood up and began to pace the room. 'I hate inactivity.' He stopped suddenly in a corner of the room, stooped and picked up some papers from the floor.

'At least I have not been deprived of this.'

'What is it?'

'Some music that I was learning with Henry Purcell. I shall practise it, whether or not he is allowed to visit me.'

'That sounds an excellent idea. As you observed, you are to be kept in close confinement. Probably you will not leave this room until your trial. Anything you can do to keep your mind occupied will help you. Your father is hoping to come to see you, but even that may not be possible. Keep yourself alert, Francis, and try to think of any weakness in Robert's evidence that you have heard. He is their trump card, and it is vital to explode his story.'

'I suppose – you have not discovered when the trial is likely to be?'

Thomas frowned. 'They are trying to rush it through, I am sure,' he said. 'I believe you will be brought to the bar of King's Bench before Parliament meets. Justice seems to matter less at such times than a scapegoat to an hysterical people.'

'For the first time since my arrest,' said Francis slowly, 'I knew fear yesterday. But it was not only fear, it was anger; anger that Robert should have treated me thus, anger that I am in danger of being condemned to death because others conspire against me.'

Thomas smiled. 'Build on that anger,' he said. 'It could serve you well. Do you wish me to take a message to your father?'

'Tell him – tell him I am not afraid. I know that I may be condemned, but I will not perjure myself. I will die with my honour intact.'

Chapter Fifteen

Eleanor wrapped herself in a warm cloak before stepping out of the garden door with her hostess, who was swathed in what appeared to be several shawls.

'We will not walk too far.' said Mrs Weston. 'It is mild, it is true, but it is only February, and I shall soon be glad to return to the fireside.'

Eleanor smiled, and tucked her hand into the older woman's arm. 'I always find a little fresh air most beneficial,' she said. 'I believe you have a seat near the river?'

'Indeed.' Mrs Weston turned to her in surprise. 'First appearances can often be mistaken. I thought you a mopey, silly thing when you first arrived. But I was wrong, was I not?'

'Perhaps I kept to my room more than was wise.' Eleanor was treading carefully. She needed this woman's friendship. 'The move was so sudden – I had to have time to understand what was happening.'

'And do you now understand it?'

'A little. I know we are safer here than at Coneybury. And I am grateful to you for giving us sanctuary. Look, here is the seat, and it is quite dry.'

Mrs Weston sank onto it gratefully, fanning her face with a handkerchief. 'There is no need for gratitude, my dear. I believe Mr Weston was glad to be able to help your uncle. He thinks very highly of him.'

'How did Mr Weston meet my uncle? We are quite a long way from Oxford.'

'Your uncle travels a good deal, as you surely know. He is always anxious to do what he can for those of our persuasion.'

Eleanor was uncertain how to reply to this, so she busied herself with adjusting the folds of her cloak.

'I am sure that you would go out of your way to help somebody you thought very highly of, would you not?' Mrs Weston's greasy face appeared entirely candid.

'I believe so. I hope I can be a good friend.'

Mrs Weston took her arm confidingly. 'Do you enjoy riding, my dear?'

'Why yes.' Eleanor was surprised. 'Though I do not know the country here. And I have nobody to ride out with.'

'Does your maid not ride? I am sure she would be thought suitable company for you. As to not knowing the country here, we are really very well placed. As soon as you are out on the road in front of the house, you turn up the hill to get to High Wycombe, and so on to Oxford, over the river if you want the road to Maidenhead. From there you can go down to Windsor, and even to London if you've a mind. I went to London myself once, a long time ago. Nasty, dirty place.'

'I have never been there. And I do not think I plan to just at present. But perhaps a little ride into the countryside would be very welcome.'

Mrs Weston beamed, as though a thought had just occurred to her. 'But of course. Jake, who looks after the horses for Mr Weston, would be delighted to take you out for a little. Your maid could go too, if that would be thought more appropriate. What do you say to tomorrow?'

'I am supposed to be going shopping with my aunt.'

'Then the day after. I will arrange it.' Mrs Weston shivered. 'But I think we have had enough fresh air for one day. It is time to return indoors.' She stood up unsteadily, and Eleanor took her arm.

*

'Ride out, Miss?' Sarah looked doubtful. 'I don't know. Sounds – well – a bit strange.'

'Sarah, Mrs Weston has offered to arrange it with Jake. I need to know something of where we are. It could make so much difference to us. And it will be no bad thing for you to sit a horse again. It is quite a while since you have done so.'

Sarah grinned. 'I used to love it, when I first come to you. We don't seem to have done it for quite some while.'

'Too long,' said Eleanor emphatically. 'I will thank Mrs Weston, and on Wednesday we will enjoy our ride – and take careful note of where we are. Now, do you think I should wear the blue silk today?'

*

Francis stood before the bar of the Court of King's Bench in Westminster Hall. Just a week had gone by since Thomas's visit, a week in which he had spoken to nobody save his faithful Will, and had not ventured once beyond the little room that was his prison. All visits had been denied him, nor was he allowed to take any exercise. Once, looking out of the window on the winter sunshine, his heart gave a bound as he saw Henry Purcell in the courtyard below, holding his lute and gazing up at the tower. Francis called to him and waved, and Purcell responded by holding the lute aloft, but he was not admitted to Francis's prison. Will told him later that Purcell had demanded most urgently to see him, but had been denied.

True to what he had said to Thomas, he made determined efforts with the anthems Purcell had left with him, he took care with his attire, though there was none but Will to see him, and he ate his meals with every appearance of an appetite.

Will made gallant attempts to be cheerful, but Francis knew that he was unhappy, and this in no way contributed to his own confidence, which appeared to be steadily deserting him. He had no idea of how his trial would be conducted, or even when it would be until the day before. The suddenness of this startled him, and confirmed what Thomas had suggested might happen; that the Whigs were trying to rush the trial through before Parliament met, to keep the danger of the Popish Plot before the country. It was only just over a fortnight since he had been arrested, and he knew that it was not unusual for a man accused of such grave crimes to spend many weeks or even months in confinement before being brought to trial. The speed with which his own case was being conducted did nothing, in these circumstances, to bolster his courage.

He had been taken to Westminster by water, for which he had been grateful, for during the short walk from the water-stairs to the court-room he had been greeted with jeers and cries of derision, and hatred staring from a hundred pairs of eyes. What an anticlimax it would be for these people, he thought, if he succeeded in justifying himself.

So now he stood before his accusers and his judges, hoping he might find the wit and the wisdom to defend himself. He looked up and found himself staring straight into the penetrating blue eyes of Lord Chief Justice Scroggs, who returned his gaze with obvious dislike. Momentarily unnerved, he looked away and saw the members of the jury, looking self-conscious and important. Nearer him, at a table covered with papers, sat the counsel for the crown, the Attorney-General Cresswell Levinz and Sergeant Maynard, the King's Sergeant at Law. Longing for the sight of sympathetic faces, he looked further across the courtroom, but all he could see was row upon row of triumphant-looking Whigs, their blue ribbons much in evidence. Even milord of Shaftesbury was there, talking behind his hand to Lord Russell. But at last he noticed, tucked away in a box at the back of the courtroom, not only his father but his mother as well, who had made the journey from Cornwall in order to be with him. She sat poised as ever, her red hair carefully ringletted, her hands demurely in her lap, but

Francis could read the signs of strain and tension in her face. For their sakes, he thought, I must fight as hard as I can; for them and for Eleanor, who may not even know where I am. Thomas was with them, and Elizabeth and Nigel sat behind; Francis made a determined effort not to acknowledge Elizabeth's attempts to attract his attention. He could not rid himself of the notion that she was there mainly for entertainment.

'Silence!' The cryer's voice was suddenly heard above the hubbub, which dropped in volume a little. 'On pain of imprisonment!' continued the cryer, and the chattering ceased. Then the jury was called, and it was almost with surprise that Francis heard his own name, as he was told that if he wished to challenge any member of the jury he must do so before they were sworn. He did not see how he could benefit himself by doing so, and once the jury had been sworn the long indictment was read. A charge had been read at the examination before the Privy Council, but this was a longer, more embittered affair altogether. He was accused that he had intended 'wholly to deprive, depose, deject and disinherit our sovereign lord the King, totally destroy his power and bring our said sovereign lord the King to final death and destruction'; that he had 'falsely, deceitfully, advisedly, maliciously, devilishly and traitorously' conspired to alter the religion of the country as by law established and to make war upon the King in his realm of England.

It included many references to his visits to Coneybury, boldly asserting that he had conspired there with Sir Henry Somerville and his brother Anthony, a Jesuit priest. Francis was weary before it was done, and was afraid that his concentration would begin to flag, though his trial was but beginning.

'Francis, Baron Trenoweth,' he was asked at last, 'do you plead guilty to these crimes whereof you stand indicted, or not guilty?'

'Not guilty,' answered Francis firmly, looking straight at his parents. He was rewarded with the shadow of a smile from his mother.

'And how will you be tried?'

'By God and my country.' At least he knew enough of procedure to get that right.

The Attorney-General now rose, coughed ominously and rustled the sheaf of papers in his hand until all eyes were directed upon him.

'May it please your lordship, and you gentlemen of the jury,' he began, 'The prisoner at the bar stands indicted for no less than for an attempt to murder the King, change the government of the nation and the religion as is by law established. This is the charge in general of the indictment. We will proceed unto particulars.

'It may seem strange and not reasonable that a private gentleman such as the prisoner at the bar should have such vast and great designs, but it is not himself alone, he is employed by others who would call in foreign help to achieve their wicked designs. He was their tool, but a traitorous tool, for he knew what designs were intended, and in what misery it would place us all, and he co-operated willingly in all their vile conspiracies.

'On November 29th last the prisoner was introduced by his cousin, Robert Carey, to the household of Sir Henry Somerville, a noted papist. This visit was to be the first of many, and on one such occasion he accepted from Sir Henry the sum of £8,000 to take the King's life. An army of papists, aided by mercenaries from France and Ireland, would then arise and enforce idolatrous obedience to the tenets of Rome, regarded as anti-Christ by so many Christians.' Francis's knuckles whitened as he clenched the bar in front of him, but he said nothing. Surely this was all too patently a farrago of lies to be believed?

'All this time,' continued the Attorney-General, 'the prisoner maintained his position as an innocent undergraduate, explaining his many disappearances from Oxford by saying that he was paying court to a lady.' He paused, to allow the ribald laughter encouraged by the Whigs to run its course. 'To a lady, of course! A fine lady, none other than the Whore of Rome, my lord! This traitor before you wished to conceal his abhorrent designs by masquerading as a love-sick boy.

'Some honest men in Oxford, fortunately, saw through this mask of deception, though it must be admitted that they allowed their zeal to outrun their discretion when they set their apprentices on to him in the hopes of ending his infamous schemes by ending his life. In this they were unsuccessful, and the prisoner, when he had sufficiently recovered from the battering he received – ' Another pause here, as laughter from the Whigs engulfed the court – 'fled to London. His treason did not end here, however, for he used family connections to gain admittance to the counsels of the Whigs,' – a protracted stare here at Sir Thomas Carey, who returned his gaze unblinkingly – ' and thus learn of the plans being laid for the Parliament due shortly to meet in Oxford. This was their opportunity, of course; whatever they had intended earlier, the announcement of a Parliament to meet in Oxford caused them to rethink their plans.

'When he had gained sufficient knowledge, or thought he had, the prisoner returned to Oxford to impart it to his fellow conspirators. By this time the authorities in Oxford were already suspicious of activities at Coneybury, Sir Henry Somerville's house, but when the magistrate was at last able to order a search Sir Henry had already taken his family into hiding. Why the prisoner came riding to the house on the day of his arrest we shall probably never know, but he came to find the magistrate and his men searching the house and was arrested. Two days later Robert Carey arrived at the justice's house and was able to give clear evidence of the prisoner's guilt.' Francis started at this. He had not known that Robert's perfidy had started so soon.

'Nor is he the only witness, my lord. Two of Sir Henry's servants have volunteered information pointing clearly to the prisoner's guilt. One overheard him discussing with Sir Henry when the King was to be "taken off"; the other saw him in earnest conversation with Anthony Somerville in a highly suspicious way.

'It is impossible for me to over-emphasise the gravity of the prisoner's crimes, as it is impossible for any sentence passed on him to be too severe. Several have already died in recent months on similar charges, but it seems their deaths were not enough to deter the wickedness of others. All honest men must shudder at the thought of what might be happening were the prisoner not now in custody; well might we then have cried "41 is come again". The nation would have been plunged into the agonies of rebellion once more, the massacre of innocents and enslavement of free men would have been daily occurrences. Let us with thankful hearts praise God that the prisoner was arrested ere his mischief was complete, and let us condemn him for his crime both as a punishment to himself and as a warning to others.'

Apart from the laughter, the Attorney-General had been listened to without interruption; even the Lord Chief Justice had not seen fit to break the flow of his remarks. Francis scanned the faces in the court; his anxious family, the impassive faces of the jury, smiling, eager Whigs. Sergeant Maynard now rose and made a speech on the safety of the nation, showing how there was a definite connection between all the earlier Popish Plot trials and that now before them. No honest man, he said, would be able to leave his house without fear if the prisoner at the bar were allowed to go free again. Francis felt his heart sink as he looked at the satisfied, approving faces of the Whigs, the jury clearly impressed with what was being said. Knowledge of your own innocence seemed small consolation in the face of such prejudice.

The first witness was Harry Jenkin, a gardener employed by Sir Henry. He looked nervous, and though dressed in faded worsted Francis suspected it was nevertheless the best clothes he had.

'Do you recognise the prisoner at the bar?' the Attorney-General asked.

'Aye. Seen him at Coneybury quite a bit. After boss's young lass.'

'Quite. Did you ever see him with anybody else?'

'I did that. Early in December it was. Still a fair bit of work outside, even then. I were sweeping the path in front of the house when this young feller comes down the steps with boss's brother. Talking a fair bit, they was, so's they didn't see me at first. When they did, though – you should have seen them jump apart! Made me wonder quite a bit, I don't mind telling you.'

'Did you see any more of them?'

'I were a bit curious, I don't mind admitting. So I follows them round the corner, an' there they was, talking together as though they couldn't get enough of it. You mark my words, Harry, I said, them two is up to something. So I follows 'em. Couldn't hear much, but Mr Somerville said summat about needing to do away with the king, an' young feller said it'd have to be done.' Harry smirked and looked remarkably pleased with himself.

'Does the prisoner wish to ask the witness anything?' asked the Lord Chief Justice wearily.

'Yes,' said Francis. 'Mr Jenkin, you say you saw me talking to Mr Somerville on the front steps of Coneybury in early December?'

'Aye. I said so.'

'Your memory conflicts significantly with mine. I well remember visiting Coneybury in early December, but the only time I saw Mr Somerville at all was at the dinner table. The person you saw me in close conversation with was Miss Somerville.'

'Don't look much like her dad's brother,' remarked Jenkin, to general laughter in the court.

'I agree. How much are you being paid, Mr Jenkin, to suggest that I was holding a suspicious conversation like that?'

'Paid? Boss pays me wage, that's all. Nobody pays me nothing for saying I saw what I saw.'

'Then perhaps you are fearful of losing your job. For I was never in conversation with Mr Somerville as you suggest.'

'If all the prisoner wishes to do is to deny the witness's evidence,' said Scroggs, 'I think we will now have the next witness. Thank you, Mr Jenkin.'

Jenkin stepped down, looking thoroughly pleased, and Robert Carey was called to give evidence. He walked jauntily, his lace cuffs immaculate, his blue satin coat looking exquisite. Francis glanced to the box where his family were sitting, and saw the muscles tighten on Thomas's face as Robert took the oath in a voice that rang with authority. The Attorney-General rose and addressed himself to the witness.

'You are first cousin to the prisoner at the bar?'

'I am.'

'And you were responsible for introducing him to the household of Sir Henry Somerville?'

'I see now what a terrible mistake it was,' said Robert. 'But I knew Sir Henry, and Francis – the prisoner – seemed so eager to be introduced that I felt it would have been churlish to refuse.'

'But it is a lie!' cried Francis. 'It was he who wished me to come to Coneybury; I had never heard of Sir Henry Somerville until he begged me to come with him.'

'You will have your opportunity to cross-examine the witness,' said the Lord Chief Justice coldly. 'Continue, please, Mr Levinz.'

'Thank you, my lord. But perhaps it would be best if the witness told his story in his own words.'

'Very well. So you agreed to take your cousin to Coneybury, Mr Carey?'

'I did; and he was exceeding well received by Sir Henry. I knew, of course, that the baronet was a papist, but thought this to be an entirely private matter between himself and his conscience; I certainly did not know of a Jesuit priest in the house. But Francis met him that same day and had much conversation with him. Many times he returned in the next few weeks; sometimes I accompanied him, for I was anxious as to what he might be doing. I had heard some vague talk of a plot to set the Duke on the throne, but nothing definite, and I thought it best to bide my time, and hope that nothing would come of it. But it was plain that something was being planned, and Sir Henry knew that I was of the Duke's household, and therefore possibly in a position to help him.'

'You had expressed yourself as desiring the death of His Majesty?'

Robert blushed. 'I was at the time a Roman Catholic,' he admitted. 'And I fear that after too good a dinner I said something indiscreet about the glorious future in store for us when the Duke should reign. It was rash of me, I know, and I repented the words at once. I feared then not to serve Sir Henry, for I did not know if my words could be accounted treasonable. I thought perhaps that if I made pretence of helping him my rash words might be forgiven me if I were able to warn His Majesty of a plot against his life.'

'You hoped, in short, to buy your pardon by betraying those you had pretended to befriend?' The Lord Chief Justice's voice was like ice.

'I sought to expose the treason I saw being plotted in front of me. I made my peace with the Church as soon as possible after that.'

Francis stared at his cousin, uncomprehending. His tale was so confidently told it might almost be true. Grimly he realised that there was no-one to witness on his behalf, so it was his word against Robert's. Since he was at the bar and Robert at the witness stand, Francis knew with a dull certainty who would be believed.

'Some weeks after that first meeting,' continued Robert, 'Sir Henry called Francis into his private cabinet. Feeling that perhaps I should hear their conversation, I slipped in before them and concealed myself behind a curtain. I heard Sir Henry offer my cousin the sum of eight thousand pounds to slay His Majesty, either by shooting or by poison. The prisoner demurred that the money was but small for so great a risk, but consented when he was told that he would also receive in marriage Sir Henry's only child, Eleanor Somerville.'

'So great a falsehood can surely not pass unchallenged,' cried Francis, heedless of the stern looks he drew upon himself. 'Whatever treason was being plotted in that house, Miss Somerville was innocent of it.'

'You admit that she was to be your prize, then?' asked Sergeant Maynard quickly.

'Most certainly not. When I first came to the house I did not even know that they were Papists. I returned to find out, if I could, whether there was any substance in a plot, and yes, to protect Eleanor from its effects if I could.'

'By committing foul treason with her father, it seems,' commented the Attorney-General. 'But let us hear your cousin out; he is being most patient with these interruptions.'

'Two days later,' said Robert, 'I dined with my cousin in Oxford, and after he was well wined he began to boast of the debt the nation would owe him when he had "taken off" the King. I besought him to think again, not to proceed with such wickedness, but he would not listen to me.'

'Then why,' asked Lord Chief Justice Scroggs suddenly, 'did you not bring this information to the Privy Council at once, instead of waiting nearly three months, during which time His Majesty might have been slain?'

Robert hesitated for a moment. 'I was still fearful that my own earlier words might be accounted treasonable. My knowledge of the law is so slender that I did not know whether what I had heard was merely hearsay, and so could not be considered evidence. And – naturally I was reluctant to bring such grave charges against one so closely akin to me.'

'Yet you have now overcome your reluctance?' asked the Attorney-General.

'When I heard of my cousin's arrest it seemed clear that I must tell all I knew of the affair.'

'You took no part yourself in this plot you say you strove to avert?'

'It was plain that I knew of their plans, but since I had done nothing, they assumed I must be sympathetic. Then when Fran - when the prisoner fled to London I hoped it might be the end of it. But he returned, and I was asked if I would act as a messenger between them. It seemed that here was an opportunity to thwart their plans – I took the information from my cousin, but forebore to pass it on to Anthony Somerville.'

'What was the information your cousin was obtaining?'

'Merely the arrangements for housing those who would be coming to Oxford for the Parliament. But Mr Somerville appeared to set great store by it.'

'Hardly treasonable in itself,' said Scroggs. 'But if you did not pass this information on, how is it that a detailed list of lodging arrangements for the Parliament in Oxford was found in Sir Henry Somerville's house?'

Robert began to bluster. There were other ways in which Sir Henry could have found out – Francis might have ridden there himself. When told that all Francis's movements had been closely watched since his return to Oxford he suggested that one of Sir Henry's servants might have been spying for him.

Robert submitted to questioning for a further half hour, but though he had been shaken on this one point, the central, damning part of his evidence remained: the interview with Sir Henry and the alleged offer of money, the fictitious boast over dinner. At the end of this Francis was grudgingly told he might put questions to the witness, and the two cousins faced each other, but it was Robert who looked away first, Robert whose eyes betrayed his fear.

'I would ask my cousin,' said Francis clearly, 'if he recalls our first meeting in Oxford, about a week before my introduction to Sir Henry Somerville?'

'Certainly,' replied Robert. 'You were moving a little stiffly, and your face was a most interesting colour.'

'It was shortly after November 17th,' said Francis. 'I had taken part in the pope-burning procession organised by the scholars, to demonstrate my abhorrence of this plot and the slavery to which the plotters would commit us.'

'A piece of deception remarkable in one so young,' said Sir William Jones quickly. 'That can easily have been the merest subterfuge.'

'But my cousin knows it was not,' replied Francis. 'For when he first suggested I should come with him to Coneybury I was reluctant, even though I knew nothing about the house, or even that Sir Henry was a papist at all. What he says about my being so eager to go there is simply not true.'

'Yet you returned to the house many times.'

'As I have said, I wished to find out if treason was being plotted – and to protect Miss Somerville if I could.'

'Then it was the offer of her hand, was it, that led you to accept Sir Henry's bribe?' asked Sergeant Maynard.

'I accepted no bribe!' cried Francis. 'I would ask my cousin why, if he was not intimately concerned with Anthony Somerville's plans, he came to the magistrate's house so shortly after my arrest. Did you have your elaborate story ready to tall the justice? Or did you make it up as you went along?'

'I – yes – of course,' stammered Robert. 'I had decided that I would make one final appeal to you and Sir Henry to stop this treason, and if I was unsuccessful then I must lay the facts I knew before the Privy Council. At Coneybury I was told that you were already under arrest at the justice's house. I therefore did the only thing I could, and told the magistrate what I knew of your activities.'

Francis was silent. His knowledge of the law was so slender that he feared he might only prejudice his chances by spending too long trying to trip his cousin. Already Robert had made two slips, but in the witness box it seemed this was allowed; at the bar it was tantamount to an admission of guilt.

The leader of the men who had accompanied the magistrate to Coneybury and who had brought Francis to London was the next witness. Francis blushed as he heard his futile attempt to resist arrest related; it had been a moment of desperation, not of guilt. He glanced up to where his father was sitting, and was rewarded by the shadow of a smile. Lord Bodmin had his own recollections of such flashes of temper. There was no need for Francis to cross-examine this witness, but Sir Henry's footman was a different matter. He declared he had overheard Francis and Sir Henry discussing when the King should be 'taken off', and gave as the date of this conversation December 15th. Francis seized his advantage.

'I do not know if the apprentices who attacked me are in the court,' he said, 'but I am sure my cousin can vouch that it was only the day before this that I was beaten and thrown into the river as though dead. Instead of plotting treason at Coneybury, on the day he mentions I lay in bed at Magdalen College, barely conscious.'

The man grew flustered, muttered something about having the day wrong, it might have been some days earlier, but he made an unconvincing witness. Francis had scored a point.

The man who had been detailed to watch his movements, however, had been thorough indeed. His journey to Coneybury was noted exactly, as was Robert's visiting him in his college. After Robert's evidence this appeared in quite a different light.

Francis grew gradually more and more dispirited. No adjournment for refreshment took place, and as the day wore on, compelled to remain standing for many hours, he knew his concentration was flagging as his mouth became dry and hunger pangs gnawed at him. There were no witnesses to vouch for him; he had not been told that he was allowed to call any, and when he asked if Sir Thomas Carey might witness on his behalf he was told that it was not possible as he had not given prior warning. The best he could hope for was to throw doubts upon the evidence of those who had been called. But though he could point out an inconsistency here, an incorrect item of information there, the weight of the evidence was too great to be set aside unless Robert's perjury could be proved. He alone, of those called to give evidence, knew that he was helping in the destruction of an innocent man, he alone wished his own actions to lie forgotten and hidden.

The questioning directed to Francis was reminiscent of his examination by the Privy Council. His guilt seemed already assumed.

'Are we expected to believe,' asked the Attorney General, 'that you journeyed to this house many times solely on account of an attractive maiden?'

'Men have travelled further for less,' replied Francis steadily. 'But this was not my sole reason; I wanted to find if treason was being plotted, so that if I went to the authorities I would have proper information.'

'You admit, then, that you shared her faith; that you were a papist?'

'I admit nothing of the sort. I spoke on matters of faith with Miss Somerville, and we were learning to understand each other. It was she who alerted me to the possibility of treason at Coneybury.'

'In what way?'

'She was unhappy with the "atmosphere" at the house. She could not be more specific, but I know that she was afraid of what her uncle and father might be doing. She also intimated – '

'Yes?'

'She believed that there was a relationship of an intimate nature between my cousin Robert Carey and her uncle, Anthony Somerville.'

For a moment there was silence in the court. Then Lord Chief Justice Scroggs turned his pale eyes straight at Francis.

'I think we will treat that remark with the contempt it deserves. It is as well that Mr Carey has already left the court. I am sure that it would pain him to hear such an unwarranted allegation.'

'On more than one occasion I saw him coming out of Mr Somerville's room late at night.' Francis was conscious that he was unlikely to make any impression, but he had to try.

'That proves nothing. Your cousin has given his evidence in all good faith. You cannot undermine him now.'

'Why did you ride to Coneybury on the day of your arrest?' asked the Attorney-General suddenly.

'I had received an invitation from Sir Henry – verbally, through my cousin. It seemed entirely genuine, and I was naturally pleased at the thought of seeing Miss Somerville again.'

'I see. Does it not seem strange, to invite a man to your house and then not be there to receive him?'

'Of course it does. I realise now that it was a trap.'

'There are other ways of looking at it. Your cousin denies ever passing this invitation to you. I would suggest that either you rode there to consult further with Sir Henry Somerville in the matter of the treason you were plotting together, or that, knowing him to be absent from the house, you saw your chance of removing vital evidence.'

'There was no evidence relating to myself there,' said Francis wearily. 'I would not be standing here at all, but for my cousin's perjury.'

'Enough!' cried the Lord Chief Justice. 'It is for the court to decide whether any of the witnesses have perjured themselves. You cannot throw doubt on your cousin's story in that way.'

The questioning finished at last, and the Attorney-General rose to sum up the case for the prosecution. Francis's knuckles whitened as he heard the now familiar tale re-told, his eager co-operation with treason asserted, his desire to expose it laughed to scorn. In spite of all Sir William's eloquence, it was evident that the part of the case relating to subverting the government and bringing in popery rested mainly on supposition, but Sir William sounded confident of persuading the jury that the prisoner was indeed guilty of being engaged in a conspiracy to slay His Majesty the King. There was ample evidence before them to convict the prisoner of high treason.

The Attorney-General finished at last, and a pause ensued before the Lord Chief Justice began his summing-up. Really, thought Francis, it hardly seems necessary now. The jury can hardly fail to find me guilty. Is there no way now that I can save my life? He looked up to the box where his parents were sitting with Thomas. His mother looked drawn and strained, and his father's face was drained of colour. Elizabeth and Nigel looked, if possible, slightly bored. Thomas was clearly trying to attract his attention and smile encouragement, but Francis was now too rigid with tension to smile back.

'Gentlemen of the jury,' began Scroggs, pressing the tips of his fingers together and directing his gaze full upon them, 'my care shall be to contract this very long evidence so you may consider only what is material. The prisoner claims he made his many visits to this popish household to expose treason and to pay court to a lady, a lady he does not trouble to deny was a papist herself, though he refuses any suggestion that he himself was tainted with the doctrines of Rome. We have evidence, however, evidence of three witnesses that he was well received by Sir Henry Somerville and his Jesuit brother, and was in fact plotting treason with them. Is it likely that he was not a Papist too? It is strange, certainly, that one brought up so loyal a Protestant should deviate in this way, for no man of understanding, but for by-ends, would have left his religion to become a papist.

'But here we have the core of it: the prisoner allowed himself to be ruled by his selfish desires. His pension was his conscience, his proffered bride his bait. He does not deny that he visited this house many times, that he associated with papists there. How can he deny the rest of his treason? It has been declared to you on oath that he accepted a bribe to slay the King, and more than one witness asserts that he heard him talk about "taking off" His Majesty. How is this paying court to a lady? Not unless that lady be indeed the Whore of Rome may we begin to understand it. Why should an innocent man seek to help one he suspects of being a traitor by gathering information for him? Why should an innocent man make such a desperate attempt to resist arrest?

'I will not go through the evidence of the witnesses again, for what they said was plain enough. Only by agreeing with the prisoner that they have perjured themselves can their evidence be disproved.

'If you believe the prisoner's assertion that all the witnesses have perjured themselves, then you must lay your hand upon your heart and find him not guilty of these vile charges. But if you believe he was endeavouring to end the life of our sovereign lord the King and bring popery into England, as several witnesses have told you, then you must not let pity sway you from your duty, nor compassion prevent you bringing a verdict of guilty against the prisoner. He comes of a noble house, and one which has hitherto set an unrivalled example of loyalty; but nobler than he have already perished for crimes in this traitorous plot.'

Francis stood immovable before the bar, rigid and tense. Five people in all that hostile courtroom had any compassion for him, and they were powerless to help him. He looked up to where his family was sitting and tried to smile, but a sob came to his throat the moment he tried to move his lips, and he looked away without seeing his mother's tears. He thought instead of Eleanor, wondering whether she was still safe. Why Anthony Somerville wished him dead he still had no idea, but he could not entertain the idea that Eleanor might be party to his destruction. For if the jury found him guilty, he knew that he would be condemned to die in a manner almost unthinkable. For a moment the horror of it was insupportable, and he clenched the bar in front of him in a desperate attempt to prevent himself falling.

The jury withdrew at last to consider their verdict, and excited chatter broke out at once, seeming to have nothing to do with the trial or with Francis. Indeed, he was largely ignored now, for the sport he had given was almost over, and there was nothing more he could do except cower when the verdict was pronounced. The Lord Chief Justice was busy with some papers, counsel yawned and talked to each other, men came and went with complete freedom. Francis watched them all with fierce concentration, anything rather than look up at his family now. For if he did that, he felt that he would break down altogether. Should a guilty verdict be returned, he would have somehow to find the strength to walk from the courtroom.

After what seemed an age, but was in fact a brief half-hour, the jury returned, and Francis's sudden, desperate hope faded as he saw their set, determined faces.

'Gentlemen of the jury,' intoned the clerk mournfully, 'are you all agreed of your verdict?'

'We are,' replied the foreman.

'Francis, Baron Trenoweth, hold up your hand,' continued the clerk. 'Is Francis Trenoweth guilty of the high treason whereof he stands indicted, or not guilty?'

The foreman looked up and paused for a moment as he stared straight at Francis. 'Guilty,' he declared.

An excited murmur at once ran around the courtroom, and many of the Whigs were smiling triumphantly. Francis permitted himself a glance towards his family, and for a curious, unreal second he thought that his mother was asleep. Then he realised that she had fainted, and was being supported by his father's arm. Francis looked at Thomas, who responded with a bleak smile. But Francis was suddenly determined that he would not give way. He knew now that he stood before the bar a convicted criminal, and that he had lost the fight to save his life, but the knowledge itself brought into being a courage he had not known he possessed. These men would kill him, but then their malice would be at an end. And he could at least withhold from them the satisfaction of seeing his fear.

'What goods, chattels, lands or tenements had the prisoner at the time of his arrest?' enquired the clerk.

'None to our knowledge,' replied the foreman.

The Lord Chief Justice paused for a long moment, then directed that Francis be returned to the Tower, and brought to court again the next day to receive his sentence. As he was led from the court Francis held his head erect, though he dared not look at his family. He knew only too well what the morrow would bring, and hoped that his mother would not be there to hear such fearful words spoken. The cries of 'traitor!' were doubly virulent now, as word had quickly passed to the crowds outside that he had been condemned. For the first time he was thankful for the protection of his guards, or he would have been trampled to death.

Will was waiting to serve him his supper, Will who could not keep the tears from running down his face as he waited on his master. Francis nearly broke down himself; his new-found courage could endure the jeers of an ignorant rabble, but not the tears of those who loved him. He laid his hand on Will's shoulder and smiled at him.

'Ah, my lord,' murmured Will. 'If there is justice in heaven – '

'I shall soon find peace and rest,' continued Francis. 'It does no good to mourn. We must look to the future; mine is now beyond the grave.'

Chapter Sixteen

Anthony sat beside the fire in his chamber, which was clearly the best in the house. He wore a long purple velvet gown, his wig curled either side of his face, which was clean-shaven. His feet, encased in soft slippers, peeped out from under the hem of his gown. He looked entirely comfortable.

Robert, the other side of the fireplace, wore a faded homespun coat over a once-white shirt. Torn breeches ended just below his knees, while bare feet were tucked into boots that held several holes. He had discarded his wig, and his cropped brown hair looked dirty and lifeless. His face, none too clean, bore the stubble of one who had not shaved that day, or perhaps the day before either.

'I am delighted that you have avoided detection in this way.' Anthony's voice was clipped. 'But now that you are here it is perfectly possible for you to dress in a more appropriate manner. You were ever one for elegance.'

Robert looked up at him in abject misery. 'He is condemned.' His voice was scarce above a whisper. 'I was not in the court at that point, but I heard it.'

'Of course he is condemned. How could it be otherwise with your evidence? Jenkin was just to corroborate you: the court will not convict on the evidence of only one witness.'

'Francis is my cousin. I have killed him just as surely as if I had run my sword through him. Worse, for he will be sentenced to drawing and quartering.'

'Sentenced, yes, but it will not happen that way. He will be beheaded, which will be just as quick as your sword.'

'He will be just as dead. And he has not committed a crime.'

Anthony sighed. 'How many more times will I have to explain this to you? We are so near achieving our great design. Sacrifices must be made.'

'I still do not understand why Francis has to be part of that sacrifice.'

'Robert, Robert.' With infinite care Anthony removed a single pale thread from his darker robe. 'Our great design is coming together beautifully. It is far too late to draw back now.'

'I wish I had never introduced him to Coneybury.'

'But you did. And he has been useful. Even his trial has bought us valuable time. They were not bothering to look for us when they believed your cousin could tell them where we were. And of course we had ensured that he did not know.'

'Then why – '

'He was getting too close. If he had gone to the Privy Council we could all have found ourselves in his position. I believe he was getting near to that.'

'You think he would have betrayed us?'

'He would not have seen it as betrayal. To your cousin it would have been some noble aim of safeguarding the realm, protecting the King, declaring his loyalty. He will probably see himself as a martyr now.'

Robert clenched his hands tightly together. 'Have I not betrayed myself by denying my faith, perjuring myself and helping in the destruction of an innocent man?'

Anthony took hold of his clenched hands and parted them gently. His eyes glittered, and Robert knew real fear even as he thrilled to the touch of Anthony's hands.

'When this country is safe in her obedience to the one true faith you will have played a significant part in bringing that about. That will absolve you from any actions you may have taken in doing so. You have, of course, described both me and my brother as traitors. Don't worry; I told you to do it, and I am sure you did it well. Do not forget the part that I must play myself barely two weeks hence.'

'You are ready for this?'

'Oh, yes. There will be many others in Oxford, but I shall feel justified if the final stroke is mine alone.'

'But – will you not be seized?'

'Of course. But we have contacts all over the country, ready to rise as soon as the King is dead. What do you think I have been doing, while you were enjoying yourself at court, and waiting on his grace of York? While the country is in a state of confusion, we shall take control. There are even troops poised in France and Ireland. Mark my words, the true faith will be restored to this country. I shall not be held for very long.'

Robert looked at him in admiration. 'You are braver than I. I am still tortured by guilt over Francis. And there is still the matter of telling Eleanor. She will have to know.'

'That may not be as difficult as you imagine. She is coming to realise that our faith is under threat, and that perhaps your cousin and others like him are part of that threat. But you should not be the one to tell her.'

'You?'

'I think this is a task that her father can usefully perform. I am no great admirer of my elder brother's abilities, but he genuinely cares for his daughter. And he will do what I ask of him.'

Robert sat silent for a moment. 'I hear all that you are saying to me,' he said. 'But I cannot rid myself of this overwhelming sense of guilt.'

Anthony stood up. 'Then I will be the priest for a little. We cannot go to church, but the prayer desk here has served before. Kneel and make confession, and I will give you absolution.'

Robert hesitated, then moved to the prayer desk with hunched shoulders and the gait of an old man.

*

Francis sat alone, locked in his little room in the tower, his head in his hands. His court appearance that morning had lasted perhaps half an hour, but it had seemed to him the longest half-hour of his life. Yesterday he thought he had found courage, but today, with the words of the Lord Chief Justice pronouncing sentence upon him ringing in his ears, he knew that he was devastated. Worse, he knew that he had allowed his enemies to see his fear. How could a man possibly listen to such dreadful words and remain unmoved? Francis shuddered. This, then, was the end. No speedy withdrawal, no single stroke, but the gallows, the drawing and the quartering block.

Only too clearly he could hear Lord Chief Justice Scroggs contemptuously advising him to diminish his guilt by making a full confession, even while assuring him that he could not hope to obtain a pardon in this way, that his life was irredeemably forfeit. Francis bit his knuckles in an endeavour to prevent panic arising.

'If you cannot with our Church,' Scroggs had pompously recommended, 'make use of contrition, which is sorrow arising from love, pray make use of attrition, which is sorrow arising from fear.' But how could he repent of a crime he had not committed? And how make confession of what were not his own actions?

Then had followed the terrible sentence, and though Francis had known it would be pronounced, he writhed within himself as he heard the tortures he must suffer described to him. His parents were not in court that day, but

Thomas was, and Francis saw the blood drain from his cousin's face as he was condemned to

'Be conveyed from hence to the place from whence you came, and that you be conveyed from thence on hurdles to the place of execution, where you are to be hanged by the neck; that you be cut down alive, that your privy members be cut off, your bowels taken out and burnt in your view; that your head be severed from your body; that your body to be divided into four quarters, to be disposed of at the King's pleasure; and the God of infinite mercy have mercy on your soul.'

Somehow Francis managed to avoid passing out altogether; somehow he managed to walk from the courtroom. It was only when he was returned to the Tower that he broke down, turning Will aside roughly, ignoring his dinner and almost wishing he could be led at once to execution, so as to fear it no longer.

Never before had he felt so utterly lonely. Eleanor was now forever beyond his reach; perhaps she would forget him soon. His parents, he suspected, were too broken-hearted by his condemnation to come to him; even God no longer seemed to be near. Should not a merciful God have saved him from such a hideous fate? Mr Purcell would make music at the Chapel Royal without him; his brother Edward would become their father's heir and eventually inherit Pelistry. The biting of his knuckles no longer served, and Francis wept, cradling his head like a child.

For a long while he sat thus, rocking himself to and fro, his body racked with sobs, face and chest aching with the effort of it. He even wondered if he had the means to end his own life at once, to die painlessly and privately here rather than shamefully in public at Tyburn. But then he thought of Eleanor, of his parents, of Will. They knew he had been unjustly condemned, and would grieve at his death, but at least they should not remember him as a coward, as one who in fear of his fate took his own life. He might never conquer his fear, but he would take the greatest care not to show it to those he loved.

At last the aching loneliness passed. God was merciful, he realised slowly, and God had not forsaken him. His death was now a settled thing, but surely that was not the end of everything? 'And the God of infinite mercy have mercy on your soul,' the Chief Justice had intoned. Even his enemies did not question the mercy of God, his willingness to receive a penitent sinner. His overstrung nerves relaxed a little, to the point where sleep was possible.

He awoke to the sound of the key in the lock, and realised that he had slept through the night. A gaoler stood by to let Will in with his breakfast, locking the door again at once. Will set his tray down and walked into the bedchamber.

'You did not eat your supper yesterday,' he said reprovingly, as Francis sat up in bed.

'You must not reproach me for such omissions now,' said Francis with a smile. 'I have little time to attend to my health.'

'But eat your breakfast now,' pleaded Will. 'The days will be arduous for you, and you will need your strength to the end.'

Francis dressed and meekly did as he was bid, picking absently at his food and asking Will how he was being treated.

'Fairly, my lord. A servant is expected to be loyal. Indeed – '

'Yes?' queried Francis sharply.

'All the servants believe the verdict was just, my lord. None wish to be called upon to serve you. But I do not heed them.'

'Nor I,' replied Francis with a sudden laugh. 'I have already withstood jeers and hatred, and shall have to again ere I am done.'

Francis sat by the window after Will had left him, looking down at the ravens in the courtyard below. It was not a great deal later, however, that he heard the rattle of keys again and Lord and Lady Bodmin entered the room. If Francis had been concerned at his father's appearance when last they met, he was doubly so now. Deep lines tugged at the corners of his mouth, refusing the smile that had been almost habitual, shadows round the eyes told of nights of worry. Even the flamboyance in dress had gone, and Lord Bodmin appeared in a suit of sober black. Francis felt almost guilty, that in some way he had let them down.

But it was for his mother that he felt the greater sorrow. Her auburn hair was carefully ringletted, her skin clear, her turquoise taffeta gown entirely right. But Francis could see at once the fear in her eyes, the way she could hardly bear to let go of his father's arm, and he knew that she was tormented with grief. The last time he had seen her she had fainted at the shock of his condemnation. It seemed as though she had barely recovered. Suddenly Francis realised that he would have to be the one to comfort his parents, rather than the other way about. He must reconcile himself to dying, but they were going to have to find a way to live – without him. He crossed the room and, smiling, took his mother in his arms. She put her hand up and touched his face, stroked his hair.

'You have lost weight,' she said, and it sounded as though speech were an effort. 'You look so much older. Still my Francis, and yet – so changed.'

'Will is doing his best to look after me,' said Francis. 'He would have me feasting every day if he could.' He released her gently from his embrace, and guided her to the one chair as though she were an invalid, turning then to his father, who stood by the window watching them both. Francis looked up at him, and raised his eyebrows enquiringly.

'Now that – the trial – is over, we have been permitted to see you,' said Lord Bodmin. 'It was not possible earlier.'

'So Thomas told me,' replied Francis. 'It seems they were afraid that I might learn how to defend myself.'

'I waited on the King yesterday,' said his father. 'He is aware that all the evidence given at your trial may not have been entirely accurate, but – '

'But I have been condemned by a court acting in his name,' continued Francis. 'I know, Father. His Majesty cannot pardon me now.'

'No,' agreed Lord Bodmin. 'I know he believes you innocent, but he cannot even allow himself to say so. But at least you need not fear – the pains – to which you were sentenced yesterday. The King will commute the sentence to beheading, and the Whigs will not grumble. They can afford to be generous on that score.'

'Generous!' cried Lady Bodmin suddenly and vehemently. 'How can it be generous to put to death a man who has committed no crime?'

'In truth it is a load from my mind, Mother,' said Francis at once. 'I *did* fear – the drawing at Tyburn. Death itself seems a little thing in comparison.'

She reached for his hand, and held it to her cheek. 'Your courage is greater than mine, Francis,' she said. 'And I must not add to what you already have to bear. At least you have my love, and my belief in your innocence.'

'I intend to have your portrait painted,' said Lord Bodmin suddenly. 'I wish to hang it at Pelistry. The artist will probably be with you this afternoon, as he must have sufficient time to gain a fair likeness.'

'Time,' said Francis. 'Have you discovered – have they – has a date been set?'

'I fear it has,' said Lord Bodmin. 'Unless – unless a miracle occurs, sentence will be carried out a week from tomorrow, that is on Friday of next week.'

'And Parliament meets on the Monday,' murmured Francis. 'They have indeed timed it well. But I am prepared. If they look for a confession on the scaffold, then they will be disappointed.'

'Thomas is hoping to trace Sir Henry Somerville and his brother.' Lord Bodmin stood and looked out of the window. 'But nobody knows where Sir Henry is, and Robert disappeared immediately after the trial.'

'Probably back to wherever Anthony is, if he knew he could get there undetected,' said Francis. 'I wish with all my heart that I knew where they were.'

'Eleanor shall know that you were steadfast. I promise you that.' Lord Bodmin smiled at his son, and Francis responded in grateful recognition of the fact that he knew he had been understood.

'I think it unlikely that we shall find them.' Francis was surprised at how calm he sounded. 'I believe they had prepared this hiding place some while ago now, and are unlikely to stir from it until after I am dead – if their plans prosper, then until after the King is dead as well.'

Lord Bodmin was silent for a little. 'What you say may be true,' he said. 'But it does no harm to search.' He stood up. 'We shall come to you again,' he continued. 'And I know that Thomas will too. Elizabeth and Nigel too, I expect. For all Nigel's – infatuation – with the Duke of Monmouth, I believe that he means well.'

'The infatuation is just as much on Elizabeth's side.' Francis smiled at his mother. 'She seems to need constant excitement.'

Lord Bodmin sighed. 'I know. Your brother Edward knows what has happened, though he will not, of course, have heard of the verdict yet. Catherine will have to be told now, though I dread the telling. She is only ten.'

'She will survive,' said Francis. 'She will probably regard it as being thoroughly exciting, having a brother executed for treason.' Lady Bodmin looked up at him sharply, but failed to match the smile on his face.

They left soon after, promising to return the next day. Lord Bodmin laid his hand on his son's shoulder in a pathetic gesture of affection, but Francis noticed that his mother could hardly bear to look back to see the door closed and locked between them.

After his dinner Francis changed into his crimson velvet coat and breeches, putting them over a silk shirt with much lace. Will polished his paste-buckled shoes, and set a feathered beaver close to his hand. Francis smiled. He was determined to look his best for his portrait; his father must not be confronted by a ragged, fearful prisoner every time he looked at it.

At the sound of the door being opened Francis turned, expecting it to be the artist his father had selected. He was surprised and delighted to find himself confronted by the thoroughly business-like figure of Henry Purcell.

'I am not come to commiserate,' said Purcell briskly. 'That would be a waste of time. I believe that a great injustice is being perpetrated. You are innocent, I know, but more powerful men than I have decided that it would be politic to sacrifice you. What I plan to do it to make music with you, for as long as I am allowed, as often as I am allowed. I hope to come to you every day.'

Francis suddenly realised that he had brought his lute with him, and some music. His last days were certainly not going to be idle, it seemed.

For the next hour he sang, and Purcell played, or they sang together. Francis was transported to the cheerful comradeship of his college evenings, or the ordered calm of the Chapel Royal. When the last note died away and Purcell began gathering up his music, it was an effort for Francis to remember that he was still in the Tower, and under sentence of death.

'I shall come again tomorrow,' said Purcell. He handed Francis a sheet of music. 'Practise this before I come. The F sharp is still a little shaky.'

'It is good of you,' began Francis hesitantly, 'to give up so much of your time – '

'Tush, man, I wanted to come! I would have come last week, only they would not let me. Some nonsense about close confinement, I don't know. But I want to hear that sung as it has never been sung before. You can do it, I know. Nobody will hear it but I, but that does not matter, nor does it lessen your achievement. Adieu until tomorrow, then.'

Soon after he had gone his father's artist was admitted, and Francis sat as in a dream while he made his preliminary sketches. He hoped his father would realise he was getting a portrait of Francis, the musician. When the sitting was complete he was shown the sketches, and realised that he looked almost happy.

*

'Eleanor.' At the sound of her father's voice, Eleanor turned in the tiny hall and looked up at him.

'Come into the parlour for a little. There is nobody there, and I have something I need to tell you.' He stroked his beard uneasily. Eleanor said nothing, but followed him into the parlour and seated herself in a wooden, high-backed chair. Her father stood in front of the fireplace, now fingering his lace collar and leaving, Eleanor saw, greasy fingermarks on it.

'You know that Lord Trenoweth visited Coneybury after we had left and has been arrested?'

'Yes, Father. I am still not certain what it is that he has done.'

'He was put on trial for high treason, arising out of this plot we have heard so much about. I am truly sorry, Eleanor, for I believe you cared for him. I fear that he has been found guilty. He is to be executed on Friday.'

Eleanor sat very still, her mind racing with the various reactions she had prepared in case she ever found herself faced with news like this. She kept her features a stony mask, and willed her hands not to move. She must say something that would make sense to her father, while concealing her real feelings.

'Then we must have been mistaken in him.' She was appalled that she could even utter the words, but she had to go on. 'I believed I enjoyed his company, but if he is guilty of such a vile crime then he deserves to die.' That at least was true; but he was not guilty.

To her surprise, her father moved in front of her, knelt down and took her hands in his.

'He has been spared the usual punishment for traitors. He will be beheaded, not drawn and quartered. These are dangerous times, Eleanor. I hope you understand now how important it is for you to stay close to your family. We can be safe here.'

'I hope that my loyalty will never be called into question, Father. I shall always be your daughter.'

'And Lord Trenoweth?'

'I am sad that such an able young man could have gone so far astray. But he must take the consequences of his actions.' She smiled at her father and stood up. 'But I need to change, Father. I have been riding this morning, and I fear there is evidence of it on my clothes.'

'Of course. Robert will be staying with us here for a week or so. This house being the size it is, you are likely to see at least something of him.' He smiled bleakly.

'Perhaps he will go riding with me. I am developing quite a taste for it.' Eleanor left the room and headed for the stairs, determined not to hurry.

Fortunately Sarah was in the chamber, sorting the linen on the bed they were forced to share. Eleanor shut the door and stood with her back against it.

'Sarah.' She spoke softly, fearing they might be overheard from elsewhere in the house. 'Francis has been condemned. He is to die on Friday.'

Sarah dropped the blanket she was holding and put her hand to her mouth. 'Miss! What did you say?'

'I pretended to my father that it was just, that I am loyal to them. But now we have no time to lose. We must escape.'

'How, Miss?'

'We have both been riding in recent days, which is good. Jake has always been with us, of course, but at least we have familiarised ourselves with the area a little.'

'But you are always watched, Miss. And Mr Carey is here now.'

'There must be some way. If we do nothing Francis will die, and I might – I don't know what I could do, but I must do something. If I could get to London it might make a difference.' She sat silent for a little, then looked up as Sarah spoke again.

'There is – a possible way, Miss. When we have been out riding – Jake was very kind to me. Perhaps you did not notice.'

Eleanor smiled. 'I think I did, Sarah. I was glad for you. But – '

'Suppose I asked him to take us towards Maidenhead, and then – I don't know. Perhaps he could pretend to fall from his horse and hurt his ankle? Then he could say we had escaped from him?'

This time Eleanor laughed. 'I can't see that working. But if Jake was prepared to ride with us to London – he would lose his place here, of course, but I believe he would not find it difficult to obtain another. Do you think he would do this?'

'I hardly know, Miss. But I can ask him. Where would we go?'

'To Lord Bodmin's house in Westminster, I think. I believe it will not be difficult to find. '

'What will you do then?'

I have not thought of everything yet. But we must get away, Sarah, we must! We have so little time. You will help me, won't you? '

'Oh yes, Miss. I shall be happy to help you.'

*

The sound of the key in the lock roused Francis from meditation, and he looked up to see his cousin being admitted.

'Thomas! It's good to see you.' He held out his arms, and Thomas returned his embrace briefly before dropping unsmiling into a chair.

Francis looked at him in consternation. Thomas was then, he recalled, barely thirty years old; he looked nearer fifty, and exhausted.

'Ah, Francis,' he murmured eventually. 'I feared we should not win – I staked much on your life.'

'Staked? In what way?'

Thomas looked up at him and smiled wryly. 'Many of the Whigs regard me as being no longer of their number. I have already been elected to Parliament, but my voice will carry little weight in debates. Exclusion will probably succeed now, and I no longer care.'

'If my death means Exclusion will succeed, then at least it is not entirely in vain,' said Francis, and Thomas looked up at him sharply.

'I am not afraid to die,' said Francis. 'I should dearly love to see Eleanor; after what I was told at Coneybury I had even dared to hope. But I have made my peace. Do not fear for me, Thomas; the sentence has been commuted, and terror overcome.'

Thomas stood up and paced about restlessly. 'I fear the fault is mine, Francis,' he said. 'I warned you, I know, but I feared even then that you and Robert could not both survive. Forgive me if I have misled you.'

'There is naught to forgive,' replied Francis. 'Indeed, I have a great debt of gratitude to you. When the sentence was passed I went through hell, but that is over now. I shall die, but I bear no grudges, not even against Robert.'

'It is good to hear you speak,' said Thomas with a smile. 'Your courage is a palpable thing now – it affects other people.' He turned the conversation to other things; to music, to Cornwall, riding and hunting, walking the cliffs. When he left Francis had such a clear vision of Pelistry before him that he almost wept to think that he would never see it again, that it would never truly be his.

But to sit and lament his fate would achieve nothing, he knew. He was mindful of the fact that he had not done the practising that Mr Purcell required of him, and then he was required to sit again for his portrait. So much to cram into one short week, he thought, then banished the idea from him so that his expression for his portrait would be serene.

Purcell came again after his sitting, and Francis was delighted that he managed the tricky F sharp without wavering. Purcell had also brought a new anthem that had not been sung at all, and Francis was honoured that he was to be the first to see what might soon be heard by the greatest in the land. It had a soaring, intricate melody that delighted Francis, and Purcell professed himself more than satisfied with his performance.

'It is such a waste,' he declared as he gathered up his music and prepared to leave, 'to kill you. You have so much to offer. If your accusers could hear you now – '

Francis smiled. 'I shall sing your melodies in heaven,' he said. 'They will be appreciated there.'

Francis soon began to realise that though he was a prisoner in solitary confinement he was on his own in fact for very little. Thomas came to him frequently, and Francis looked forward to his visits. A slight shake of the head at the outset would be sufficient to tell him that neither the Somervilles nor Robert had been found. After that, by mutual consent, they talked of a world where death did not enter, where treason found no place. Thomas would bring a smile to his cousin's lips with his tales of fashions, of scandal-sheets and tavern gossips. Not so Lord and Lady Bodmin; they came sad-eyed, unsmiling, unable to offer a word of comfort to the son they were so soon to lose. Francis felt uncomfortable in their company, for they needed consolation, and his own halting words seemed totally inadequate.

They could not stay away, yet it seemed they were almost glad to leave, for Francis had built up an armour that they could not penetrate, though his heart was wrung by their unhappiness. Making music with Purcell seemed refreshingly straightforward in comparison.

Elizabeth and Nigel came briefly, but it was clear that neither of them really knew what to say, and Francis did not know how to respond to them. They were both so full of life, and his approaching death had forced a whole new perspective on him.

As well as talking to his family and singing with Mr Purcell he had the sittings for his portrait, and of course there was time spent with Will when his servant brought his meals. Francis began to value the time spent on his own; he was going to need it if he was to set his affairs in order. He was allowed pen and paper now, and he spent a long time composing a letter to Eleanor, which he hoped she might one day see. Then he wrote to Edward and Catherine, Christopher Wentworth, and even Robert. The chaplain came to him early every morning, bringing words of comfort and healing. If he was able, Francis would follow this with a period of meditation, for God was very close then, and he wanted to hold on to the tranquillity brought him. At other times he might know fear and loneliness, but never then. God, he knew, could penetrate his armour, but God, he believed, would be ready to receive him, and he had no fear of the men who had rejected him, for theirs would prove but a barren victory.

Chapter Seventeen

'Eleanor, are you sure you wish to go riding today?' Mary and Eleanor faced each other across the dining table. 'Only I think it is likely to rain soon.'

'Oh yes, aunt. The exercise does me so much good. Jake will come with us again, and he is very reliable.'

'Mrs Weston speaks highly of him, it is true. But can it not wait until after we have dined?'

'But, aunt, we always seem to dine so late in this house. The best of the day will be gone by then.'

'Very well, since you are so set on it, I suppose it can do no harm. But only for a short while. Dinner will be in two hours, and I think your father will need you later. He is closeted with your uncle at the moment. Affairs press on them both, and I know your presence cheers him.'

'I will not be very long, aunt. I will go to change now, so that we can be back before very long.' She almost skipped up to her chamber, where Sarah was excitedly pushing some of their clothes into bundles.

'We cannot go out of the house carrying those, Sarah.'

'No, Miss. Jake will be in the yard in a moment. I am to toss them out of the window to him, and he will put them in the saddle bags. Nobody will see.'

Eleanor laughed. 'Oh, Sarah, that is wonderful!' She became suddenly serious. 'Am I betraying my father, Sarah?'

'You are trying to save the life of an innocent man, Miss.'

'Yes. I can look at it no other way. You have my riding clothes ready?'

Not many minutes later they were riding over the bridge out of Marlow. Far from the rain that Mary had prophesied, it looked a clear spring day, and Eleanor's heart rose as they jogged along.

'I think we may not make Westminster today, Miss.' Jake sounded uncomfortable. 'Perhaps if we were to head for Ealing, we would be able to make it easily tomorrow.'

Eleanor almost stopped in alarm. 'But – it is already Wednesday. The execution is set for Friday. It leaves us very little time.'

'We should not be travelling after dark, Miss. It would not be safe. If we get to Ealing we could be in Westminster on Thursday morning.'

'I think I have no alternative,' said Eleanor. Let us press on now. And, Jake, I am grateful to you. You have risked much to help us.'

'Tis nothing, Miss.' Eleanor heard the gruff note in his voice. She turned, and saw to her surprise that he was blushing. But he was looking, not at her, but at Sarah.

They were a few other travellers about, but not a great many. Even so, Eleanor was glad that they had Jake with them. Had it been just herself and Sarah she realised that they would have been very vulnerable.

It was after two by the time they reached Maidenhead, and Eleanor was more than ever glad of Jake's presence. Although she could see it was only a small town, hardly bigger than Marlow, with one rather muddy street through it, she was nevertheless immensely glad when Jake led them straight to the better of the town's two taverns.

'They will bring us cheese, bread and beer,' said Jake easily. 'And they will see to the horses. We need not be here long, and we can be on our way again.'

'They will be wondering in Marlow where we are soon,' said Eleanor. 'Though if Mrs Weston realises, she may hold her tongue for a little. I am sure she was trying to suggest earlier that I should get away.'

'She's the only reason I stayed there.' Jake turned his hat in his hands. 'Not quite sure why they had to get rid of so many of us, but I felt sorry for her. Must be something he did.' He tore off large pieces of bread as soon as it arrived, washing it down with his beer.

Sarah ate cheerfully enough, but though the smell of the food was not unappetising, Eleanor found she was now so tense that it was difficult to eat. She managed a little, and swallowed some of the rather bitter beer, but was infinitely relieved when they were underway again. It seemed their stay at the tavern had not aroused any suspicion, but having made her decision Eleanor was more anxious than ever to press on.

They moved at a steady pace, coming on the river so many times that Eleanor was moved to comment on it.

'We follow the river to London, near enough, Miss.' Jake smiled. 'Did you not know?'

'No. that is, I have never really thought about it. Have you ever been to London, Jake?'

'No, Miss. When there were more servants, Mr Weston would always take someone else rather than me when he went. And now there's so few of us he doesn't go. He wanted to turn me off as well, only Mrs Weston said she must have someone to see to the horses.' He paused. 'S'pose she'll get someone else now.'

'If you wanted to go back there, Jake, I believe Mrs Weston would have you. When I first met her -- but never mind, I know now that she has a good heart.'

'She does that, Miss. Reckon you're right. She'll have guessed what we're doing. An' she'll think it only proper.'

'But will we be in time? Suppose they still kill him?'

'They may do that anyway, Miss.' Sarah spoke gently. 'But at least you will have tried.'

'But – ' Eleanor found herself blinking back tears as she considered the enormity of what she was doing. With just two servants, one of whom she hardly knew, she was riding to London in an attempt to stop a due process of law from taking place. However much she believed Francis to be innocent, who was going to believe her? The sob in her throat turned to a rather strange laugh, and Sarah moved towards her and took hold of her reins.

'Careful, Miss. We don't want you falling in some ditch. You just concentrate on where we're going. Time to think of other things later.'

Eleanor blinked and smiled ruefully.

'Yes. Thank you, Sarah. Look, there are catkins on the trees.'

By mid afternoon they had reached Slough, but the earlier sunny weather had disappeared, and the clouds were gathering ominously.

'I hope we can make Ealing tonight.' Eleanor tried to keep the anxiety out of her voice. 'We must get to the house in Westminster in good time tomorrow.'

'Reckon we can, Miss.' Jake looked at the sky. 'Rain'll hold off for a couple of hours yet. Not too tired?'

'I haven't even thought about it.' Eleanor laughed. 'Though I don't know when I last rode so far. But I cannot stop now.'

Dusk was gathering by the time they reached Ealing, and now Eleanor did know that she was perilously near total exhaustion. Sarah appeared to be in a similar condition; fortunately Jake was entirely capable of arranging accommodation at a tavern, and seeing to the horses. It was none too clean, and the food was execrable, but she made the best of it, ate what she could, and fell onto the straw mattress beside Sarah.

*

Will was delighted that his master's appetite appeared normal, for Francis had declared that since his time was so short he would make the most of the fruits of this earth. His servant held firmly to the conviction that 'they' could not, in the final instance, put to death a man who had committed no crime. And Francis did not disillusion him.

The portrait progressed well, Francis sang every day with Mr Purcell, and knew that it was good, he exercised in the courtyard and tried to comfort his parents on his own approaching death. It was strange, he thought, that though his death was now inevitable, he had rarely felt so well. He wanted to gallop along the cliffs at home, to sing in the Chapel Royal again, to walk the banks of the Evenlode with Eleanor. He would never marry her now; somehow he was going to have to regard himself as a bridegroom on Friday.

But he woke with a shock on the Wednesday morning to realise that he had two days more to live, two days to eat and breathe, to walk and speak. He had resigned himself to death, or so he thought, but as it drew nearer he felt panic endeavouring to reassert itself. These last days he had known only kindness, so that he had almost forgotten the hostility that awaited him outside the Tower. The final sounds he would hear would most likely be the shrill cries of the crowd, condemning him yet again, when he had thought to surrender his life with the blessing of God. Thomas had not succeeded in tracing the Somervilles or Robert, so of course Francis did not know where Eleanor was, or even whether she knew of his fate. God had failed him at the last; he had brought him to the brink and then deserted him.

Limp and inert, he lay flat on his back, engulfed in a mood of black despair, knowing only desolation. When the chaplain came Francis could not face him and feigned sleep so that the man would not remain. Will attempted to wake him, but Francis brushed him aside and told him he wanted no breakfast.

For most of the morning he lay in bed, too listless and dispirited to rise, too shaken in his faith to attempt a prayer. The little chamber was a prison indeed, threatening to close in on him and crush him, to destroy the edifice of his peace of mind in crumbling ruin. Gone was the tranquillity he had known, as he realised how swiftly was the appointed hour for his death approaching. He wanted desperately to live, to love, to marry, and all this was to be denied him because of the lies and perjury of others. His limbs felt leaden, and it seemed as though he would need to move through treacle even to get out of bed. Though he was hot, the thought of even leaving the bed made him shiver. Could anybody understand his anguish, his loneliness? He was too restless to sleep, yet the world beyond the bed appeared to hold even more terrors. He turned his face to his pillow, and wet it with his tears. Sleep was not possible, but neither was true wakefulness. He hoped his parents would not come yet. How he would face them he simply did not know.

The sound of the key in the lock roused him, and he realised that Purcell was in the outer room. He sat up, shamefaced; even music had been forgotten during his morning of terror.

'I am sorry,' he muttered. 'I had not meant to greet you thus.' Purcell smiled.

'There is no need for apology,' he said. 'You have fought a battle this morning; one glance at your face is enough to tell me that. But I have brought a new piece with me today, which, with your permission, I wish to dedicate to your memory. It is based on Christ's Word from the Cross: "Today shalt thou be with me in Paradise".'

Francis was silent. Then he asked Purcell to wait in the outer room while he dressed. Afterwards he sang the counter-tenor line of the new piece from sight, without an error. It had been written for him, and he must do it justice.

After Purcell had left Francis realised that his morning of agony need never have been, that God had not deserted him, but he God. He sang Purcell's new piece again, which he had already committed to memory, and asked forgiveness of the God he had for a short while ceased to trust. As he ate the dinner Will had prepared for him he knew that he need have no fear, that a God who could bring peace in the face of death would look mercifully on Eleanor too.

Thomas came to see him that afternoon, a Thomas whose lined and drawn face told of sleepless nights and anxious days.

'I fear me we shall fail, cousin Francis,' he said as he sat heavily in a chair. 'Until now I have hoped we might win, but – ' he raised his hands in a helpless gesture. 'I have fought for your life, Francis, fought as I have never done for Exclusion, and all in vain, it seems. Whether or not the Duke of York succeeds his brother on the throne now seems to be of little account.'

Francis looked at him, uncertain what to say. The pretence had gone, conversation on other matters could no longer continue in the face of imminent death. Francis himself felt calm and serene, perhaps more so now that the horror of the morning was no more. For it was not oblivion that awaited him, but peace; the refuge he had sought had come very near. Thomas did not stay long, for there was a constraint between them, and Francis could find tranquillity by himself. Each moment now was precious, to be savoured, caressed, and not thrown lightly by. Loneliness had been defeated since the morning's desolation, and fear was now a thing of the past. Death was a fleeting pain, a sad adieu to friends on earth, but it could not be a final tragedy. Francis felt certain that the mercy of God would not permit such a travesty.

Soon afterwards his parents were admitted, but it was a difficult meeting. His mother was clearly having difficulty holding back tears, and his father seemed not to know whether to comfort wife or son. Within minutes of their leaving the artist came to complete his portrait. At the end of an hour he began packing up his brushes and invited Francis to view the finished picture.

'Let it stand there for a while,' he said. 'And tomorrow you may give it to your father.' Francis stood and looked at it, noted the serenity in the eyes that gazed calmly back at him, the luminosity introduced into his red hair. He tried to imagine it hanging at Pelistry, but somehow the thought brought home to him more forcibly than ever that he would never see his home again, and he turned away from the portrait.

'It is a good likeness,' he said. 'Thank you.'

'You were a good sitter,' was the reply. 'Quite amazing, under the circumstances.'

'I can hardly let my father see an expression of panic every time he looks at it,' said Francis with a smile. 'I am sure this is what he wanted.' He turned away, not wanting to acknowledge that he would never see this man again.

He began to sing Purcell's anthem that he had brought that morning; it was difficult now to know what to do, and he suspected that if he did nothing he would find panic arising. So he sang, and ate the food Will brought him with every appearance of lightheartedness. At dusk he lay down, and slept contentedly.

*

Robert thought he had never seen Anthony look so angry. There were white patches either side of his nostrils, his mouth was a tight line when it was not open bawling orders at any servants who were left, at Robert, at Sir Henry, at Mary.

'You let her go riding with just her maid and that half-wit from the stables? Are you out of your mind, woman?'

Mary's normal composure had completely deserted her; she looked thoroughly frightened.

'They have done it a number of times before.' She was almost whimpering. 'Eleanor has really behaved very well these last days. I never thought – '

'No, that's your trouble. You never think. They have several hours' start on us now, and we cannot even be certain where they are going.' He paused as Robert coughed.

'As to that – some little while ago I did tell her where Thomas and my uncle live in Westminster. It seemed a harmless thing then.'

Anthony wheeled on him. 'You did what?'

'At the time you were wanting me to woo her. She asked, and I told her.'

Anthony took a deep breath. 'We cannot go after them. It will be dark soon, and there are any number of inns they could have stopped at.'

'Is there really so very much mischief she could do now?' Sir Henry stood by the fire, his wig askew, his hands clenching and unclenching.

'We must hope that they are too late.' Anthony took a deep breath. 'The very soul of the nation hangs on this; I cannot have it brought to nothing by a slip of a girl!'

'How much does she know?' Robert spoke quietly.

'Enough, I believe.' Anthony's anger was clearly mounting, and Robert's fear increased. 'She has been so meek and mild, I was almost taken in myself.' He turned to his brother. 'And you have told her plenty, haven't you?'

'No, brother. I think she has simply been listening, and put things together for herself.' He smiled. 'She is my daughter, after all. She is not unintelligent.'

Anthony stood up, and began pacing the room. 'The plan goes ahead,' he said. 'I shall go to Oxford tomorrow. If the rest of you wish to take yourselves beyond seas, that is up to you. I am sure my learned brother could arrange it.' He cast a look of contempt in Sir Henry's direction, and left the room.

*

Eleanor did not sleep a great deal that night. The noise was considerable, and the bed extremely uncomfortable. She knew that Jake had done his best, but she was not used to a communal room with several others, and she strongly suspected that there were fleas in the straw mattress. Certainly before the night was very old she found herself scratching, even while she tried to obey Sarah's whispered instructions not to, as she would only make it worse.

On top of all that, she was filled with forebodings as to what the next day might hold. What could she do when she reached Lord Bodmin's house? What could anyone do? The lies of others, it seemed, had condemned Francis to death, and she did not know whether she could achieve anything by standing up and saying that he was innocent, and that she knew where the guilt really lay. She only knew that she had to do so.

They were up at first light, and after a hasty breakfast that was marginally better than the supper of the night before, they went out to find their horses. To their surprise these had been well tended and fed, and walked out willingly enough to take them on the road again.

'We shall be there before very long, Miss.' Jake helped her mount and then swung himself easily into the saddle, brushing almost accidentally against Sarah as he did so.

Unfortunately it was raining steadily, and soon all three of them were soaked. The horses were plainly unhappy, though they plodded steadily through the mud. But any thought of maintaining a fast pace was doomed.

They spoke little; Eleanor was uncomfortably aware of the magnitude of her mission, and she suspected that Jake and Sarah were as well. But they pressed on, and gradually realised that the distance to go was becoming less. Acton, Shepherd's Bush, Paddington, and still the rain continued to soak them.

There were more people about now, but nobody gave a second glance to three travel-stained and weary travellers coming in from the country.

'At least we know where we are headed,' said Jake. 'Though I have never been to London or Westminster. We will need to keep our wits about us.'

'We are a little way from the river, I think.' Even to herself Eleanor thought her voice sounded muffled.

Jake smiled, though in the gloom of the downpour Eleanor did not notice. 'I hoped to avoid taking you past Tyburn, Miss. I thought it might distress you. But there is a lane a little way ahead which will take us nearer to it now.'

They were in the village of Marylebone, but Eleanor was paying scant heed to her surroundings, intent only on reaching her goal. The lane down which they travelled now was rutted and very muddy. Sarah cried out as her horse slipped, but Jake was quick to grab the reins and avert catastrophe. She smiled at him gratefully.

'I hope that at least we may find dry clothes soon.' Eleanor was finding it difficult to hold the reins, her hands, even in gloves, were now so wet. Water streamed from hats, noses, coats and boots. In truth the rain was only one of their problems, and not the greatest; they were filthy, cold, hungry, and Eleanor was unhappily aware that she was still not certain how to reach their destination.

At last they came to the river, slipping sullenly between its banks. In spite of the weather there seemed to be a large number of craft of many sizes plying up and down it. Eleanor paused, and the others waited with her.

'I must think carefully. It is fortunate that Robert told me where this house is, before he realised what use I would make of the information. But I must think a little which way we are to turn. Then to the surprise of the other two she turned around and moved away from the river.

'Miss!' Sarah was plainly discomfited.

'We are the wrong side of Whitehall Palace. From what Robert has told me we could go straight through, but I think we would lose our way.' The other two followed her, and Eleanor rode on, showing more confidence than she felt. The two servants smiled in relief when she exclaimed excitedly.

'There is a gate across the street here. This must be King Street. It is just as Robert described.'

They moved slowly down the street, considerably wider than the alleys they had come down, but now they were being jostled by a constant press of people. It was another half hour of slipping in the mud, wrong turnings and getting even wetter that Eleanor led them into a fair sized yard, where the houses proclaimed that those who lived here were certainly not among the poorest.

'This is it, I am sure.' Eleanor knew that she was not, but one look at her companions' faces told her that she must try. 'Jake, can you help me dismount? I don't want to fall in the mud. I'm dirty enough as it is.'

Jake held the reins as Eleanor slipped to the ground and staggered up the steps of the house she had indicated.

'Be off!' said the servant who opened the door. 'There's no call for the likes of you in a house like this.'

He was about to shut the door, but Eleanor was desperate. 'Please,' she said. 'Can I speak with Lord Bodmin, or – or Sir Thomas Carey? My name is Eleanor Somerville.'

'Yes, and I'm the King. Now be off with you!'

The door was almost shut when a voice from further in the house called 'John! Who is that at the door?'

'Says her name is Eleanor Somerville, Sir Thomas. I'll send her on her way.'

'No.' The door was opened wide again and Eleanor, by now hardly able to stand, found herself looking into a pair of bright blue eyes over a firm straight nose and a mouth that was smiling in welcome. Robert, she thought, but older. And definitely kinder.

'For you not to be who you say you are would be too great a coincidence. So many times we have hoped that we could find you. We must find you dry clothes at once. Who is come with you?'

'My – my maid and another servant.'

'Good. John! See that these three horses are taken to the stables and looked after. And take Miss Somerville's maid and her companion where they can put on dry clothes and have some refreshment.' He turned to Eleanor. 'And we must do the same for you. Lady Bodmin's maid will help you when I explain the situation. In truth I understand very little of it as yet. I only know that it is a miracle that you are here.'

Eleanor, by now streaming water onto a polished wood floor, looked up at him gratefully. She was past speaking. Some half hour later, however, clad in a yellow muslin gown that was only a little large for her, her feet in comfortable slippers and sat by a blazing fire, she felt recovered enough to tell her story to Sir Thomas Carey, who listened without interruption.

'I am amazed,' he said when she had finished. 'These last weeks all my energies have been devoted to finding your family – and my brother. Now you are here there is just a chance – only a chance, but we will take it – that we may be able to save the cousin who is dearer to me now than any brother. I had intended to go to see him when his parents returned, but things are very changed now. I am going to have to take you on a journey.'

Eleanor looked down at her borrowed gown anxiously, and Thomas laughed.

'We shall take my carriage,' he said. 'Lord Bodmin would no doubt advocate going straight to the King, but I am a Whig, not a Tory, and I know one whose arm at present is just as long. My standing with Lord Shaftesbury has slipped a little of late, but when he sees what good reason I had for my actions he may perhaps revise his opinion. Come. You are sufficiently refreshed?'

'Thank you, yes. I wished we could have arrived here yesterday, but it was not possible.'

'John has brought the carriage round. Do you wish your maid to accompany you?'

'She and Jake have been very good to help me this far. Let them rest.'

Thomas smiled. As you wish. Then I shall take you to Thanet House.'

*

Francis woke on Thursday with a curious sensation. This was the last day permitted to him to live, and he felt as though he must do everything with the greatest care. Washing, shaving, dressing: all these must be done to perfection. It felt desperately important to him.

His parents were with him almost before he had finished his breakfast. They were both making a determined effort to be cheerful, for this would be the last time they would be able to speak to their son. It was hard to know what to say; Francis did not know how to say goodbye to his parents, and they felt it useless to tell him that a final appeal for clemency had been turned down.

'Certain bills I fear are left unpaid at Oxford,' said Francis suddenly. 'Most of my papers are there, but I have tried to draw up a list of those that require attention.' He handed Lord Bodmin a paper, which was pocketed silently. 'And – look after Will for me,' continued Francis. 'He still does not believe anything is going to happen tomorrow. Perhaps – later – he might accompany Edward to Oxford.' Francis smiled at his mother, who tried in vain to return it.

'I cannot tell you not to weep, Mother,' said Francis gently, 'for I know that you will. Try not to remember me caged like this, but riding through the park, hunting and losing myself in Cornish mists. Maybe they will allow you to bury me there.'

'I have already approached the King on the subject,' said Lord Bodmin quietly, 'and received his royal assurance that it will be so.'

'Why, then there is nought to fear!' cried Francis. 'And this is not a final adieu; I shall come with you to Pelistry. I had thought my head might have been stuck on Tower Bridge! Can't you understand that there is nothing for which to grieve?'

Lord Bodmin smiled and stood up. 'Your courage has not deserted you, Francis,' he said. 'Your going will leave a void, and I am sure you would not be content if your mother and I felt no sadness. But you have made your peace, I can see that; and so is our loss easier to bear.' He picked up the portrait. 'I am delighted with this; it will hang in the great hall at Pelistry. No man is going to require me to be ashamed of my son.'

It was hard for them to leave; in the end the gaoler had to come and tell them that they might not remain. Lady Bodmin put her arms about Francis, and could hardly tear herself away. Even his father embraced him before they finally left.

Francis sat by the window and allowed his thoughts to wander over happy times; his childhood in Cornwall, making new friends at Oxford, the awakening of his love of music, drinking ale with Christopher Wentworth, missing disputations on a spring morning to ride or play tennis. Inevitably then his thoughts turned to Eleanor; walking with her in the park, making music with her, meeting her eyes at dinner and answering glance with glance. He smiled to himself as he thought of his friendship with Purcell, and the knowledge that but for the plot that had brought about his condemnation it would not have occurred.

Darker thoughts he refused to admit, since it seemed they could do no good: Eleanor's absence now, her uncle's plans, the possibility that she no longer cared for him. His father had taken the letter that he had written, and had promised that she should see it. With that he must be satisfied.

After his dinner a Warder came to him and told him he might exercise in the courtyard if he wished. It had rained heavily in the morning, but now a watery sun had appeared between the clouds, turning the grey stone into diamonds. This was not the sloping cliffs and green hills of Cornwall; harsh paving underfoot instead of lush turf and wet earth, but still he was out of doors, looking up at blue sky and grey cloud, the same, perhaps, that Eleanor was even now looking at elsewhere. As he walked round the confined space it seemed that the clouds disappeared and the sun shone more brightly. Surely she is faithful, he thought. I should know if it were otherwise.

He returned to his room – he refused to think of it as a cell – to find Purcell waiting there for him.

'I had to hear this once more,' said Purcell, waving the music of the new anthem. 'Forgive me if your time is too precious for such pursuits.'

'I am delighted to see you,' said Francis. 'I will gladly sing with you. I am truly touched by your dedication.' He sang the anthem, and several others that Purcell had brought, as well as some songs and odes. Before they had finished the gaoler who had admitted Purcell was in the room with them, listening with frank admiration. Eventually he had to tell Purcell to leave, and Francis smiled, sensing the man's reluctance. To his surprise, his parting with Purcell was entirely unconstrained.

It was not until dusk that Francis realised that Thomas had not been to see him that day. Was it that his cousin did not, in the final instance, know how to say goodbye? Or was there some more sinister reason for his absence? Francis was puzzled, and knew an element of disquiet. Surely Thomas would have come today, the last day of his life? He went over in his mind all the possible reasons, and could not find one.

He must not let this deflect him. Thomas was his friend as well as his cousin; he must hope that there was significant reason for his absence.

It seemed strange, he mused, as the evening drew on, that he should still wish to sleep this night. Should he not keep vigil, spend the night in prayer, rather than attend to the needs of his body which was soon to be no more than dust? But he was tired, the fire burned low, and he would need a clear mind to face the hostile crowd he knew would confront him on the morrow. So he commended his loved ones to the care of a merciful God, climbed into bed and slept as peacefully as ever he had done.

The chaplain was with him at dawn, bringing, at Francis' particular request, the Sacrament that he normally took only at festivals. Francis smiled as he listened to the words of comfort spoken to him; he felt like a traveller well prepared for his journey. Will brought his breakfast soon after, and though it seemed hardly likely that he would need it, he fortified himself with a piece of mutton pie and a mug of ale. He was not able to say goodbye to his servant, but laid his hand on Will's shoulder and turned away. When he looked back into the room Will was no longer there, but four Warders, halberds in hand, were waiting to conduct him to his execution.

Chapter Eighteen

'I will bind your eyes if you wish,' said one of the Warders. 'The crowds are – not sympathetic towards you.'

'No matter,' replied Francis. 'I would look upon the light for the last time.' He placed himself between them and marched down the stairs. He was surprised when, on traversing the courtyard, they came to a closed carriage and he was told to enter it. There was no sign of hostile crowds, or the scaffold he was expecting to mount. He obeyed without question, however, feeling very vulnerable and uncertain. Two men dressed in black were waiting for him, silent and unsmiling. He sat between them and dug his nails into his palms to prevent panic arising. Such a short time now and it would all be over; merely a few more minutes and he would know eternal peace.

Perhaps the execution was to take place on Tower Hill, but the carriage was taking a very long time to reach it. He could not see outside, but it was strange that after several minutes they were still travelling. He could hear laughter and voices, the voices of ordinary people as they went about their business. To prevent his thoughts from dwelling on what lay ahead he tried to make out what they were saying, but only disjointed fragments of conversation came up to him as he jolted along towards his death. Surely they had turned more corners than necessary? He turned to ask one of his guards the reason, but as he looked at him, silent and impassive, he could not form the question. But a sudden panic arose in him that he should find himself at Tyburn after all, there to suffer the pains from which he believed he had been released. He had not been bound to a hurdle and dragged through the streets, but even so...

He could not tell which way they were travelling, but it seemed impossible to suppose that Tower Hill would be their destination. With something of a shock he realised that he had never expected to live until now, that the time set for his execution was already past.

At last the carriage was brought to a halt and Francis was curtly told to alight. As he did so he found, not the open space of Tower Hill, and certainly not Tyburn, but a city street, wider perhaps than some, and with houses of a certain size and elegance. There was no sign of a scaffold, no black-clad executioner, and no hostile crowd. Two more men were waiting for him as he left the carriage, and walked either side of him into the house outside which they had stopped. His bewilderment increasing every second, he walked with his new guides up a fine oak stairway and into a large, plainly furnished room, with damask hangings and a moulded plaster ceiling. Before the fire, looking smaller than ever by reason of his stoop, stood Lord Shaftesbury, with determination and resourcefulness in his eyes. By the window, looking out on to the garden below and with his hands clasped firmly behind him, was Sir Thomas Carey. Seated before them, her normally pale face flushed with apprehension, her yellow muslin gown looking as though it had been over hastily donned, sat the one he had thought of more than any other these last days and weeks.

'Eleanor!' he gasped, and could say no more, nor was he able to move, but stood looking to left and right in utter confusion. She rose from her chair, walked to him and smiled, touching his hands, which hung loosely at his sides.

'Yes, Francis,' she said.

Francis looked around the three occupants of the room with rapidly approaching bewilderment. He saw the calculation in Lord Shaftesbury's eyes, the relief in Thomas's, and, yes, at last he could acknowledge that he could see the love in Eleanor's. With a gesture Lord Shaftesbury indicated that he could be seated, and he sank gratefully into a chair.

'What – what has happened?' Even to himself his voice sounded like a croak. 'I was to have been dead by now. Where am I?'

Eleanor looked down at her hands, Thomas looked questioningly at Lord Shaftesbury, who returned Francis' questioning gaze with an unblinking stare.

'New evidence has come to light.' He spoke precisely. 'I was not able to hear it until yesterday evening. Having heard what Miss Somerville had to say it seemed that justice – and the country – would not be best served by your death today.'

'Then – I am reprieved?' Francis looked across at Lord Shaftesbury, trying to keep the pleading out of his voice.

'You are still under sentence of death.' Lord Shaftesbury was clearly choosing his words with the greatest care. 'But it is possible that you are destined to play a part at Oxford next week. We knew, of course, that your cousin had – embroidered – his story a little, but until Miss Somerville came here we could not tell by how much. Your knowledge of the household at Coneybury places you in a very advantageous position.'

'But – if I am still under sentence of death – ' Francis found he was unable to finish the sentence, but Lord Shaftesbury smiled.

'At least now we know where Sir Henry Somerville has been hiding. You will ride there this afternoon with a magistrate, who will arrest Sir Henry, his brother and any others there who may be implicated.' Francis sensed Eleanor stiffen, but he said nothing.

'If Robert Carey is there then he too will be taken into custody. Afterwards you will ride to Oxford. If there is a plot to be launched against His Majesty there, you are to discover it and thwart it. Certainly if you manage that you will have earned, not a reprieve, but a full pardon.'

'Forgive me – I will not be expected to work with Sir William Corner, will I? Only – our earlier meeting could make that a little difficult.'

To his surprise Lord Shaftesbury threw back his head and laughed.

'No. Sir William is well-meaning enough, take my word for it. But this is not work for which he is at all suited. I have picked one of greater abilities for you.' Thomas coughed, and Lord Shaftesbury's slightly sinister smile appeared again.

'Yes, Sir Thomas, I was coming to that. Your cousin believes, Lord Trenoweth, that you should be allowed a little time alone with Miss Somerville. After that you will return to your father's house, where the magistrate will come for you to ride with you to Marlow.' He stood up and bowed slightly to Eleanor, then left the room with Thomas.

Francis moved towards Eleanor, put out his hand and let it fall again.

'I was so certain,' he began, 'that I should die this morning, and never be able to tell you that – that I love you.'

She coloured, then smiled shyly. 'Cookie suggested that it might be so.'

'An estimable lady, your cook. She is still at Coneybury, I believe. But I was able to speak with her a little before – I was arrested. It was she who suggested to me that you cared for me.'

Eleanor touched his hand then, and he felt a sudden thrill. 'It is true. I think we both believed it was doomed, yet now – everything seems different. And only by pretending to my father and my uncle that I did not care could I hope to achieve anything.'

Francis sat down, and reached for her hand to seat her beside him.

'How is it that you are here? I cannot think that your father wanted it.'

'No. It is my uncle, of course, who dictates what is happening. But even he could not object to my riding a little, provided I was suitably accompanied.'

'Then – '

'Sarah, my maid, has caught the eye of the groom who came with us. He has probably lost his position in helping us, but we simply rode away from the house and did not return. They are both at your father's house now. I wish we could have come earlier, but it was not possible.'

'And – your father?'

Eleanor studied her hands with great intensity. 'I suspect he has taken my aunt to France. I heard my uncle suggesting this for me as well, if he did not like the danger.'

'But your uncle?'

'Without him this plot would not exist. He is become a fanatic, and is not afraid of laying down his life in what he says is this country's salvation. You are to go to the house this afternoon, I know, but I think it unlikely that my father or my uncle will be there.'

'Will he have returned to Coneybury?'

'No. I believe he is already in Oxford. I was able to learn a little after we left Coneybury. My uncle is certain that the King will leave Christ Church to visit the Duchess of Portsmouth at Merton. That is when he will strike. I hated the house at Marlow – but the fact of its being small made it easier for me to find out things.'

'But have you not put yourself in danger?'

She smiled delightedly. 'A little, perhaps. I am sure that my uncle was less circumspect because he believed there was nothing I could do. Yet I have never felt so safe. And tomorrow I leave with your mother for Pelistry! I hardly think that my uncle will look for me in Cornwall.' She stood up. 'Come. I think it is time that we returned to Westminster. Will not your parents be wanting to see you?'

Richard's carriage was ready to take them to Westminster in what seemed very little time. Thomas came with them, and the three of them made the journey in silence. As they left the carriage and began to walk up the steps to the door, however, Francis began to laugh; to such a degree that he turned to grab Thomas's arm for support.

'Francis, what is it?' asked Eleanor, puzzled, but he only shook his head, wiped his eye and continued up the steps. Thomas was chuckling as well now, and by the time they reached the door to the parlour all three of them were laughing helplessly. They stood grouped about the door, none of them making a move to open it. Their laughter died away as the door was flung open from inside and Lord Bodmin stood gazing at them in mock solemnity. Then he burst into a peal of laughter: they smiled in relief, and followed him into the room, where Lady Bodmin rose from a chair by the fire to take Francis in her arms. She held him wordlessly for a moment, then released him to embrace Eleanor.

'I still can hardly believe that this has happened,' she said. 'I was so certain that we were to lose you, and now – you are here, and Eleanor too. We are to travel to Cornwall tomorrow, my dear; it is all arranged.'

'I wish I could come with you, Mother,' said Francis. 'But it seems there is work I must do before I am entirely free again. I have not even been reprieved yet; milord Shaftesbury could have me back inside the Tower if he so desired.'

'He may have desired your death,' said Thomas, 'but he desires the success of Exclusion more. If you can prevent any plot next week, then you will be the nation's hero; but even if not, I hardly think that you will be executed now. But you are right that there is work for you to do: Uncle, could we perhaps dine straight away? I know it's a little early, but Francis and I will have to leave you shortly, when the magistrate comes to accompany us to Marlow.'

'You are to come with us?' asked Francis.

'If you have no objection,' replied Thomas, with the hint of a smile. 'Robert has caused us both a great deal of trouble recently. I want to be there when he is cornered.'

'I shall come to Oxford tomorrow,' said Lord Bodmin, 'when I have seen Eleanor and your mother start their journey to Cornwall. But you are right, Thomas, we must eat. Francis, are you not hungry?'

'Now that you mention it,' said Francis, 'I realise that I am. I had not thought ever to be hungry again.' For a moment he looked confused, then he started to laugh again. He was still laughing when they sat down to dinner, and were waited upon by Will Peters.

'Will!' cried Francis. 'How is it you are always here when I need you most? I suppose – '

'Of course Will is coming with us this afternoon,' said Thomas. 'The magistrate and his assistant, myself and my servant James, you and Will. Six of us; I think we shall find it is enough.'

They had scarcely finished eating when the magistrate arrived; Francis then discovered that Will had brought all his possessions from the Tower, and packed them in saddle bags ready to take, first to Marlow, then on to

Oxford. Francis embraced his mother, and asked her to take care of Eleanor.

'She'll do that, Francis,' said Lord Bodmin. 'You've no need to ask. Eleanor's maid and her sweetheart will go too. He looks to be an admirable companion.'

'He helped us a great deal.' Eleanor looked up. 'He is an honest man.'

'Then work can be found for him at Pelistry.' Lord Bodmin turned to Francis. 'This is an easy goodbye; we shall meet again very shortly.'

'Amen to that,' said Francis. He held Eleanor close, then blushed, as he realised he had never done so before. But she did not appear to object. 'We shall be together again soon, my dear. I feel sure of it.' Then he swung into the saddle and they started to move away.

They came out of London along the Bath Road, then turned to follow the Thames valley through Maidenhead and so to Marlow. They had dined early, and it was scarce past noon, though cold, and a suggestion of frost coming in the evening. Sir Nicholas, the magistrate, was anxious to complete the journey in daylight. Francis was happy to try to oblige him, but Thomas, riding at a brisk trot beside his cousin, was more cautious.

'It is over thirty miles,' he said. 'The horses are fresh now, but they will tire.'

'Tush, man, we can do it!' exclaimed Francis. 'We can change the horses at Maidenhead. We have several hours in front of us. I mean to enjoy them.' And he spurred his horse to a gallop, so that it was several minutes before Thomas, breathless and laughing, caught up with him.

'You have made your point, Francis,' he said. 'But we had best not leave the others too far behind.'

Francis smiled, slowed his horse to a trot, and suddenly began to sing.

Thomas turned to him, his face alight with amusement.

'It is a long time since I heard you sing, Francis,' he said. 'But I do not recognise the piece. What is it?'

Francis blushed. 'Henry Purcell has become a good friend these last weeks,' he said. 'Only two days since he brought an anthem he had written and dedicated – to my memory.' He laughed, embarrassed. 'I have it by heart: singing with him was wonderful, this last week.'

'I am sure it must have been. And now you can do so again.'

'Yes. I suppose I can. I had not thought of that – yet.'

They paused for ale in Maidenhead, and changed the horses. It was still well before four, and even Thomas was now confident that they could complete their journey before dark.

There was daylight enough when at last they crossed the bridge in Marlow; that very still, even light that precedes the dusk. The house they sought was easily found, a three-storey building of warm red brick fronting the street. Mr Weston must have been prosperous enough when he built it, but the white paint had all but rotted away on most of the sash windows, suggesting a lack of care, or of cash.

A short flight of stone steps led up to the front door. They all dismounted, and Will, James and the magistrate's assistant took the horses' reins, while Francis and Thomas followed Sir Nicholas up the steps. The magistrate hammered vigorously on the door with his riding crop; the sound seemed to echo all around them, but as it faded away the silence seemed almost eerie.

Sir Nicholas hammered again, more forcefully. 'Open, in the name of the law!' he called.

Silence again: then footsteps could be heard, the sound of the bolts being rattled back, and an elderly man stood before them, in the dingy garb of an inferior servant, his wispy hair clinging to his scalp. His hand shook as he held a tallow candle high to try to identify the visitors.

'See to the horses, my man,' said Sir Nicholas curtly. 'We have business with your master.'

Looking thoroughly flustered, the servant descended the steps and began to lead the way round the side of the house to the stables. Francis and Thomas looked at each other, then at Sir Nicholas.

'Well, here we are,' said the latter. 'Did you recognise that surly fellow, Lord Trenoweth?'

'No,' replied Francis at once. 'I think he must be a servant of the house.'

'Then he is no concern of ours,' replied Sir Nicholas. 'But there are others here who are.' He strode across the threshold and flung open a door on his left, revealing a rather musty and decidedly empty kitchen.

'I think the parlour must be the other side of the hall.' Thomas moved away, and they found themselves in front of a door that was slightly ajar. Sir Nicholas pushed it wide, and the three of them walked into a parlour hung with faded muslins, where an elderly man, dressed in threadbare broadcloth, sat before an inadequate fire.

'Mr Weston?' demanded Sir Nicholas, and the man nodded, rising shakily to his feet.

'Where is Sir Henry Somerville? I know you have been hiding him here, you need not trouble to deny it.'

'And where is my brother?' cried Thomas. 'He is here too, I know it.'

'Your brother?' said Mr Weston, and his voice, in contrast to his appearance, was that of one used to giving orders. 'How should I know where your brother is?'

'Because my brother, so help me, is Robert Carey, and I have information that he has been here many times.'

Slowly the old man smiled, and turned to face them with a look almost of satisfaction.

'Yes. Oh yes, what you say is true. He has been here.'

'Then where is he?' asked Francis. 'We must have them all here now.'

Mr Weston sat down again and spread his hands to the fire. 'But you are too late,' he said. 'They were here, oh yes, I sheltered him, of course I did. But they have gone.'

'Gone?' repeated Sir Nicholas. 'Where?'

'By now,' said Mr Weston slowly, 'I expect they are in France. How could they remain? I keep a boat at Southampton, and put it at once at Sir Henry's disposal. He was to board it either yesterday evening or this morning, together with his sister and Mr Carey.'

'Then the plot has been abandoned?' asked the magistrate.

'Oh no. Oh dear me, no. You did not think that Sir Henry was essential to this plot, did you?' His voice had grown stronger as he spoke, and there was a hint of triumph in his eyes. Francis just had time to note that he did not even trouble to deny the existence of a plot before Mr Weston went on.

'Even Robert Carey had more of a part in it than Sir Henry Somerville. His house was extremely useful, as was his influence, but the person who has organised this plot is Anthony Somerville, his brother. And he is not in France. Without him the plot would fail, and there is too much at stake for that.'

'Then – where is he?' demanded the magistrate, anxiety making his voice even more curt than before.

Mr Weston was entirely calm. 'You surely do not expect me to tell you that? You may arrest me – oh yes, I know you are going to do that. But ask me to betray my friends? You have underrated me if you think I will do that.'

Sir Nicholas looked around the room for a moment, then he turned to Thomas and Francis.

'Fetch the servants,' he snapped. 'Search the house. Mr Weston, you spoke truly of your own arrest. For today it will have to be in your own house. Tomorrow you will be conducted to Oxford gaol.'

For a moment the old man looked crestfallen. 'My wife,' he whispered. 'She is not well – she is in bed.'

'If she had no part in this treason, then no harm shall come to her,' replied Sir Nicholas.

The searching of the house did not take long, and it was soon established that Sir Henry, his sister and servants were not in the house and neither, to Thomas's chagrin, was Robert.

'The birds have flown,' said Sir Nicholas. 'Well, it is too late for us to continue our journey tonight. I will take the key to Mr Weston's room, and we will ride to Oxford in the morning.'

It was a strange night. Francis, to his delight, found himself sleeping in the bed that Eleanor had occupied only a few nights before. There was even a gown that was clearly hers draped across the bed. He was extremely tired, but his mind was too full and too elated for sleep. He had come, these last days, to regard his approaching death as a settled thing, and now it appeared he was not only to be allowed to live, but to enjoy Eleanor's love. Eventually, settling himself into the comfort of the bed, he tried to imagine Eleanor there with him, and slept at last.

Will and James were efficient in procuring breakfast for them the following morning, ignoring the protests of Mr Weston's two servants who still remained. Then they prepared for their journey to Oxford; only Mr Weston was to come with them, and he was not bound, though his horse's saddle was secured to that of Sir Nicholas. His wife appeared as they were about to set off, looking anything but an invalid, and regarding her husband with something approaching scorn.

'You should have gone to Southampton when you had the chance.' She turned to Francis and her face softened. 'Look after her. You are clearly the one she fled for.'

As they approached Oxford Francis suddenly realised that he had no idea where he was going to stay. People were flooding into Oxford from all directions, and as most people believed him to have died the previous day, it seemed hardly likely that his room at Magdalen would still be free. The thought of it being taken over by some officious Tory made him feel suddenly angry, so that Thomas turned to him and asked him what he was thinking.

'Only wondering where I should sleep tonight,' said Francis. 'You have lodgings arranged for you, I expect?'

'Yes, in Exeter College. Your father will be there too. I daresay they might find room for you, if your room at Magdalen has been appropriated.'

'I will go to college first,' said Francis. 'Christopher Wentworth had permission to remain this week. I must at least go to see him.'

They came into Oxford over Magdalen Bridge, and even here Francis could see that the city was busy indeed. Blue ribbons were to be seen in abundance, dominating the cheerful colours of Whiggish clothes, and the Tory red of Oxford's university. Thomas and Francis exchanged glances, and smiled. Both could see at once that the opponents of Exclusion were going to have quite a fight on their hands.

'If you wish to go to your college then we part here,' said Sir Nicholas, reining in abruptly, so that Mr Weston lurched in the saddle. 'I must see my prisoner safe into custody at the castle, and make sure they have some accommodation for me. You are hoping to remain at Magdalen, Lord Trenoweth?'

'If possible,' said Francis. 'Otherwise I shall join my cousin at his lodgings in Exeter College.'

'I shall need to know where to find you,' said the magistrate. 'It is vitally important that we apprehend as many of Sir Henry Somerville's servants as we can – and particularly his brother. I am sure that he is in Oxford. He might even be among these crowds around us now.'

Francis looked about him. 'I cannot see him,' he said. 'But I suppose he would consider himself safe enough. He believes me dead, and probably thinks there is nobody here who could identify him.'

'You'll not find him,' said Mr Weston suddenly. 'He's too clever for you. Just because you avoided the axe yesterday, you think everything's going to be so easy. What do you think he'll do, the moment he spots you? All the rest will do the same. Count yourself safe, my clever little nobleman? Pah!' And he spat into the street.

'Come,' said Sir Nicholas. 'I must get this fellow away. I shall look for you at Magdalen, then, Lord Trenoweth.' He moved away, taking his prisoner with him, his assistant discreetly the other side of Mr Weston.

'I must find my lodgings,' said Thomas. 'Do you see if your friend is here, Francis; we shall meet again soon, I have no doubt.'

Francis dismounted and stepped into the college, Will closely behind him. He was immediately aware of how the parliament had changed it. St John's Quadrangle was full of self-important looking members of Parliament, most sporting an abundance of blue ribbons.

The porter recognised him with delight, but confirmed what Francis had suspected, that his own rooms were now occupied.

'But Mr Wentworth took your possessions into his room,' said the porter. 'He had permission to remain in Oxford, you recall; maybe he's there now.'

'Thank you,' said Francis. 'I will see if he is. Will, could you take the horses to the posting station? They are reasonable animals. We might use them again.'

Will began to unstrap the saddle bags and Francis, impatient now with the possibility of seeing his friend, ran into the Cloister Quadrangle, up the stairs leading to his own rooms and hammered on Wentworth's door. He would not be in, of course; he would be quaffing ale with the Whigs or searching out what news he could. But he heard movement inside, the door was opened and his old friend stood there in his shirt-sleeves. For a moment it seemed he was too surprised to speak, but drew Francis into the room and shut the door, pointing helplessly to a settle on which Francis seated himself.

'I thought you were dead,' said Wentworth at last, sitting down and passing a hand over his brow. 'You were to have been beheaded yesterday.'

Francis smiled. 'I know,' he said. 'At times I have to convince myself that it is otherwise.' He told his friend all that had happened since they had parted, and though Wentworth had heard some of it by rumour, he soon discovered how inaccurate were the tidings he had received.

'So you are here for the Parliament after all, as you intended to be?' asked Wentworth. 'Faith, I am glad now I did not leave Oxford. Almost I did, then I reflected that since I had been given permission to remain, it would be a pity not to use it. At least I can offer you accommodation; this room will easily hold us both. I am sure we can find space for Will as well. But what are you going to do now?'

'I hardly know,' said Francis. 'But I expect I shall soon find out. The magistrate expects to be able to find me here, and it seems that any I identify as having been at Coneybury will be immediately arrested.'

'Supposing any of these people see you first? Are you not in some danger, here in Oxford?'

'Yes,' said Francis simply. 'I am. But at the moment they believe me dead; I shall be looking for them, whereas they will not be looking for me. I shall at least have the advantage of surprise.'

'All the same,' replied Wentworth, 'it might be as well if you did not venture out by yourself. There would seem to be little point in your escaping the scaffold yesterday, only to fall victim to assassins tomorrow. Do you think that this plot will still go ahead?'

'If Anthony Somerville is in Oxford, then yes, I do. He is determined, and resourceful.'

'And you would love to outwit him?' asked Wentworth with a smile. 'And to do that it has to be seen to be you that exposes this plot.'

'Eleanor did say that nothing would happen before Exclusion had been introduced,' said Francis. 'Her uncle wishes to make it quite plain that he is acting in this drastic fashion to prevent Exclusion becoming law.'

'Yet it is because of plots such as his that Exclusion was ever thought of,' said Wentworth. 'A clever way to go about things.'

'The King is here already, I suppose?' asked Francis suddenly.

'Yes, he arrived a few days ago and spent Thursday at Burford races. He seems mighty confident that things will go his way. I have been watching the people arriving, and a fine showing they have made. Many of the Whigs have come with armed attendants, and 'No Popery, no slavery' is to be seen in everybody's hat. But come; my lord of Shaftesbury is expected to arrive in Oxford soon. His entry should be quite a spectacle; let's join those who have gathered to welcome him. You should be safe enough: there will be quite a crowd. Nobody will try to shoot you down in that.'

Francis was filled once more with admiration for the little, elderly earl who left nothing to chance. His entry into Oxford was clearly arranged to impress. Magdalen Bridge and the High were packed with crowds shouting 'Make way for the Earl! No Popery!' and the blue ribbons they sported seemed somehow to mock the royal standard flying from Tom Tower. Francis felt the same stir of excitement he had when he took part in the pope-burning procession, and realised with a start that that had been barely four months since.

Soon there was movement on Magdalen Bridge, and the crowds began to press forward. A number of horsemen came by, finely dressed and well armed, the horses stepping fastidiously and delicately. Two or three coaches followed, containing some of the earl's gentlemen, looking mightily pleased as they waved to the cheering crowds. Further behind were more coaches, containing among others the earls of Stamford and Salisbury, and a great many armed horsemen in the rear; but in the centre, on a great chestnut horse, rode Lord Shaftesbury, unsmiling, but acknowledging with his hand the cheers of the people. He was dressed in black, but with blue ribbons adorning his coat and hat, and plaited into his horse's mane. He rode on slowly, his penetrating eyes darting hither and thither among the crowd. For a moment his gaze rested upon Francis, who knew that he had been seen, but the earl gave no indication to those about him.

'No Popery! No slavery! The Bill! The Bill!' shouted the crowd, and Francis and Wentworth shouted too. Soon the procession turned aside, to seek the rooms prepared for the earl in Holywell. The crowds waited until the last horseman had disappeared, then turned reluctantly to go about their own business.

'There goes the hope of the nation,' said Wentworth. 'All this shouting has made me thirsty. I don't suppose you brought any wine with you? You always had better wine than I did.'

Francis laughed, but admitted that on this occasion he had none.

'However, I think we can dispense with University regulations and seek a tavern this time,' he said. 'We are not here as undergraduates at the moment.'

The Boar in St Aldate's was full, and it took them some little time to procure themselves refreshment. It was noisy and stuffy, and more than one strange glance was thrown their way, which they both ignored.

They returned to Magdalen to find Sir Nicholas waiting for them.

'I needed to see you, Lord Trenoweth,' he said without preamble. 'No, I have not been waiting long – we had not arranged a time. But we have to make some plan for the coming week. It is vital that this plot is thwarted.'

'Come upstairs,' said Francis at once. 'I am sharing rooms with my friend Christopher Wentworth here, but he knows almost as much of this as I do.'

'I have seen my prisoner safe into custody,' said Sir Nicholas, as soon as they were seated. 'And I hope that soon he will be joined by others. You have not recognised anybody in Oxford yet?'

'Only Lord Shaftesbury,' replied Francis. 'And I hardly think it would be a wise move for us to arrest him. But I believe that Anthony Somerville is in Oxford, though I confess I hardly know how we are to find him.'

'Those lists you were required to make,' said Sir Nicholas, 'concerning where Sir Henry's friends were staying. Can you remember who any of them were?'

'Some of them,' said Francis. 'But they were not really relevant. Most of them were people Anthony did not even know; he just needed to know their whereabouts – and, at the time, to keep an eye on me.'

'I see,' said the magistrate. 'Then what do you propose to do?'

'Tomorrow morning,' said Francis, 'I think I will see if the King will grant me an audience.'

'The King!' said Wentworth and Sir Nicholas together.

'Yes. Until we know where we can find those who would assassinate him, we can at least warn him. '

'But he does not believe in the existence of this plot,' said Wentworth. 'Even though you were condemned for having taken part in it.'

'I know,' said Francis. 'But when he hears what I have to say – he may choose to be on his guard. At least I know when he is going to be most vulnerable – we must ourselves guard the exits to Christ Church every night after dusk next week. That is when they are most likely to strike.'

'But not before Monday?' asked the magistrate.

'No. They will not act until Exclusion has been introduced into Parliament.'

'If you are sure – ' said Sir Nicholas doubtfully.

'I am. Believe me, I know these people.'

'Then I will meet you in Oriel Square at six on Monday. I will bring others with me, so that every exit to the college can be guarded. And any you can identify as having been in the service of Sir Henry Somerville will be immediately arrested.' He stood up, and reached for his hat. 'Until Monday, then. And I wish you luck with His Majesty.'

'How will you seek your audience?' asked Wentworth, after Sir Nicholas had gone. 'Present yourself at Christ Church and ask to see the King?'

'I think not,' said Francis with a laugh. 'Though under the circumstances it might be possible. 'But he will most likely attend service at the cathedral tomorrow – I will go myself, and try to speak with him as he comes out. You need not come with me; I am sure I shall be safe enough.'

Francis reached Christ Church in good time the following morning, and installed himself unobtrusively towards the back of the cathedral. Just before the service began the King entered, with the Queen on his arm. Francis found that though his mind was very much on his reason for coming, he still found a corner of it to spare to listen to the music. It was better than at Magdalen, he had to admit, but it still could not attain the heights of the Chapel Royal. To his delight the anthem was Purcell's 'Behold now, praise the Lord', which first drew his attention to the wonders of Purcell's music. He smiled softly to himself: certainly the performance here was more polished than had been the case at Magdalen. Even for this it had been worth coming.

At length the service ended, and the great doors were flung back. Francis stood just inside them, and advanced a little as the King and Queen walked down the aisle, bowing low as soon as he realised that the King had seen him.

'What – ' clearly the King was considerably startled, but was just able to check himself. 'A moment, madam,' he said to the Queen, and drew Francis aside.

'Come to the Dean's lodging in an hour,' he said in a low voice. 'You will be conducted to an apartment more private. Au revoir until then.' He smiled, raised his hand and rejoined the Queen. Francis left the cathedral as soon as he was able, and decided against leaving Christ Church altogether. He wandered round Tom Quad for a little; it seemed so much grander than the Cloisters at Magdalen. The people taking the air here were Tory to a man; Francis smiled softly to himself at the thought of Whigs sullying the hallowed ground of Christ Church while the King was in residence. He had prudently left his blue ribbons behind.

He went up the stone staircase and stood in the dining hall, gazing up at its great hammerbeam ceiling. Everything at Christ Church was clearly on a more lavish scale than the other colleges, Magdalen included.

Chapter Nineteen

At the end of the hour he presented himself at the Dean's lodging, where he was at once conducted into a large, airy chamber with windows looking out across the garden and towards Corpus Christi.

His guide held the door open for him and withdrew. Francis vaguely noticed the elegant furnishings of the room, but his attention was focussed on the figure before the fire. Dressed in a suit of rich black velvet, with fine lace at collar and cuff, His Majesty King Charles the Second stood with his left hand on the hilt of his sword, his right on the mantel. He looked up in almost casual fashion as Francis entered, and extended his hand, which Francis kissed, dropping on one knee to do so. Then the King smiled, and Francis felt a surge of joy, for he had feared royal anger, even a royal command that his execution be carried out forthwith.

'It is unusual for me to hold a conversation thus with a dead man,' began the King, as Francis stood up. 'No, I knew of course that you had not kept the appointment prepared for you on Friday, though I confess I know not how, nor how you come to be apparently free in Oxford, when I thought you close prisoner in the Tower.'

'If it please Your Majesty,' began Francis hesitantly, 'the plot for which I was condemned exists in truth, though I am innocent of any part in it. But Miss Somerville reappeared just in time, and I found myself at Thanet House instead of on the scaffold.'

The King threw back his head and roared with laughter. 'I can well imagine that such a move would have appealed to my lord of Shaftesbury,' he said. 'So there is not even any reprieve yet. And does our interfering earl know of this plot?'

'He does, Sire. He knows that you are in considerable danger while you are in Oxford.'

The King did not reply at once, but drummed with his fingers on the mantelshelf.

'My life would not be so dear to him if I had given assent to a Bill he hopes to pass,' he muttered. 'But, by God! He shall not have me that way. So you are here, as you once promised you would be, to protect my life. Is that it?'

Francis blushed. 'I – I suppose that it is,' he replied. 'It was thought I could be useful in Oxford, as I know many of the members of Sir Henry Somerville's household.'

'And how do your friendly assassins propose to achieve their ends?'

'They will be watching every exit to this college every evening after sundown. Your Majesty's figure is not difficult to recognise, even at night.'

The King drew himself up to his full height and glared down angrily at Francis.

'And whither,' he asked, with a steely edge to his voice, 'do your fine plotters believe I should be bound?'

'Why, to – to Merton,' stammered Francis. 'Is not her grace of Portsmouth lodged there?'

'She is,' replied the King, his voice still cold. 'And if I should visit her?'

'You will walk past those hired to kill you,' said Francis bluntly. 'There are so many exits. If I could but know which – '

'I doubt that it is common knowledge, though some may know of it,' replied the King. 'But my father had a gate cut in the wall between this college and Corpus Christi. He was here in Christ Church for some years, with the Queen my mother at Merton. It gives direct private access from this college to Merton, with just Grove Lane between Corpus and Merton to cross.'

'I have seen it,' said Francis. 'A small path that emerges into Christ Church Meadow.'

'Precisely. So you see I have made my arrangements. And, of course, my timing is entirely of my own choice.'

Francis blushed, and the King smiled. 'No doubt your fine plotters believe it would be virtuous to cut me down at such a time,' he said. 'Though my brother has his mistresses too. Just ugly ones.' The King held out his hand, and Francis knelt to kiss it.

'I do not know what you hope to achieve this week, Lord Trenoweth. I am weary of stories of assassins who lie in wait for me; I should be dead a hundred times over if half of them were true. If I can outwit Shaftesbury and his minions you shall have a full pardon, though I imagine milord Shaftesbury believes he is well able to reward you himself.' He smiled again, and Francis rose and withdrew in some perplexity.

The King had been angry with him, it seemed, yet had acknowledged that he had been wrongfully condemned. The fact that he was still under sentence of death seemed now to be a point that most were prepared to overlook; but it did little for Francis' confidence. Could anybody who killed him be guilty of murder while that state of affairs remained? Perplexed, Francis took little heed of where his footsteps were taking him, but was not really surprised to find himself outside Exeter College. Hopefully his father would be here by now, and after his somewhat curious dismissal by the King he felt in need of reassurance.

He found Thomas with his father, engaged in a heated discussion as to the merits of Exclusion, and its possible success. They broke off when they saw Francis, and his father asked him whether he had made any progress.

'Thomas has told me of your findings in Marlow,' he said. 'Hardly surprising, I suppose, but disappointing. Your mother and Eleanor have begun their journey, by the by. I shall be delighted to offer young Jake employment. He has admirable qualities, in particular a strong sense of what is right.'

'I have not met him.' Francis smiled. 'But it would seem he has helped Eleanor considerably.'

'I think it possible that she may be looking for a new maid very soon.'

'What? Oh.' Francis laughed, and began to tell them of his audience with the King. Lord Bodmin let out a peal of laughter when told of the King's anger that his relationship with Merton College should be so particularly noted.

'Most likely he was putting on a sudden show of virtue,' said Lord Bodmin. 'In the circumstances he would not care to be reminded that he has brought two mistresses as well as a queen to Oxford. But his anger is not directed against you; I have reason to believe that he is quite well-disposed towards you. What do you propose to do next?'

'I am to meet the magistrate at six tomorrow,' said Francis. 'I think His Majesty will be most vulnerable as he crosses from Corpus to Merton, particularly if Anthony Somerville knows of this route. Perhaps I ought to be wandering Oxford now, seeing if I can recognise any of Sir Henry's servants.'

'And suppose they recognise you first?' asked Thomas. 'What then?'

'Christopher urges caution on that score,' said Francis. 'He thinks I should not go out into Oxford alone.'

'And he is right,' said Lord Bodmin. 'I will come with you, if that is what you want.'

'Not without eating dinner, surely,' said Thomas. 'Or am I always to be hungrier than the pair of you?'

In fact there was little that Francis could do that day. He dined with his father and cousin, and afterwards walked around Oxford with them, but this was more for the pleasure of doing so than any particular hope of catching would-be assassins. The events of the last weeks had already taken on an unreal, dream-like quality, so that Francis began to wonder whether any of it had really happened. It was only when he returned to Magdalen, and the necessity of sharing Christopher Wentworth's room, that the dream once more became reality.

Oxford was busier than ever next morning. Menials, members of Parliament and peers were bustling everywhere, all endeavouring to give the impression that Parliament would be useless without them. The very fact that Parliament was sitting at Oxford and not, as was customary, at Westminster, made this one more important, but there was not a man there who did not know that this was to be the final test. Exclusion would not come again, and for once there seemed every chance that it would succeed. The Bill would pass the Lower House easily; and the Upper, unless Lord Shaftesbury had seriously miscalculated. And would the King then find any means whereby he might refuse his consent? The Commons, with their power of refusing him vital grants of money, thought not.

Francis and Wentworth joined crowds of others in the Schools Quad, hoping to discover a little of the proceedings of Parliament. The Commons, having heard the King's speech in silence, withdrew to Convocation House to debate it, and after the morning session was over the two young men caught sight of Thomas crossing the Quad. He smiled as he saw them, and walked across to join them.

'Well, we have begun,' he said. 'We have quite a fight on our hands, but I think in the end we must win. The King has offered "limitations" on a Popish successor, and some seem prepared to accept it. But I think there are enough who will settle for nothing less than Exclusion.'

'The Bill! The Bill! Let us have the Bill!' was shouted by the crowds around them.

'You see?' said Thomas. 'We are winning. But I must leave you now; a group of us are to dine together, and plan how we may push the Bill through quickly.' He waved his hand to them, and was gone.

Promptly at six Francis and Christopher presented themselves in Oriel Square; Will had insisted on coming with them, and Francis had not demurred. Will knew some of the servants at Coneybury better than he did.

They were met by the magistrate, together with a number of assistants he had banded together. Francis told him of his meeting with the King, and of what he had learned of the King's likely route to Merton. Sir Nicholas walked the short length of the little path with them and scratched his head.

'I agree this is the likeliest place,' he said. 'And the front of the college is well enough guarded. But we cannot entirely ignore Oriel Square. Fortunately I have been able to assemble several assistants. Some will stay in Oriel Square, some here. What about the Dean's garden at Christ Church, or Corpus?'

'The colleges are well enough guarded,' said Francis. 'The plot is fraught with danger, which would only be heightened if they tried to strike the King within the college itself. Yet it all seems very casual. I wish we had some better plan.'

The magistrate smiled. 'We shall just have to be very observant. Let us return to Oriel Square for a little. Do you recognise anybody?'

Francis looked about him. 'No, I don't think so. Are you sure this will work? We don't know how many conspirators there are, how long Parliament will last, or when the King will come.'

'We can but try. Do you and your friend, with Peter and Michael here, return to Grove Lane. I will remain here with the others.'

Francis turned and was moving away when Will nudged him.

'My lord – look!'

Francis followed the direction of Will's finger and grabbed the magistrate's arm. 'By thunder, Will! There – just turning out of the lane into Merton Street! It is Ferriman – James Ferriman, I think his name is. He is Anthony Somerville's manservant.'

Sir Nicholas looked at him intently. 'You're sure?'

'Oh, yes. Will noticed first, but I recognised him at once.'

Sir Nicholas summoned his two men, and the servant was arrested before he had taken a dozen paces. He looked round in blank incomprehension, then understanding dawned as he saw Francis.

'You!' he cried, as he was led away.

Francis returned to Grove Lane just in time to see the King stepping casually across it to Merton College. He did not even look at Francis, but continued on his way, apparently unconcerned.

Francis found that this was to be the pattern of his next few evenings. He grew weary of wandering from Grove Lane to Oriel Square and back again, linking with Sir Nicholas, recognising a servant from Coneybury on a couple of occasions, more often not. Both Will and Christopher were tireless in accompanying him, and Francis was grateful for their support, particularly when Will spotted a youth he declared had been a kitchen hand at Coneybury. Francis was initially surprised that Anthony Somerville even knew of the existence of such a one, but he was learning that he must not under-rate his opponent.

There were many guards between Christ Church and Merton, and Francis was beginning to see why it was that the King was sceptical about the plot. He continued to try to show caution as to his own safety, though he soon began to believe what he had said earlier, that Sir Henry's servants believed him dead, and were not looking for him. Though he knew that the sudden blow to the back of the head was not impossible, he found he was not walking Oxford expecting to meet death at every turn.

Two days later he saw the King again, striding jauntily and entirely safely towards Merton. He began to get depressed, and said as much to Wentworth, when they were hovering in the schools quad on Friday morning, hoping for news of the debates.

'I thought you had all the world to live for,' said his friend. 'There are surely enough people alerted to any possible danger to keep the King safe. Your pardon is assured, your marriage too, by the sound of things.'

Francis smiled. 'I suppose so,' he said. 'But if I am to be reprieved, why hasn't it been done already? Suppose Lord Shaftesbury intends to have me back in the Tower if things go wrong for Exclusion or if, heaven forbid, the plotters are successful and the King is killed?'

Wentworth put his hand on his friend's arm. 'I will stay with you again tonight,' he said. 'You want to come out of this affair in a blaze of glory, it is obvious. And you'll certainly not shift Will in a hurry. We have to keep you safe.'

But their watch that night was no more productive than on previous occasions. Sir Nicholas was plainly restless that Francis had failed to identify Anthony, but Francis recognised no-one that evening, and the King they did not see at all.

'At least the King is still safe,' said Sir Nicholas. 'But I wonder how many more cold evenings we are going to have to spend here before his safety can be assured?'

Next morning, before they had even breakfasted, Francis and Wentworth were visited by Lord Bodmin. Will had discreetly disappeared; Francis sometimes wondered how it was that Will always managed to be there when he was wanted, but never at the wrong moment.

But Francis was delighted to notice that the lines of worry round his father's eyes were fast disappearing, the infectious smile had returned, the laughter sounded freely again. Lord Bodmin could never do without hope for very long, and his natural optimism had reasserted itself. He set both young men laughing with his tales of the debates in the House of Lords in the Geometry School, the King formidable as ever.

'It will be a close thing, though,' he mused. 'Exclusion has already passed the Commons, but then we knew that would happen. It still may not pass the Lords, and the King is implacably opposed to it.'

'But can he resist,' asked Francis, 'if the Lords pass it?'

'He will be under a great deal of pressure if that happens,' said Lord Bodmin. 'But even then – I have seen him in tight corners before, and he is adept at getting himself out of them. He does not look like a man facing defeat.'

'You will vote against Exclusion, then?' asked Wentworth.

'I? Yes. James is his brother's heir, and has done nothing to show he may not be King after him. We are offered limitations on a Popish successor so that he may not interfere with our religion, and that should be enough.'

'Will it, though, I wonder?' asked Francis.

'It is all we can hope for. I have not forgotten, in the last Parliament, when your friend Shaftesbury suggested outright that the Duke of Monmouth should be legitimised and declared heir.'

'He said that?'

'He did indeed. And Monmouth was there, smirking and backing him up. I was near enough to hear what it was His Majesty said when Monmouth sat down, though it was only in a low voice. It was "The kiss of Judas".'

Both young men began laughing at this, and Lord Bodmin smiled.

'But now I must leave you,' he said. 'The sittings of the House of Lords are far too enjoyable to be missed.' He swept up his hat and was gone, leaving Francis considerably amused, though Wentworth was perplexed.

'I cannot understand your father,' he said. 'Civil war is still not an impossibility, yet he seems to regard the affairs of the nation as being a fit subject for laughter.'

Francis shook his head. 'He holds his own opinions and will not be shaken,' he said. 'Though I disagree with him on this, I believe that many in the Lords would do well to listen to him. But he can find amusement in the most unlikely places, and is a lost person if he cannot. He knows the Popish Plot is not a joke.'

'A pity the King does not also,' replied Wentworth. 'Shall we go down to Schools Quad this morning? It would be interesting to discover what the Lords are making of the Bill.'

The Commons had stationed guards under the archway leading to the Quad, but they made no attempt to prevent the friends entering. It was not crowded, though several people were idling about and talking to the guards who, bored with the monotony of their positions, were disposed to be conversational. It was a pleasant morning with a light breeze, and the quad seemed filled with sunlight, sunlight made all the warmer by the mellow stone of Bodley's library, of the Schools, each with its name in Latin written above the door. It was somewhere utterly familiar to Francis, yet suddenly become strange. He looked at the corner where the Geometry School lay, and thought of the Lords assembled within it, the King glaring at them from beneath heavy brows. Across the other side lay Convocation House, where the Commons were now debating, while upstairs, tranquil, peaceful, defying all human crises, Duke Humphrey's library, its vaulted ceiling so magnificently restored by Sir Thomas Bodley, offered a haven to all who would come to read, to learn, to study.

So absorbed was Francis in contemplating all this that he had almost forgotten why they were there, and was considerably startled when Wentworth grabbed his arm and pushed him forcefully into one of the doorways.

'Over there,' whispered Wentworth. 'That little man in dingy broadcloth. Do you recognise him?'

Francis looked, and drew his breath sharply.

'He was employed as a footman at Coneybury,' he said. 'Do you think he has seen us?'

'I am sure of it,' said Wentworth. 'But he realised that I was with you, and no doubt thought it prudent to withdraw for the moment. I am glad that you were not alone.'

'But now he can tell all the other conspirators that I am alive and in Oxford,' said Francis. 'For how long?'

Wentworth looked across the Quad. 'He is gone now,' he said. 'You are safe for the present. Maybe we will see him tonight, and the magistrate will be able to arrest him.'

'But how many others will be looking for me by then?' said Francis. 'Come, we had best return to College. I think I shall remain there until it is time to meet Sir Nicholas. If he has alerted his fellows – ' He did not finish, but walked towards the arch and turned towards Magdalen.

At six they were both in Oriel Square, alongside Will, who had armed himself with a stout cudgel. They met Sir Nicholas, who looked anxious.

'I have men at all the exits to the college,' he said. 'But I am beginning to agree with you, Lord Trenoweth, that our arrangements are far from satisfactory. I think I shall join you in the lane this evening. I know that for the moment His Majesty is safe, but – '

'And so am I,' said Francis, and told him of what had passed that morning.

'Then let us hope he comes here tonight,' said the magistrate. 'But it does complicate the situation somewhat.'

'I will stay with Francis the whole evening,' said Wentworth at once. 'I do not think he should be alone – he is in some danger.' Will said nothing, but fingered his cudgel thoughtfully.

'And so is the King,' said Francis. 'Now that they know I am here, it might force their hand. Christopher, let us walk a little – I'm unable to stand still at the moment.'

They walked up the lane to Christ Church Meadow, then began to retrace their steps. Just as they reached the further end of the lane they both saw the ex-footman together. He was walking up Merton Street in the direction of Oriel Square. Sir Nicholas was a little way behind him, clearly having no idea of the man's identity.

'If he sees you he may shoot in alarm,' said Wentworth. 'Can we come up either side of him, and so secure him?'

Speed, they both decided, was more important than caution. They ran towards the footman, who saw them and put his hand to his waist, but before he had time to draw a weapon Wentworth had seized one arm, Francis the other. Will moved round in front, holding his cudgel firmly. Sir Nicholas had drawn level with them by this time, and was quickly told who this was.

'You may think you're safe now,' said the man, looking at Francis. 'But there's others besides me out for you. Which of us will still be alive in the morning?'

They led him into Oriel Square, where three of the magistrate's men were in waiting for them. One of them produced a length of cord and quickly bound the prisoner's wrists.

'I will take this fellow into custody,' said Sir Nicholas. 'Peter, do you come with me. Michael and John, return to Grove Lane with Lord Trenoweth and Mr Wentworth, and apprehend anybody, anybody, you understand, who appears to be behaving suspiciously. I will return as quickly as I can.' He and Peter set off towards Carfax and the castle, and Francis and Wentworth fell into conversation with Michael.

Some little while later Sir Nicholas still had not returned, and Francis grew restless. He walked up and down Grove Lane, hardly standing still at all.

'Tonight seems different, somehow,' he said, as Wentworth caught up with him. I find I am particularly uneasy.'

'Yet you must not move off on your own,' said Wentworth. 'I still believe that you are in danger.'

'Mr Wentworth is right, my lord,' said Will. 'What good will it be if we avert this plot, yet you are killed?'

Francis did not answer, but walked a pace or two into Christ Church Meadow, then moved swiftly into the entrance to the lane, looking suddenly frightened.

'What is it, Francis?' asked Wentworth, who was almost immediately behind him. 'What have you seen?'

'Anthony Somerville,' said Francis. 'Coming towards us from the Meadow. And Sir Nicholas is not here!' The expression of fear left his face as suddenly as it had come, and he ran out into the Meadow again, with both his companions following closely. Michael stayed in the lane, looking bewildered.

Anthony saw him almost at once, but even as he raised his pistol Wentworth gave Francis a fierce push, so that he landed sprawling on the wet grass, and the shot passed harmlessly between the two of them.

Francis had fallen easily, picked himself up at once and threw himself at his adversary, by now almost at the entrance to the lane. He was just able to prevent his drawing his second pistol, but Anthony still had hold of the first, and turned it to use as a cudgel on Francis's head. The two of them were rolling on the grass now, locked in a tight embrace, knowing now that both could not come out of this alive. Already Francis could feel his senses dulled as blows were rained on his head; his own fists seemed but puny opposition, and he realised that despite all their precautions, Anthony was very near achieving his goal. His sword seemed more of an encumbrance at the moment; he could not even draw it.

Suddenly the blows ceased, and Francis twisted round on the grass sufficiently to see that Wentworth had managed to wrest the pistol from Anthony's grasp even as his arm was poised for another blow. Will was raising his cudgel, clearly aiming it at Anthony's head, but by this time Francis could hear voices; his companions of – was it really only a few moments ago? and another he recognised at once.

'Stop this unseemly wrangle!' commanded the King, and Francis found himself thrown aside, landing on his back in the Meadow again. Anthony leaped swiftly to his feet, drew his remaining pistol and stood pointing it directly at the King.

'Now I have you,' he said, and his voice seemed almost to purr. 'Now this country shall know a Catholic King.' Everybody else seemed frozen into immobility, but Francis, jumping swiftly to his feet, realised that he was a bare two yards from his assailant, and slightly behind him. As Anthony raised his arm to fire, Francis drew his sword and brought the flat of it sharply up under the would-be assassin's wrist. The bullet soared into the air high above the heads of all those present; Sir Nicholas and Peter turned into the lane almost at the same moment. They came either side of Anthony at once, and with the aid of Michael and the guard he was soon disarmed and bound.

The King stepped forward and turned to Francis with a smile. 'We seem ever wont to meet in strange circumstances, Lord Trenoweth. I have not been disposed to believe in this plot of yours, particularly when I have walked this way twice this week unmolested.' He looked at Anthony, who was now standing proudly upright, the magistrate's men still holding him.

'My brother will succeed to my crown in due course.' The King's voice was altogether pleasant. 'But it seems you could not wait.'

'No,' replied Anthony. 'We could not. Because we could not trust you. You would have given in to these Exclusionists; anything rather than go on your travels again.'

'You mistake me,' said the King. 'It will not be so. But your mistake will cost you your life.'

'I am not afraid to die for the cause I hold dear,' said Anthony. He looked at Francis. 'I heard that you were at liberty. I would have killed you, if I could. I suppose my niece thinks she has acted out of loyalty, does she? She has betrayed her faith and her father. If ever he sees her again, it will not be to call her daughter.'

'Enough!' cried the King. 'Take him away. Lord Trenoweth, I bid you good evening.' He turned to the crowd that had quickly gathered.

'Well, what are you staring at? Begone, or I'll have you set in the stocks!' He set his hat on his head and strode away; the crowd parted in silence to let him past. Only when he had disappeared into Merton did pandemonium break loose, and Francis was carried shoulder-high into the nearest tavern. Toast after toast was drunk to the nation's saviour, and even to the King, who did not wish these people to have their way. Francis was delighted to see Thomas there among the crowd: the more so, when at last people began to drift away, as he found the support of both Wentworth and his cousin necessary to get him back to college.

Next morning Thomas was with them again, with the news that Francis was to wait on the earl of Shaftesbury at his lodging in Holywell after the morning service at St Mary's. This was very different, Francis soon discovered, from the grave stateliness of Thanet House. The earl received him in a small first-floor room with a plain plaster ceiling and muslin hangings. He was seated at a table by the window, busy with some papers, but looked up as Francis was shown in and bade him be seated.

'I did not expect you to achieve what you have this week,' he said. 'I thought that either we should in truth have found the King slain, which would have been a disaster, or it would transpire that this plot did not exist at all, which I confess I thought more likely. Your trial made people more aware of the dangers of Papists, and particularly of a Papist heir to the throne, but you have now done much more. The nation lies deep in your debt; but for you we would now have to acknowledge James, Duke of York, as King, and many of us would be fleeing for our lives.'

'As my cousin Robert Carey has done already,' said Francis.

'Indeed. He will never be able to return, of course; he will be condemned in his absence. But Exclusion is bound to succeed now; this has very likely given His Majesty the opportunity he needs to abandon his brother without loss of honour. Parliament will settle for nothing less, and the King must see that his own safety lies in accepting it. There will be a reward for you, young man; it will be for Parliament to decide what is suitable, but you may be sure that you have the nation's very grateful thanks. Stay in Oxford for a while; it seems probable that you will be called to the Bar of the House ere long.'

That the nation was grateful Francis could not doubt as he stepped once more into the street. Word had spread that he was closeted with Lord Shaftesbury, and as Francis emerged he could scarcely move for the press of people. Apprentices, shopkeepers, servants, and a fair sprinkling of the gentry in Oxford for the Parliament were there to cheer him and to cry long life to him. Again he was carried shoulder-high into the Broad, and it was a little while before he could escape from these somewhat embarrassing attentions into the calm of Exeter College; he was minded that he had not yet seen his father.

'Well met, Francis!' cried Lord Bodmin, as soon as Francis appeared. 'So you have covered yourself in glory? Yes, of course I have heard about last night's doings; there can hardly be a soul in Oxford who has not. What do you propose to do now?'

Francis sat down. 'Lord Shaftesbury told me to wait in Oxford for a little,' he said. 'It seems that Parliament may want to reward me – after they have at last given me a pardon, I hope. But then – I must travel to Cornwall as soon as may be. Father – ' he hesitated, and Lord Bodmin looked at him questioningly.

'Sir Henry Somerville is now in France – I do not know where. All I know is that I wish to marry his daughter, and that he would refuse his consent.'

'Yet before your arrest I understood you to say that he was encouraging you to pay attentions to his daughter. That he would have preferred her to marry Robert need not concern us. She is out of his power now; he will be condemned for treason in his absence, and can do nothing to prevent your marrying Eleanor. He will not, of course, give her a dowry, though by the time that you have had Lord Shaftesbury's "reward" that may not matter.'

'It hardly seems to matter already,' said Francis. 'I wonder what will become of Coneybury, though?'

'It will be forfeit to the Crown,' said Lord Bodmin. 'But come, noon has long since struck, and even without Thomas to remind me I grow hungry. Let us wine and dine and forget all cares.'

That meal was a long time ending, and afterwards Francis walked round Oxford with his father, suddenly conscious of the fact that he was probably about to leave the city for ever.

Next morning he announced that he would stay in his room in case he was sent for to appear at the Bar of the House of Commons, though he was clearly impatient to be elsewhere. He dressed carefully, choosing a laced cambric shirt, dark blue velvet suit and buckled shoes. His red hair was well curled, and he selected a feathered beaver ready to put on his head. Wentworth smiled at him.

'You cannot wait to be off,' he said. 'Instead of a hostile court you will face a House of Commons falling over itself to express its gratitude. It is no more than you deserve.'

Francis said nothing, but went to the window, looking out on the quad, peaceful in the morning sunlight.

'I shall be sorry to leave Oxford,' he said. 'But I think my life is taking a new direction. I hope I shall be able to spend at least part of my time in London, and sing with Purcell as he invited me.'

'Perhaps we may meet in London, then.' said Wentworth. 'For I shall soon be going to the Inns of Court. You have no wish to know more of the law?'

Before Francis could answer there was an imperious knocking at the door, and though they were expecting it they both started. What followed, however, threw them into utter confusion: they had expected a messenger come to summon Francis to the Bar of the House, and sat back while Will Peters came forward to open the door. At once a tall, swarthy individual strode into the room, and so startled was Francis that he stumbled as he left his chair and knelt to kiss the hand of the King. Wentworth followed him at once, but the King impatiently motioned them to rise.

'Enough,' he said. 'I have no time for such idle ceremonies. Lord Trenoweth, this, I take it, is the young man for whom you requested permission to stay in Oxford?' Feeling thoroughly bewildered, Francis murmured assent.

'Well, well. You have done well, sir, to have protected your young friend thus far.' The King moved across to the fire and stood with his back to it, facing Francis and Wentworth, who stood uncertainly in front of him. 'Doubtless you are wondering what has prompted this curiously timed visit. I do not make a practice of visiting undergraduates in their colleges, but the circumstances are unusual, and call for unusual measures. If I do not tell you, you will soon discover from other sources that I have dissolved Parliament; nor do I intend to recall it yet awhile.'

'Dissolved?' Francis was unable to conceal his surprise. All that Thomas had told him went racing through his mind; how the Commons would grant the King no money unless he consented to Exclusion, how they had refused alternatives and rushed the Bill through, confident of success. How had the King found the means to thwart them?

'But,' he heard himself stuttering, 'I thought the Commons were to move into the Sheldonian.'

The King smiled, a sudden mischievous light in his eyes. 'So did they,' he replied. 'But they have already outlived their usefulness, and their insolence passes belief. Many of them believe I have troops from Ireland and France to pursue them. They will cause no trouble, and there will be no further talk of Popish Plots or Exclusion Bills. My assailant of Saturday night is beyond pardon, and both Sir Henry Somerville and Robert Carey will be condemned in their absence. But there I believe the lust for blood must stop; already far too much has been shed these last two years in the name of protecting the nation, and only incidentally my life.

'As for you, Lord Trenoweth; it may be that you were expecting to receive a formal pardon at the hands of Parliament. That cannot be now, but as one deeply in your debt I offer you my sincere thanks and this ring, which I desire you to keep in token of a King's gratitude.' From the little finger of his left hand he drew a plain gold circle in which was embedded a fiery ruby and handed it to Francis, who accepted it silently, then suddenly dropped to his knees.

'As your debtor I do this much for you.' The King's voice had changed in tone, sounding for a moment almost severe, and Francis remained on his knees, nervously fingering the ruby ring. 'As your King, I absolve you from any penalties imposed upon you by courts acting in my name and declare you to be entirely free, untainted by any treason whatsoever.' Francis looked up, and was rewarded by the King's most dazzling smile as he was told to rise.

'You will receive a formal pardon as soon as the chamberlain's seal can be set to it,' the King continued. 'But to other matters. If Sir Henry Somerville is indeed declared guilty of treason his estates will, of course, be forfeit to the Crown. It would seem appropriate that you should receive them as a reward for your loyalty; I believe you are likely to become his son-in-law. He has not carried his daughter off with him, I trust?'

'No, Your Majesty,' replied Francis, thankful for a straightforward question to answer. 'She – she is in Cornwall with my mother.'

'Then I give her the dowry her father refuses,' said the King lightly. 'If there is any difficulty I shall delight in making her a royal ward. And tell your father to bring you to Whitehall. Mr Wentworth, I trust we shall see you there also. My young protector is fortunate indeed to have so true a friend.' Wentworth bowed, his pale face suffused in colour.

'And now I fear I must leave you,' said the King, moving towards the door. 'There is much to be done, and it is imperative that I reach Windsor today.'

He held out his hand, which both young men kissed, then he was gone as suddenly as he had come.

They sat back in silence for a moment, looking at each other in some perplexity. Then Francis stood up and shouted with laughter.

'Will!' he called. 'I need my riding clothes. And we must pack.'

'Pack?' Wentworth was clearly puzzled.

'Yes. I must ride at once, and fast, Will, I trust, with me. You as well, Christopher, if you have a mind to it.'

'But – but where? Are you going to London at once?'

'London?' Francis laughed again, but more easily than he had done for many weeks. 'No indeed. I am going to Cornwall. London later, perhaps, but every hour, now, that keeps me from her, I deem an hour wasted.'

'Then I will not encumber you with my presence. We shall meet again soon, Francis, I have no doubt.' Will Peters appeared from the bedroom. 'Your riding clothes are ready, my lord. Shall I go to see to the horses?'

'Yes, please, Will. Get us good posting horses, for we ride hard, and fast.' He moved towards the bedroom. 'I will not stay even to see my father or my cousin. I shall see them soon enough, and I am sure they will understand. But now I am bound for Pelistry.'

Author Bio

Photograph by Geoff Luckman

Felicity Luckman is a history graduate of London University, and lives in Tavistock, West Devon, with her husband. From an early age she knew she wanted to write, and has formed a particular love of historical fiction, especially the seventeenth century. She is a member of the Historical Novel Society, and belongs to a writers' group in Tavistock. 'Writing can be a lonely craft,' she says. 'It is good to receive the views of others and to exchange ideas.'

She has worked as a journalist, a carer, in an open-air museum and on her local newspaper. In her spare time she loves reading, listening to music, walking on Dartmoor – and looking after her grandchildren!

If you enjoyed *Sacred Music,* please share your thoughts on Amazon by leaving a review.

For more free and discounted eBooks every week, sign up to the Endeavour Press newsletter.

Follow us on Twitter and Instagram.

23182273R00148

Printed in Poland
by Amazon Fulfillment
Poland Sp. z o.o., Wrocław